DAY AFTER DISASTER

Sara F. Hathaway
2016

THE CHANGING EARTH SERIES

DAY AFTER DISASTER

SARA F. HATHAWAY

TATE PUBLISHING
AND ENTERPRISES, LLC

Published by Tate Publishing & Enterprises, LLC
127 E. Trade Center Terrace | Mustang, Oklahoma 73064 USA
1.888.361.9473 | www.tatepublishing.com

Tate Publishing is committed to excellence in the publishing industry. The company reflects the philosophy established by the founders, based on Psalm 68:11,
"The Lord gave the word and great was the company of those who published it."

Book design copyright © 2014 by Tate Publishing, LLC. All rights reserved.
Cover design by Rodrigo Adolfo
Interior design by Jimmy Sevilleno

Published in the United States of America

ISBN: 978-1-63122-134-7
1. Fiction / General
2. Fiction / Thrillers / General
14.10.20

DEDICATION

FOR CYNTHIA. MAY happiness shine upon you like your endless love and support has always shined upon me.

For T.R. May your passions always guide you like the fire you have lit in my heart.

CHAPTER 1

ERIKA WOKE UP in a panic to the smell of must and wine. She was frantic and could not move. Where was she and why did an immense pain overwhelm her? She tried to calm herself and let her tears rinse the stinging out of her eyes so she could focus, but there was darkness all around her. As her pupils began to widen, adjusting to a dark room, she realized her body was buried from her neck down under some immoveable mass.

Her mind started racing. She remembered going to work that day just the same way she had done so many times before. She worked in a small restaurant in the Sacramento Valley. It was called El Primero. This high-class Mexican restaurant was located in a beautifully remodeled Victorian home. The home had been built in the 1800s, and had always been perfectly maintained by its owners. Four years ago, an ambitious entrepreneur had bought the home to turn it into a restaurant that would bring Mexican food into the fine dining spotlight. True to its purpose, the chefs produced gourmet Mexican delicacies on a nightly basis in one of the finest kitchens in town.

The restaurant was only a recent phase for the home, though. Its main purpose had been a residence for multiple families. Sometime during the Cold War, a paranoid homeowner had built a bomb shelter underneath the area that became the restaurant's kitchen. The bomb shelter itself had remained virtually unchanged after its installation, and rather than sealing it shut, the restaurant owner decided to make use of it instead. It made an excellent storage area for just about any supplies the restaurant needed to operate efficiently, and it wasn't long until the employees started utilizing it as a break room as well.

The only way into the bomb shelter was through a heavy door that sealed tight when shut. The stairs descended downwards, and the walls were lined with cabinet space. The wooden cabinets stored everything from dry foods to napkins to cleaners. At the end of the stairs, the room opened up into an area that was originally meant to be living quarters for nuclear bomb survivors. Since then, it had been strategically stacked with plastic water jugs for the water coolers and shelves for more storage. There was also a table with a few chairs around it for workers taking a break and a huge oak wine rack that contained the expensive wines that the restaurant boasted, which were specially chosen to accompany the Mexican dishes.

Erika had run down to grab a new bottle of Merlot. She hated going down into that dark dungeon. The door would slam behind her with a bang that would make her jump. She had no choice, though; a disagreeable customer had insisted he would only drink their very finest bottle of Merlot, and the waitress had asked her to grab it for her since she had an order up. Erika had seen the bottle on the shelf, but as she grabbed for the bottle, a severe shaking began. California always shook from time to time. In this area of the world, the Earth's plates shifted regularly enough for the inhabitants to become accustomed to the nauseating shaking, but this time it was different.

The Earth, rotating on its course outlined in the depths of space, is a precious miracle of life. It has been a bountiful provider for its inhabitants for generations and generations of countless species. But these new inhabitants, the humans, they developed as no animal had before. They have an insatiable urge to grow, to expand, and to change the natural process that had sustained life for so long, and it was killing the great Mother Earth. The humans had finally gone too far. Not only had they cut, carved, and dug at the delicate skin in ways that had opened huge gaping wounds in the surface, they trampled the natural environment and destroyed all other animal species with little regard for any life but their own. They built everywhere. The Earth's own materials had been stripped from her, manipulated, and then stacked on her fragile surface like huge warts glowing and gleaming in the night. Mother Earth had taken enough abuse. She began to shake like a dog trying to expel fleas that had been biting it and scratching it for too long.

Erika, unaware of the extent of the Earth's fury, had been too close to the wine racks when the rumble began. She bent her legs to maintain her balance, but the wine rack began to rock back and forth. Before she could dodge it, the large oak rack teetered its last totter and fell smack on top of Erika. The incredible weight of the wood held her to the floor, and the scattered shards of glass from the broken wine bottles made her very apprehensive about her situation. She felt a stinging pain in her left arm and leg, but between the darkness of the bomb shelter and the moisture of the wine puddle she was lying in, she didn't know how badly she was hurt.

She tried to force the wine rack off of her as hard as she could. When she realized she was not going to be able to lift this rack on her own, panic overtook her again. She began to produce a sound as loud as her vocal cords could muster. She shouted and wailed, but her desperate pleas went unheard. Finally, exhausted, her crying ceased. Her throat was too sore to continue. She stared up, through the darkness, at the heavily sealed door and realized that no one could hear her, no matter how loud she yelled. It was useless.

"If no one can hear me, I'll have to wait for someone to find me. They'll probably notice I'm missing in no time." Erika's worn-out vocal cords scratched as she spoke. While she waited for help, the pain began to eat into every fiber of her being. She had to think about something else but her mind was in a panic. The dark and quiet made it even harder to block out the pain, so she began to talk to herself. "I wonder why no one has come to look for me. They must know I am missing. That guy is probably grumbling more about his wine. I wonder what time it is. I wonder if Vince had made it home from work with Dexter before the quake hit. I wish I could call him."

Her cell phone was in her green bag that she carried to keep her personal belongings in. It was stacked right over there on a shelf with the other employees' purses and backpacks. She looked toward it through the blackness, wishing she could reach it and call the man she loved so much. She knew he would always be there to help her, and she desperately wished he was there now to help lift the load that seemed to be crushing her into a pancake on the freezing cold cement floor.

Pain, shock, and fatigue finally took their toll on the pinned woman, and she fell into a daze filled with dreams. She dreamed of her husband, Vince, with his brown curly hair and matching beard, his eyes that could see into her very soul, and his tall, lean body that was perfectly accentuated by his little round belly. He had a great smile, and he was never afraid to announce the sheer joy being married to her brought him. She dreamed of her son, Dexter. He was already five years old, but it seemed like just yesterday that Erika had given birth to him. Erika had a fairly easy pregnancy, and on that day that she did finally hold him in her arms, she embraced a baby for the very first time in her life. At that moment, she learned that there was a type of love that was so unbreakable and remarkable it made her breathless even in her dreams. She had watched her precious baby grow into a little boy. His blond hair formed a perfect outline around his fine-looking facial features. His eyes were a steely gray, and they seemed to hold an ancient wisdom within them.

Erika's dreams were shattered when she awoke to another rumble that made the heavy oak rack grind into every bone of her body. Her pain was searing. She felt like the herbs between a mortar and pestle, but these herbs were being marinated in Sauvignon Blanc and White Zinfandel.

"What the hell is going on? They have to be looking for me by now. How long have I been here? Where is everyone? Gosh darn it! *Someone help me*! What if no one knows I'm still down here? Well, I have got to get out of here. My leg is throbbing and my arm is too, for that matter. What if I'm really hurt and I've been trapped here for... for... God knows how long." She finished speaking in a frantic tantrum of frustration.

The rant of emotions seemed to give her a new strength. With a sudden flash of fierce determination, she decided she would have to free herself. She had to lift this thing off of her, but she could just barely recoil her arms enough to give a desperate heave on the rack. With all her effort, she lifted the heavy rack a tiny bit, but that was all she could do. It was so heavy she had to quickly let it go, and it fell back on her bruised body again.

"What am I going to do? This thing weighs a ton. I have to get out!"

Erika's mind reeled; logic was unreachable, but the instinctive survival side of her took over. Her eyes had adjusted as much as they could to the darkness of the shelter. She swiveled her head around, and in the shadows, she thought she could see a milk crate that had been used to transport the wine to the rack. It didn't look too far out of reach; if she could just free her right hand, maybe she could reach it. She heaved up on the oak rack again. This time she only tried to move it enough to move her arm. She found that the little bit she could push it up was enough to squeeze her hand up toward her head until she had it extended out above her.

She couldn't hold the rack up for long though. When she dropped the rack back down on her, there was only one arm to support the weight of the oak, and it fell hard onto her ribs. She exhaled as the wind was ripped out of her lungs. After she caught her breath, she knew that she had to free herself as quickly as she could. She needed to find out if she was seriously hurt because at that moment she felt like every bone in her body was broken. She reached out for the crate. She knew that it was essential to get a good grip on it. Any attempt to just touch the crate might push it further away and diminish the possibility of escape from her wine-rack cage.

All in one movement she thrust the rack up and grabbed the crate. Her fingers slid through the square holes in the milk crate and she pulled it closer. The next step would be the most critical part of her escape. She gathered her strength, got the crate into position, and sent a silent plea to her God asking him for his help and the strength she needed to do this. She shoved as hard as she could. It was working. She moved the oak rack higher than ever before. With extreme precision, she held the rack with one hand and slammed the crate into a space just barely big enough for it to fit with the other. She did it. There it was, right next to her shoulders.

A huge load had been lifted off of her chest, but Erika could still not breathe easily. The incredible weight of the oak rack was only being held by one tiny milk crate. The crate began to bend under the heavy load. A wash of anticipation and adrenaline took control of her emotions. Even though her legs were stilled pinned, she was going to be free soon. The next step was not nearly as critical but all the more physically straining. She had devised a process of pushing up enough on the rack so she could keep sliding the crate further and further toward her legs. Then the crate, straining and bending under the pressure, finally reached the middle of the rack. Working the rack like a teeter-totter, she rocked it back so it rested on her chest and slowly bent her stiffened legs up toward her. She was amazed her left leg moved, and more importantly, this meant that—despite the throbbing pain emanating from it—the bone was not broken. After her legs were curled into her abdomen, she began to rock the rack back where her legs had been. Free from the restraint, she wormed her way out.

CHAPTER 2

ERIKA TRIED TO stand immediately, her exuberance overcoming all pain, but she quickly fell back to the frigid cement. Her legs were too stiff from being pinned to support the weight of her body. She felt as if her whole body was bruised and scabbed. She lay on the chilly cement for a moment to gather her strength. Then she tried to stand again but slower this time. Erika was not tall but always stood proudly. She had straight brown hair that fell down over her shoulders and matched her dazed brown eyes. She had a little nose that she quickly wrinkled when she smelled the foul smell that came wafting her way. In the dark, she would never know what the stink was or how messed up her body was.

She stumbled over to the table in the center of the room and found her purse on a shelf nearby. She pulled a lighter from it. Using its flickering light, she found a candle that was left on the table and lit it. She looked down and saw why there was such a stink in the air. Her clothes were completely stained with wine.

Her white blouse, which she always took such good care of so it would not get stained, was now a rosy color, and even her black pants looked brown because they had absorbed so much wine off the floor. Erika pulled out a pack of Camels from her bag and sat down to puff on a smoke as she looked her body over. Nothing was broken or too abnormal-looking, but she had sustained a deep laceration down her left leg, and her left arm was very bruised and sore. The laceration was scabbed, which looked good. Erika had been certified as an emergency medical technician while in college and had dabbled in herbal medicinal techniques. She knew enough medically to know that no red around the scab was a good thing. Appreciating the fact that she was just sore and not badly wounded, she sat back and puffed deep on her smoke. When she was halfway through the smoke, she jumped to her feet.

"What am I doing just sitting here? I'm going to get out of this dungeon." With that, Erika sprang to her feet but moved a little more cautiously when the pain reminded her that she was black-and-blue and had a huge cut on her leg. She gingerly climbed the stairs to the landing at the top. This area was shaped like a square and featured the big metal door. Everything around her was cold and dark, and she could not wait to bust through that heavy door into a brightly lit kitchen that smelled rich with carefully prepared dishes. As she reached for the door, she somehow knew that it was not going to budge. When her suspicions proved correct, she fell to the floor and began to wail again. Her struggle had not ended by freeing herself from the wine rack; it had just begun. Determination took over again, and she slammed into the door as hard as she could. Unmoved but clearly dented from her frantic efforts, the door stood quietly unyielding.

"What am I going to do now? Can't they hear me banging? Why won't someone open the door for me? Wait… at least I can turn on the lights and look at this picture in a different light."

Erika flipped the switch but nothing happened. She kept flipping it again and again, expecting the light to turn on and illuminate the room, but the light never came.

"Darn it, darn it, darn it! One thing after another. I will never get out of this nightmare." Tears began to form in her eyes, but she quickly regained her composure. "Wait… my cell phone. I can call Vince, and he can come and get me. He must be worried sick about me by now."

Erika launched down the stairs despite her throbbing leg and scrambled back to her purse. She reached for her phone and turned it on.

"All right! I actually remembered to charge the battery last night."

She dialed the numbers and waited for the phone to start ringing. It dialed, but then there was nothing but silence. Erika looked at the front of the phone to see how many bars she had. The phone was searching for service. She began to shake the phone in alarm.

"It always worked from in here before. There is power. Why can't it find a signal? What the hell is going on? Why is this happening to me? Okay… calm down. I'll just wait for it to find a signal and try again. It has to work." She put the phone on the table and relit her smoke. She sat and puffed looking at the phone, willing it to find a signal, but it never did. She picked it up and dialed again just to try anyway, but there was nothing but an eerie silence. She tried to hit the emergency button to summon someone—anyone, but there was nothing, just more eerie silence. The silence crept into every corner of her brain, and she yelled out just to break it apart.

"Well, looks like I'll be here till someone finds me. I can't just sit here; I have to do something. Look at me, stained red with wine and blood, and I'm really hungry too. I wonder how long I've been here already."

She checked the cell phone, and it was still on the same time and day when the earthquake happened. Erika knew that couldn't be right, but couldn't figure out what would be going on. She didn't wear a watch anymore because her cell phone had always provided her with the information she needed.

Erika was at a loss. Again, she was trapped and wondering what to do next. She eyed the stack of purses on the shelf and went to them.

"I will just look for a working cell phone or a watch and nothing else. I'm sure they wouldn't mind."

She rummaged through the purses, trying not to be rude and not look at anything but cell phones or watches. Not one purse had a watch, and all the cell phones she found had the same date and time, and could not find service. Erika was not surprised, being that nothing had been going her way for a while now.

"Well, so much for *that* idea. I guess it is time to worry about me. I'm a mess, and I'm starving. There are more uniforms in the cabinets, and there's water in those jugs in the corner. There are crackers and some fruit in those baskets. At least I could get somewhat clean and fed."

Erika jumped up, excited to have something else to do besides worry. She picked up her candle, which was nothing more than a cylinder candle in a coffee cup so it could be moved easily. She went over to a corner toward the back of the main room by the dreaded wine rack. Here she found a stack of five-gallon plastic water jugs. She grabbed a full one and pulled the jug over to a corner by the stairs that was more or less unused and contained a drain for moisture runoff. Then she went up the stairs to look in the cabinets. They were a gold mine for someone in Erika's current position. They contained pants that the cooks wore in the kitchen, button-up shirts, and T-shirts for cooks. Besides the clothes, there were candles, napkins, cleaning products, baskets filled with assorted varieties of nuts, fruits, potatoes, noodles, and rice. There were herbs that had been used for cooking, a first aid kit, and much more. Erika gathered up one of the large cooking bowls and a small one too. She took some soap that had been used to fill the containers in the bathroom and figured she might as well take some of the lotion that had been used for the same purpose. Then she grabbed a pair of pants that the cooks had worn in the smallest size she could find. They were not very attractive-looking, with their green jungle scene covering every inch of them, but she figured they would have to do. She also snatched up one of the matching green T-shirts. Erika decided that it would be wise to bring along the first aid kit as well. She could put antiseptic on the gash on her leg and the cuts she had received as a result of being crushed under the wine rack and then lying there in the glass for days. She did not have new socks but figured she would just rinse and wash the ones she had on and hang them on the shelf to dry.

She went back down the stairs with her hands full of the materials needed to give herself a makeshift cleaning. She moved back over to the corner, where she had placed the large jug of water. She poured some of the water out of the huge jug into the big bowl she had brought from the cabinet. Then she set up the soap nearby. As she began to undress herself and expose her bare skin to the cold, she realized she forgot something to dry off the water with. Naked from the waist up, she ran back to the cabinet. The biggest towel she could find was one that had been used for drying off dishes, but she figured it would have to work. She went back to the process of undressing once she reached the corner again.

She couldn't help but think that this is when her rescue would come. The rescuers would come busting in, and there she would be, naked in the bomb shelter giving herself a cat bath. She blushed at the thought, knowing she would be so embarrassed, but at this point, she just had to get the wine smell off of her. She sat down and removed her shoes, which had once been white but were now rosy just like everything else. Then she peeled off her newly dyed rosy socks. She delicately removed her pants. The cut on her leg still pained her greatly and, coupled with the bruises she had sustained, this was an uncomfortable process. It had to be repeated again to remove her underwear. Standing fully naked in her cement enclosure, goose bumps covering her, she began to shake.

She worked quickly to get the job done. She would dip the little bowl into the big bowl and pour it over her. The first time she did this, she screamed when the freezing water ran over her, but she kept going until she was drenched. Erika always hated taking cold showers. Even when it was one hundred degrees outside, she would make the shower just as hot. But she didn't have any hot water, and this washing had to be done. She was filthy and had cuts that had to be attended to. Once she was rinsed off, she grabbed the soap. Shivering in the cold, she washed from head to toe. She washed her hair with the soap too. Her hair would probably end up a mess of tangles, but it stunk so bad she went ahead and did it anyway. Although her skin was stained pretty bad, most of the red wine coloring was lathered up into piles across her body. She picked up the small bowl again, dipped it back into the water and re-soaked herself. Once she was free of the wine and blood coating, she picked up the small towel she had found and patted herself dry.

Erika was violently shaking in the cold, concrete room. She dressed quickly, not bothering to put on any underwear under her pants or a bra under her shirt because they were both badly stained. She thought about attending to the gash in her leg before putting on the pants she had found. Luckily, the uniform pants were baggy and the pant leg rolled far enough up her leg to expose the cut on the left one. So she put them on, rolled up the pant leg, and opened up the first aid kit. There was a bottle of hydrogen peroxide in it and a big roll of gauze with medical tape. She poured the peroxide over her wound and watched it bubble, angrily expelling any infection that might have escaped an unintentional alcohol cleaning from all the wine she had been lying in. When it stopped bubbling, she poured peroxide over it again just in case. When there was no sign of infection left, she covered a rectangular piece of gauze with Neosporin and put it on the gash. She taped the gauze to her leg so it would not fall off and rolled her pant leg back down.

After she was clean and her cuts were attended to, she turned to the task of cleaning her undergarments and socks. She poured more water into the large bowl and put her clothes in, too. Then she took out each one and soaped them up. She poured clean water into the large bowl and rinsed the garments. Then she walked across the floor. Her bare feet were sore with cold from the freezing cement, which made Erika realize she could not wait for her socks to dry; she would have to cover her feet sooner than that.

"Why did I even bother washing those stupid socks? I should have just put them back on, but they're so gross. I can just put on my shoes without socks for now. Well, now I'm clean and I know my legs are all right; let's see what I can find to eat. I wish I had some meat, but I couldn't cook it anyway. Oh well, I can have some of those nuts, and fruit too."

Erika went to the cabinet and grabbed another plastic bowl. She filled it with assorted nuts, a peach, and a pear. There were new knives still sheathed in their cardboard casings that would have eventually been used in the kitchen. She took one of those too. She spied a loaf of bread and snatched it up. She grabbed a cup out of the cabinet and went back downstairs. After putting her meal on the table, she went over to the corner where she had been washing and dragged the huge jug of water over to the table. She filled up her cup, and once she began drinking the water, she gulped down one glass after another, realizing she must have been very dehydrated. After she had her fill of water, she sat at the table and began to munch. She chomped down the pear; then handfuls of nuts; the peach was next; and lastly, she had a slice of bread accompanied by more nuts. She finally sat back in her chair. She was full, and now her problems flooded back into her mind. Before they encompassed her every thought, she jumped up and grabbed a smoke out of her pack.

"I've only got a half a pack left; I'll have to conserve them. Wait, weren't there more smokes in those purses? I can't take them, though. Once someone finds me, they'll know I was going through their things. Screw them, I'm stuck here; they won't care." But in Erika's mind the guilt over taking someone else's things was driving her nuts, so she decided she would just worry about that later. "I wonder if all the bottles of wine broke when the rack fell. I sure could use a drink."

Erika took her smoke with her as she walked over to the rack that was still supported by the crate and began to examine the remains. Although there were many broken bottles, she found half a dozen or so unbroken ones. She gathered them up, put them in another milk crate, and hauled them over to the table. The next problem—of how to open the wine bottle—was solved when Erika went rummaging through the cabinet. She found corkscrews reserved for future use in the restaurant. She opened a bottle of Merlot. Ironically, it was the same bottle that she had come to get in the first place! The bottle that had started this whole fiasco. She found that fitting. She filled her glass and sat back to think.

"No one has come yet. I must have been pinned under that wine rack for a while; who knows how much time has passed. What happened out there? I wonder what kind of damage that quake did. It was the biggest one I've ever felt. If no one has come for me yet, I wonder how long it will take. If I would have waited for them to free me from that wine rack, I would still be there waiting. I got myself out of that mess. I bet I could figure out how to get that door open."

Erika took another drink of her wine. She had decided that if no one was coming to save her, she would have to save herself.

She had finished her second glass of wine and was filling her third when the effects started to take hold. She had never been much of a drinker, so a little was all it took. Erika's husband had always poked fun at her for this; he called her a "cheap date." Thinking of her husband brought tears to her eyes; every part of her being ached to be with him. She thought of her husband's warm, safe arms and wanted to be there so bad. She thought of her son and how he would be calling for her. It annoyed her in the past to be constantly pestered by him, but now she just wanted to hear him and be with him.

"Are they okay? Did they survive? Was Vince at home with Dexter, or was he on his way home? I know they are alive. I just know it. I can feel them with me. I'm going to get home to them. I'll get out that door; you just watch."

There was no one there that Erika was addressing, but she could not stand the silence. Seldom was she alone, and she hated every minute of it. In the past, she had tried desperately to find a couple of minutes of quiet. Now, overwhelmed with it, she was going crazy. Tired and half drunk, she looked for a place to rest, but the bunker was concrete and the sleeping platform was removed a long time ago. She stumbled over to the cabinets again, but she didn't find any blankets or anything like that. There were boxes of cloth napkins and a few tablecloths. At least it was something to separate her from the cold floor. She made a pile of napkins on the floor. Then she covered them with two of the tablecloths. Finally, she carried over a bundle of cook's shirts from the cabinet. She polished off the last of the wine in the bottle as she snuggled under one of the tablecloths and covered the tablecloth with the bundle of shirts to keep warm.

In the drunken stupor that Erika was in, her dreams did not come easily. But, she slept soundly nonetheless: exhausted from the experience she was trying to struggle through. Late in her sleep, dreams began to come.

She was in her little house in the foothills of California, cooking dinner. Her son was running all over the house, and she began to scold him for getting into the cupboard which contained shiny pots and pans used to cook the daily meals. She told him to go and play with his toys. As he rounded the corner and left her sight, her husband rounded the corner and came into it. Her eyes soaked in every detail of his persona. She ran over to him, holding him in an embrace that left her glowing with his love. He stepped back from her and stared directly into her soul with his hazel eyes that had yellow stars outlining his black pupils. He said in a low rumble, "Come home to me. I will always be here waiting for you. I will never leave without you. I love you, and I know you will come home to me."

Erika awoke overwhelmed by the reality of her dream. "I know he is okay; I have to get home to him. But first, I have to get the hell out of this hole!"

She slowly arose from her bed with a throbbing head that reeled from the after-effects of her wine indulgence. She went over to the cupboard and rummaged through the first aid kit to find some Tylenol. Then she hesitated, knowing her supply of pain-relieving medicine was limited and probably not replenishable any time soon. She opted not to take the medicine for such an insignificant ailment as a hangover. Instead, she went to where the fruit baskets were and chose a peach that was beginning to turn brown and soften. Usually, the fruit baskets were replenished every week, but it did not appear that the new supplies would be coming any time soon.

She went to the table in the corner of the room, filled her water glass, and sat down to think of a way to escape her concrete cell. She felt like she had been asleep in her little nest for a week, and her mind was groggy and slow. She thought through the haze; the space in front of the heavy metal door didn't appear that big. She began to remember when she was young, and her brother, Bob, used to lock her out of the bathroom. She would wedge herself between the door and the hallway wall and push. Her back would create pressure against the door, and her feet—pressing against the drywall lining the hallway—would give her push much more force. The lock barely held in its metal casing, so the door would fly open, giving her access to the sink she needed to prepare herself for the day.

Erika was looking back fondly on the incident, and she reached into her purse to get a smoke from her depleting supply. She refilled her water glass and lit the smoke. The water was rehydrating her body, and she began thinking clearly again.

"What happened out there? How long have I been down here? If no one has come for me, will they ever? Why is there no rescue effort? If I do get out of here, what is going on out there? Maybe no one can come for me because the house collapsed and is blocking the door. Regardless, I have to find out."

All the while Erika had no sense of time. She had no idea how long she had been trapped under the wine rack and had no idea that her night on her bed of napkins had been more like days. After she awoke, the days passed on in this same fashion; Erika had no idea of day or night. She would rummage through the cabinets for food when she was hungry and sleep whenever her lack of energy overtook her. She had found some books that the owner had stored in the cabinets and read them to pass the time, while she was waiting to be rescued. Her thoughts always seemed to go back to how she was going to escape. She had tried and tried but could not get that door open. Her supplies were rapidly depleting, and Erika was growing very tired of this predicament.

She was claustrophobic and felt very irritated when she was confined. She began to dwell intensely on the fact that she had no idea how much time had passed. She had no window access and could not judge the movement of the sun to clock her days. Erika was an avid outdoorswoman, and she longed to see the sun and frolic through the forests as she had done so many times before. Tears began to roll down her face, and she began to cry out in terror. Her cries were stopped short when she remembered her dreams that she had often dreamt in her nest of napkins and tablecloths on the floor. *Vince... Dexter. I have to get home.* This thought of her beloveds would become her savior and push her through times when all she wanted to do was give up the struggle.

One day, Erika woke up with a new determination. She was now pretty certain that no one was ever going to come to rescue her. She felt like she had been locked down there for years. She declared to the silence, "That's it. Somehow I'll have to get myself out of here. First, I'll need more light. Then I'll figure out how to get the hell out of here so I can get in my car and go home. I'll put an end to this nightmare and see my family again, with or without a rescue party."

Erika went to the cabinet to get another candle from the box. She decided it would be worth it to grab two of them, so she could light the area in front of the door with a small candle and the downstairs area with a large candle at the same time. After she had lit the candles and had them in place, she looked intently at the door as if it would melt under the pressure of her intense stare. She pushed a shoulder into it and tried, again, to push as hard as she could. Nothing happened. Erika kept thinking of the story of her brother and getting into the bathroom. Erika sat down in the position similar to the one she had used when she was young and was struggling to gain access to the bathroom her brother had locked her out of. She just barely filled the space in front of the door, but she realized she could not reach the door handle and push at the same time. The door handle was not a round one but one that jutted out from the door in an L-shape. She figured that if she could hook a string to it, she could pull on the string, which would then turn the door handle, all while she was pushing from a sitting position.

She got up and ran down to the last cupboard, where she found a ball of cooking string. It was shrink-wrapped in plastic and would have been bound around a stuffed tri-tip and roasted. She grabbed the string and ripped off the plastic. She used her knife to cut a length of string, and proceeded to tie one end to the tip of the door handle and the other end in a loop that she could pull down on. Then she assumed her pushing position. As she pulled on the string and pushed with her legs, the door moved a couple of centimeters, but her legs didn't reach across the space in front of the door well, and, even with her legs fully extended, she could not open the door far enough to even let a little light in. She quit pushing and her centimeters of progress toward escape quickly vanished with the slamming of the metal door.

"At least I moved it! Whatever is holding it shut is really heavy. If I weren't so short, I could push it all the way open."

As she said that, she thought of her son. Whenever he was in the kitchen with her, he always wanted to know what was going on. On occasion, she would get him a chair to stand on, so he would be taller and could see how the dinner preparations took place.

"That's it. I'll get one of the chairs and lay it so I can push it against the wall. Forget that, I might as well get the table. It will give me an even longer reach, and it will be sturdier."

This time, she launched down the stairs, skipping every other one all the way down. She put her drinking glass and the candle that were on the table on the shelves by the purses and lifted up the heavy square of oak. Even though the task of dragging it up the stairs was arduous, Erika was no lightweight. Years of weight lifting and martial arts training had transformed her body into a finely tuned machine. When she reached the top of the stairs, the table was laid on its side with its legs facing the concrete wall. The table was bigger than she thought and covered almost three-quarters of the landing in front of the door. There was just enough room for her to fit in the space with her legs totally bent into her chest.

When she was in place and pulling on the door-handle string, she began to push. First a couple of centimeters, then an inch, then two, then there was daylight, and to her surprise, water began to rush into the bomb shelter. The water—green and brown—was a toxic mix, and it was pouring into Erika's only salvation from the devastation that awaited her on the other side of the door. Suddenly, Erika felt an immense pain down her lower back, over her butt, and down the back of her legs. She quickly quit pushing, jumped to her feet, and let the force of the water outside slam the door shut again.

CHAPTER 3

ERIKA HAD TO react fast. The water was melting her skin! She flipped the table up on its legs and climbed on top to escape the flow of toxic mush that had entered and was aiming to melt her flesh right off her body. The stench it released was incredibly horrible. She stood on the table in awe, but was quick to realize the implications as the back side of her body began to burn with pain. She knew she had to get washed off, but the water had come in much faster than she had realized, and it had filled her cement cavern with a foot of toxic waste.

"Great! Now what am I going to do?" she sobbed, "I'm going to die right here on this table. No! Pull it together. You have to wash this muck off."

Her survival instincts had begun to kick in again. She remembered the little bottles of water they had kept for certain picky customers. Erika didn't know if the toxic sludge—that had flooded the landing, the stairs, and had run down to fill the floor area—would eat through her clothes and shoes as well as her skin. It didn't appear that it had done so yet. Only the skin that had been exposed was enflamed. She stepped off the table into a toxic film that still barely coated the stairs. The cupboard door flew open as Erika tore into it, desperately reaching for a case of small water bottles. She took them to the table. Then she carefully took off her clothes and flung them into the watery abyss below. She was not going to tolerate the threat of any more of that sludge getting onto her skin.

She poured the cooling water over her screaming burns and wondered what they looked like and how bad they were. She would be able to coat some of the burns with the healing power of the little tube of Neosporin, but some on her back were unreachable. She wished her husband was there to rub lotion on her. She remembered his soft touch as he had rubbed sunblock over her sunburned body, but now it was just her. She would have to just leave them to heal on their own.

Once she was rinsed off and had some salve on the throbbing skin, she went to the cupboard that contained the uniforms. She had to stretch out over the sludge in order to reach the fresh clothing. She dressed but then quickly removed the clothing. Her blistered body had flared out at the soft cotton, and it was more than she could take. Erika thought she could just go without clothing, but the cold that was encased in the cement crept up on her until she could not decide which was worse: the cold air, or the pain of the clothing. In the end, she devised a way of wrapping her body in what little gauze she had and the cheesecloth that the chefs had used to supplement the gauze. This gave her some protection and cushioned her body from the rough elastic waistband.

In her new wrap, the pain subsided, and after redressing herself, the warmth began to comfort her again. Her candle was burning low by the time she was done caring for her wounded body. Knowing that she had no way to obtain her lighter, which provided her with flames, she grabbed another candle, a bigger one this time, from the box in the cabinet. When she originally lit the candles, she had used the larger one for the lower area, figuring that she would need that one longer, but her current dilemma had proved that assumption wrong. She was at a complete loss on how to put an end to this nightmare, now that things had managed to become even worse than they were before. She puzzled at why the water did not seem to drain from the lower floor even though there was a drain. Then she realized that the water was more like slime, and it was so filled with debris that it clogged the drain instead of flowing through it.

Erika's stomach rumbled, and she responded to its needs. She was hungry for something more than fruits and nuts, so she began to search the cupboards for anything else that could be eaten without cooking it. Some dehydrated milk with oatmeal and water became her final choice. She devised a way to heat it in a pot over the candle and ate a dinner of warm oatmeal with a tangerine. She ate, still standing in that toxic film. Her blistered skin was a constant reminder of just how dangerous the water that had run down the stairs and filled her chasm was. After eating, she had nothing to do but think. Standing there, skin burning, she stared into the abyss below. Suddenly, a thought flashed into her mind.

"There was daylight when I opened the door. The whole restaurant was gone. Of course, it was the dam. I bet it broke when the quake hit. The water flooded in. I wonder how much water is out there. Did the water sweep everything away?"

Erika was somewhat correct in her estimation of the problem. She had gone to college, and while she was there, she did a report on the implications of building a new dam by her house. She knew that once the reservoir behind the dam was filled, if anything should ever happen to the fragile structure, a one-hundred-foot wave would descend upon the Capital building in Sacramento within an hour. In its wake, it would leave a disaster area resembling a nuclear catastrophe. The dam had been built despite the demonstrators that visited the building site daily while construction had been in progress.

On that particular evening, while Erika had been at work, the great Mother Earth smashed the dam with her vicious shaking and let the destruction sweep her pestering children away. Hardly anything of a capitol city remained. People, houses, cars, pets, crops, everything had been drowned in water. It unleashed thousands of tons of toxic chemicals that had been stored by humans for various purposes. The sludge that remained ate anything alive that dared to challenge it.

Erika had been saved by that grumbly customer who had sent her down to the shelter for their very best bottle of wine. She was the only one left alive in Sacramento. Her situation was bleak, and she knew it.

"What am I going to do now? No one is ever coming to get me. How would they know I survived? I'm half burned by that slime. I can't swim through it; I can't even walk through it. I'm going to die here. I'll never make it home to my family. Maybe Vince wasn't even home when it happened. He could be dead too, for all I know. *I can't even sit down!*" Erika was frantically screaming and wailing in sheer misery.

Tears rolled down her face, and Erika flopped down on her stomach on the table. Lying on her stomach was fine. Her back was straight, and her body fit perfectly across the table. Completely drained of all will to survive, Erika continued to stare down at the water that now filled the floor area. She desperately wished she could get to the supplies that she had utilized down there. As she stared, the candle that she had lit down there before the water came in began to dance and flicker like a strobe light. One of the empty plastic jugs that had formerly been stacked in the far corner was floating by. Its movements were accentuated by the strobe lighting. As she stared at it, an idea came to her.

"If only I could float on top of that water jug, I could float out of this sludge. Wait a minute... maybe I can. The water delivery guy was going to come tomorrow, and there were even more empties than normal to collect because it was a holiday the week before this. There must be at least ten of those things floating around. But how would I sit on them without getting wet? If only I had a piece of wood to hook them to."

The implications of her statement clicked as soon as she laid her head back down on the oak table that she had lugged to the top of the stairs before the water came in. She stood up and jumped down to the concrete landing. She placed the table onto its side and began to kick the legs off of it. Once the legs were lying in a heap on the floor, Erika began to wonder how she was going to hook the huge water jugs to the solid oak slab she had created. Before she could attach the jugs, she would have to fish them out of the toxic sludge. How to do that was a mystery in itself. She needed a very long pole, but her space was limited to the stairs. She went to the cupboards and began to rummage through them. She did not find a pole, but she found items like the cooking string and a box of duct tape that might come in handy for building her craft once she had obtained the essential materials to make it float.

Erika began to think of the daily operations of the restaurant, and what they would have used that would suit her current needs. She remembered the high vaulted ceiling lavishly painted and the giant chandeliers hanging from it. When dust had accumulated, they had used a giant feather duster hooked to a long pole to reach the otherwise unreachable heights. They had stored the long pole in a piece of plastic PVC piping that had been cut in half and hooked with U-bolts to the ceiling of the shelter over the stairs.

She looked up and saw the familiar tubing. Her eyes lit up, and she ran up to the landing. Standing on her tippy toes, she could just barely reach the PVC pole. She pulled it from its sheath and began to wonder what she could attach to it to make a hook at the bottom. She was at a loss. Finally, she decided that the two-pronged fork they had used for stabbing meat off the barbecue could be bent so that the tongs formed a hook. She took the fork and pressed it against the concrete until the tongs rounded up toward her hands. When she was done, she grabbed a roll of duct tape and attached it firmly to the pole where the duster had formerly been attached.

Now, with her new tool in hand, she was ready to start fishing. She was excited by this new purpose, and it eased the pain of her injuries. She grabbed her candle off the table but then decided she should just light another one. Erika could not afford to lose the only light she had when her lighter lay on the other side of the toxic pond. After she had the additional flame burning, she went down the stairs to the last one not covered by the sludge. She put the candle down on the stair by the cupboard door and began to move the pole toward one of the jugs.

As Erika predicted, ten of the plastic jugs floated in the mush, but only half of them would be reachable. Erika decided she would deal with that issue later. Erika reached out with the pole and began to roll the jug around until she could see the handle. Then Erika hooked the bent fork through the handle and pulled back. It worked! The jug was moving closer. The only problem Erika could foresee was how she was going to pick the jug up when it was coated in the toxic goo. Erika thought fast. She was too excited about getting her raft built to let this problem slow her down. All she had to do was stand up to reach the cupboard that held the box of rubber gloves. She put a pair on and grabbed the jug out of the green water. She put the jug two stairs up from where she sat, so it would not hinder her fishing the next one out, and once she had collected them all, they could be washed later. She pulled the next two jugs out in the same fashion. After some problems hooking the handle, she decided it would be easier to just drag the jug in with the pole.

The rubber gloves worked perfectly at protecting Erika's frail skin from the burning sludge. On the fourth jug, though, Erika put her hand too far into the water and a drop had burned her arm as it ran down the inside of her rubber glove. She had to remove the glove and get a new one. She also washed her skin carefully with water to avoid further burning. Erika came up with a solution to this problem while she was washing. She went and got one of the long-sleeved cook's shirts and put it on. Then she held the cuffs while she slid her arm into the rubber gloves. The last step she took was to wrap the area where the rubber glove met the long-sleeved shirt in duct tape. With her arms covered, she could work without the fear of reaching too far into the water or having some of the water run down into her gloves.

The delay that the burning drop had caused was actually a blessing in disguise because all but two of the jugs had floated into the reach of the pole during the cleaning. Before long, three of the last four stairs were stacked with the eight water jugs. Erika rinsed the jugs lightly with as little water as possible because she only had two flats of water left. She had no idea how long it would take her to find more water once she left the shelter.

Now all her materials were together, and she began constructing her raft. Erika's biggest difficulty was figuring out how to attach the tabletop to the water jugs. She was tired and hungry, so she went rummaging through the goods in the cabinets again. She picked out a peach, an apple, and a banana that were really starting to look gross, but she mixed them with oats and nuts and ate them anyway. She sat down on the top stair to eat. As she ate, she contemplated her dilemmas. She had quite a few rolls of duct tape and figured it would work, but how much would it take? She didn't want to deplete her whole supply with just this one task.

She moved the oak table flat on the floor of the landing. By now, the sludge had all drained off, and she figured it would make a great area for construction. Erika envisioned a craft kind of like a makeshift pontoon boat. Erika thought the most resourceful way to put it together would be to attach a row of four jugs to one another with the duct tape to form one of the pontoons. She would have to seal the tops up tight so that only the air would fill the space at all times. She covered the opening in the five-gallon jug with the rubber glove and then held it in place with the sticky duct tape. Then she started to attach one jug to another with the tape. Pretty soon, there was a line of four jugs all put together and securely fastened. She laid that one aside and made the next row. Now she had all the pieces to the raft assembled, but how could she put it all together? She thought about just using the duct tape but that would be a whole lot of tape, and it had taken a lot just to connect the jugs together. Her supply was dwindling quickly, and she didn't know if she had enough. She needed something that, when wrapped around an object, would cover space faster than duct tape, but was waterproof and sticky like the duct tape.

She thought back about when she and Vince had gone skiing. They needed the four-wheel drive that the truck had, but if it was snowing, their gear would get all wet. To avoid this, they had wrapped their gear in plastic bags. Erika dismissed this idea because the plastic bags would only loosely wrap things. She needed to connect the jugs to the table.

It made her feel good to think about her husband. She kept thinking about him and her dilemma. She remembered talking with him about what his boss did when he was driving his truck in the rain and needed to keep his tools dry. He had wrapped them in cellophane. The plastic wrap had formed to the tools and had kept them dry. That was it! There was a whole box filled with individual rolls of cellophane in the cupboard.

Erika ran over to the cabinet and grabbed a roll of the prized wrapping. She laid all the pieces for her craft out together in the way they would be put together. She began to wrap the jugs and the table in the plastic wrapping. She started wrapping the length of it first and then the width, until the plastic wrap covered everything and was holding it together well. She had used every roll, except one, to wrap the craft but knew it was a good investment of resources. Erika was not sure that the cellophane alone would hold her craft together; she would have to use some tape to help it out. She had enough duct tape so that, once she had reinforced the craft in a coating of it, she had four rolls left.

The craft was finished. She took it down to the water for a test float. She put it in the water and the jugs held the table top far away from the toxic sludge. She was triumphant but very hesitant about climbing aboard. Whenever you rode in a boat, especially a raft this size, you got at least a splash of water on you. Usually this was no big deal, and a welcome relief from the summer heat, but in this case it would be very painful. She had protected her arm skin from the burning liquid. She remembered her plastic gloves she had used to reach for the jugs and looked at her craft. That was the solution. She would wrap herself in the same fashion as the boat. She decided a coating of cellophane under a layer of duct tape should be worn over her clothes. That way it would allow her to move around but still protect her from the sludge. She left a gap at the waistline that could be unsealed and resealed so she could still relieve herself.

Her body was completely covered in gray duct tape except for her yellow rubber hands and her completely unprotected head. Finally feeling a little safer, she boarded her raft. She had brought the pole that she had used for fishing out the jugs so she could direct herself around the watery space. It worked perfectly, and she moved with ease. She headed right for the shelf that held the purses. She pulled them off the shelf and piled them in a heap on the raft, and she grabbed a hooded sweatshirt as well. There was nothing else of use above the water, but she thought about the drinkable water and wine that lay below. Just then, her eye caught the gleam of the wine she had stashed by the table before the water came in.

After trying to hook the pole to the milk crate that held the full bottles and pull them directly up to the craft, she found that leaving her head unprotected was a bad idea. The water had splashed as the raft bobbed under the weight of the crate, and even though only a small drop got her, it had burned a spot on her neck under her ear. She had decided that nothing was worth the risk of suffering more burns and left the bottles where they lay (Erika was not aware that the toxic sludge had eaten away the corks in the bottles anyway).

Once she docked her craft at the stairs, she took her reclaimed goods to the top. She went into her purse and got one of her few remaining cigarettes, lit it, took a deep drag, and sighed. She knew she had a lot to do if she was going to escape this dungeon alive.

As Erika began to consider what she would need for the long voyage ahead, she thought of food first. There were lots of nuts and oats left; there were also raisins, dried apricots, prunes, and some very overly ripe fruits. She really had no idea how long she had been living on this diet but thought maybe she had been there about two weeks or so. Regardless, she was starting to feel the effects of the lack of proper nutrition; she longed for some protein, but this was all she had. She needed bags to pack her goods in and thought the purses would work well. She would also take one crate filled with the remaining fruit that was actually worth taking.

Since the landing at the top of the stairs had dried out, Erika laid the last tablecloth she had on the landing and began to empty the contents of the purses. The first one she picked up was a black leather bag that had one large pocket for all its contents. First, she took out the wallet. She was riddled with guilt about going through somebody else's things but figured that it didn't matter now anyway. She opened the wallet and looked at the California driver's license inside. It had belonged to Kelly Burns, a sixteen-year-old girl who had just gotten a car and a job at the restaurant as a busser. She had a hundred dollars in her wallet, and Erika took it. She also found a pack of rolling papers and took those out too. She threw the wallet in the watery depths when she found that there was nothing else of use in it. Even though Kelly was not legally old enough, she had developed a habit of smoking, and Erika removed a full pack of Marlboro Reds from her purse. The rest of the contents had little value right now, so she just threw them in the water.

Erika continued emptying the contents of the other purses in the same fashion. She would check the ID, remember the person it belonged to, look for valuable items, then throw the unneeded things into the water to meet the same watery fates as their owners. It was a solemn event, but she had found five hundred dollars, five full packs of smokes and two half packs, six lighters, a knife, some mace, a pair of sunglasses, and four books of matches. The last purse she had to clean out was her own. She pulled out her own wallet. She rubbed it slowly like a genie lamp to relinquish all its memories. She thought of her mother-in-law, who had bought it for her. Her in-laws had been vacationing in Washington when the quake hit, and Erika wondered if they had felt the effects of it. She opened her wallet and looked immediately at the picture of her beloved Vince. It was a picture from the year they had gotten married. Vince stood regally in his black dress shirt, and his loving eyes glared into her soul. *I will make it home, I will make it home*, was the only thing Erika could think of. But as Erika turned the page to reveal the picture of her son and her mother, she wept huge tears of pain.

"I will make it home! I have to. I know they are alive. I can feel them pleading with the Lord to allow me to come back to them, and I will. I always said that if something happened to our fragile environment, I would survive. I read all those books about herbal healing, hunting, survival techniques, and martial arts: all to learn how to survive if I had to, and now I do. I have to pull it together, get what I need to get to land, and get the hell out of here."

She closed her wallet and continued cleaning her purse out. She emptied out old receipts and shopping lists; she would need to make room for more important things now. She opened the last pouch and saw her slingshot. It was a weapon not commonly used, but Erika had trained herself proficiently with it. Erika also had her hunting knife there because she had gone out looking for a pesky raccoon that had gotten into the chicken coop at her in-laws' two nights in a row. The circular metal ball thrown with the slingshot had not proven fatal, but that pesky raccoon would definitely think twice about bothering those chickens again. Along with the slingshot, she noticed an unused tampon. She did not need it now, but Erika had never kept good track of her cycle. It was often unpredictable and could be delayed when she was under stress. She wondered when it would come. This made her think about future supplies for that certain female problem, and she was relieved when she found a big box containing smaller boxes of the protective cotton in the cabinet. She took out five boxes. This many boxes could last her at least five months, and she said a silent prayer that she would not need that many before she hit land. She figured that once she reached shore, she could buy more and would not need such a large supply.

All the purses were now empty, and she began packing. She thought that if she could get the door open all the way, the raft would float out the door. She dragged the raft back up the stairs to the landing. She could stock it there, and then when she opened the door, the shelter would fill with water, and she could just float out. Erika put the crate of fruit onto the back of the raft and then two purses full of oats, already mixed with dehydrated milk and nuts with the dried fruit. She decided it would be best to put everything into crates so she could wrap the sides, and attach it to the raft so it would not fall off. She put all the remaining water on the raft, along with more knives, and extra clothes. She also loaded on one of the extra outdoor table umbrellas. She brought Tupperware bowls and cut the sides off a square Tupperware container so it could be attached to the pole and used as an oar. She packed all the candles and reached for the first aid kit.

She had ransacked the kit since she had been there and realized there wasn't much of use left. She had used the entire bottle of antiseptic and the tube of Neosporin on her burns. She still had half of the bottle of Tylenol, and there were still some gauze left so she took them out. But then she changed her mind. The first aid kit was plastic, maybe waterproof, and it would probably float if it ever fell in the water. So Erika threw out the empty items and put the gauze and Tylenol back into the kit. Even though Erika had studied a little about herbal medicine, she was not confident enough with it to know what she should use for which ailment. She didn't have a book or anything with her. She grabbed some spices that she thought would be helpful and packed them into Ziploc baggies before putting them into the first aid kit to make the most of any available space.

Erika continued pillaging the cupboards. She packed a medium and small sauce pan into one of the wooden crates that she had hooked to the craft. Erika had attached the crates to the craft in a sort of U fashion. This would give her an area to sleep, an area to row in, and plenty of storage space. Erika constructed the paddle for the craft by removing the hook from her PVC pipe and attaching the square Tupperware piece that she had cut to it. It would not be ideal, but it would have to do. After she had her raft loaded with everything her brain could imagine she would need, she decided to refine her attire one more time. She had removed the top half of her cellophane-and-duct-tape suit so her hands would be free to work, but she could no longer afford this luxury. She remembered the new burn on her neck and knew she would need to protect her head as well.

She thought the hooded sweatshirt would work well as upper body and head protection. Over the sweatshirt, she wrapped cellophane. Then she wrapped the duct tape over it to complete the suite once again. Except, this time, she tucked her hair into the hood of the sweatshirt and duct-taped as much of her head as she could without covering her eyes, nose, or mouth. She would probably pull her eyebrows off when the tape was removed, but if it would keep her alive long enough to reach land, it was worth the loss. Finally, she put on the sunglasses she had found to protect her eyes and put the rubber gloves back on too.

She was all ready. One last rummage through the cupboard assured her she had packed everything she could. She looked over the raft and decided it would be wise to cover the tops of the crates for the initial launch. When she was through, she had a half of a roll of cellophane and one roll of duct tape left. The most dangerous part of the launch would be getting the door open again. She would have to trust that her suit would protect her, because it would take everything she could muster to budge that door. She remembered that the table was what helped her push the door open last time, and she would not be able to set it up the same way this time. She decided she would have to wedge herself in between the raft and the door and push on the side of the table. It gave her a smaller area to push on, but, hopefully, it would work just the same.

In position, with the door loop in hand, and her legs bent for pushing, she decided it was time. Erika pushed, and as the door opened, the water flooded in, but this time it did not burn. Her suit held, but she did not know how long it would hold out for. She used all her might and forced the door all the way open. The raft was beginning to float, so she climbed aboard quickly. The force of the water wanted to push the raft down the stairs, but the slope of the ceiling and a strategically placed oar prevented it. Soon, she forced the raft out the door.

CHAPTER 4

ERIKA'S EYES WINCED in the daylight. After all that time in the dark with only a candle to light the way, the sun pierced her pupils and made them water even with the protective glasses on. When her eyes adjusted to the blast of sunlight, Erika could not believe what she was seeing. The buildings that had once towered above the city in every direction had been pummeled into piles of rubble. Some of them had been sheared right in half by the rapidly moving water. Debris floated all across the surface of the sludge that had formed when the water crashed into the toxic substances that humans used to sustain life. The cars that had once congested every street were smashed into more piles of debris surrounding the building shells. The people that had filled the city with the noise of life were all gone. Erika was thankful for that. She could not imagine the scene that had played out here all the while she was trapped in concrete below. The capital city of California had been blasted with green, slimy water spanning as far as the eye could see. The smell of urban life was gone and the stagnant, toxic stench of the ooze was all that remained.

Erika was thankful for the sunglasses she had found in one of the purses. They softened the extreme sunlight and through the glare, she could see the familiar peaks of the Sierra Mountains in the distance that always welcomed her home. They were there in the east, standing gloriously above the sludge. She started paddling her vessel toward where the freeway that she had driven so many times before to get home used to be. It was difficult paddling with only one PVC paddle in hand. The craft was awkward and wanted to veer left or right depending on what side she was paddling on. As she neared the area where the freeway should have been, she noticed that it was easier going, almost like there was a current flowing down the freeway. She just hoped it would be flowing in the direction she needed to go. She finally made her way onto Interstate 80, or what she thought was the freeway. It was hard to tell with the amount of rubble that had gotten moved around, but she did see what looked to be like freeway overpasses strewn about on either side of an alley. To her dismay, the current was flowing against her. She should have known. None of the forks of the American River flowed up to the mountains; they ran down from the mountains to the ocean. Even though the rivers had been inundated with toxic sludge, it was still these same rivers acting as a driving force and moving all this water around.

The flow of water made it even more difficult to maneuver the bulky craft, and the sun beat down upon Erika. All of her struggling to paddle the raft against the current and her cellophane-and-duct-tape suit intensified the heat; she was feeling rather faint. She quickly remembered the outdoor umbrella that she had laid across the crates on the back of the raft. She grabbed it and set it up to shade her from the heat. Much to her surprise, even though the current was going the opposite direction that she wanted to go, the wind was not, and it caught at the umbrella. Erika quickly realized the implication of this and used some of her last roll of duct tape to attach the umbrella as a sort of sail to catch the wind and help move her along her desired path. The wind in the umbrella also helped to stabilize the craft, and Erika found that if the wind was constantly pulling the craft to the left, she could just paddle on the right and the raft would be balanced. It was much better than rowing a couple times to the left and then a couple to the right.

Erika's first night on the craft was awe-inspiring. The sun blazed red, orange, and pink as it dipped out of sight beyond the horizon of destruction to the west. Then a beautiful crescent moon peeked up over the mountains. The stars twinkled like diamonds in the sky, and Erika was taken aback by their beauty. She couldn't figure out why they looked so bright and then it dawned on her. There was no light on the Earth. She scanned the horizon and did not see one light anywhere. The city used to look like a sun lying in the mountains at night. The light dimmed the stars and made them dull. Now the stars were back in their full glory, and they were awesome. Erika saw the Milky Way as bright as the first settlers of this place had seen it so long ago. The darkness made Erika realize how tired she was. She had spent all that energy on her escape and then the very last of her strength paddling. The lack of calories finally caught up with her, and she dozed.

Erika woke up very distressed. She did not remember where she was. She was on her craft but there was no sun overhead. She felt the craft bumping against something. It was dark and for a moment she thought that she was back in her concrete cell, but it was not the deep dark of that hole: somewhere there was sunlight shining. She sat up quickly so she could assess the situation.

"I must have fallen asleep and the current took me. But where did it take me?" As she looked up, she quickly realized what had happened. "I'm in a building! The current must have pushed me in here."

Her craft had been bumping against the wall of the building that was still holding back the flood waters, and a roof was overhead. She was in a pile of debris that had been caught in this building from the flow of water.

As she started to paddle away from the debris pile, she screamed, "Oh my God!"

There were bodies, bloated and floating, along with her in the pile. The stench assaulted her nostrils with rotten flesh, and she had to put the paddle in between the bodies or push off of them directly to free the boat. She started to paddle frantically, completely freaked out. She rounded the corner in the building and saw where everything was coming from. This building had survived fairly well and only one large window had broken on the front. The flow of water had entered that window and was now creating a huge eddy inside of the building. She paddled as fast and as hard as she could to that window, with the faces of the dead still flashing in her mind.

She found her way toward the freeway once again and vowed that she would tie up the raft to anything she could find before she fell asleep; that way, she could not drift too far while she was resting. All in all, her raft held together well, and she was making decent time. One day began to blend into another as the mountains came closer, and her water and food supplies were depleted. It was tough, at times, to tell how deep the water was because she couldn't see through the green slime. Occasionally, her pole would hit what Erika thought could be the bottom. This would cause her to hope that before too long, she would be reaching some kind of a shore. But more than likely it was just some unseen debris lying under the slime, because she could not even see an edge to the toxic film on the horizon.

On the fourth day of traveling on the raft, Erika awoke at first light. She lit her candle so she could make some oatmeal and tea. Usually, she hated tea, but it was nice to throw some herbs into her water and heat it up. It gave it a totally different flavor, and at least it was some kind of flavor. She thought how nice it would be to have a big old cup of coffee but that was not an option. Her fruit was totally gone, and all that remained were oats and nuts. When she gazed toward the mountains, excitement washed over her. They were very close. Today was the day she would finally reach them! She finished breakfast and lit a smoke. Then she sat back to finish waking up before she would have to pick back up the oar and paddle. She scanned the landscape of sludge. Was that smoke from her cigarette or from something else?

"What the heck is that? It looks like a huge fire. Maybe it's a wildfire, but with all that water, how can it be burning? It looks like it's coming from that huge cone. Is it a volcano? It *is* a volcano. Look how thick and black that smoke is. Oh well, it's a long way off. It probably won't affect anything this far away, especially since there is nothing left. I don't care anyway because today, I'm going to reach that land. I'll find someone to drive me home. I'll walk all the way if I have to but soon I will be there, home with my husband and my son in my arms again."

Erika picked up her paddle and rowed with a vengeance. She held her pace all morning. What she noticed in the distance had indeed been a volcanic eruption. But her assumption that it would not affect her was wrong. Even though it was hundreds of miles away—and thanks to a sudden change of wind direction the smoke would not affect her area—the lava followed freshly opened cracks in the earth. It flowed into the newly formed lake in Sacramento where the lava cooled and the temperature of the water increased. Erika didn't notice until she paused her paddling that the water had begun to steam. When she noticed, she was concerned but unaware of the implications. She figured it was best to just keep going. The shore was very near, but as she traveled through the super-heated sludge, the plastic jugs that held her afloat began to melt. She was only half a mile from shore when her raft began to take on water. Erika's suit held off the burning effects, but paddling an overweight piece of wood through ooze was not going to get her to shore fast enough.

The excitement of reaching shore overwhelmed her, and she was thinking impulsively. She figured she wouldn't need her supplies because she could get whatever she needed if she could just make it to shore. Erika plunged into the gross sludge, keeping her head out and depending on her suit to protect her. She began to swim to shore. The heat from the water began to overwhelm her, and she swam hard to make it to shore faster. Pain began to take its hold and, with her limited energy supplies depleting quickly, she struggled on. She finally swum to a shallow-enough area that her feet reached for ground. Her last energy reserves were expended on her walk to dry land. Erika collapsed as she reached down to hug the soft dirt.

Erika awoke in a dimly lit room, and she anxiously looked around to make sure her escape from the bomb shelter and struggle through the sludge had been for real. Her eyes confirmed that it had been reality. It had been so long since she woke up someplace that was familiar; the panic she felt upon waking up was beginning to feel normal. She took a deep breath and looked around. She was in a barn that had been damaged by the earthquake but was sound despite the abuse it had taken. As she tried to sit up, pain pierced every inch of her body, and she screamed.

"Don't move, honey. You're in no shape for it," a sweet woman's voice commanded.

"Where am I?" Erika's mouth hurt to talk, but it had been so long since she had someone to talk to that she couldn't refrain from doing it.

"Well, we're in what used to be Newcastle, and we're in the barn because the house was completely destroyed in that horrible earthquake."

"How did I get here?"

"Well, you see, honey, my husband has been out looking for survivors since the dam broke and flooded the valley. Being that we never found anyone alive, he wasn't going to go out the day that he found you. You know with the volcano eruption and everything, but he went anyway. It's a good thing he did because he brought you back in the wagon. He went back and got your supplies the next day. That suit you made was a very smart idea. It kept the water from burning your skin. Unfortunately, when I cut it off, I noticed the hot water had melted the plastic wrap to your clothes and skin. So you still got burned pretty badly where the plastic touched your skin. But you're alive, and you will be back on your feet in a few weeks. I am just so glad someone made it out of that disaster alive. I didn't think we would ever find anyone after the weeks that we searched in vain."

"Where is everyone? Why were no rescue attempts made by the fire department? I never even saw one helicopter."

"Well, everyone took a beating in the quake, honey. We thought that it only affected our area at first, but now… well, I am not so sure. There have been no relief efforts. No National Guard, nothing. After months of waiting for rescue, we're fearful of people altogether. People have been killing each other for food since no food has been delivered in months."

"Months? No food? What the hell is going on? What about transportation? How will I ever get home now?" Erika's mind was scrambling to understand the implications of everything this woman was saying so flatly.

"That's right, honey. The main quake happened two months ago now. All the roads are pretty damaged. The cars that are okay can't clear the gaps and chunks that were opened or strewn about. We have our garden and animals, and we have been doing fine besides having to move into the barn. The fighting has been around the city centers mostly. My husband rode one of the horses into Auburn to get help. It took him a half a week to get there and back. Once he got there, he just turned around and came home. He didn't want to tell me what he had seen and simply said it was horrible."

"Two months? That means it's…" Erika was trying to calculate with a head so full of fog she was finding it hard to think at all.

"It's July 2, actually, honey. Just two days until Independence Day. Not that there will be any celebration this year." The lady mumbled that last part under her breath.

"Oh no, what am I going to do now? I figured I would be home free once I got to shore. This is the worst nightmare ever. I have to get home to my family," Erika sputtered with tears in her eyes.

"Don't worry about all that now, honey. There's plenty of time to worry about how to get home. Right now, you just need to rest and get healthy. Here, eat this."

The woman handed Erika a bowl of soup that had meat chunks finely cut so Erika's famished stomach would not become upset. It also had carrots, peas, and onions. It was like heaven to Erika—real meat and vegetables that weren't dried out, hot broth, oh yeah. After Erika ate it, she slugged down a glass of water and fell back asleep.

CHAPTER 5

SHE FELL BACK into a deep sleep. She dreamt of her tiny home that was white and trimmed with green. She dreamt of her son running through the backyard. The green grass was blowing in the wind. Her son was climbing his play-set. He would zoom down the slide right into the dog and then the two of them rolled through the lawn. She was lazily working in the flower bed, just enjoying the sunshine and the peace and quiet. Erika heard the wooden gate to the yard close behind her, and her husband walked up. She gazed into his warm eyes and reached out to feel the ripples of his muscular body. She wrapped her arms around him and drank up all the love he could possibly offer. His embrace enveloped her, and she knew she was in heaven.

Erika awoke. She almost wished she could sleep forever, so she could just stay wrapped in Vince's love. Realizing that the dream was too real to just be a dream, she knew she had to get home. He was still there. He was trying to reach out to her just as she was trying to reach out to him. They were soul mates, and they would find one another no matter what.

Erika looked around the barn. She was in the hayloft, which was furnished with items that had obviously been salvaged from a home. It was hard to believe it was a barn at all, but the smell of hay and animal reminded her. She sat up slowly. Her body was still sore and scabbed all over from the burns she had sustained. She drew back the blanket but quickly brought it back up when she realized that she was completely naked. Then she heard the creak of the wooden stairs that led up to the loft. She heard the footsteps come across the barn floor, and then the blanket that was hung as a door to her room was pulled back and in popped the head of the sweet lady Erika had talked to before.

"Oh dear, you're up. I'm sorry I wasn't here when you woke. You look much better." She entered the room and sat down on a chair next to Erika's bed. "My name is Carol Duncan, and what is your name… or should I just keep calling you honey?" Carol asked.

Carol was an older lady with gray curls encompassing a round face. She was small in stature and walked stiffly. She had brought a pitcher of water with her. She filled a glass that was next to Erika's bed and put the pitcher down next to it.

"My name is Erika. How long have I been asleep?"

"Two days since you woke up last; it's the Fourth of July," Carol said cheerfully. "I doubt we'll see any real fireworks today, but seeing you sitting up is fireworks enough for me. You must be feeling much better."

"Besides feeling like I have been hit by a truck, I am not feeling too bad." Erika said, stiffly moving her arms around.

"That will pass, honey. I just wish I could do more for you. I'm no doctor and even if I was, I don't have any medicines left. I don't even have any of my arthritis medicine left."

"I studied a little about medicine. I was on Ski Patrol up in Tahoe for a while, and I studied some books on herbs for healing, but when it really comes down to it, I'm no doctor either. I remember some of those herbal remedies, though. Maybe I could get up and find something for you and me." Erika was really anxious to be up and about after sleeping so long. She figured she was a lot closer to home now, and she wanted to know just how close she really was. Looking for healing herbs seemed like a good excuse.

Carol was not as convinced as Erika that she was ready to be up and about yet and quickly countered, "I don't know, honey, you're in no shape to be going out yet. Maybe if you could tell me what you need, I could get it for you, and you could show me how to prepare it."

Erika was disappointed but decided that it was probably best to listen to this woman. After all, Erika did owe the couple her life at this point. She replied, "That sounds like it will work. I need a plant called plantain. It is really common in this area and grows in the grass. It looks like really thick blades of grass growing from a singular plant. This time of year, it might have sprouts like flowers coming out of the middle. Also, if you could get me my clothes, I could try to get these legs moving again." Erika tried to slide the last part in real nonchalantly, hoping that Carol would at least let her get out of bed and move around some.

"Oh, I almost forgot all about your clothes. Hold on one second." Carol enthusiastically stood up and left the room. Erika heard her steps across the floor again. They faded away and then returned. "Look here, honey. We had to cut your clothes off your skin and the cellophane you wrapped yourself in melted all over them. You have some more of those cooking clothes with your gear, but I made this outfit out of an extra pair of sheets. They shouldn't irritate your burns as much as those thick cotton cook's clothes." Carol held up a simple outfit and placed it on Erika's bed.

"Thank you. That's absolutely perfect. Carol, I really have to thank you for all you've done for me. I owe you my life," Erika said sincerely.

"Oh, nonsense." Carol shrugged the comment off. "I am just glad we could help. Like I told you before, we have been looking for survivors since the quake, but you are the only one we found."

"I'm the only one… Are you serious? What happened to everyone?" Erika was shocked.

"I don't know. We think that when the water hit the valley, it simply washed everything out toward the coastal mountains and the ocean. The volcano that erupted over that way probably covered all of the aftermath," Carol stated with a sad, wondering look in her eyes.

"I've wanted to ask you, Erika, how did you survive that mess?" Carol was looking very inquisitively at Erika. Then she shook her head and said, "Actually, don't answer that now. You can tell my husband and me at the same time after dinner tonight. That way you don't have to tell your story twice. Now, I need to go and find that plant you need before it gets dark."

"Thanks, Carol."

Without the enthusiasm for the outfit that Carol had made for Erika, Erika noticed that Carol rose very stiffly from the rickety wooden chair that had been placed by Erika's bed. Erika was guessing that Carol had watched over her the whole time she had been sleeping. All this talk of medicine and watching Carol's stiff body made Erika remember something from her herb books.

"Carol, do you have any evening primroses planted in any flower gardens?" Erika questioned inquisitively.

"Why, yes, I do. I have a whole bed. At least, I had a whole bed but some survived. I just love those flowers."

"Great! If you can find some seeds from them, the oils that they contain can bring you some relief from that arthritis. Also, you can eat the young roots as a vegetable."

"I'll be darned. Who would have guessed that I have a flower bed full of the medicine I need. Here I've barely been able to walk and bend, and the whole time the medicine was right there," Carol exclaimed as if completely dumbfounded by this information.

"I wouldn't say it's an instant cure, or even that it will work as well as the medicine you used before, but it will help," Erika countered.

"Honey, you have made my day. What a joy having you around is going to be," Carol said cheerfully.

"I can't stay long, Carol. I have to get home to my family, and I have already been gone for two whole months," Erika said, grimacing with pain as she tried to sit up straighter.

"I know, honey, but you will have to heal first. Just relax and concentrate on that."

With that, Carol headed down the stairs with two empty baskets. Erika picked up the garments Carol had left for her. The shirt was light blue and made of very soft cotton. The collar had a V slit cut into it with strings so it could be tied shut. The pants were also the same light blue color, and the only feature was an elastic band around the waist to hold them in place. Erika pulled the covers back again and threw her legs over the side. Something was poking her in her very sore legs. She looked down and saw that her bed was made of hay bales with a thick foam pad laid over the top. Then the sheets were put over the top so that it was soft and looked almost like a real bed, until you felt the side. She stood up and slipped her pants on over the sore, scabbed, and blistered skin. Erika thought the pain from the elastic band would be excruciating, but it actually wasn't that bad. That was a good sign, indicating that the wounds were healing quickly, and, although she would be pretty scarred, nothing was seriously damaged.

She looked down at her bare feet. They were cold but they were not painful. Erika figured that the shoes she had on had protected them. She strolled across the floor and looked out the window that was located in the kitchen over the sink. The window looked out to the Northwest. At one time, it looked over a wooded area that gradually molded into a valley that contained a city named Sacramento. On a clear day when the smog was not too thick, you could have seen skyscrapers looming in the distance, and the endless shops, people, and cars. Human life and their creations as far as the eye could see.

It was all gone. The forest area now ended abruptly at the edge of a toxic lake occupying what had been the Sacramento Valley. The new toxic beach was about five miles west of the barn. The barn that used to be home to just animals stood soundly and had provided Carol and her husband a sanctuary from a world that was turning itself upside down. A tear fell from Erika's eye when she began to think of the hundreds of thousands of people that had died there. Why had she been spared? She was there, in the middle of the toxic sludge, and made it out. She was alive and in decent condition: Why her and no one else?

"What am I doing just standing around? I need to get ready to go."

CHAPTER 6

SHE KNEW THAT Carol had told her to stay put, but she headed toward the stairs anyway and started to descend the steep stairway. When she reached the bottom, she was shocked. The barn below was split into quadrants by beautiful wooden planks. There was an aisle down the middle and each quadrant was reserved for a different type of animal. Feed bins for each type of animal were located along the inside of the individual quadrants. That way, whoever was feeding the animals just had to walk down the middle and fill the bins. Each kind of animal also had doors leading to spacious pastures outside. As she walked down the aisle, she saw cows, sheep, pigs, goats, chickens, ducks, and horses. The end of the barn opened into a covered patio. One side had been made into a work area for butchering meat and tanning hides, and the other side was a general work area containing tack for the animals, woodworking tools, and mechanical tools. In the middle of the two areas was a table and chairs.

Erika jumped when she heard a large man standing in the tanning area say, "Howdy, missy, how are we feelin'?"

"Good, well… better," Erika answered in a startled voice.

The well-statured man stood six foot seven inches from the ground and towered above her. Erika knew by the wrinkles on his face that he was as old as Carol, but that was the only way to tell. His body gleamed in the sun; it was as muscular and strong as he was tall.

"My name's Henry Duncan. I'm glad to see you up and about." His voice was deep and boomed when he spoke.

"Nice to meet you, Henry. My name is Erika Moore. Sorry to bother you while you're busy, but Carol told me you brought my supplies back here too."

"Why, yes, I did. They're right over there by the workbench. That was quite an ingenious contraption you rigged up there and that outfit you had on. I didn't even know if you were human when I found you," Henry rumbled with a great chuckle. "It worked, though, by God it worked, and here you are. I can't wait to hear about your adventure."

"And I can't wait to hear about yours," Erika countered slyly.

"What's that?" Harold said in a very confused voice.

"Carol told me you went to Auburn. I have to know what you saw because I will have to go that way to get home." Erika was focused on her family and eager to know what she would be up against.

"Aw… home." Henry was trying to quickly change the subject. "I knew you would want to leave right away. Anyone who could make it out of that mess down there safely must be very determined to get somewhere. That's why I'm out here trying to finish this bull hide. Your shoes were totally destroyed, and your feet are much smaller than my wife's. I am finishing this so I can make you some moccasins. It's not much and I hope you're okay with wearing moccasins, but there's nothing else we can do for you and you are going to need some shoes." Henry was not sure how she would react to the idea of wearing moccasins. It was not really a typical shoe anymore.

"You're making me moccasins! That's a great idea. I had a pair at home, but at work I had to wear those cruddy non-slip shoes. I would love that, and I really do appreciate all that you have done for me already. I have no idea how I could possibly thank you two enough." Erika was overwhelmed by their kindness.

Henry was encouraged by her reaction and replied with pleasure, "It's no trouble, little miss. I heard you in your dreams crying for your loved ones. I knew that if I was in your position, the first thing I would want to do is find Carol."

Henry had a fierce determination in his eyes. Their brown gleamed into almost a golden color as he thought of her. It made Erika realize how distraught her husband must be. He would think she was dead. She wanted to tell him somehow that she was all right. She longed to hold him, to kiss him, and caress his body.

"And you have a son, I believe," Henry continued, interrupting her thoughts.

"Yes, he's five now. His name is Dexter. He's so funny and full of life. He has pure blond hair with steely gray eyes." As Erika described her son to Henry, tears started flowing down her face. "I miss him so much. I just hope he and his daddy are okay. I have to get home to them. Vince will know I'm alive," Erika said to reassure herself. She was almost talking to herself now. "I always told him that if some great catastrophe ever happened, I would be a survivor. I learned how to survive in nature and studied basic herbal medicine just because I knew that one day it would come in handy. Other women teased me and looked at me funny because I hunted and wore moccasins so I could feel the earth. Well, now all that is going to pay off. I just have to get myself together and get home." Erika talked with a steady voice as clear as crystal while the tears still streamed down her face.

Henry knew he shouldn't have touched on such a fragile subject, but he wanted to test Erika's strength and determination. He was completely satisfied. The woman that stood before him, although short in stature, had a very strong heart and an unrelenting mind that once set to a goal would not stray. Her body structure was solid, and he was sure she had been an athlete before the world had changed. The fact that she hunted made her journey home not only possible but likely to succeed. Henry knew what the world beyond this snug barn had become. Erika's chance of making it to her family depended on her being self-sufficient. For that, she would have to be physically and spiritually strong.

"Sorry I've been babbling on and on. You probably want to get back to work, and I should check on my supplies." Now it was Erika's turn to interrupt Henry's thoughts.

"Erika, you will make it home to them, and I'll do anything I can to help you get there." Henry already knew when he found her on the beach that she was a special person. He only had to confirm it.

"Thank you, Henry. I will gratefully appreciate any help you can give me, and I only hope that I can do something to help you out while I am here to repay you for all your generosity."

Erika was feeling a lot better. Her talk with Henry had given her a way to vent her sorrow and rekindle her determination to get home. She strolled over to the craft she had made. The plastic jugs on the bottom had melted into a mass of plastic and duct tape. The wood table was in good shape and the crates looked to be intact, for the most part. She started looking through the purses when Carol came around the corner. She had two baskets in her hands and almost dropped them when she saw Erika.

"*Oh my goodness*, honey, what are you doing down here? You don't need to be going through them things right now. You need to be upstairs resting."

Erika swung around as if she was being scolded by her grandmother. She dropped her head down.

"Now, just leave her be. Her legs just needed a good stretch, Carol," Henry shushed his overly concerned spouse, and when Erika looked up with surprise, he winked at her.

"I just wanted to check on my things and have a smoke," Erika chimed in.

"Well, you know those things will kill you, and I don't think in your current condition that is the best idea, but I guess a little fresh air won't hurt. Hurry upstairs though, and we'll try to fix one another up. I'm going up now to get dinner started," Carol said in a motherly tone.

"We'll be up later, hun," Henry bellowed in his deep tone.

Carol walked through the aisle of the animals to the stairs and disappeared from sight.

"Girl, did you say you had a cigarette?" Henry questioned.

"Yes, do you mind if I have one?" Erika was used to the anti-smoking stigmatism that so many people displayed nowadays and wondered if she should have brought it up at all.

"Only if you can spare one for the old man who saved your life. Carol made me quit a few years back, but I guess a lot has changed lately. It would make me feel… normal again."

"Sure, I found quite a few packs in the restaurant I used to work in. What kind do you want?" Erika was thrilled that she had something Henry valued that she could share with him.

"You got a Marlboro Red?"

"Yup, I got one of those. Here you go." Erika handed Henry a cigarette that was only slightly bent from the trauma of the trip to the coast.

Erika and Henry lit their smokes and stood at the edge of the porch looking out. The greens and blues filled Erika's eyes, and she realized just how long it had been since she was outdoors, on solid ground, breathing fresh air and letting the wind blow through her hair. She had been trapped in the bomb shelter and then she had been wrapped stiffly in duct tape; after that she had lain unconscious in bed. She tried to soak in every bit of life she could, but it overwhelmed her, and her legs were beginning to ache. Henry had noticed Erika beginning to stagger a little. He offered her a chair, but she refused because she was afraid of sitting on her scabbed legs. When their smokes were gone, she thanked him again and left to go and talk with Carol.

As she climbed up the steep hayloft stairs, her legs wobbling with pain, she realized Carol might have been right. She needed to take the time to rest and recover, even though all her thoughts centered on leaving and getting home to Vince and Dexter.

CHAPTER 7

PAIN AND FATIGUE caused Erika to pause when she reached the top of the stairs. She looked out at the layout of the loft. The remaining hay that Carol and Henry had stored in the barn after the quake had been stacked into walls to make rooms. The first area at the top of the stairs had been made into a kitchen area. In years' past, Carol had insisted that Henry drag a huge old stove into the hayloft. It was the kind where you built the fire inside and didn't rely on conventional energy sources. Henry had wanted to sell it in a yard sale but Carol was his only love, and she loved that antique stove. So he had hauled it up to the hayloft as she insisted. The stove was now one of the focal points of the kitchen and one of two heating sources in the barn. Across from the kitchen area was an eating and sitting area. There was table with a couple of chairs and a side table with an oil lamp in the corner. After that, there was a hallway right down the middle of the loft formed from the blankets that were hung as doors in between the haystack walls. The first room on the right looked as if it had some other purpose, but all the other rooms were clearly made for sleeping. The final room in the back left corner of the loft was still stacked full with hay.

Carol was busy fixing a meal of roast beef, carrots, corn, and potatoes. Her back was to Erika, and she jumped when Erika asked, "Carol, is there a restroom I can use?"

Carol turned around with wide eyes and said, "Oh my goodness, honey, you can't sneak up on an old woman like that. I am sorry, though. I should have showed you when you woke up. Look over here."

Carol wiped her hands with a damp towel and put it down on the counter Henry had made for her. It was a piece of the counter from their old house that he had recovered out of the wreckage. Carol began walking down the hallway but stopped at the mystery room on the right. Once the curtain was pulled back, Erika could see that there was a hay bale with a dish of water and some soap on one side and a portable potty from an old boat in the back.

"It's not the best toilet, and it smells pretty bad if it's not changed often. We ran out of the blue stuff to knock the smell down last month. Never thought I would need that much of it. Oh well, no matter, my wonderful Henry keeps it clean. We do have an outside place to go, but until you get healed up a little more, I think you better stick to using this one."

"Thanks, Carol… for everything." Erika had tears in her eyes when she said this, overwhelmed by the amount that this couple had done for her and her inability to repay them.

Carol had seen this and quickly said, "Now, don't you worry about everything all at once. There will be plenty of time for that later."

Carol walked away and Erika proceeded into the bathroom. The toilet wasn't very smelly and had probably just been changed. It was nice to finally do something almost normal. It seemed like nothing was normal anymore. Nobody had come to save anyone.

To Erika, the whole world was wrong. Whenever a disaster happened, there were people to help. They would fly across the whole country to help those in need, but this was different. In Erika's little pocket of the world, she could not see that it wasn't only a local disaster, or a national disaster, but a worldwide disaster that no one in any corner of the world could escape. No one came to help because everyone needed help, even the helpers. People were fighting to save loved ones and survive in an environment that was just beginning to unleash its fury.

When Erika was done, she went over to the basin to wash her hands. She dipped them into the chilly water and then rubbed her hands with the bar of soap. While she was scrubbing, she noticed the beautiful designs on the rim of the basin. They looked like small dragons flying around the edge. Her son was born in the Year of the Dragon. Suddenly, Erika was snapped out of her daydream when Carol asked if everything was all right.

"Yes, I'm fine, just finishing up," Erika answered. Then she dipped her soapy hands back into the water. When she opened the curtain, Carol was there waiting for her.

"Come back here, I want to show you something. I know you like to look outside and this used to be a big old wooden door, but Henry turned it into this." Carol pulled back another blanket that was draped over an area of the wall in the back of the barn. This area was obviously their sleeping area. Erika was standing in front of a huge window. "Now whenever you want to look out, you don't have to waste your energy on those stairs; you just come back here and enjoy yourself."

"Thanks, Carol, there is just no end to your generosity, and I'll never be able to thank you enough."

"You don't have to. The Lord teaches us to be charitable. In his infinite wisdom, he has blessed us with minds that we can use for great good and great evil. His path leads us to the use of the mind for great good. I believe rescuing you was part of some grand plan of the Lord's. You are special, Erika. If you weren't, you would have never made it out of there at all. No one else that I know of did. The Lord has to have some reason for saving you, so don't thank me, thank him."

Erika had never thought about her experience or her life in that way before. The thought that the Lord individually crafted each one of us for some unknown purpose was rattling around inside her mind. Carol and Erika stared out the window, lost in thought. They could see to the very edge of the forest, to where the toxic lagoon began.

"I used to have a lot of friends down there, and the Lord did not save them," Erika said with a quivering voice. "Actually, two of my very best friends and their daughter were probably down there."

"Lots of people died down there, Erika. When the quake hit us, everything was rattling like a freight train was coming right through the house. Then the house started coming down. Henry had been outside, and he came running in the door. We ran out to the wine cellar, and we hid down there. All the bottles were shaking, but they stayed put and we made it. When we opened the door, the whole house was gone. Trees that had stood for 180 years were shaken from the ground. The roads, everything was broken, except for the barn. Henry says it has something to do with how the foundation was laid, but I don't know about those types of things. I tend to think that it was a miracle, or maybe the will of our Lord kept our barn standing. Now it's our sanctuary. I don't know what happened to everyone else. Besides Henry, you are the only person I have seen since the quake. We used to go every day to the lagoon to look for survivors but now we only go once a week, and Henry always insists on being with me when-ever we go anywhere off the property." Carol was rambling. She was just happy to discuss life with another individual.

Erika and Carol were still staring out the window while they were talking. Far off in the distance, the cloud from the eruption could still be seen. "That cloud may come this way if the wind shifts. Hopefully, our luck will hold," Carol said as if to herself. "Oh well, we'll worry about that when the problem comes. Until then, we will just pray. Dinner is just about ready, and I bet you could use a rest. Why don't you go sit at the table while I get dinner served and call that man in from his tinkering?" Carol was already walking into the kitchen, so Erika followed her and sat down delicately on a chair at the table. It had a nice soft cushion so Erika's burns didn't sting too badly, and it felt nice to rest her legs. Carol hummed as she worked around the kitchen. The roast smelled awesome when Carol took it out of the oven and pulled off the lid. Erika's mouth was watering, but Carol proceeded to neatly set the table and then went down the rickety stairs to get Henry. Erika was so hungry and the meat smelled so good, it felt like forever before she heard voices and then two sets of feet coming up the stairs.

"Well, well... still on the move?" Henry bellowed as he reached the top of the stairs.

"Now just leave her alone and sit down, you big moose," Carol countered in Erika's defense.

"Yes, I am still up and the smell of Carol's wonderful dinner is keeping me wide-awake," Erika replied in sheer anticipation of the feast as Henry sat down next to her.

"Well, that wonderful cooking has kept me going for a lot of years. I'm sure you'll feel as good as new in no time." Henry chuckled.

"I hope so," Erika said with a far-off look in her eyes.

"You'll see them soon enough. Right now let's worry about getting you healthy enough to make the trip to see them." Henry had seen the look in Erika's eyes and knew her thoughts were of her family. Erika wondered how he knew but felt that he was right. Her mission was to get well enough to get home to them.

"That's enough chatter out of you two. Let's eat before it gets cold," Carol said in a cheerful voice trying to break the tension. She was carrying some meat sliced on a platter and a bowl full of veggies.

Once the food was served, Erika went to dig right in, but Carol abruptly stopped her. "I know you are hungry, honey, but we must give thanks to the Lord for providing us with such a bountiful meal, especially in these uncertain times. Plus, it's the Fourth of July, and I think our country could really use a special prayer right about now."

Erika withdrew her hand and folded it with the other. Then she bowed her head and waited for Henry to finish the blessing. Erika's prayers went out to her family, and she asked the Lord to give her enough strength to make it home to them. When Henry was done, they dug in and Erika ate like never before. Everything was so good, and it had been so long since she had a wonderful hot meal with big chunks of juicy meat. When she had packed every corner of her belly full, she sat back in her chair. Henry and Carol were watching her.

"Well, you must be feeling better. I haven't seen anyone eat that much since my son was sixteen," Henry said, chuckling again.

"Now, Henry, you leave her be. She needed it," Carol countered.

"I have been saving something for a special occasion," Henry declared.

Henry ran down the stairs like an excited schoolboy. Then the door that was under the stairs opened and closed.

"I wonder where he is off to. Oh well, I better get these dishes done. Don't want the ants coming in for our leftovers."

"Let me help you," Erika insisted and got up to help. Her body hurt, and she winced a little.

"No, honey, you just rest. I got it," Carol replied.

"No! I insist, Carol. You have done so much for me already. I will feel horrible if I can't make it up to you," Erika pleaded.

"Just don't overdo it, honey. You are just like my daughter, Christy. She joined the Marines at eighteen and stayed for life, always so strong with an unquenchable sense of duty. She never had any kids but has worked hard for our country." Carol was just making small talk as she washed the dishes in a big basin. Erika cleared the table then began to dry the dishes that Carol was washing. "Now my son, Harold, on the other hand, was always such a lover. He liked hugs and was such a good baby. Now he has three kids of his own. His oldest is a girl named Jen, Kim is the middle child, and his son Rob is the youngest."

"Do you know if they survived? Where did they live?"

"No, I don't know, but my faith in the Lord will protect them. They lived in Colfax, but it took Henry four days just to get to Auburn and back, so who knows how long it would take them to get here," Carol answered with hope in her voice.

"Yeah, and who knows how long it will take me to get home," Erika wondered.

"Just have faith, honey. You have made it this far and that is much farther than most. Everyone will get where they need to be in time," Carol replied assuredly.

"Are you two up here bumming each other out?" Henry questioned from the stairway. He thought often of his son and hoped that Harold had the same determination to get home as this young lady in front of him did. But now was not the time to think of the many troubles that were plaguing them. "This is supposed to be a celebration!"

Erika and Carol both jumped. Having been so involved in work and conversation, they did not hear his approach.

"Here's the surprise." He held up a bottle of King James III Cognac. "Now let me help you get those dishes put away, and we'll work on drinking away those sorrows."

"Henry, you devil," Carol said with a twinkle in her eyes.

They all worked together to finish up the dishes then sat down around the table together. Henry opened the bottle and poured them all a glass. Erika took a sip of the potent spirit. She had never been a big lover of alcohol, and this was extremely strong but strangely smooth as well. She drank down the first glass and held her glass out for more.

"Now, we can't drink it all," Henry said as he was filling her glass. "I'm saving at least half of this bottle for when Harold gets here with Betsy and the kids." He almost kicked himself for bringing the kids up again and quickly added, "Anyway, like I said, this is a celebration. How about some tunes while we drink?"

Normally, a radio would have been turned on but now, with no electricity, Henry reached for a case holding a fiddle. He began to play a happy tune and while he played, they drank from their glasses. All of Erika's pains began to melt away. After a while their glasses were empty and Henry put down the fiddle to refill them.

"Now that we are all feeling better, let's hear that story of yours, little lady." Henry was full of anticipation.

"Before she starts, why don't we go down onto the porch to enjoy some air? It just feels wrong to sit inside on the Fourth of July with no fireworks blasting away down in the city." Carol stood up and went to get the lantern in the corner so the three of them could bring it along. She was moving with more grace and ease. *Probably the alcohol was having a pain-relieving effect on her too*, Erika thought.

"Sounds like a wonderful idea to me, darling; I'll bring along the fiddle so we can have some music too." Henry packed his fiddle back into its box and started heading for the stairs.

Erika got up too. She was still dumbfounded by the fact that it was the Fourth of July. Usually, she would be one of the people blasting off those fireworks in the city. Even though they lived in the country, Erika, Vince, and Dexter had always gone down to their friends' house in the city for the Fourth. They would all pitch in and buy one or two of those gigantic boxes of fireworks that they have for sale at the roadside stands. Then they would all delight in setting off fountains, smoke bombs, and sparklers until the road in the city looked like a war zone, with explosions going off in all the driveways and the street filling with the smell of sulfur. Erika never really thought that the Fourth in California was all that great. You weren't allowed to fire any fireworks into the air because of the wildfire risk. Since Erika hailed from Michigan, where there were all kinds of fireworks going off every Fourth, she didn't think that the fountains were all that spectacular. Plus, Erika hated the new sparklers. They were designed to be safer but they sucked. They didn't light well and would burn out quickly. She longed for the old-school wire sparklers. Sure, they burned you a little, but they stayed lit for a lot longer and burned a lot brighter.

When the three of them got out to the porch, Erika knew that Carol had the right idea. It was so fresh outside, but there was a smell in the evening air that Erika knew immediately was the smell of a major wildfire.

"Carol, it smells like a fire, but there was no smoke today. Was there a fire?" Erika wondered.

"Don't really know, Erika. After the quake, there were days when the smoke hung thick for long periods of time. It would clear and then come back. Without the TV, we have no idea where it came from, but this is California in the summer, and, with all that has happened, I bet some big wildfires burned in more than one place," Carol answered honestly.

"Wow! Crazy."

"There you guys go bringing our celebration down again. I know what will cheer us up. You guys just sit tight," Henry insisted.

Erika pulled a smoke out of her pack and lit it. Carol and Erika sat in silence, each preoccupied with their own thoughts. They sipped their cognac, and Erika puffed on her smoke while Henry went to get another surprise.

"You know," Erika said, while twirling her glass so the liquid made a little whirlpool, "I once saw a shot of this cognac sell for $100 a shot."

"Oh yes, I believe it. We were just kids when we bought this bottle, and it just about broke the bank. Henry never opened it, though, and he has been saving it for a lot of years. He always said we will know when the time has come to have a glass," Carol answered.

"It's not so bad, but I could have never paid $100 for a shot. It better get me drunk for a week at that rate," Erika laughed.

"Some people like to show how important they are by paying way too much for good alcohol."

"Yeah, I guess all that doesn't really matter now, huh?"

"No, I guess not. Maybe all the rich people are held up in rich-person sanctuary. All day long, they sit in their comfy bunker sipping cognac and eating caviar." Carol was laughing out loud as she said this.

"Well, I guess I am in rich-person sanctuary," Henry rumbled as he came in, "because I am surrounded by beautiful women, sipping cognac, and eating better than crummy old caviar."

"Henry, you are just full of the devil tonight. I will have to sleep with one eye open," Carol giggled.

"You better-woman," Henry replied flirtatiously.

They all laughed. It was nice to laugh out loud with friends again. It seemed like it had been years since Erika had partaken in this banter and laughed. There is something to be said about laughing with friends. It brings joy to the heart and is something that should be appreciated. People used to take this social interaction for granted, never realizing that one day it would be so precious. It relieved stress and gave hope to those who could not see it.

Erika had begun to slur her words slightly and was having so much fun goofing around. She was doing a fine job of forgetting the recent past and was not looking forward to retelling the story of her horrible experience in the cell, as she had begun to call it. Henry could see this but wanted the story anyway. Now was a perfect time for the telling. The senses had been dulled, and he knew its telling would not affect her as much now.

"Well, you better get used to telling your story because you may have been the only one to survive. Many people will want to know how you survived the flooding of the Sacramento Valley," Henry said matter of factly while staring Erika directly in the eyes.

Erika looked up, startled. How could this man read her mind so well? Was she so transparent? She wanted to escape, but she knew that he was right. She would have to tell and retell the story until one day it would become legend—the legend of the girl who survived a toxic flood because of cellophane and duct tape. *Oh boy, what a legacy*, Erika chuckled to herself.

But Henry knew that Erika was a very special individual. Not just strong but deep in spirit and in possession of a very big heart. If she was going to get home, she would need all of these strengths. There was no time to be weak. Erika would have to face the reality of this situation. She would have to face what she had gone through and the bleak situation she was now facing. Henry knew it and would take every opportunity to destroy her weaknesses and prepare her to harness all the strength she would need in the future.

"So, let's hear the story." Henry was looking at her again, his fierce brown eyes piercing her. Erika saw a man that demanded respect, and she knew that she could never refuse a direct request from him.

Erika began, "I woke up just the same as any other day. Dexter was running all over the place, and I had to keep telling him to calm down. I got the dishes done and I went down to my in-laws to check on the house. My in-laws were up in Washington visiting my husband's grandmother. I could see some raccoons were bothering the chickens at night. I know they are nocturnal, but I was eager for something to do and Dexter was so antsy. So I went back home, which wasn't very far away, and loaded up Dexter's BB gun; my dog, Ripper; and my slingshot. I called Vince on my cell phone and let him know that I would be spending the day there." It was hard for Erika to talk about her family, and her voice began to quiver.

"We didn't find any coons, but we did have fun running around, shooting. I knew my slingshot wasn't really going to work, but I figured Dexter would have fun with it and his gun. We had a blast running around in the woods. Then I went and dropped Dex and Ripper off at my mom's house. We talked about our days for a while, and then I had to change and go to work. I hugged and kissed my mom and Dexter. As I drove off in my car, I looked in the rearview mirror, and that was the last time I saw them. I called Vince on my cell. He was on his way home. I let him know we were safe and sound after a day of coon hunting and that I loved him. That was the last time I spoke to him. After that, I drove down to work at El Primero. I was late because of traffic so I threw my stuff in the break room and went to work, prepping food in the kitchen. Halfway through the night, this girl I worked with, Casey, came in and asked if I would grab a 'bottle of our best Merlot' for this frequent customer that always acted like an arrogant bastard." Erika stopped for a minute and realized her language may have been too strong to use in front of Carol. She felt like she had just said the "F" word in front of her grandma and had to apologize. "Pardon my French, Carol, but he really was a jerk."

"Don't worry, Erika, just don't stop now." Carol was more irritated about the break in the story rather than the harsh language.

"Okay, where was I? Oh yeah, so I went down to the basement and as I was grabbing the bottle the quake started. Now this was not just any old basement, it had originally been a bomb shelter constructed during the Cold War by some lunatic fanatic that owned the house." Erika's story was starting to flow now, thanks in part to the alcohol.

She went on to tell Henry and Carol all about being trapped under the wine rack, sleeping on tablecloths and napkins, living off of oats, fruit, and nuts, her first failed attempt at escape, and how she thought up the suit and the raft. Then she explained her escape, her first night under the stars when she got caught in the eddy, and, finally, her long voyage across the toxic sludge. By the time she was done, it was very late, and the oil lamp needed more fuel. Carol got up to fill it.

"That is some story, young lady. You truly must have a guardian angel at your side. I wonder how many other people may be stuck under the sludge," Henry pondered.

"I don't know, Henry. I didn't even think about other people stuck in basements or crazy bomb shelters. I didn't even try to look for anyone else alive. All I could think of was getting to shore, getting home to my family. Believe me, Henry. I saw my fair share of bodies above the ground, though." Erika was freaked about the idea that more people could have been stuck in situations just like hers. Maybe they were still there in cells under the water. Maybe one day the water would recede, and they could open their doors into the air instead of a lake, if they made it that long.

"That's not what I meant, Erika, don't go crazy over it. You will learn that in life it is never good to think of the 'what could have been,' only what was, and what will be. You must stay focused on the future. No one could have survived without a suit like yours, and you wouldn't have made it yourself if you got to shore any later than you did." Henry was kicking himself for planting that thought in her head. He had looked for survivors for so long that he couldn't help wondering.

Carol brought the lamp back to the table and announced, "I am going to bed. It's too late for an old woman to be up worrying." She was looking tired, and she kissed Henry before she headed up the stairway.

Erika had watched them embrace and kiss the way she and Vince always did when they shared passionate moments together. She longed more than ever for the touch of her man and his warm love that always made her feel better no matter what. Everyone has hard days, and Erika had her share as well, but the love of this one man could light up her whole world. He would always find a way to make her smile no matter what, and sometimes when Erika was trying to act really mad, it drove her nuts. What she wouldn't do to feel that feeling now.

"Good night, guys, and don't keep her up all night talking," Carol yelled down the stairs as she reached the top.

"Yes, dear, good night," Henry answered as the light at the top of the stairs went out. All that was left was the dancing light from the lantern on the table.

CHAPTER 8

ERIKA SEIZED THE moment and looked Henry directly in the eyes. It was her turn to make a request of him, and she was not going to miss this opportunity. "Henry, you know I will have to go towards Auburn to get home. What is it like out there?"

"Well, I guess it's only fair that since you have told me your story I will have to tell you mine. You must promise me, though that you will never, ever tell Carol. To her, the world is still a beautiful, safe place filled with the good will of men. That is the way I would like to keep it." Henry demanded.

"You have my word, Henry, but I must know," Erika stated with an extreme desperation in her voice.

"Okay, okay. I will tell you then, but give me another one of those Marlboros first."

"No problem, Henry, take as many as you like. Just tell me the darn story," Erika replied impatiently as she tossed him a smoke.

"All right, all right, don't get all fussy." Henry chuckled a little as he lit the smoke, holding Erika in suspense. "I'll just start at the beginning: I packed up one horse to go to Auburn to get some supplies we were running low on. You see, at that time I did not know the extent of the earthquake damage. Around our house was a mess. We had lost our home and our roads were impassible, but I figured it could not be like this everywhere. There was no way of getting to the car. It had been buried in the garage. The horse was the only option, so I rode off on my horse toward Auburn. It was very difficult because when the earth moved, it created a completely foreign landscape. Valleys that had not been there before were now deep cracks in the earth, and many obstacles had been created when this upheaval happened. The road was split into pieces around these valleys. After a day and a half of traveling, I started to smell the foulest stench of death imaginable. It wove its way into every one of my senses and made me sick a few times before I finally saw what used to be Auburn. It was literally a pile of rubble, Erika. The road that I was traveling used to be Auburn-Folsom Road, but as I said before, it was in pieces wedged between newly formed valleys. I use the past tense, Erika, because there is nothing left. The homes and stores that were there are all gone. Rubble and sunken land was everywhere." Henry sat back and took a big puff of his smoke. There was a sense of fear and horror in his eyes that Erika had never seen before. She knew that this scene had an immense impact on him. It took Erika by surprise. When Erika looked at him, she saw a huge, immensely strong man, and she couldn't believe that it could have been that horrifying. She knew she would have to follow that same road and the hair on the back of her neck stood on end.

Henry took another puff and returned to his story. "Up until now, I had not seen anyone. I was completely inundated with the overwhelming smell and sense of death, but I did not see anyone. I was still really curious though, where was everyone? Many people must have died but a lot of people used to live in that town, and I had not seen one of them. I knew there had to be other survivors like ourselves but where were they? Just then, a shot from a gun rang out. I was shaken and quickly turned my horse and ran toward what used to be Old Town Auburn. The gunman was in the rubble at what used to be the 7-11. I did not know it at the time, but now I know why he was there."

"Why, Henry?" Erika was completely enthralled in the story now. Erika should have known the answer and immediately felt like an idiot for asking it in the first place.

"He was hoarding the food that was left by the store, and he wasn't going to let me anywhere near it. After I ran into old town, I chose a path that would lead me to what used to be a grocery store. I was hoping I could just get a few of the most important supplies that we needed and then I was going to get the heck out of there. I learned from the experience at the 7-11, though. I left my horse down in a secluded valley and climbed up a hill a little ways away so that I could scout the area that I was headed for first. I could not believe what these people had become. All of the buildings that used to comprise the shopping center were piles of rubble, and anything that was worth anything had already been pilfered. There was a group of people that were using the area as a compound. They had made new buildings out of the rubble that surrounded the whole shopping center. Then they gated all the openings and used all the surrounding buildings as walls that they could guard so no one else could get the supplies that were left there."

Henry lowered his voice a bit and said, "Erika, the dead bodies were piled everywhere outside the complex. They put people's heads up as decorations on the walls to deter attackers and thieves. It was absolutely sickening to see how fast society deteriorated when faced with disaster and no sign of relief. That is why I am telling you, you must never, ever go toward people. I know you will want to, and I am not sure that it is the same everywhere, but you must not take those familiar old roads home. You will need to chart a new route with my help and your memory. From here, you must follow the road but stay far off of it and go directly toward the river. Then you will have to go to where the original road went down before the dam was built and weave a new course down and up the canyon. Stay away from Auburn, always."

"What did you do? Don't get off track now. Did you get the supplies? What happened next, Henry?" Erika was not happy with the sudden change from hearing an intriguing tale to listening to a lecture and wanted to know how the story would end.

"Well, after seeing what happened at this shopping center, I had no idea what to do, and I wasn't expecting to need a gun so I went back to my horse and found a quiet way to ride home. I did not get the supplies, and it was a very long ride home without any food. See, I had only taken enough to get to Auburn and figured I would restock there. Also, I didn't expect it to take me so long to get there in the first place, so I was already running low on the trip there." Henry paused for a moment and took a long drag off of his cigarette.

"I made it home to my sweet Carol, and I realized then how stupid I'd been. What if people looking for shelter had come while I had been gone? God knows what they would have done to my precious Carol. I realized then that we probably should not burn fires during the day so that we do not attract any attention. I just hope my son gets here soon. We could really use the help, and a bigger group is a safer group. With all the supplies we have, we would be easy pickings if they knew we were here."

Erika did not know what to say. She figured it would be a long trip home without a car, but this news was heartbreaking. Now she would have to travel through this new alien world, and she could not depend on anyone but herself to get her there safely.

She sat there for another minute, silently reflecting on all that information she had just learned. She put the cigarette she had been smoking out then said, "Thanks, Henry, for telling me. At least I know what I will be up against."

Henry put his smoke out and looked Erika dead in the eyes. He had a very intimate stare. "Look, Erika, you don't have to go. You can stay with us. I hate to say this, and I know that you will not want to hear it, but you may have to face the fact that your family may be gone, and all you will return home to is chaos and heartache." Henry knew she would never stay, but he had to let her know she was welcome. If there were any doubts in her mind, she must stay. Not many people actually survived, and those that did were more concerned about essential supplies for their survival, not banding together as a people to recover.

"Henry, you know I can't stay. I have to go; I have to see for myself. Who knows, I may be back someday, but all the same, I have to know," Erika said without question.

"I know you can't stay, but you must understand the extreme danger the world presents for you now. Anyway, that is enough talking; I am off to bed." Henry had made his point, and now he would let Erika simmer in the juices of her new knowledge.

Henry and Erika headed up the stairs into the hayloft. When Erika climbed into her bed on the hay, it felt good. It was a million more times comfortable than the pile of rags on the cold concrete she had gotten accustomed to in the hole, but she longed for her bed—her warm bed—where she could snuggle up with her boys and melt away into relaxation. Sleep did not come easily despite her comfort, and she lay awake for long time thinking about her upcoming journey.

CHAPTER 9

ERIKA WENT ON living with Carol and Henry for a couple of more weeks. Every day, Erika grew stronger and stronger, but each day she also grew more and more anxious to leave. She knew her family would be waiting, and she knew she would have to go to them soon. How long would she wait if the shoe were on the other foot? If she was safe at home with Dexter, how long would she wait and wonder if Vince was alive or dead? She didn't know, and that's why she knew she had to go.

Erika was never very much of a morning person, and, usually Carol and Henry were up long before she was. One day, she woke up to a great commotion. Harold had finally arrived with Betsy and the kids. They were all healthy and came with four more horses. They also brought some supplies that the household badly needed, like rice and sugar.

Although their coming was a very joyous occasion, Erika was feeling like a third wheel and could not help but feel that her place was not here. The hugs and tears flowed that day, and Erika was distraught. All she could focus on were the hugs of her own family and how much joy they would share when she returned home.

All day, they shared food and stories. The first story told was how the family had fared during the quake, and then how their journey to Henry and Carol's had been. Harold and Betsy told the story marvelously. One would literally finish the other's sentence, and you could feel the love was thick between them. They said that when the initial quake hit, the family had been outside, and their house and barn were destroyed instantly. Luckily, they and the horses had been outside, and everyone was all right. They had no idea what to do, and they—like most people in California—waited for help that would never come. While they were waiting for some kind of help, they started pillaging what goods they could from their destroyed home. They built a temporary shelter and stored the goods there. They also started looking for neighbors. Unfortunately, they found only three people that were still alive.

They waited in makeshift survival shelters with the others they had found until stocks began to run desperately low. Then it was decided that they would disband to look for their families and more supplies. It was quite evident by then that help was not on its way, and everyone had different priorities. Harold and Betsy's priority had been to get to Harold's parents since they were the closest relatives. Betsy's parents still lived in North Carolina. Betsy said she was praying that they were safe, and Erika understood her pain only too well.

Betsy's thought of her parents made Erika think of her own mother and father. She sent a silent prayer out to them and hoped they were safe and in good hands. Her immediate focus had been on her husband and son. There was just too much misery to think of everyone she loved at once. It could drive a person mad.

The conversation then shifted to lighter issues. Harold and Betsy's oldest child, Jen, who was fifteen, told all about what had been happening in school, and how their basketball team had been doing so great this year that it really was a shame all this had to happen. Her younger sister, Kim, who was eleven, and spoke loudly so her older sister would not interrupt, told all about how she was a champion horse jumper, and was very excited about nationals this year because she was going to be a part of the junior Olympic team. She didn't know if there would even be nationals now but was very excited because she got to ride her horse here just like in the Old West.

Then it was Rob's turn to tell his story. He was only nine and spoke very softly. He was so cute, and it was very annoying how his sisters broke in to finish his sentences for him. In the end, Erika heard all about how he loved to play soccer and was going to Harvard one day and would play soccer there just like his dad had done.

It was nice to talk of normal things but at the end of all the stories were the same questions of: Would it still be there? Or would the event still happen? Erika even wondered if a school as old as Harvard could have survived this nightmare, but like most other things, Harvard was gone. The earth had swallowed up the university, and any person inside went right with it, to a grave in the newly opened earth.

After dinner, Henry played a song on his fiddle and out came the Cognac again. After the song, Carol and Betsy put the kids to bed. Harold and Betsy were sleeping in the room between Henry and Carol's and the bathroom. The rest of the kids would be sharing the bedroom next to Erika's room. Once the kids were in bed, Carol and Betsy came back to the table, and the subject changed to more pressing issues like supplies.

Harold and Betsy had to leave the other livestock they had behind because it would have been way too arduous to make the trip with them. They gave them to the folks that were staying behind at the survival camp, waiting for their own families. It was decided that it was a good decision because they only had one stall of hay left, and now there would be four more horses to feed. The garden was still going to produce well besides having a few new grooves in it. There were babies on the way. The cows, sheep, and goats all had pregnant females. They would only kill the adults as needed so they would always have meat. The only question was, how they would sustain a feed supply for the animals with all of the feed stores closed.

Erika couldn't help but feel guilty during the conversation. She was feeling better again. She knew she was just a drain on the family resources, and she was taking up precious space that the family needed. She decided that it was time for her next journey to begin. She knew Carol would protest her leaving and decided to go quietly tonight when everyone was sleeping. As her decision became finalized in her mind, she looked up, and Henry was staring right into her soul. They both knew what she had been thinking, and Henry simply looked over to a saddle and a horse pack. Erika knew he was giving her permission to take that saddle, and she began to go over supplies in her head. She knew she had most of what she would need and figured she would find the rest along the way. After the discussion at the table was finished, Erika made sure she had said a special good-night to everyone and thanked Henry and Carol again for their kindness. Henry banked the fire, and everyone went to bed.

Erika lay awake waiting for everyone to fall asleep. From the other room, with only the hay-bale walls and blankets for doors, she heard Harold and Betsy making love. Probably a celebration romp for having arrived safely, but Erika could only picture Vince, his big arms and loving eyes. That was it; she was leaving now. She got up, grabbed her moccasins, and got dressed in some fresh clothes that she had carried with her from the bunker. She put her personal effects in the saddle bags and went downstairs to pack everything up.

She ran to the end of the barn, where the rest of her supplies were, and stopped short when she saw Henry was there, cinching up the horse pack onto one of his horses.

"You can go ahead and put that saddle on that little, black mare over there. Her name is Artaz, and she will be your new friend for your journey. Since we seem to have a couple of horses too many right now, you can also take this little brown one. His name is Kit, and he will ride well, carry a pack, and even pull a cart. He is steady and will not lose your things," Henry said quietly.

"Henry, I can't take them; not two of them. That is way too kind," Erika replied.

"Oh yes, you can. How will we feed them all? Take them and put them to good use. They will get you home quickly and be good friends as well. You can return them later once things have settled down again." Henry said this but Erika could tell that he never thought for a second that she would be back. Henry silently wondered how far she would make it, but he knew she was strong and had to make this journey.

"Now, I have loaded the goods you had along with some others you will need. You should have enough food, and remember to stay away from people. Carol will be angry as a crocodile getting her eggs stole when she wakes up and finds you are gone, but I know you have to go." Henry said this in a sarcastic manner, but Erika could tell that he was choking back tears.

Erika snickered as she dug into the pack for something and found it. "Here, Henry. I know it isn't much, but I want you to have this pack of Marlboros. The only ones gone are the few you've had. I know it isn't much, but they should last a while at least." Erika was digging deep to try to repay him somehow.

"Well, thank you. That is a gift I will accept. Now get your butt going." Henry was uncomfortable with good-byes, especially when he did not want to see that person go.

"Henry, there is no way I can ever thank you or your family enough. I... I don't know how... I could even..." Erika was now in tears.

"Now just stop right there, missy. You don't need to thank me. What goes around comes around in life, and if not in this life then in the next. We were just hoping to find one body alive out of that mess down there. We knew what we were getting into, and I wouldn't have traded it for anything. You are a good girl, Erika. A strong woman who is totally devoted to the ones you love. This will carry you home and be your light in dark places. You will get there. Now you jump on that horse and ride." Henry was putting finality to the conversation.

The good-byes were over. Erika did as she was told, jumped up on the saddle, and gave Artaz a firm kick to start her journey back to her family. Henry's red hair shined in the candlelight as she rode away. Erika looked back and waved. As Henry waved back to her, he turned to rejoin his wife and try to make some sense out of this backwards new world. He was safe with his family for now, but in this period of uncertainty he knew it was only a matter of time till danger came knocking at their door.

CHAPTER 10

AS ERIKA LEFT that night, it was with a heavy heart and very mixed emotions. She was glad to be on her way back to her loving family, but she didn't even know if they would still be alive if she did make it home. So much had changed in just a few months that Erika had no idea what to expect from anything. Henry and Carol had been so kind to her. They helped her when she could not help herself, and they fed her and nursed her back to a healthy condition that would allow her to make this journey. Then, when Henry and Carol's family arrived, the barn had been so full of life, and the sounds of children were very soothing. But in the end, Erika knew she could not stay. What would that accomplish? Would she ever know if her family and loved ones lived or died? She could not bear the pain of not knowing. So she had left the comfort of the secure barn and started her journey home.

Henry had provided her with all she would need for the trip home, plus he had given her two horses as well to make the trip faster. Erika could not get the conversation about the people in Auburn out of her head, though. Henry and Harold had warned her that the people's desperation was the worst kind of evil, and even the normally docile people were stealing and killing to survive—and who could blame them?

In the beginning, it was quiet and easy riding for the most part. The moon was full and the night was bright. The horses had to pick their way carefully along this alien landscape, but the stillness of the air was strangely comforting. Henry had warned her to stay close to the road so that she would know her way, but to beware of it as well. The roads continued to be major transportation routes even though they were scarcely recognizable as the roads they once were. Refugees from the disaster, thieves scrambling to take the goods of others, and displaced wildlife were all using these routes as a way to get around, but they were not the smooth concrete structures of the past. They were now pitted with cracks and piled with debris. It made travel with automobiles very difficult and ambush very easy.

Even still, Erika could not fully wrap her head around the severity of this situation. She figured that somewhere, someone was mobilizing to rescue the people. Maybe San Francisco and LA had been hit much harder, and her area was just too remote to be receiving help yet. She just didn't know. In reality, San Francisco and LA had been hit much harder. They were little more than rubble piles with fires burning everywhere out of control. Volcanic eruptions had covered them with ash and dust so thick that it was becoming impossible for survivors to move. Thousands and thousands of people lay dead in the streets. People on cell phones that would never ring again, mothers still clinging to their babies, and fathers laid out in the streets, fancy foods forever uneaten scattered across floors that had once been the staging for grand balls, all of it was destroyed. Mother Nature had taken all she could, and her wrath was not over. It was just beginning.

Erika plodded along a course that led her through the trees, and she had to be careful not to get rubbed off by a branch, and even more careful that none of her goods were lost along the way. She could not take time now to get more goods. Even if she had the time, where would she go? Who would she ask? There was far too much uncertainty involved, and as long as she was careful, she would not have to worry about it. The dirt itself seemed different. It was fluffier than the compact soil that usually existed in California. In the upheaval of the main quake, the dirt itself was displaced and even further displaced by the falling trees and cracking roots. The horses' hooves sunk deep, and it made her very aware of the tracks she was leaving.

She pushed that thought out of her head, though, because she knew she was not far from home in reality. When the roads were the smooth concrete routes of the past and the cars sped along the unbroken roadways, it would have only taken her about a half-hour to get home from where she was. But now, it was a very different world. With dangerous roads that would be too treacherous for most vehicles, she was left with good old traditional horsepower. But at least she had that. Henry and Carol had been so kind, she was sure a place would be reserved in heaven for their souls.

As the sun began to come up, Erika was weaving through the trees, watching and listening for any other sound but hers when she heard a vehicle. She quickly chose a place in the trees where she and the horses would be hidden from anyone coming down the road. Then suddenly a jeep came into view. Erika thought it was a very sorry-looking vehicle, basically just a frame with an engine and two seats. There were two men inside and they looked ragged. They could not travel very quickly along this broken road and had to slowly crawl along, as the jeep bobbed violently and they rocked from side to side gripping the roll cage for dear life. The driver was a dirty blond man, with a strong build. He was wearing a baseball cap. The other man was darker skinned with a slight build. As they slowly crawled past, Erika could just make out their conversation as they yelled above the roar of the engine.

The dirty blond man was saying, "We really need to bring back some meat to the camp; with all those people there, I don't know how we will keep feeding everyone."

The dark man replied, "I know. If those scavengers hadn't robbed us blind, we would not be in this position. I am telling you, dude, we aren't going to trust anyone any more. They can all die and go to hell for all I care. We are going to take care of our group and anyone else is just in the way. We will survive this."

"Hell yeah, we will, and once we get that surveillance balloon in the air this evening, we will be able to monitor this whole area. Then we will weed out the little pockets of survivors and take what they are surviving on. They can join us or die, and personally, I would rather they die because that will be less mouths to feed."

Erika was getting uneasy hearing this cruel conversation. She was thinking of Henry and Carol and hoping they were far enough away that they would not get bothered. She had traveled a long way, but if these people had vehicles, they could make it. She was also worried that she would not make it through wherever they were camped without getting spotted by this surveillance mechanism that would go into effect tonight. Her uneasy thoughts relayed to the horses, and they began to fidget around a little. Erika tried to soothe them, but she was getting panicky herself.

All of a sudden the dark man hit the dirty blond man and said, "Hey, stop the truck, Dave."

The sandy-blond man named Dave abruptly halted the jeep. "What, Doug?"

"I thought I saw something in those bushes over there."

"What was it?"

Erika was holding her breath and it seemed that the horses knew what to do as well. They all held perfectly still, and Erika prayed to God that they would not see her. She didn't know what would happen if they did. Would they kill her? Would they kill the horses? Would she ever get back to her family?

Finally after what seemed like a lifetime, Doug said, "Oh, forget it. If it was a deer, we must have scared it off. We will send out a couple of hunters this way tomorrow to see if they can find it and bring us home some meat."

"You are right," grumbled Dave. "Let's finish the perimeter check and get back. I'm sure someone back at camp is pitching a fit about something."

Dave got the jeep bumping along again, and their conversation and engine noise faded away into the distance.

"Oh, Artaz, was that close," Erika exclaimed to her horse as she let out a huge breath and slumped down to pet the horse. "We almost got ourselves into some big trouble. Let's make sure we stay away from their 'perimeter' and get the heck out of here as fast as possible. What about Henry and Carol? Should we go back and warn them?" Erika knew in her heart this was not really possible. It would take her too long to get back and then what good could she really do them. Henry and his son were setting up defenses anyway. They knew what was out there.

In the end, Erika decided to continue on as fast as the horses could go in this broken landscape. It was very tough because every bit of ground everywhere had been rippled by this earthquake; there was no escape. Trees that once stood tall and straight—delicately outlining the road—were now pointed sideways because the earth they were rooted in was so skewed. Erika's attempt at traveling in a straight line turned into more of a zigzag around this tree and then that one. One would be shooting off at a left angle and then the next one to the right, and all the while she had to keep the road fairly close but not too close. Plus, she constantly had to be aware of who might be on it.

The sun came up big and bright. All that day, Erika was completely freaked out. The horses felt her anxiety and stammered and tripped because they were trying to use their great big ears to pick out even the smallest of sounds. Erika did not even stop to eat. She was too nervous. She figured if she could just keep going, this whole ordeal would come to an end all the sooner. When she found her home and her family, they could hunker down together and wait for the help that was bound to come sooner or later.

To settle her mind down, she thought about riding when she was young. Erika had a quarter horse named Red, and she and Red had many great adventures together. They had gone soaring through cornfields, jumping irrigation trenches and fences as they dashed along. Her mother had always worried about her out riding alone. She had made Erika take her cell phone with her every time, and Erika wished now more than ever that she could call for help. But the phones did not work; Erika was on her own. If she lived or died now, no one would know. They would never know how far she had come, and anyone who found her would have no idea who she was or where she was even going. *In these desperate times, they probably wouldn't give it a second thought to begin with*, Erika thought to herself.

The sun began to dip down and Erika knew she would have to stop soon. If anything, she would need to feed and water the horses. They were thick with sweat from the day's anxious traveling, and Erika's tummy was rumbling as well. The stress of the day and the lack of food were finally catching up with her. She made a mental note of where the road she was following was and decided to turn further into the woods to hide for the night. Tomorrow, she would have to go through part of town to get across the river, and she knew this would be the most dangerous part of the journey she would encounter.

After going a short way off of the road, she found a little clearing and got off the horse. Erika used to ride a lot when she was young but she had not ridden a horse in a while and definitely not for a whole day. Her legs were so sore they didn't even want to move. They stayed all bent and crooked and her butt felt like a couple of basketballs stuffed in her pants. She hobbled over to the pack that was on Kit and got grain for the horses. She decided to take their bridles off so they could graze in their halters for a while. But she did not unsaddle or unload them all the way because she was afraid she might have to make a fast getaway. She got out a little beef jerky and chewed on it, but she mostly ate the fruit and vegetables that Carol had packed for her. She knew that the beef jerky and trail mix would last for a long time, but the fruits and veggies would soon perish if she did not eat them. Erika fully realized that wasting those essential vitamins could be a fatal mistake. After she and the horses had eaten and had some water, Erika got a blanket and put it down on the ground. She laid back and closed her eyes. The ground was hard and dirty and she wished she had something more comfortable to lie on, but at least the blanket created a barrier between her and the bugs. Erika had never liked bugs, and Vince had often been her savior. He would be the great white hunter that would leap in and squash that nasty bug deader than a doornail. This made Erika smile, but it also made her realize how alone she was. At least she had the horses. They were on the ready, and she knew they would alert her to anything approaching. She quickly dozed off but had dreams of her family and the warmth of their arms. Then they turned away. She screamed for them to come back, but they did not hear her. She tried to scream louder, but it did not matter. All of a sudden, she sat up, screaming and crying. All she saw was darkness and the horses. After that horrible dream, she was too restless to sleep. She re-bridled the horses and set off through the darkness.

It may not have been the best idea, but Erika did not care. She was going home and the faster she could get there, the sooner she could see her family. Plus, she convinced herself that maybe it would be easier to get through the city without too much interference at night. So, she got out the one little flashlight she had and headed back to the road. It was harder-going in the dark because she could not see the branches that threatened her and her goods as well. She was worried about losing her stuff and kept shining the flashlight at the tightly packed bags to make certain they were still there bouncing on Kit's back.

She found the road and was strategically using her flashlight as she went along it. She figured as long as she was very careful she could travel along the road, because it was dark and she could go much faster. She also did not have to worry about the continuous barrage from the branches. Traveling along the broken road did turn out to be much faster, and soon she was riding next to piles of what used to be houses. They were all broken. Just pile after pile of rubble. There was a stink in the air of death, and soon, she began to realize that the stink was coming from the bodies that still lay there in various stages of decomposition in the piles of rubble. It was at least two months since the main quake, and still the bodies rotted here. Where was everyone? Why didn't anyone do anything? She stopped to look at one of the bodies and noticed that one body had been dragged out of the rubble pile and meat had been cut off the bones. It looked like it was done purposefully. Erika couldn't fathom what had happened. She had no idea people could so quickly become so desperate.

The darkness was at its peak, and suddenly Erika heard a muffled scream in the distance. Someone was up and around and it sounded like something was going wrong. She felt like riding away as fast as she could, but something deep inside her was telling her to help. She slowly and quietly guided the horses toward the sound of the scream. As she neared the sound, she did not want to put her precious horses and cargo in the path of danger, so she found an area where the walls of an old home made a hidden cove and tied the horses there. Then she crept along as stealthily as she could toward the cry for help. When she finally spotted the cause of the commotion, she was shocked.

A big man dressed in raggedy clothes with a huge beard and belly was holding a woman down. She was struggling against him with all her might. Her body was being ground into the rubble that was strewn all around. He was tearing her clothes off with a frenzied hate. She was screaming and screaming, but he still held her and then tied her mouth shut with a piece of her own clothing that he had ripped off her. Before long, she was naked in the dirt. The man was rubbing her breasts and touching her crotch. She was whimpering and begging him to stop but he didn't. He kept on rubbing, touching, and squeezing her breasts. He put one of them in his mouth and bit down hard on her nipple, and Erika heard her scream through the gag. He had drawn blood, and now a trickle of blood ran down her breast as it shown in the moonlight. Erika was frozen. She didn't know what to do or how she could help. The man was far more powerful than her. She would have to wait for the perfect moment to intervene if she was going to at all.

The woman made a desperate attempt to shove the man off of her, but this just angered him even more, and he hit her multiple times across the face. The woman's face began to swell and bleed. She slumped into the dirt that surrounded her naked body. The man had a sickening smile on his face as he reached down and undid his pants. As she lay there almost knocked out, he let his pants fall to his knees and then he took his penis out of his pants. Erika could see it glowing in the moonlight, and she knew that her moment was coming. The man forced his body back on top of the naked woman, and then he shoved his penis into her. He was ramming it in and out with a fierce rage and pretty soon he was sweating and getting closer and closer to orgasm.

Erika knew this was her moment. If she was going to do anything, now was the time. She ran out from behind the wall and kicked the guy as hard as she could right across the head. He flew off the woman with a look of shock. Then before he had time to take in the new circumstances that had developed, Erika picked up a wooden two by four that was lying in the rubble and knocked him out with a carefully aimed blow that she landed right to his face. His nose smashed in an explosion of blood, and the man collapsed back onto the pavement. Erika was blown away by her actions and the graphic outcome. She stood staring in awe at the horrible scene. The man and the woman both sprawled out on the ground in unnatural positions; she thought they were both dead. She had never meant to kill anyone. She was frozen with shock when suddenly a tiny girl with golden-blond hair came flying out from behind another wall that was hidden in the dark. Even though the girl was little more than eight years old, she launched right at the knocked-out man. She jumped onto his limp body and stabbed him right in the area of the man's heart with a knife. The knife hit home but the little girl's strength was not enough to kill the man. When the knife sank into the man's skin, he suddenly woke up. He flung the tiny girl off of him into a pile of rubble. He got back on his feet and came right for Erika and began to choke her with his huge, bear-like hands. The knife was still stuck half-way into his chest. In a frantic gesture, Erika grabbed the knife and shoved it all the way in. Then she twisted it around. The man fell to his knees as the knife pierced his heart. He was still clutching Erika's shirt as he sank to the ground.

Erika opened the tightly clenched hands and let his body fall. Then she quickly scanned around for the girl and found her wrapped in her mother's arms lying on the ground. The woman was not dead. Erika quickly realized she must have just been knocked out. The small girl was sobbing, and her mother was trying to console her through a bloody and bruised mouth. Erika did not know what to do now. All she wanted to do was get home, but how could she leave these people behind with nothing? This was a mother and child lost in a ruined world. A world that we thought was stable; a world that had protected us for so long. Now nothing was certain. Erika knew that if she had heard the commotion, then others would too, and who knew who was where. Plus, what if someone had found her horses and supplies, then she would be in some major trouble. Her heart pounded as she thought desperately for solutions. She decided to drag the woman over to the horses. At least that area was more sheltered and easier to defend. She grabbed the woman quickly by the shoulders and began to drag her toward the horses.

The little girl screamed, "What are you doing to my mommy?"

Erika replied quickly without even looking at her, "My horses are over there. We will be safer."

The little girl grabbed her mom's legs without question and began helping Erika drag her mom over toward the horses. When they got there, the horses were fine and all the bags were in place. Erika sighed with relief. The little girl was in shock. She just stood there, wanting to know what to do next. Erika felt exactly like the small girl looked, but she wanted to be strong and help this little girl.

"You can let her legs go now. I will get her a blanket," Erika said to reassure the little girl.

The girl gently let her mom's legs go and sat down next to her. Erika grabbed a blanket from the pack and put it over the woman. She groaned and said a muffled thank-you through her swollen mouth. Bubbly blood came out of her mouth with each breath the woman took. Erika did not know what to do next. She wanted to leave as soon as possible but what was she going to do about these stragglers. Erika got some water and a rag out of her bags. She washed the blood off the woman's face and began to assess her condition. It did not look good. Her face and skull were very swollen, which meant she might have some serious internal damage to her brain. Her body was completely bruised, especially the area around her ribs. That was also a very bad sign, and judging from her labored breathing, Erika guessed that she had a punctured lung. She sat back when she was done. Her hands were bloody and she was exhausted.

"It doesn't look good, does it?" the girl questioned quietly.

"No, honey, it doesn't look good. We will have to wait and see though you never know what will happen. What is your name?" Erika said, trying to sound convincing.

"My name is Star."

"How old are you, Star?"

"I am eight."

"Where is your daddy, Star?"

"Daddy is dead. He died when the house fell down. Mommy and I have been hiding here for a long time, and we have always done a good job of hiding from the bad people until tonight."

"What bad people, Star?" Erika's curiosity was piqued by Star's comment.

"The bad people that took all the cars; they have a base where they stay. Remember where the grocery store used to be with the other stores around it? Well, they took over the grocery store and ate all the food. They used the other stores for supplies and turned the whole area into a big walled castle. Mommy and I went there to try to find more food, but we were scared of the men and decided to turn back and just stay hidden. One night, Mommy went out and she got some fresh steak. It was so good, I ate it all, but we haven't eaten in a while now," Star rambled innocently.

Erika went back to her packs and got out a big piece of beef jerky and an apple and gave it to Star. Erika thought she heard a thank-you pop out of that little mouth as she gobbled the food like a ravenous dog.

"Don't eat too fast-honey," Erika warned. "It may give you a tummy ache."

"I don't care. This is so good," Star said with her mouthful.

"Here, have some water too." Erika handed Star a canteen that Henry had given her.

"Oh, thanks."

When Star was done eating, she looked at Erika and asked, "What is your name, lady?"

"Oh sorry, my name is Erika."

"Where are you going, Erika?"

"I am trying to get home and find out if my family is still alive. I was stranded at work when all this happened. Some very kind people gave me these horses and here I am trying to get home now."

"I hope you find them," Star said this with a distant look in her eye as if she already knew that she had no family left. "My Daddy is already dead, and now look at my Mommy. I will probably die too."

Erika could feel her extreme desperation and uncertainty. "Don't you worry, Star, you are not going to die. You are going to survive. You will see. Why don't you curl up in this corner and try to get some sleep." Erika pointed to a corner that was nestled close to the wall. That way, if there were any happenings during the night, she would be farthest from danger.

"What about my mom?"

"Don't worry. I will take care of her. We need to get some rest, though. It will not be safe to have the horses here during the day so we need to keep moving. We will leave in a couple of hours."

"Okay." Star seemed strangely agreeable. Most kids would balk at the prospect of sleep, but Star just curled up in a little ball by the wall as she was told and she quickly fell asleep.

Erika was deep in thought watching the child sleep. She already knew deep down that she would be taking Star with her, and Erika would care for her like Star was her own. There was no one else to take care of her, and there was no way she was going to leave a child to die on her own or worse. Star's mom was very bad off. Her breathing was much more laborious now and she was coughing up more blood. These spasms roused the woman, and she looked up at Erika through black and blue eyes.

"I… I'm not g-going to make it, a-am I?" she slowly sputtered.

"Honestly, I don't think so," Erika said. Her eyes began to fill with tears.

"Thank you s-s-so much for helping us. N-no one else would. You and S-Star must leave me here. You must g-g-go. I-I am dying."

"I can't just leave you here," Erika said frantically.

"Y-You have to. The p-p-people from the compound. T-they will come. S-Star will die and you will die. You must go a-and you must go, *now!*" The woman was trying to find the strength to save her rescuer and her child. She knew that Erika did not know the dangers of staying here. The people from the compound came looking for food and supplies all the time.

"Star will never let me take her away from you while you're still alive," Erika countered.

"Then you must end it. Y-you must make her leave, and if killing me accomplishes that then s-so be it."

"Kill you? I am not a killer. I can't do it." Erika was even more frantic now. She knew the woman was right, and she knew the woman was going to die anyway, but she had never even dreamt of taking another person's life until tonight, and now this lady was asking her to take two lives in one night.

"Y-you have to. I-I can b-barely breath anyway, and I-I want Star to live. A-are you a m-mom? W-would you die to s-see your child live?"

Erika knew the answer was yes, and she slowly reached for the other blanket that she had. She would snuff out this life so another could live.

CHAPTER 11

ERIKA CHECKED TO make certain that Star was still fast asleep. Erika wadded up the blanket and slowly leaned down toward the poor, battered woman that she had just rescued. Her mind raced. On one hand she was thinking: Why couldn't she save her and build a cart to bring her along? But, on the other hand, she had no supplies to build a cart. The men would be back around, and eventually, those scavengers would find her, the woman, and Star. They would take her supplies and do God knows what to them.

The reality of the situation built and built in her head, until the thoughts finally frustrated her so bad that she found the courage to bury the woman's face in the blanket. Her labored breathing ceased and Erika sat back and checked on Star again. She was fine, all curled up and dreaming of days' past, wonderful days of carefree goodness, days that would never come again.

Erika curled up in her own corner and cried and cried. What was this world? She had never even dared to dream of the horrors that she experienced on this night. Her world was so desperately changed. She knew in her heart her family was out there, but would she ever survive this chaos, this anarchy, and this savagery to make it home? How would she face them knowing the realities that she survived through and the things it caused her to do? Erika sobbed until finally she slept under the blanket that had taken Star's mother from her.

Luckily, it wasn't long until Star roused from her dreaming. She scuffled around in the dirt then quickly remembered the events that had transpired before her nap. She looked toward her mom and saw her there resting, or was she? Was the blanket going up and down as she breathed? She ran over to her mother and flung herself onto her.

"Mommy... Mommy... No!" Star cried so loud Erika bolted out of her sleep and was there in a flash with her hand on Star's mouth.

"Star, you must be quiet," Erika warned the little girl.

"But Mommy?" she mumbled.

"I know she is dead. She died while you were sleeping. She told me to take you with me. You must come with me, Star. We have to get moving; we have lingered here for too long," Erika pleaded urgently.

"What about Mommy? We can't leave her here," Star begged Erika to listen.

"We have to, Star. We have no choice. You saw that man. There could be more of them out there. We have to go. *Now!*" Erika said this with extreme resolution. "You must trust me now. I will protect you. Okay?"

"Okay." Star's reply was barely a whisper.

If Erika thought her world was upside down, Star's world was a swirling vortex. Her mom and dad were dead, and she had only a stranger to trust. As a child, she had no option but to comply. She could not feed herself or protect herself from the unknown.

She could only hope that this stranger, who had offered a bit of help in a helpless world, could care for her.

Erika packed the blankets up on Kit and grabbed a couple of pieces of beef jerky and some water for her and Star. Then she got up on Artaz. She turned toward Star and grabbed her arm. Then she swung Star up behind her. When they were both seated comfortably, she handed Star a piece of beef jerky.

"Well, we're off," Erika said trying to sound cheerful.

She gave Artaz a kick and off they went. Erika always tried to keep the horses hidden behind this pile of rubble, or that one. Each time she rounded a corner, there was a chance for encounters with the other survivors grasping for life. This kept Erika on the very highest alert. She said a little prayer for her and Star and luck smiled upon them as they munched on their beef jerky.

Erika was going to have to make a major decision soon, though. The route that she was taking led to a bridge that used to span a dam that formed a mountain lake. She knew that if the dam had gone in the quake, which obviously it had, then the bridge would not be there any longer. This meant she must cross the river itself and climb through a mucky swamp to get there. Even though the canyon area had once been a beautiful river ecosystem with forests and wildlife, it was all destroyed. The forest had been turned into lumber, and the stumps were all that remained at the bottom of the lake. Dirt and soot that once coated the bottom of the lake formed a mucky ground, and it was steep. Erika knew of a road that used to exist before the dam was built, but lots of other people knew of it as well. Erika feared it might be a major place of congregation and decided that way would probably not be so good.

"Hey, Erika," Star whispered as she tapped Erika's shoulder.

Erika jumped a little when Star touched her and replied, "What is going on, Star?"

"I have to go."

"Okay, let's stop here and have a break."

Erika got them both a dried apricot and waited for Star to finish relieving herself. Erika watched as Star approached. She was a pretty girl with hair so blond that, even covered with dirt, it was still golden. She was skinny and had blue eyes that looked like a cloudless sky.

"Here, eat this, Star," Erika demanded. She did not like the look of how skinny the girl was.

"Thanks." Star took the apricot and quickly ate half of it. Then she savored every bite as she ate the other half. "What's wrong, Erika?" she asked.

"Nothing, why?" Erika was defensive because she did not want Star to worry anymore.

"Well, you are looking right at me, but it feels as if you don't even see me. What you thinkin' about?"

Erika was amazed by how astute Star's observation was and knew that she could not hide these realities from Star. She decided to tell her the situation and see if this young mind could help.

"Well, I have to decide what will be the best way to get us home," Erika admitted.

"Home? Your home? Do you think it is still there?" Star wondered out loud.

"I don't know, but we are going to find out." Erika was sure that even if her home was not there, her family was, and continued thinking out loud. "I think we will ride the forested edge of what used to be the lake for a ways up river, and then, hopefully, we will be far enough up to avoid major groups of people."

"Okay, if you say so. I've heard lots of talk about the river from the mean men while mommy and I were hiding. The bad people may be there, Erika. I am scared," Star said fearfully.

"Don't worry. We're going to make it. We just have to find a good area to cross. Regardless of how we cross that river, the sun is just about up, and we will need some place to hide for the day."

"Where are we going to go, Erika?"

"That's a great question, Star. There used to be some apartments at the edge of the canyon. They were built a long time ago and probably got destroyed. That should have left an area with lots of hiding places and not many survivors. We can hide the horses in the rubble there." Erika was hopeful her assumptions would be correct.

"Okay, if you say so." Star was still convinced she was going to die. It was sheer instinct driving her to trust in this stranger and continue on a road to survival.

Erika and Star got back on Artaz's back and urged him on. The lead line pulled on Kit's bridle and he followed behind. The travel through this area was very slow. There was debris from businesses and homes strewn everywhere. In the same way traveling through the forest had been a challenge because of the angled trees, traveling through the city was challenging because of the angled telephone poles, walls, fences, and whatever else men had planted in the ground. None of Auburn had been built to withstand an earthquake of this magnitude and no one had been ready. Erika had once wondered why no help had come for her in that bomb shelter when the truth was there was no help for anyone. Then, when Erika thought of global implications, she was really disheartened. She knew that if no help had come from the federal government, it meant that California was not the only place suffering.

Oh well, she had no time to worry about that now. She was finally getting close to home, but what about the river? How would she know if people were down there or not? Would they be friendly people? Or had everyone freaked out like those weirdos in Auburn?

Truth is, that although some individuals took the anarchy idea too far, the people in Auburn were just trying to survive too. First of all, the stress of actually surviving that horrific day pushed most people to a point of consciousness that they had never been to before. The vast quantity of carnage that they saw laid out before their eyes would haunt their dreams forever. Then, after surviving the initial shock, they had to fight off their neighbors for their dwindling food supplies. A group of survivors had banded together to start taking over grocery stores, gas stations, and whatever other resources they could find from the random looters. Most of the stores had been reduced to rubble so the group of survivors had used the remains to build compounds around these areas to keep other survivors away from their precious supplies. They formed raiding parties to go and search the small city for anything of value that remained. They ransacked solar panels for power and tried to supply some normality of their former life. Finally, even those resources started to dwindle, so these groups started attacking one another for supplies, which hardened these survivors even further. Murder, death, and war were not just a movie on the TV anymore; it became a reality. These people were not afraid to kill to survive.

Artaz was leading the way to the area where the apartments had once been, and Erika snapped back to reality. She said another silent thank-you to the Lord for an uneventful trip to the area and prayed that she would not find anyone there.

"This is it, Star," Erika whispered.

"Do you think anyone will be here?"

"I hope not." Erika knew what Henry had said about the marauder camp's location. They were far enough away to not be heard but close enough to still be very cautious.

Slowly, Erika urged the horses into the debris. They were very anxious and Erika quickly saw why. It was a horrible scene. The many floors of apartments, that had been stacked on one another, came down hard. The roof had been shaken to bits, and more of the decaying bodies laid half buried everywhere. They were old and young. This tragedy did not discriminate. Erika could tell that the remains of the building had been picked through, but the bodies were just left to rot. At least they had been dead and exposed to the elements long enough that they didn't really smell too bad anymore.

"Erika, I don't like it here. I think we should find someplace else," Star whimpered.

"We don't have the time; the sun is coming up," Erika replied sharply. She didn't like being here any more than Star, but she knew they had to get hidden fast. The night was gone.

Erika found a corner with a wall and no bodies. She quickly pushed the debris out of the way then led each horse in against the wall. She piled walls of debris all around them, and even found some boards she could put across the top in a disheveled manner to camouflage them further. She felt bad about always leaving their gear on them but knew no fast getaway would be possible if she had to load up gear first. She made a promise to them that once she found her husband she was going to give them at least a week without a saddle or a pack.

Once the horses were hidden, Erika set to the task of feeding everyone. She liked the fact that she now had companionship, someone to look after. It gave her a welcome distraction to her overwhelming mission of getting home.

"I think we will have some beans tonight. A whole can! We need to keep our strength up. Of course we won't be able to heat them up but I bet they'll taste good anyway." Erika was trying to make small talk with Star just to keep her mind off of this life. She felt horrible about Star's mother, and now Star was hers, and Erika would protect her to the end. She looked around, and to Erika's surprise, Star was busy with her own plans.

"Okay, I don't mind cold beans. Bring a blanket too. I cleared a place for us, and even made a little roof just like you made for the horses. We can eat our beans there."

It was a great little place Star had made. There was no wall space left, so Star had made a little hole in the rubble right next to the debris wall that Erika had made for the horses. It was expertly done and all the piles looked natural. Erika handed her the sitting blanket, and off Star ran to the makeshift tent. Erika got oats out for the horses and fed them in feed bags. Then she gave them some water from the bottle she had. She wished she had some hay to give them but grazing would have to wait for another day. In the meantime, oats would have to do. She got out the can of beans, a couple pieces of beef jerky, and some raisins. She thought of having one of her remaining cigarettes but opted not to, for the same reason a campfire was not possible. She didn't want anyone to see or smell the smoke. When she had what she wanted and was satisfied that the horses were sufficiently camouflaged, she climbed over one of the rubble walls and entered Star's tent.

It was not big but it was the perfect size for two people to sleep in. The blanket felt nice when Erika climbed onto it. It was so soft. She was surprised that she even took notice of the comfort provided by the cloth. Before, she would have hardly cared. She opened the can of beans, but without utensils she and Star had to pour them into their mouths. It wasn't so bad, and Erika was amazed at how good cold beans could taste, when all you have had was beef jerky and dried fruit for days.

After they ate, Erika lay back just for a minute to listen for people. If she heard anyone, she would follow them for information, and if she heard no one, she would go out and scout out the river to see the best way across with the horses. But, lack of sleep and the high intensity level of the day finally caught up with her, and she fell into a deep sleep.

CHAPTER 12

STAR AWOKE ERIKA with a shove. "Erika, I heard someone. Wake up!"

"Okay, okay, I'm up," Erika whispered groggily. "What is going on?"

"I heard a vehicle pull up and turn off, over that way." She pointed toward the old road. "The guys that were in the truck went that way." She pointed down the old road that ascended into what had been a winding canyon road at one time.

"Stay here and be quiet," Erika commanded.

She quickly grabbed a couple of broken wooden dowels that had held clothes in a closet. If Erika did have to defend herself in a pinch, she figured she would at least have something. She was fairly proficient at wielding the three-foot-long fighting sticks known as Eskrima sticks but that had only been for fun or demonstration in the past. Erika was fairly well dressed for stalking the men. She had a green hoodie on that Carol had given her. With the hoodie, she could keep warm without wearing a huge, bright, white cook's shirt. On her legs, she still wore the cook's pants, but the motif of the restaurant had been a jungle theme, so at least the pants were mostly green and brown and provided excellent camouflage. Her clothes still had a splattering of Star's mom's and that horrible man's blood. On her feet, she wore the moccasins that Henry had made her. They were finally breaking in from the constant use and were snug on her feet. Her moccasins helped to ensure that her steps were not seen or heard. Her hair was brown, so it did not stand out, and the dirt that now covered it helped give it a little more camouflage even though Erika thought it was gross and could not wait to give it a good shampoo and conditioning. She bent down outside of the tented area and rubbed her face with some mud. She did not want her face to be a beacon of white in a camouflaged area. She was not about to get caught by these weirdos, but she had to know what they were up to.

Erika knew that they had gone down the old road but she wondered at the speed at which they had done so. How far had they made it since Star had heard them and roused her? There was no way to know, so Erika proceeded with absolute caution. It was easy to make out their tracks in the mud, and Erika was very careful not to leave any of her own that would be noticed by the men when they returned. She made sure she was following their tracks, but stayed well to the left of them and up another ravine. This way, her tracks were hidden on the top of the little ridge, and she was always uphill from her quarry.

This was a treacherous route to choose. At one time, the canyon road had been a beautiful drive. Along the way, oaks, pines, and manzanitas reached for the heights of the canyon. Waterfalls cascaded down the sides and eventually joined the meandering river. Huge rock outcroppings made wonderful sitting areas for all of the travelers to enjoy the view, or just simply have a rest. Mountain bikers and hikers with dogs dotted the whole area, and during the summer, the activity was immense as people flocked to the river to avoid the heat. The brilliant forest that the canyon supported teemed with animal life as well, and the day that the dam was finally finished, many people cried for the wildlife that would have to find new homes.

Man liked the area so much, they decided it needed to be altered and turned into a lake. They built their dam and flooded the land with water. The dam itself was a bridge from the town of Auburn to the town of Cool, and there was another bridge that had stood long before the dam was built. This bridge had been one of the tallest in North America before the land below it was flooded, but then it had originally been built to stand in the water anyway. Years of waiting for the flooding had already started to deteriorate it. Crazy people used to skydive off the bridge and Hollywood movie producers used it in their movies, but once the water inundated the area, it was just another bridge on a road. This bridge connected the town of Auburn to another mountain town called Foresthill.

Before they flooded the land, man had to rape it one more time. The trees were all cut down because it would have wasted the wood to leave them under the water, and they were too tall and would affect the boats riding on the water above. They cut down vast swaths of forest, and the nearby residents, all eager to get their beachfront properties, could hear the screams of birds and animals crying for their homes that they would never return to again. Now, only a ghost forest of stumps remained; the ground was a sloppy mush of dirt that had been saturated with water for years. But the months since the dam had broken had left the high areas of the former mountain range exposed. A crust formed on the top of the exposed dirt. Luckily, Erika was a little woman and very light. With her moccasins on, she could walk flat footed and float over this crust without disturbing it too much. Any tracks would be disastrous, so Erika continued cautiously on, delicately stepping from one stump to the next.

Finally, she heard them in the distance. They were just on the other side of the hill around the next bend. They were posted up behind a couple of stumps. They were looking down the river and engaged in conversation. Erika seized the moment to slowly creep around to a stump that was on a cliff, almost directly above them. The area they occupied was a small cove that had a fair amount of stumps to keep them hidden from whatever they were looking at below them.

Erika strained her eyes to see what was down there. She noticed a walled area down on the muddy edge of the wide river. Obviously, the walled area had been erected to keep out intruders like the ones lurking around below her. She paused from her thoughts to listen to their chatter.

"Do you see any obvious weak spots, Steve?" Erika thought she recognized that voice. It was the darker-skinned man she had seen before. What was his name? Oh yeah, Doug. It was that same man that she had overheard in the jeep. She had averted him then, and now, here she was overhearing him once more.

"See where the fence is just made of that sheet metal?" Steve replied.

"Yeah."

"Well, if we could throw something sharp through it, with a barb on it like a fishing hook, we could tie it to a rope and use them to break those walls wide open."

"All right, Steve, I'm buying what you're selling. With a big barb, we might be able to take those walls right down. Too bad we couldn't find those horses that left those tracks the other day. We would be more mobile down there. We only have the one truck that can make it down there and back up again through this muck. Plus, you know what our gas supply looks like. I almost hate to waste any on another raid. Animals like that could make a big difference. We could tie the ropes to them and use them to rip those walls down in no time."

"We have what we have, boss, and that's it. Unless we can get more from those tree huggers down there, and I think the grapplers would do the trick. I know just the materials we can use at the compound to make them. You know those iron fence posts? All we need to do is sharpen them and weld on barbs and we are set. If all the guys pitch in, we could be ready by nightfall." Steve's plan was formulating.

Erika was starting to develop a much bigger picture of what was going on here. She ascertained that this guy, Doug, was the leader of the group in Auburn. He had brought his guy, Steve, here to devise a plan to attack these people! What was she going to do? She couldn't attack two fully grown men. They had been hardened from all this fighting. She was one little woman with two sticks, who was she kidding. She had her family to get home to. Not to mention Star and the horses, who were still waiting for her. This was not her fight, but why did she feel she had to help? She could not deny this overwhelming urge to protect these people on the river. The ideas were running round and round in her head. All her thoughts were brought to a screeching halt when the men below started to move again.

Erika shrunk back as she saw Doug and Steve slowly and cautiously start to make their way back up the canyon. They were so concerned about not being seen themselves that they never bothered to look for footprints of anyone who may have followed them. Erika followed them back up. She was concerned about being spotted but wanted to learn more of their plan.

"Steve, do you really think we could have the grapplers ready by tonight?" Doug questioned.

"Yeah, I do, boss," Steve replied confidently.

"Good. Because there is a rumor that they are preparing to leave," Doug said in a concerned voice.

"Leaving? Where would they go? Where would anyone go?" Steve questioned curiously.

"I don't know and I don't really care, but they are blocking a good spot to access the river, they have food supplies from somewhere, they have some smart fellows down there that made that generator they run. I even heard that they have at least half a dozen women in that camp. We have to overtake them before they leave," Doug insisted.

"What are you talking about, Doug? If they leave, we can have their camp without a fight. I understand that we need supplies, and raiding and killing have been necessary to keep us alive and safe, but we can't take people. What would we do with them? How would we feed any more people than we already have in camp?" Steve sounded shocked by Doug's suggestion.

"Think about it, Steve. Those men are smart enough to get us connected to someone who might still be out there, waiting to rescue us. They already have power down there, and they can make more at our camp. They can figure out how to fuel our vehicles. Plus, if we capture them by force, what say will they have in what they do or eat. If they don't do what we say, then they won't eat, or we will just beat them for a while.

"As for the women, I don't know about you but I could use some action. We have thirty guys and five women at camp. It is a regular sausage fest. Plus, four of those women are married, and the last is already taken by Bill. We could take those women down there and hold them at the compound. They can cook and clean and if we need some action, well, they can take care of that to, if you know what I mean." He grabbed his groin and thrust it forward as he finished his statement.

"I guess you're right. I could really use the company of a woman. There are some people at the compound who will protest." Steve still sounded concerned despite his partial agreement to Doug's plan.

"Probably just those mouthy wenches anyway. If they don't like it, let them leave and try to survive on their own. They will be crawling back in no time," Doug said in a very cocky tone.

Erika could not believe what she was hearing. What century was she in? What country? How could our super-civilized world decay so quickly? What Doug was talking about was slavery! He was going to take those people as slaves. She knew now she had no choice. She had to warn these people. She had to get them to leave or life for this once-sleepy little town was going to rapidly be transferred back to the eighteenth century.

After what seemed a very long time, the men finally reached the top. They were full grown men in their twenties and thirties, and as they walked, they crushed through the top layer of crust on the mud and slipped and slid everywhere. Plus, the mud got stuck to their boots on each step, and they had to pull the boots back up through the crust. It looked very arduous and Erika was glad for her soft steps. Finally, they were scrambling up the last hill. They kicked the mud off their boots and pants for one last time. Then they went over the top of the hill and disappeared into the ruined city. Erika waited to hear their vehicle start up in the distance and, in a flash, she was climbing back into the hole that contained Star.

CHAPTER 13

"COME ON, WE are leaving now!" Erika barked at Star. Star didn't even reply. She just began quickly packing the blankets and food she had brought from the packs. By the time Star was done, Erika already had the horses ready to go. They finished packing the things that Star had brought to the tent into the horses' packs and mounted Artaz. Erika no longer cared about tracks, and she rode directly into the road and started down the canyon.

Erika was very frightened for the horses all the way down. She had thought that the heavy men had slid a lot on this mud but that was nothing compared to the horses' pounding footsteps. They slid and scrambled. Star clung to Erika like a tick. Erika never liked riding downhill. She had grown up riding in the flat midwestern land. When she did ride downhill, she did it with grace, but it was never one of her favorite places to be. Now, not only was it going to be a long downhill ride, but the slippery mud made it a horrific experience. There was no grace here. Erika thought of getting down and leading the horses to reduce the weight they carried, but it would have taken twice as long to reach the bottom, and time was not something they had very much of right now.

Erika followed the old road at first, but soon she would have to leave it and start going directly down the steep mountainside. She had decided that she would try to wind down the side of the mountain in the classic S-formation. She thought it might take a little more time, but it would be much safer for the horses. Erika found it kind of ironic that these people, that Doug had referred to as hippies, now camped in an area which had been a nude beach for free spirits back when the river flowed unabated through the canyon. She wondered if the energy in the area had called them back and chuckled to herself about the idea.

Now, it was time to leave the road. Erika had liked traveling the old road because when they were on it, she knew that somewhere beneath them a road did exist. Some remains of solid, paved ground remained there in some form and provided support for the horses' footings. Now she was stepping off into the abyss. Before the lake, this ground was pockmarked with cliffs and mini canyons. Since it had been made a lake, the silt at the bottom had filled in those nooks and crannies, making all the ground look smooth. Erika knew better. She knew that under that smooth layer she might be stepping off a cliff.

There was no option; she had to go. She didn't know how passable the river was. She had no idea what may be down there, but she had learned a lot from those scoundrels. Now, she knew there were people down there. People surviving off the river and not allied with the ruffians above. The scoundrels also gave her something else: a bargaining chip. She knew when and where the attack would come, but she didn't know if this knowledge alone would provide her with safe passage.

So far so good, Erika thought. Artaz and Kit were sure-footed and chose their steps carefully. They slipped and slid but continued on. Erika and Star didn't bother to eat all morning. There was no time. They rounded a bend in the canyon and they finally saw the camp. It was very creative. They had used huge pieces of iron and concrete to build a fence around their compound. It was secure. They also had access to the river, and it looked like their compound protected a potential crossing spot. Most of the river was still very wide from the flooding, but this area seemed to pinch off at the width of the original river, which was very easy to cross.

Erika knew that if she could see the compound, they could see her. No warning came, and she continued forward. Soon she was up alongside one of the iron walls. She continued until she found a section of fencing that looked like a gate. Her suspicions were confirmed when she saw the marks in the mud from the gate being opened.

"Hello there," she called, eagerly anticipating a response. Star jumped a little as Erika broke the silence with her yell.

"What do you want?" A voice had come from a hole in the iron that was located at the top of the wall.

"I only want to use your crossing, and in return, I can give you information regarding the marauders in Auburn," Erika responded, laying her cards out on the table.

"How do you know about them? Maybe you are one of them. How else would one small woman with a child make it past them on two horses? Maybe you were sent here to take our guard down." The voice seemed leery.

"No one sent me here. I am just trying to get home to my family in Georgetown. I only want to cross the river safely with this girl and my horses."

"How do we know that you are what you say you are?" This time it was a female voice from the window.

"I only have my word," Erika screamed back. "I have already been through hell and back and thought maybe, just maybe, I could find one decent person left in this world. I overheard an attack plan on this compound this morning and thought I could help, but if you don't want my help, fine. I will cross somewhere else and hey, at least I know the marauders won't be looking for me for a while." Erika was trying to entice their curiosity about what she knew and could tell them.

Erika had turned Artaz in a direction that would follow the wide girth of the river in hopes of finding an alternate crossing, when she heard the clanking of metal beyond the gate. Star squeezed Erika in fear and excitement, and Erika quickly turned back toward the gate. The gate slowly creaked open toward Erika, and she had to back the horses up a little so it could open far enough to let them in.

She was met with grim faces inside the gate. They were not very dirty but they were thin, and everyone bore the pain of this situation. Three of the men had rifles and the rest of the people were armed with sharpened makeshift spears of one type or another. Erika urged the horses inside the gate. The ground inside had been covered with pieces of iron and concrete that the survivors had sunk into the muck to make a flat, clean area. There were walls inside built of this same material. The group inside the compound had formed a circle around her, and one of the men with a rifle stepped forward.

"Well, you better start talking, sweetheart." It was the same voice that she heard at first from the window. It had come from a dark-haired man with a mid-sized build. He seemed highly protective, and who could blame him.

"How do I know that if I tell you what I know, you will help me to safely cross the river?" Erika questioned. She did not want to be stuck inside their camp with her can of beans opened, depending on the honesty of these people.

"You should not ask so many questions when you have a gun pointed at you and nowhere to go," the man replied angrily.

"Oh Sam, don't act like one of those jerks out there. Show her the crossing and let her go if that is what she needs. She is not asking for food or water. She is offering help, so shut up." It was the woman from the window. She was huge, a really tall, really big woman with long brown hair and brown eyes. She could definitely have been a lumberjack or an Amazon woman in a past life.

"My name is Jane. We aren't going to harm you, the girl, or your horses," Jane said this with pure honesty and directly met Erika's gaze so there would be no doubt.

Erika dismounted, leaving Star seated on Artaz, and went to shake Jane's hand. Erika was so small compared to Jane, she felt as if she was sitting in the front row in a movie theatre when she looked up to talk with her.

"Hello, my name is Erika."

"Nice to meet you, Erika, please follow me. I will show you the river crossing and a place where you can keep your horses while we talk." Jane turned and started to walk away from the gate.

During this time, Erika had been inconspicuously surveying the compound. The circle was made up of about twelve people in all. There was Sam, who was always close to Erika, waiting for her to make the wrong move. There was a man who was fairly small with a gray beard and dancing green eyes. There were three other men that looked to be in about their thirties. There were four teenagers there—three boys and one girl. Two other women were there as well as Jane. They had all lowered their weapons and turned along with Erika to follow Jane along a passageway.

The area to the left of the passage they were following looked like it was used for bathing and clothes washing. It was along the river, and had some towels and clothes hanging on lines there. The space on the right of the passage looked like it was used as sleeping areas. There were smaller rooms blocked off by walls that were not as tall or fortified as the outside walls. At the end of the passage, the group emerged into another open spot. Here, the river was loud. It looked like a section for eating and talking, and to the left was an actual bridge they had made to cross the river.

"This is not a crossing. This is a bridge!" Erika was ecstatic—finally a stroke of luck coming her way. She would not have to worry about how to keep her things dry or make sure Star was safely across. They could simply clippity-clop across an actual bridge.

"Now that we have shown you our secret, you must tell us yours," Jane said this with the same honest determination in her eyes. "You can tie your horses up over there by the river."

Erika led her horses to a half wall that had iron rebar posts sticking up out of it. This made it perfect for tying the horses to. The horses could reach the water from their tethered area, and they drank heartily after days of trekking across the mountains depending on Erika's dwindling supply. Then she walked over to the sitting area with Star in tow.

"Please, sit here." Jane was indicating a seat near her that was in a circle with other seats, and everyone sat down. Sam was the only one still standing, and he left to go take his place at the guard house. Star sat on the ground beside Erika.

Erika started to speak. "I have come to tell you all about an impending attack," she said calmly. She felt weird. Like she was in an old-school war movie, and she was the messenger of death.

"What! When?" Now it was Jane's turn to get frantic.

"Tonight." Even though Erika was flush with emotions, she tried to make her statements very matter-of-factly. This was not her fight. She had to get home, and even though she really felt that she needed to help, she was also thinking of herself, Star, and her family. Putting herself at risk for a fight that was not hers would not be a smart move now. Not when she was so close to home.

"How do you know? What else do you know?" Jane wanted all the information now so she could plan. So Erika spilled it. She told Jane about her close run-in with those horrible men in Auburn, how Star had come to be in her care, and then the spying she had done when the men were at the top of the canyon and all that she had heard.

"They are going to use grapplers to bring down the walls? They are not aluminum, they are iron. Will it work?" Jane asked.

"I really don't know. My knowledge of the situation ends there. I don't know what kind of grapplers, or metal, or any of that. All I know is what I heard them say, and it seems their estimation of the situation was wrong to begin with, but I really thought you all should know what they were up to so you could have a chance to protect yourselves," Erika replied. She had nothing left to offer. She had given them all of the information she knew, and she did not really have any idea of how to successfully attack or defend something.

"Taylor." Jane was speaking to one of the teenagers; he was tall and lean with brown shaggy hair. "Go relieve Sam at the guard post and send him here."

"Okay," Taylor quickly replied as he loped off.

"Steve, you worked in construction and you designed a lot of this place, what do you think?" Jane questioned calmly.

It was obvious to Erika that Jane was in charge here. It was a weight she bore well. She had been frantic when she heard the immediacy of the situation, but that franticness quickly melted into calculated calmness. To be calm here in this world was truly commendable. She was quickly working out a plan and would carefully evaluate all of her resources before coming to a conclusion.

The man she had questioned, Steve, was a big man with blue eyes and very strong-looking hands. He had been one of the riflemen when Erika arrived. Now, with his rifle stored away, he looked much friendlier, and Erika was eagerly anticipating his reply.

"If what she says is true, we have very little time to worry about defenses anymore. They will be tested tonight, whether we like it or not."

Just then, Sam arrived with a questioning, panicked look in his eyes. Taylor had informed him of the situation while relieving him. Sam was a smart guy with lots of mechanical knowledge, but this lack of emotional control explained why Jane was in charge and not him.

He came into the circle and sat down. "What did I miss?" he questioned. "What in the heck is going on?"

"Taylor must have told you what Erika told us, Sam. We need to decide what we are going to do and I was just asking Steve about our defenses," Jane replied and looked at Steve again.

"As I was saying, the walls are stout and not made of sheet metal like those crazies think. If they attack they will be determined, and a grappler thrown over the wall may be able to hook it and pull it down." Steve was cautiously calculating the possibilities involved with this attack. Erika had brought them vital information, but there were still many variables unaccounted for.

Erika interrupted the conversation, "Do you mind if I see to my horses and the girl? We have a long way to go still."

"It is your plan to leave, then?" questioned a woman Erika had not heard from yet. She had blond hair that was starting to gray. It hung to her shoulders. Her blue-green eyes told a story of deep pain and many nights of crying herself to sleep.

"Yes, I am leaving. I know the situation here is critical, but I must get back to my family. I am not a member of this group, not that you aren't all great people, but I am simply passing through. Plus, I heard those guys saying that they plan on taking prisoners for their own use, just like slaves, or worse. I do not plan on being one of those women they are so short on," Erika replied honestly.

She knew she was being cold for not staying to help them defend this place, but she also knew she could not afford further delay. She had been gone too long already. Who knew what horrors Vince was facing and how long he could wait for her. How long could he hold out and hope that she was out there, somewhere, alive?

"I'm with her," the woman replied. "My kids may be alive, and I have to know. I am leaving too."

"Jaclyn, we talked about this. There is no crossing the river towards Foresthill. The bridge is gone and they dredged the lake over there. It is deep and wide. The upper Auburn clan guards the few crossings that exist. It is certain death," Jane replied.

"Don't you see, Jane? It doesn't matter anymore. If my kids are dead, then I am dead, or I might as well be. Who wants to live in this messed-up world anyway? What am I going to do? I have to go back. I have to know, and if it means my life to find out, then so be it. I am going." Jaclyn said this with finality and got up to go and pack her things.

"I'm sorry," Erika said. She felt like this sudden discord in the group had been her fault. She got up and walked towards her horses with Star following right behind her.

When she reached the horses, she got out the sitting blanket for Star. She knew it would be the only time they could rest before they must move on again. Erika dug deep into the food bag. They were running really low on food. There was a piece of beef jerky left and some raisins. She ripped the jerky in half and gave Star the bigger one. Then she divided the raisins. Erika figured it might be their last meal, so it might as well be a good one.

Erika gave Star's share to her but put her own food aside for a minute. The horses were enjoying themselves so much that Erika unsaddled and unpacked them. They had not been unpacked since leaving Henry's and they were thrilled. Erika scratched them and rubbed them down with water. In her head, she was thanking them for bringing her so far safely. She was also saying a prayer for their continued safety in this last step of their journey. The horses seemed to sense her emotions and nuzzled her gently with their heads. Finally, Erika got out some oats that she had left for them and put some in their feed bags. When she was satisfied that the horses were well cared for, she sat down to enjoy her meal with Star.

Erika glanced over toward the circle of people that was still in deep debate. Sam, Steve, and one of the young teenage boys named Randy had set off to start working on some unknown task. Jaclyn had never returned to the circle. Soon the discussion ended, and the rest of the people set off to take care of the tasks they had been given. Jane was walking toward Erika.

"Well, we have decided to leave as well. We have survived here well enough but what of the future? Those men are just going to keep coming until they have accomplished their goal, and we are all captured or dead. Plus, once the rainy season starts, this river is going to rise and our comfy home might not be so comfy then. So we are packing. We do not know where we will go but we will go, and hopefully, we will come to a better place," Jane said halfheartedly. This was a no-win situation for her. Stay here and defend a walled mud hole that was eventually going to flood, or venture out into an unknown that might be worse than the situation here.

Erika could not believe what she was hearing. She thought she would just ride through and travel off again, just her and Star, but now everything had changed. The group was leaving too, and for some reason she trusted these people, and Erika wanted to reach out to them.

Erika almost jumped at Jane in her excitement. "Well, Jane, suddenly we find ourselves in the same predicament, heading in the same direction, so why don't we travel together? My supplies are running low and Kit's pack is light. We could build a cart and carry more of your group's goods out." Erika was thrilled that she would be able to help and still keep moving. Everything was going to be okay.

"That would be great! I do not know how we could thank you for that. Many people have wondered how they would carry out all their stuff. I want to let you know we do not plan on leaving here quietly. We have water cannons that Sam and Steve are rigging to go off automatically. Once the marauders have made it through the walls and the water cannons, we will rig our generator in the bridge to blow up and hopefully take some of those jerks with it. This will make it difficult to follow us and hopefully it will convince them to turn back." Jane laid the plan out before Erika, and she was impressed. In just a few minutes of planning, Jane had composed a great defensive strategy. They would not stay here and let stubbornness kill them all in a useless defensive plan to keep their compound. They were survivors, and they knew moving on could keep them that way, surviving. But they were not sulking and dragging their heels out in defeat: they would provide these intruders with an unexpected surprise.

CHAPTER 14

DURING THE NEXT couple of hours, everyone was immersed in preparations. Jane went around supervising and making sure her belongings were ready to go, her loud mouth directing and answering questions. Sam, Steve, and the boy, Randy, had finished readying the defenses and they started packing their own belongings. When Randy was done, he went and relieved Taylor at the post so Taylor could pack. The small guy who was older, Jim was his name, used to work as an electrician. He had engineered the generator and was busy working on turning it into a bomb. The generator was built into the bridge and used the water flowing through turbines to generate electricity.

Jane went over and enlisted the help of Sam and a young teenage girl, Kim, for the building of the cart. They used an old car axle and quickly had a cart rigged up. It would be a challenge for Kit to pull this cart in the mud so it was decided that it would be loaded immediately. The group with this cart would leave as soon as possible, so they had a very good chance of making it to the top of the canyon without being followed or caught. A quiet couple that had survived with their four-year-old son was chosen to guide it. It would be dark, so Erika had given them some candles. The light from these candles would guide the groups to one another at the top.

This couple, Rich and Joan, had also found a three-year-old boy who was wandering around in their neighborhood. He was part of their family now and would accompany this group. Since they had most of the valuable supplies, it was decided that Taylor, Randy, and Kim would travel with them as well. It turned out that Kim's brother, who had died, was very involved in the restoration of classic automobiles, and since she had helped him often, she had considerable knowledge of mechanics. She could be instrumental if anything went wrong with the cart.

Sam and Kim also devised two carts that could be pulled up the hill by hand. Two more groups were composed to take these carts to the top. All of the groups would head up the canyon in different directions and meet at the top. This way, any marauders that decided to follow the group up the hill would only be able to find one group, and there was no way of catching the complete caravan with all the goods and people together. Erika had supplied them with some candles as well. She just knew she had lugged those things all over for something. They had come all the way from the restaurant. When she thought of the restaurant experience, it seemed like a lifetime ago.

One group was composed of Jim the electrician and Steve the contractor. The other group was composed of Jimmy, or Jimmy D as he was called, and Tom Jensen, a seventeen-year-old teenager who had been on the football team and was out running on the track when the big quake hit. It had saved him, but, unfortunately, his family had not been so lucky.

Erika had to pack her own pack back up quickly so Kit was ready to go. Erika was sending her supplies with him and Richard and Joan. This was a huge risk, but she wanted to be mobile if anyone needed help. She tried to convince Star to stay with Rich, Joan, and the other kids, but she absolutely refused to leave Erika's side. Star had been so content to follow Erika's direction, and this was the first time that she put her foot down and would not comply. She was not going to lose Erika too. Erika finally gave in and let Star stay with her and Artaz.

As Erika packed up her things, she took stock of what she had left. She packed up her three blankets, her sauce pans, the first aid kit, and her box of candles (even though there were only twenty left now, it was still enough to justify lugging them around). Erika fondled the soft fabric of the outfit that Carol had given her and then wrapped it up in one of the blankets and packed it away with the others. She still had a bag of rice that she hadn't been able to eat because she didn't want to risk building a fire or wasting the water. She also had three months worth of tampons, and she had been thankful that she was lugging them around as well. She had no idea what the other women were doing at that time of the month but was thankful she did not have to worry about that yet. She had a few packs of smokes left and decided that right now was as good a time as any to have one. This gave her a minute to relax and enjoy some sense of familiarity. When she was finished packing her belongings in as small a pack as possible, she led Kit over and got him hitched to the cart. She tried one more time to convince Star to travel with Richard and Joan but she would not budge and went over to stand with Artaz.

Kit and the main supply cart were fully loaded with supplies from the compound. After some hugs and promises of meeting at the top, the first party left. After crossing the bridge, they began to carefully ascend the hill. Erika watched Kit go. He was so strong, and he worked so hard to pull the cart up the hill. By the time dusk was setting in, the other two parties had left as well. They only had the three rifles and one had been given to Richard upon his departure. This left two rifles and two individuals behind to wait for the attack and trigger the bomb.

The two individuals staying behind were Sam and Jane. They were going to have to trigger the bomb, cross the bridge, and run for safety. They decided that Jane would trigger the bomb and Sam would cover her as she completed her task.

Jaclyn, the woman who was leaving, had kids in Foresthill. She was all packed up and ready to go. She was saying her good-byes now and left Jane standing at the gate watching her go. Just as Sam was closing the gate behind her, Jane saw the marauders coming down the side of the mountain from the right-hand side.

The gate was still closing and only had an inch left to go then *bang!* It slammed shut. There was no way to get it open again in time to get Jaclyn safely inside before the marauders ascended upon them.

Jane screamed to Jaclyn, "Run Jaclyn, run and hide! They will catch you!"

"Jane, get that gate open again just enough for a horse to get through," Erika barked the order while she was running toward Artaz.

Jane was frantically pulling the gate open. Jaclyn started to run along the edge of the river where the flowing water had pulled back the mud and left stone that was not as slippery. Erika lost sight of Jaclyn when she ran to Artaz. Star was already mounted and Erika jumped up in front of her.

"Whatever you do, *do not let go!*" Erika yelled while driving her legs into Artaz.

Artaz leaped forward, and in a flash, they were flying through the opening of the gate. She heard the water guns start blasting on the left as Artaz's rump cleared the right-hand gate. The mud flew in the air as they pounded along the river bed. Then, she saw Jaclyn running in fear as fast as she could. Artaz was soaring now; his hoofs were clacking across the rocks but somehow, he found solid footing every time. Erika was a short distance from Jaclyn. They were going to make it. Then, all of a sudden, a truck came into her view from her left. The engine roared as the truck bounded across the mud. They were closing in on Jaclyn. Erika realized she would never make it before the truck and pulled back hard on Artaz causing him to come to a sliding stop.

As Artaz spun around on his heels to scamper back to the safety of the compound, Erika heard Star scream, "They have her!"

"There is nothing we can do now except get the heck out of here." Erika was out of her head to be running after Jaclyn. All that would come of it was her and Star getting captured as well. Then she heard the men from the truck shouting.

"There it is! The horse, that girl is riding it. Get it!" They quickly turned and started chasing Erika down, but before they could get their truck rolling through the deep muck, Erika was through the gate and Sam was closing it behind her.

Erika turned back as the gate closed and saw Jaclyn tied up like an animal in the back of the truck. The men were laughing at her and hitting her. She screamed in horror for someone to help her, but again, there would be no help. She would just become another victim in a world that no longer had sympathy for the defenseless.

Erika could not help her now, and she had already lingered here too long. The walls were starting to get pulled down by the grapplers that had been thrown over the top of them. She saw Sam and Jane pulling back to the designated point for the final retreat. The marauders were shooting guns and throwing spears at Jane and Sam. Jane and Sam were firing back, but their ammo was very limited, and Erika knew it. Sam ran back to the cover point. Erika had been forgotten in the fray. The bridge would be blown and Erika was on the wrong side!

She dug her heels deep into Artaz and they galloped toward the bridge. She could see Jane getting ready to hit the switch, but in a second, Jane was standing there with a spear directly through her eye, and it was coming out the back of her head. Sam screamed for Jane and shot the spear-thrower dead in his tracks. Sam went to fire again and the only sound was *click, click*. He was out of bullets and the marauders were closing in. Erika jumped off a galloping Artaz and rolled over to the generator. Artaz hit the brakes quickly on the bridge as soon as he felt Erika jump. Star instinctually moved up and gripped the reins. Star yanked on one rein and Artaz wheeled back around toward Erika. Erika hit the switch, and as she looked back, there was Artaz with Star at the reins.

Erika leapt up in front of Star and they tore across the bridge that was blowing up almost underneath them. They turned to get Sam and saw a bullet rip through Sam's chest. As the last of the bridge blew, the debris went flying along with ten men who had been on the bridge, following closely behind Erika, hoping to take her down as well.

Artaz was now in a wild gallop, completely freaked out from the guns and explosion. He barreled up the hill uncontrollably, but then *bang!* Star screamed out in pain as a bullet ripped through her calf and struck Artaz in the guts. He flinched but the pain just fueled his wild scramble. He ran like never before, but as his life ran from his wound, he collapsed halfway up the canyon in a lifeless mass.

Erika and Star were thrown off Artaz as he fell. With that final crash, all that could be heard was the quiet of an unbelievable night. Star was knocked out, and Erika lay still, completely dazed from the experience. As Erika lay there somewhere between reality and unconsciousness, she thought again that this was all just some horrible nightmare and she had to wake up eventually. What was this life? Would everyday be like living in hell? There must be a nice normal life to be had somewhere. How fragile everything had been. People walked through life everyday taking it all for granted, their cars, cell phones and their lattes, their dramatic social issues and medical problems that spawned from obesity and laziness. Well, welcome to the real world, to life where you had to fight for survival with people who used to be neighbors, or at least civil.

CHAPTER 15

ERIKA SAT UP quickly. She wiped a tear from her eye when she saw Artaz sprawled out at her feet. The life was gone from his limp body. She continued scanning the broken terrain for Star. Then she saw her. She was curled into a ball, which must have been her natural reaction when Artaz started to go down because she was out cold.

Erika scrambled over to Star and checked her over. Her head looked okay; there were some new scratches but nothing of too much concern. Her chest was okay and she was breathing well. Her arms weren't broken but when Erika began to scan her legs, she saw lots of blood on the back of her left calf. She quickly saw that it was a wound from the same bullet that had killed Artaz.

Oh no, oh no! that's all Erika could keep thinking. Normally, the child would have been rushed to the hospital in Auburn, but now, what was she going to do? She had a little knowledge of treating minor cuts and scrapes, but not this. This was major. Erika could not take it anymore and screamed out, "Why, God, why?"

At that moment, as if in answer to her prayers, a few things happened all at once. First of all, Star woke up, and even though she was trying hard to be tough, she started to whimper like a lost puppy because of the pain in her leg and the shock of this escapade. Erika turned to shush Star because Erika thought she had heard something in the bushes. She thought maybe she had been followed by the gang but then a sight, more welcome right then than anything she could imagine, hit her eyes. It was Jimmy D! He had met up with the others but when no one else came up the hill, he went back down to see if anyone had survived the blasts and gunshots he had heard. He was just about to give up the search, figuring everyone was dead, when he heard Erika scream.

"I thought you guys were goners. I figured with horsepower, you would have been to the meeting spot hours ago. So, I had to come and see what happened, and this definitely explains it," he said just as dryly as ever.

"Oh, thank God, you came back!" Erika exclaimed desperately. "Star is hurt, Jimmy. The bullet went right through her leg and it killed Artaz."

"What? Star is hurt?" He hadn't realized she was hurt because of the darkness and the huge dead horse spread out in front of him. He quickly turned his attention to Star. "Hey, you okay, sweetie?" he asked softly.

Star snapped a quick reply. "No, I have been shot!"

"I guess you are right." He couldn't help but laugh a little at the irony of the little girl. The great thing about kids is they live in the moment so they can adapt to severe tragedies faster.

"Well, what are we going to do?" Erika asked impatiently. "We can't just sit here." She couldn't get the thought of those Auburn guys sneaking up the hill behind them out of her mind.

"How I see it is we need to do two things: get Star up that hill to some kind of help and cleanliness; and get that meat off that horse and up the hill so we can eat," Jimmy replied matter-of-factly.

"You want to do what?" Erika was shocked. "We don't have time for that, Jimmy."

"Look, Erika. That's a lot of meat right there and we have people, including ourselves, that need to eat. Now, I was a paramedic for a few years so I can patch the kid. Do you know how to deal with that?" He pointed to Artaz.

"Well… yeah… I guess so. I have dressed out a lot of animals but never a horse." Erika was still stupefied.

"Well, get to it," Jimmy said as he turned his back to Erika and started to tend to Star's wounds.

"Jimmy!"

"What, Erika?" He was getting very impatient now. "Are we going to get through this night, or what?"

"I don't have a knife!" Erika snapped back.

"Here!" He threw the knife to her and then he flipped Star onto his shoulder and turned to go.

"No, no, I'm not leaving Erika," Star pleaded with Jimmy.

"Yes, you are, sweetie." He was starting up the hill and Star began kicking and screaming.

"Star!" Erika snapped. "There's no time for that now. Jimmy is helping us. I can't get you and the horse meat both to the top but Jimmy can get you up there and come back for me. Now you just act like a good girl and I'll meet you at the top. I promise."

Star was not pleased but knew Erika was right, and Erika's eyes looked wild. She relaxed; Jimmy took one look back at Erika and trotted up the hill.

Erika flipped the knife open and looked at poor Artaz. He had been so faithful and carried her so far, but the simple fact was, he didn't make it. Jimmy D had been correct. The meat from this animal would be most welcome, even though the thought of eating horse meat was still freaking her out.

It was still very dark but she had to work quickly. The sun would be up soon, and if any of those guys from Auburn were following her, she would be a lot easier to find in the daylight.

Thinking of those crazies in Auburn started to really eat into her mind. What if they were already tracking her? What if they were coming up the hill right now? Jimmy had heard her scream; what if they did too? Her mind was racing out of control now, and her hands began to shake.

"Oh God, please help me now. I have to get this done." She flipped the horse so that his belly was facing downhill and began to carefully cut his skin away from his abdominal lining. As she cut, the stomach began to expand and she was extra-cautious not to pierce it. She knew the immense stink that it would cause. It wasn't long until she was cutting off the last remaining pieces of connective tissue in the interior cavity, and Artaz's guts rolled down the hill. Some people would have savored the liver, heart, or kidneys, but Erika had always found it absolutely disgusting to eat any of the organs out of an animal.

On any other day, this would be the time when the animal would be hung and the skin would be removed before the animal was broken down into individual parts. Right now, Erika had no time for this. She also knew it would be way too hard to drag the whole animal to the top. The quickest way to get as much meat as possible was to quarter it. This was basically removing the leg and the giant pushing muscles that areas like the shoulder and hip contain. With the skin still covering the precious meat below, she began to frantically hack at the pieces she wanted. This made it very difficult because she had to actually cut through the skin and then the connective tissues to remove each quarter of the animal.

Erika was just finishing hacking off leg two when the first rays of the sun shot over the mountainside. Usually, Erika was not really a cheery person in the morning, but on this day, the sun's pure glory overwhelmed her. She wanted to take a moment to revel in its glow, but she was being pushed, physically and mentally, to a limit that she had never known. Emotional stresses were everywhere: those crazy guys were out there, she hadn't slept in days, and food had been awfully scarce. She heard a noise and looked up. Jimmy D was back, just as he had promised, and he had brought Kit and the cart with him as well!

"Look at that, you're almost done!" he said gratefully. "Sorry I took so long. I decided to unload Kit's cart and bring some backup help."

"Oh, am I glad you did." Erika's eyes began to tear but she kept on working frantically, trying to get leg three cut free. She was done and Jimmy grabbed her arm.

"Erika, we have to load up and go now."

"Why? What's going on?" Erika was delirious, and all she could think about was completing this task. That meant leg four was next, and she was not leaving all that meat behind.

Erika slumped back on her heals to take a rest and focus her attention on Jimmy. She surveyed the landscape in a far-off stare. She could almost see herself sitting in a bloody mess, with one cut-off horse quarter in one hand, and two others piled in a heap. She came back into her mind, and her eyes were tracing the blood stain up her arm. She looked at herself and saw she was completely covered in blood as well.

Jimmy D broke her gaze. "On my way down, I could see a couple of guys stirring around at the river compound. Luckily, they were still on the other side, but still, I'm not sure if they are on this side or not. Plus, there are always scavengers in this area. Let's go! We have enough meat."

Erika and Jimmy D loaded the gigantic horse quarters into Kit's cart. The horse stood patiently, but the smell of death was in the air, and he seemed to be on the edge of spooking and running for his life.

"Easy now, Kit, we'll be out of here in no time." Jimmy D's calming voice reassured the horse and Erika as well. Jimmy led Kit up the hill, and Erika walked with them as if she was in a dream.

Her thoughts went toward her source of strength—her home and her loving man. As her feet stumbled on, she could only think of him. She was looking into his eyes and they filled her with strength. Her steps seemed to lighten as their march up the hill continued on. She felt absolutely gross blood and dirt covered her from end to end, but she didn't care. All that mattered was getting home to him. Danger swirled all around her and blocked her every move, but she no longer cared. She would walk through fire if she had to but she was going to get back to her soul mate.

"*Erika!*" Star came limping over.

They had finally made it to the group at the top and she was met with hugs and statements of appreciation, but Erika was so exhausted that her vision began to blur, and she fell into the arms of Jimmy D. He had been watching her on the way up and was hoping she would make it all the way. She was a proud woman and probably would have been opposed to adding her weight to the immense load Kit was already pulling up the slippery canyon side. She had tripped multiple times, but halfway through, she seemed to pick up the pace and now here they were at the top. Jimmy was amazed by her. He had never really expected that she actually did know how to butcher the horse, and butchering that animal took a lot of strength. He had to wonder where she drew this immense power from. When they got to the top, he saw Star's yell break Erika's concentration, and her swaying body told him she would not be conscious long.

Star was alarmed when Erika fainted, "Erika! Erika, wake up!" she wailed.

"It's all right, Star," Jimmy said confidently with Erika's limp body in his arms. "She's just exhausted. She'll be fine in a couple of hours. You wait and see."

"Come on, Star. Let's go see what little Jim and Tyson are doing. They have some toys in the cart. Let's just let Erika rest for a while." Joan came in to reassure Star.

Joan was married to a man named Richard Cunningham. They had their own son and another boy, Taylor, they had found all alone after the quake. It was better for Star to relax and be with the kids. She was hurt bad, but she still would not rest. They told Star what a big girl she was for helping with the little boys, even though she was hurt, and this gave her a real sense of purpose. Those boys were her responsibility, and she was going to take good care of them no matter what.

"So, now what are we going to do, Jimmy?" Randy asked. Randy was one of the teenagers that had been instrumental in getting the supplies to the top of the canyon in one of the handcarts they had designed.

"Great question, Randy, and honestly, I really don't know. First, let's get everything in that handcart loaded into the other one and the horse pack so we can put Erika in that cart and keep moving," Jimmy suggested.

Even though they had won a sort of victory last night, it was not without some great losses. They were free but they had lost their homes again, and they had lost their leaders. Jimmy was racked with indecision, but he knew he had to get as far away from this canyon as possible.

"Jimmy, I know we need to go, but we all had a really long night, and I, personally, would love to eat something before we go," Kim whined.

She was a heavier-set teenage girl, and even though her mechanical knowledge had been a huge asset for the cart building, she could be a bit of a nag sometimes.

"Yeah," Steve said. "Look at all that meat you guys hauled out. I am starving."

"I know, Steve. I'm ravished as well, but I think we should move on to someplace safer before we feast on that meat. Plus, we will need some place to smoke some of it so we can save it. There is no way we can eat all that, and most of it will go bad." Jimmy just wanted to get going. He could see the vultures circling the carnage in the canyon, and he knew the scavengers would see them as well. It wouldn't be long until they were fighting for their food all over again if they didn't get going soon. "So, come on guys, let's move!"

Joan and Richard kept the kids occupied while the others quickly worked to re-sort their limited supplies again. They put Erika into one of the handcarts and started to move. It was a sight out of the past and certainly one not seen in America for a long time. Kit led the charge with Jimmy D guiding him. Second in the caravan was Erika's handcart. It was being pulled by Randy and Taylor. They had decided to put Star in the cart with Erika since her leg was not in any condition for a long walk. After that, Joan and Richard followed along with the kids so they could keep a watch over Erika and Star. Next in line was the second handcart that was overloaded with supplies. Tom Jensen and Steve were pulling that one. Bringing up the rear and on lookout for any followers were Jim Harlow and Kim.

CHAPTER 16

WHEN ERIKA FINALLY woke up, it was to the smell of roasting meat. It smelled so good. Her stomach rumbled and her mouth watered. She opened her eyes and realized she was in a tent that had been erected between all of the carts they had made. It looked to be early morning, because it wasn't dark but it wasn't extremely bright either.

"Hello, hello, sleepy head." Joan had noticed her begin to stir. The kids were still sound asleep from the distressing night they had the night before, and Joan was taking care of housekeeping duties and keeping her eye on them.

"Good morning, Joan," Erika said sleepily.

"We made it, Erika, and I want to thank you. If it weren't for you I doubt I would still be here with my family, all together. We would have been totally unprepared for that attack. I don't really know what else I could say other than thank you. Thank you so much." Joan was in tears as she said this.

"Oh, Joan, I'm just trying to get home to my family too, and it wasn't anything that someone else on my journey hasn't done for me. I just thought it was the right thing to do." Erika had tears in her eyes as well.

The two embraced in a deep hug. It felt so good to be sharing someone else's pain. Feeling Joan's energy was making her stronger, at the same time Erika's energy was making Joan stronger.

"Okay, enough blubbering. Where's Star? How is she?" Erika quickly remembered her traveling companion and the fact that a bullet had ripped through her leg.

"She's fine. Look." Joan pointed to Star nestled between the two boys, all sleeping peacefully and snuggly.

"Wow, they are so precious." Erika was impacted by the peaceful scene and could not help but see Dexter there in one of the boys' faces.

"She has been such a blessing. We told her it was her 'job' to look after the little kids and make sure they stayed safe. Girl, let me tell you, Star sure did step up to that plate. She has been watching them like a hawk, even with her leg. She must be in pain, but she is not showing any of it." Joan was obviously relieved for the help with these two rambunctious young men.

"Where is everyone? Where are we, Joan?" Erika noticed the silence around the camp and was hoping everyone was okay. Besides that, she had no idea what had happened after she passed out, or where they took her to.

"Let me fill you in. After you and Jimmy D made it to the top, you passed out, and we decided that it was best to keep moving and try to get someplace safer. We crested the top of the mountain yesterday and made it into Cool. The people that are occupying Cool were very leery of letting thirteen new people into their group so they let us camp over here. We are on the hill across from town. They have been really nice though, not anything like those crazies in Auburn. Right now, we are preparing a big meal for both groups to eat. With all the meat we have, we thought sharing might be a good way to break the ice and get to know one another. We cut up some of the meat from one of the horse's hind legs into strips for drying, but the other group has about thirty people in their camp, and they look really thin. Now Jimmy D and Jim H are out at the Cool camp talking about the group in Auburn and the future of our two groups. Taylor and Randy went out to gather firewood because we will need fires long into the night for cooking and drying meat. Kim and Tom Jensen found some friends in the Cool group. Tom was on the football team in Auburn and used to play and party with some of the kids in Cool. We let them go and hang out. Figured they need some sense of how life used to be. Steve is in charge of drying the meat, and he has been cutting meat and putting it on the racks since we finished making camp last night." Joan finally had Erika caught up with what had been going on.

"That must be that wonderful smell I keep getting a whiff of." Erika was still getting her senses together for the day and that roasting meat was all she could think of. "Joan, I think it is me who should be thanking you all. You could have left me and taken all the meat and supplies, and I would have never known it."

"Don't be silly, Erika. We owe you our lives; we will watch out for you always." Joan couldn't believe her suggestion.

"Wait a minute. We're in Cool? This is great! I am almost home. I am right down the road. Oh, I can't wait. All I have to do is get to Georgetown." The reality of her location made her mind race. How long would it take her to get home now? She was so close.

"You will never make it without some food in your belly, and you don't want to see them again after all this time looking like that, do you?" Joan pointed at her.

Erika looked down and realized she was still soaked with horse blood. It had dried across her skin, and her clothes were a mess.

"Come on. I'll help you get cleaned up. We have a bath ready for you." Joan was gesturing for her to leave with her.

"You have a bath ready for me?" Erika was surprised.

"We knew you would certainly need it when you woke up, and we have all used it already so I wouldn't say it was just for you, but we did put clean water in it for you," Joan explained.

"What about the kids?" Erika questioned.

"I'll keep my eye on them." Joan assured her.

Star had roused during the conversation Joan and Erika were having, and she whispered from in between the two snoozing boys. "Hi, Erika."

"Oh, Star, I love you." Erika was kind of surprised to hear that come out of her mouth, but she really did love that little girl. Their union had happened so fast. She looked over at her beautiful new daughter. Then Erika got up and went over to kiss Star on the forehead.

"How's your leg feeling, baby?" Erika remembered the searing bullet and could only pray that Star would recover.

"It hurts really badly, but there was a doctor here in Cool. He looked at it and said I should keep it very clean and rest a lot, and as long as I do that, I should be fine. So, I'll just wait right here. I have to heal fast so I'll be ready to go with you." Star was reassured by Erika's affectionate words toward her, but she was still frightened that she would be left behind because of this injury.

"I'm not going anywhere without you, Star, so you just rest easy." Erika was serious and Star knew it. Star relaxed and snuggled back in between the boys.

Erika got up to go with Joan out to this bath she was talking about. As they walked out into the sunlight, Erika was completely dumbfounded. She had expected to walk out into familiar territory and into a town that she had once known so well. All she saw was blackness in every direction, except the one that went down into the dreadful canyon they had just come from.

"Oh my God," Erika gasped.

It had all burned down, all the trees, all the buildings. Everything there now had been built out of the ruins of the old town. The broken wood and scavenged metal had been made into makeshift buildings where the town once stood. The concrete from the old parking lots was still clearly visible, but it even looked crusted over from the fire.

"This area was massively damaged when the quake hit, Erika. That's why we never came up here before. From Auburn, we could see the smoke thick in the air, so we didn't know what we would find. The river was a ready source of water, and the fire had stopped at the quarry. A lot of wildlife found refuge in the woods between here and the river, so we just stayed at the river. We had water and food, so it seemed like the logical decision, until those idiots started to rally up in Auburn." Joan was reflecting on decisions of the past. "Come on, Erika, let's get you cleaned up," she said cheerfully, "and then we'll worry about all this." Joan was trying desperately to keep Erika's attitude positive the middle of all this misery.

Joan led the way to the bath while Erika's mind raced. If the whole place had burned, how far did the fire go? The fire had stopped at the old quarry that was located on this side of the canyon, but what about the other direction towards Georgetown? She thought of Vince and Dexter and sent her prayers out again as she had done so many times before on this journey. What about Coloma and Lotus? Was her mom safe? This whole idea had thrown a huge monkey wrench into her grand plans of returning home. What home? Was it still there?

Walking through the camp, Erika was really impressed. It seemed like the group had been here for a week, but Erika knew they had only arrived yesterday night. Directly in front of the tent was the main campfire with an eating and preparation area set up next to it. Kim and Tom had returned, with some other older teens, from the Cool camp and were preparing food for the big feast tonight in the preparation area. Further away to the left, there was another fire burning. This one was elongated and burned with a steady low flame. There was a rack set over the top of it, and Erika could see the meat drying on the rack. Steve was standing attentively by that fire with a gentleman that Erika did not recognize.

Joan's and Erika's footsteps crackled on the burnt and crispy landscape as they continued on to a small roughly made tent. There was a basin of water outside of it and next to that were two sticks planted in the ground with a line in between them. The tent itself was made of old burned wood and the roof was just a blanket laid over the top. Joan pulled back a panel, and inside was a very small fire with a large metal basin over the top of it.

"I know it's not the Holiday Inn, but at least the water will be warm," Joan said encouragingly.

"It's a whole lot better than nothing." Erika was actually really glad she could get clean in a hot bath. She felt disgusting.

"Now you just get in there and hand me your clothes, and I'll wash them for you while you get clean." Joan sounded so motherly.

"Are you for real? Wow! Thanks, Joan." Erika was kind of shocked to find this much kindness in this hopeless landscape.

"Well, if it weren't for that blood all over you and your clothes, we wouldn't be having a feast tonight and food for many more nights to come. Plus, I wouldn't even be alive if it weren't for you," Joan replied. "Just give me your clothes, it's the least I can do."

"Thanks again, Joan." Erika had never been good at taking compliments and didn't really know what to say, so she quickly got into the little tent with the washtub. There were stones placed on the ground in front of the tub. That way, when Erika took off her moccasins, her feet stayed somewhat clean. Erika had to take a minute and revel in the ingeniousness of this setup. The little stones to keep your feet clean, the tiny fire keeping the water warm under the metal basin, it all made perfect sense. She took off all her clothes and wadded them into a ball.

"Here you go, Joan," Erika called out while she turned her back to the door.

Joan cracked the door to grab Erika's clothes, and she gasped when she saw the scars that covered Erika's body. Erika turned her head when Joan gasped and their eyes met.

"It's a long story, Joan." Erika felt really uncomfortable about this turn of events. She didn't want to face the fact that her body had been altered. At least she was alive and close to home. Hopefully, her beloved, Vince, would feel the same way.

"I'm sorry, Erika. I didn't mean to... I..." Joan was now stammering with her words. She could feel Erika's tension heavy in the air.

"It's okay. I am alive, but I have some scars to prove it." Erika was regaining her confidence. She knew the Lord made everything happen for a reason, and God made every person just as they were meant to be. Each imperfection made each individual perfect.

"That is one story I would love to hear." Joan could feel the tension lighten, but she did not want to push it any further right now. She grabbed Erika's clothes and headed over to the wash basin.

Erika picked up a little wooden bowl that was floating in the water. She washed the warm water over her skin and tried to wash off as much blood as she could. She wanted to try and keep the basin water as clean as possible so she could soak away her worries in the nice, clean, warm water.

Once she had rinsed herself, she got into the tub and immersed herself in the warmth of the water. It was a tight fit into the tub, and it was definitely weird to be in a tub of water directly over an open fire. She pictured herself as a lobster for a minute and had to chuckle at the thought. Even with all her worries, the bath felt great. Soaking in this delightfully warm water, she almost forgot how much she loved long, hot showers. Erika saw a little square of something that looked like soap and when she scrubbed it on her body it started to get sudsy. The water was reviving her, and her mind started wandering. She could not believe how far she had made it. She thought about Henry and Carol and all they had given her. They just gave. They didn't ask for anything in return, and without them, where would she be? Thinking of Carol and Henry made her remember the outfit made out of old sheets that Carol had made for her.

"Hey, Joan," she yelled.

"Yes, Erika," Joan replied. She was busy washing Erika's outfit in the basin outside.

"If you go into Kit's packs, I have an extra outfit there. It is the only other clothes in there, so it should be easy to find. I wrapped it up in one of the blankets I have. Would you mind grabbing it for me?"

"Sure, no problem, then you won't have to wear wet clothes," Joan responded cheerfully.

Erika could hear Joan leave by the crackling footsteps. She also heard more voices over at the camp. She thought it sounded like maybe the boys came back with some more folks from the Cool camp. Erika decided to get out of the tub so she could drip dry for a while before Joan got back. She always hated putting on her clothes when she was too wet. They stuck to you and were always a pain to get on. She didn't have a towel, but luckily, it was warm both inside and out, so it felt pretty good to just let the water drip off of her. Then she heard Joan's footsteps outside the tent, and Joan slid the door open.

"Here you go, Erika. Those sure do look comfortable," Joan commented on her sheet outfit. "When everything went down, all I escaped with are these jeans. I'm not complaining, but some-times, I wish I could just throw on a pair of my old sweats."

"They are really comfortable. A sweet lady who helped me recuperate made them for me," Erika said thinking of Carol.

"Oh, and here are your… moccasins?" Joan said questioningly.

"Thanks. Yeah, I have moccasins. Not something you would expect, but they were made by the husband of that same lady. My shoes didn't escape the mess that I made it through," Erika said with a dreamy look in her eyes. "The moccasins were better than nothing."

Joan was getting very curious about this story but remembered the tension that it had aroused. She remembered Erika saying something about escaping from Sacramento when she had first reached the River Compound, but there was so much going on at that point. Joan had only focused on what Erika's story meant for them and not really about what Erika had been through. The effects of her ordeal were rather obvious by Erika's skin but Joan didn't want to push. She knew Erika would have to tell the story over and over, and eventually she would hear it.

Joan walked over to the wash basin and Erika followed. Most of Erika's clothes were already hanging on the line, and Joan just had to finish washing her jungle pants. The blood had permanently stained her clothes. They were now a brownish-green color. There was no Tide out here, but they looked a lot cleaner and smelled a whole lot better.

"Cute pants. Good color," Joan teased.

"Yeah, tell me about it. You got jeans and I got jungle pants. The cooks at the restaurant I used to work at had to wear them. That's all I could find after mine got wrecked," Erika explained.

"Okay, we're done here," Joan declared. "All we have to do is let them dry. I think it's going to get rather warm later today so it shouldn't take long. Let's go get some food while we wait."

The smell of meat was wafting every direction through the air, and Erika's stomach was going crazy. There were lots of people at the campfire now, and everyone seemed to be busy doing something. Erika could not wait to get a bowl of the soup that everyone seemed to have in their hands. Their footsteps crackled through the burnt grass as she and Joan approached the fire. Suddenly, she saw a very familiar face in the crowd. One of her best friends from before the accident, Greg. For a minute, she could not believe it was him. As they approached, Greg saw her as well, and there was no question it was him, not that it was easy to mistake him for anyone else. He had always been one of the most handsome and charismatic people that Erika had known.

There were no words that could explain their feelings of elation in recognizing one another. They ran at one another and hugged. He picked her up and swung her around. There were times in the past when Erika's husband had been tired and Erika was out on the town with the girls. Greg had always kept his eye on her and protected her from the drunken advances of silly men. This was his big chance to get her back under his wing and home to her husband and his best friend. The tears were rolling as they began to separate.

"You're alive, Erika! Oh my God, you're alive!" Greg was ecstatic. He could not believe his eyes. He had gone on watch at the Cool camp many days, and each day, he would hope to see her coming up the canyon.

"I am, G-man," she teased him and used a nickname that he had gone by in the past. "I am. I wouldn't be here if it weren't for some really great people I met along the way. Including these folks that I'm with, but I made it. I'm home."

"He survived, Erika, and Dex too. They made it," Greg said, looking straight into her eyes. She did not even need to ask the question. He knew Erika and knew what she would be worried about. He could always read her like a book.

The tears started to flow down Erika's face. Her family had made it. They were really alive. She had known it all along. Someone brought her a bucket to sit on as her legs went weak. She knew her family had been waiting, and they actually were.

"You saw them, G-man?" she gasped.

"Yup, Vince has been coming down about once a month to see if you have turned up anywhere. Everyone told him that there was no way anyone made it out of that pit that Sacramento became, but he knew you would. He said he could feel you. He knew you would survive because you always said you would. Last I heard though, the Georgetown group was thinking of heading further up into the mountains because of the conflicts down by the river and the lack of housing for them," he explained

"What happened around here, Greg?" Erika wondered.

"The fires burned most everything from here to Icehouse to Coloma. Georgetown actually fell into all the old mines that were under the city so those people got double screwed. Now with all the aftershocks and all, who knows what's going to happen?" Greg said with a faraway look in his eyes.

"Oh my God, he's okay. I knew it. I have to go now!" Erika got up and looked like she was going to go running across the hill.

"Just wait a minute, Erika. I just found you, and I'll be dammed if I'm going to let you go running off into that," Greg stated firmly as he pointed out at the burnt landscape.

"Plus, think about Star," Joan said in Erika's ear.

"Star?" Greg questioned.

"Along the way, a lot of crazy stuff happened, Greg, and now I have a daughter. Her name is Star," Erika stated as a matter of fact.

Greg knew that there were a lot of orphaned kids out there that had to be taken care of and all he said was, "Can't wait to meet her. Look, Erika, I know that you want to see him, so I'll send out two guys to run to the Georgetown camp and bring Vince back here. We have horse power too, and we have a pretty good route scouted to the Georgetown camp. They should be able to move pretty quick, and with it being so early in the day, they should be back by nightfall. Okay, Miss impatient?" Greg always had a quick wit and here he was solving problems with humor just like always.

"Woo-hoo!" Erika yelled. "I'm home and my family is safe!" She screamed through the air in sheer delight. She jumped up off the bucket and spun around in the air. It had been a long, hard road but she knew for certain they were safe, and they were coming here tonight. She fell back down onto the bucket as someone shoved a bowl of delicious horsemeat soup into her hands.

CHAPTER 17

GREG LEFT TO go and talk with the other guys that had come with him from the Cool camp. Erika thought she recognized one of them but wasn't sure. She sat immersed in her thoughts and soup until the spoon was finally scooping up the last pieces of meat in the bowl. Now that she knew her husband and son were alive and safe, her thoughts began to roam to other people she loved. She thought about her mother. She lived in Lotus, a town not too far from Coloma, and Erika hoped her mother was safe. She thought about her father over in Michigan and hoped he was safe as well. Then she thought of her brother, Bob. He lived in Canada. He had taken a job there and had really liked living there. His wife on the other hand was not too pleased with leaving California and missed the weather. She thought of her husband's parents, who had been on a trip to Washington State visiting her husband's grandmother. There were lots of people that she was wondering about and felt frustrated that she could no longer just send out a text to see if they were all right or not. All she could do was pray to God for their safety or their acceptance into his Kingdom.

Greg had noticed that Erika was looking way too somber and hit her in the arm.

"Owww! What was that for?" Erika quickly snapped out of her thoughts.

"Just seeing if you still got it," Greg replied sarcastically.

"Oh, I still got it. At least I'll still kick your butt anyway," Erika returned the jest.

"Well, let's see it," Greg prodded on. He stepped back with his hands in fists and began to dance around.

Erika put down her bowl and got up with her hands balled into fists and gave him a swift kick in the bootie.

"See, told you I'd still kick your booty." She smiled wide.

"Oh, you're gonna get it," Greg replied, and he started chasing after Erika, punching in the air after her.

It felt great to Erika to act normal again, goofing with her friend in a very old game. Both Greg and Erika were trained in martial arts, and they often play-fought one another.

"Okay, G-man, you better knock it off." Erika was getting out of breath and realized the stress of her recent life might have taken a toll on her body. She needed a little more rest before she would be at full strength again.

"Oh, are you getting tired?" Greg poked on.

"Yeah, actually, I am," she admitted.

"Well, let me show you around then. I'll show you the new town of Cool and the awesome pad I'm kickin' it at now," he said. His words were thick with sarcasm.

"Is that where you get your chillaxing on nowadays?" Erika teased.

"You got it. My dad is over there anyway with Mike Nostrem." Greg's voice sounded very cheerful.

"Really? Mike made it and your dad. What about Mike's kids, Chris and Burt?" Erika wondered.

"Chris didn't make it, and we still haven't heard from Burt." Greg's cheerfulness suddenly turned somber.

"Oh man, I'm sorry, Greg." Erika almost felt bad for even asking.

"Look, Erika, lots of people are gone and the quakes keep coming. All we can do is live each day and hope that one day we can get things back to normal," Greg replied, trying to keep his voice steady.

Erika could see that talking about the past was something that was hard for everyone to do. Not everyone had been as lucky as her. They had lost their families and now faced a bleak future alone. Erika decided right then that it would be better to leave the past there, in the past, and just focus on the future.

She quickly changed the subject. "Are those guys you were talking to going after Vince?"

"Yeah, remember Denton from high school?" Greg played right into her change of subject.

"I think so. He looked kind of familiar." Erika was thinking hard. She always remembered faces much better than names.

"Well, Vince used to coach him in wrestling. He is going over there with Rob Burton. I don't know if you remember him but you had met him a couple of times at the bar. He was in the military and loves to go on adventures," Greg stated.

"How long will it take them?" Erika said impatiently. This was a moment she had been dreaming of for a very long time.

"Don't worry. They'll be here before you know it. The guys should make it there by midday, and they'll be back before nightfall," Greg said with a gleam in his eye. He knew Erika hated surprises and her anxiousness delighted him.

"I guess I'll just have to wait then," Erika said with a sigh.

"Yes, you will." His delight was obvious. "Let's go see everyone over at the camp," Greg said, urging her to come with him.

"Before we go over there, I need to tell Star what's going on." Erika didn't want Star to wonder where she was. Star needed to rest easy, not worry about being left behind.

"Great, let's go see her." Greg's enthusiasm for life was contagious, and they smiled as they walked lightheartedly over to the tent.

When Erika pulled back the blanket that formed the doorway, she took in the interior for the first time in the daylight. Everything they had carried with them had been used for the tent's construction. The carts had been used for the corners, but they were covered on the inside with blankets. A tarp formed the top and the remainder of the blankets formed the floor sleeping area. This made a cozy interior whose only purpose was for sleeping. It looked like one big, giant bed, which it basically was. The only separated area was at the end, just on the other side of where the kids slept. This area was made for Richard and Joan because they were the only married couple with this group.

Star's condition had the kids staying inside and amusing one another with dice and card games. Little Jim still had a transformer toy that he retained from his former life, and Tyson still had a small red fire engine whose batteries were dead. Tyson made a great sound for the toy in an effort to mimic the sound it once produced. Erika had to laugh because, in the past, she had said how horrible it was that the kids didn't have to use their imagination to play anymore. She noticed they learned pretty quickly once they had no other option.

"Erika!" Star yelled enthusiastically. She was obviously feeling better, even though the pain in her leg was keeping her in bed. Erika was surprised to see her in such a joyous mood.

"Hey, baby, how are you feeling?" Erika questioned. She was so concerned about Star, hoping her leg would not be permanently affected by the shooting.

"I'm doing okay, Erika. The doctor came by this morning while you were in the bath. He rewrapped my leg and said it was doing much better. He said if I did a good job of resting today, I may be able to go out tomorrow."

"That's great, Star. We'll have to see how it goes." Erika was thinking that she would have to stop by and talk with this doctor. It was weird to have the group taking care of one another so much that she had not even talked with the doctor treating her newly adopted daughter yet.

"Who's that, Erika?" Star interrupted her thoughts with her question while she was pointing at Greg.

"This is Greg. He is one of my very best friends." Erika put her arm around Greg and gave him a big hug.

"He's cute," Star blurted out, turning a little red.

"Yeah, real cute," Erika said sarcastically while giving Greg a poke in his ribs.

"Well, I think you are very cute too, little lady," Greg said flirtatiously to Star, which made her blush an even deeper red.

"Anyway," Erika broke up the playful banter. Greg always did have a way with the ladies, and even a girl of just eight years old picked up on it immediately. "We are going over to the camp in Cool to talk with some folks, and I want to check it out. Will you be all right here with Tyson and Little Jim?"

"Yeah, they're not so bad. We're actually having a lot of fun." Star had a sincere glimmer of youth and hope in her eyes again, and Erika loved it.

"What's up, Tyson and Little Jim?" Greg questioned trying to include the two boys in the conversation.

Little Jim shied back and hid behind Tyson, but Tyson replied, "Nothin'. What's up with you?" and stuck his chest out a little.

"Oh, a big tough guy, I better watch out," Greg said playfully.

"That's right, you better," Tyson said, feeling a bit big for his britches.

"Well, in that case." Greg grabbed Tyson and rolled around with him on the blankets. Then Little Jim jumped on Greg's back and the three of them wrestled and laughed. Erika just stood and watched. It was healing for her heart. Finally, Greg got up and told the boys, "and now I am going to give this fine lady here a tour, and I will see you tough guys and cute girl later." He gave Star a wink and the boys a high-five before he turned toward the tent opening.

"Okay, Star, you be good, and you two rascals be good too. I'll see you all in a little bit." Erika gave Star a big hug and headed toward the door with Greg.

As the two stepped back into the bright sunlight, Greg said, "That's some girl there, Erika."

"I know. She really needs me, and how could I not take her with me? How she came to me is something I don't know if I'm really ready to face yet, so please don't ask." Erika knew Greg's thought pattern and had a good feeling that the question of where she came from would be on his mind. She wanted to stop that conversation before it even began.

"It's cool, Erika, you can tell me when you're ready. Let's go see my dad." Greg was actually trying to stay cheerful anyway and a depressing story wasn't going to accomplish that.

"All right, let's go," Erika said with a bounce in her step.

The two walked on, consumed in their own thoughts. So much pain gave people a lot to reflect on and the silences that might have been uncomfortable before were now quite welcome. It gave you time to put things in perspective and decide how a person would go on living, having seen and done the horrible things they had to for survival.

The ground still made a *crunch, crunch* sound as they walked along. The season was coming to the end of a very long and profound summer, but summer was not done yet. The hot sun in California usually turned most plant life crackly by the end of summer, but with all the burnt debris around it was like walking on a charcoal grill. The two made their way down the hill toward the area where a Chinese restaurant and post office had been. The long building had burnt to the ground. The leftover wood had been built into a watch tower that overlooked the canyon area that led up to the camp.

"Howdy, Greg," a young girl with a ditsy smile shouted from the top of the watch tower.

"Hi, Michelle," Greg replied halfheartedly.

"Are you going to be around the fire tonight?" Michelle asked flirtatiously.

"Of course I am. Where the hell else would I be?" Greg replied, kind of annoyed.

"Well, I'll see you then," Michelle yelled, as Greg and Erika kept crunching along to the Cool camp.

"Nice, Greg, got a little honey on the side?" Erika poked at him in fun.

"Hey now, let me tell you how hard it is to find a booty call around here. The pickings are pretty limited, you know," Greg replied arrogantly.

"Same old Greg, still 'pimping the hoes'," teased Erika.

"Hey, just because the end of the world is coming doesn't mean that good old G-man ain't going to be screwing his brains out. We have got to repopulate and everything, right?" Greg was obviously thrilled to have this excuse to use on the ladies.

"Whatever, Greg, some things just don't change and your libido is obviously one of those things." Erika absolutely loved this. Walking along with her friend, making fun of the same old things, it made her realize that life would go on. People would adapt to this new life. They would find their old comforts and rebuild their broken lives.

The two friends finally crossed the old highway, or what used to be the highway. The earthquake had left its mark in a big way. It was all twisted like half of a taco. It was as if the whole mountain had heaved up and rolled it like a delicate dessert.

"Well, you definitely won't have to worry about the traffic on that road anymore." Erika often used humor to explain the shocking things in life, and right now she was feeling very humorous.

"No kidding. I used to complain and complain about that traffic, and why did they have to build that darn bridge? The canyon used to keep all those people out, but I guess we won't have that worry anymore. The bridge snapped like a twig, and who the heck is going anywhere anyway? Where do you think you could go, Erika? I mean, if you were to go somewhere, where in this world would you be safe?" Greg was suddenly very serious.

"I don't know, Greg. Maybe up into the mountains further? Definitely around some water. Speaking of water, Cool is not close by a river. What's everyone drinking?" Erika countered his direct comments at the reality of this new world.

"We have a big well that is still working, and they rigged up this cool bike that you can ride on and it pumps the pump. That way it's easy to get to a lot of water. Where do you think that wonderful bath water came from?" Greg was teasing her again.

"That's why I was curious, you jerk," she replied.

"Hey, I lugged half that water all the way up there for your bath. They told me it was for their 'savior' and it was very important that they give you a hot bath. Little did I know that the 'savior' was little Erika. I would have let you carry your own darn water," he said, giving her a shot to the arm again.

"Oh thanks," Erika said seriously. He laughed at her. "No, for real, thanks. I really appreciated that bath."

"So what's up with the 'savior' talk?" Greg pondered.

"That Auburn camp over on the other side of the river was going to attack that little river camp. I was on my way across and heard the plan so I warned the river people and they left with me. I guess they think I saved them, but really, we saved each other." Erika didn't feel like a savior and was playing it off.

"That makes sense," Greg said flatly.

CHAPTER 18

WHEN GREG AND Erika entered the Cool camp, Erika was completely awe, stricken. She thought she had seen suffering riding across Auburn. All the dead bodies stacked up and the smell of death in the air, but this was a totally different story. The bodies were alive and dirty. The people formed a foul stench, and they looked at Erika as she walked by the small shanties and tents that were built throughout the parking lots of the former shopping centers located there. The people looked sad and hungry. Their eyes all showed pain, fear, and desperation. Erika was almost scared to walk through the throng.

Then an older lady came up to her and said softly, "Thank you for the meat you brought."

Erika quickly realized that the people were watching her because they had heard of her arrival. They had heard that she had brought a whole dead horse to share with the two camps and how she had saved the river folks from certain death or, worse yet, capture. All these people were curious about her story, but none of them had heard it yet. She was the big news story for these people and they were eager to see the program.

Greg could feel Erika's uneasiness. "Don't worry, Erika, they are all good folks. We are all stuck in the same boat now. Nobody knows where to go or what to do. Nobody knows if help will ever come. We are all lost, but we are together, and together, we can survive."

"You're right, Greg. I guess after spending all those months alone, or almost alone, I am just not used to seeing this many people yet." Erika had always hated crowds, though, and her fear of people had not gone away.

"Yeah, and you're the talk of the town, Erika. You're famous," Greg said with a big grin.

"Oh boy, just what I always didn't want to be," Erika said as she smiled. Greg could feel the tension lift and wanted to continue on.

"Come on. Things aren't so bad. The American River Grill almost survived without a flaw. Come and see." Greg was getting excited to be walking around with the person everyone wanted to see and having the privilege of showing off the compound to her.

They walked through the rows and rows of makeshift tents and shanties. Some people waved, some people just looked, and the children usually pointed while their mothers corrected their behavior. Other people were just laying in their tents, lost in thoughts or depression. As they continued on, Erika saw they were coming up to a rather large tent that had been constructed off of the entrance of the old restaurant. They walked into this tent and the light dimmed. Erika saw tables and blankets with pillows scattered around. The smell of food was heavy in the air, and Erika quickly saw that this tent must have been constructed to give the people more space for eating and preparing food than at the random fires that were scattered throughout. Erika noticed that the crunching sound under her feet had stopped. Someone had made a great effort to clean this area up and keep it that way.

Her moccasins made no sound as they walked through an actual door into the restaurant. The building itself had been tweaked a little, but it was amazing how sound it was. The owners had fought back the fires that quickly followed the quake, and their building was the only one that God had spared.

"Oh, it smells good in here," Greg said in a loud voice so he could draw the attention of the owners.

"Well, it ought to," A heavier-set lady with graying hair replied from somewhere back in the kitchen.

"Is that Greg out there making all that ruckus?" a man asked as he walked out of the back of the building into the eating area. He was also graying a little but he smiled warm and welcoming. "Oh my Goodness, it can't be, is that Erika?"

"In the flesh, how are you doing, Clay?" Erika said cheerfully. She had been familiar with the owners of the restaurant before the quake, and she was happy to see faces she recognized.

"Oh, I've been better, but it is so great to see you. Laurie, come out here. Erika made it home," Clay said joyfully.

Laurie came hustling out of the kitchen, and both Clay and Laurie gave Erika a big hug. She quickly started rambling at Erika, "You know, your husband has been here time and time again wondering if you came home. I'm sorry to tell you, but we all told him he was crazy to think you would ever make it back, but by God, here you are. You just make yourself at home; I got to get back to my cooking. We are making up some goodies to eat with that meat that the river group brought in." All of a sudden it clicked in Laurie's head. "You came in with the river group, didn't you? Were you there the whole time, or are you this 'savior' I keep hearing about?"

"Oh my Gosh," Erika said rolling her eyes. "I guess I am not going to be able to escape this for a while. I am the 'savior,' I guess. It was more like I was in the right place at the right time and I helped them get away from some really bad men, but we didn't save everyone, and in the end, I needed as much saving as they did."

"Well, either way, it is nice to have you home. I assume someone has sent for Vince," Laurie replied, hoping that Vince was on his way. She had known how desperate he had been to hear news of her and knew that he would want to be notified immediately.

"Yeah, Greg sent Denton and Rob to go and find him. He wouldn't let me go." Erika glanced at Greg.

"Well, that's good, looks like you could use some rest anyhow. Why don't you guys sit down and have some coffee. We still have a little left. Clay can grab you some while I get back to my kitchen," Laurie said as she walked away.

"Oh yeah, that's no problem," Clay said quickly.

"No, that's okay," Greg broke in. "I am going to show Erika the rest of the camp."

"Well, there's not much to see; everything got destroyed. We had to fight tooth and nail to keep our building standing. It is still a miracle that it is standing now with all these darn aftershocks," Clay replied sadly.

"I know but Erika hasn't seen any of it, so we will see you later when the food is served," Greg said, grabbing at Erika's hand to lead her away.

"Sure, that's all you worry about, where's the food?" Clay said in a playful tone. "That's okay. We'll see you later."

"Bye, Laurie; bye, Clay," Erika yelled while she waved and walked out the door with Greg.

"Nice to know at least something is still standing," Erika said to Greg.

"Oh, that's not all, but I don't want to ruin the surprise," Greg said with a gleam in his eye, knowing of her resentment toward surprises.

"What, Greg?" Her hatred for surprises was apparent. Now was not any different than before; it would drive her nuts trying to think what the surprise might be.

"Just come on," Greg said. He knew he had her now and was going to revel in it for a moment. "You wanted to meet the doctor that was treating Star anyway, so let's go do that now and we can worry about surprises later."

"Oh, give it up, Greg, I don't even care what the surprise is." Erika said this but she was actually bursting with curiosity. She made herself content with meeting this doctor instead.

The two of them walked all the way to the other end of town where another restaurant had once been. They passed tent after tent and campfire after campfire. Once they reached the other side of town, Erika saw that the restaurant had been destroyed, but they had cleaned up the aftermath enough to look somewhat respectable and turned it into a makeshift hospital. The entire structure had tarps over it and was lined wall to wall with cots and sleeping mats. People filled all of the beds, and a stocky man with a round head and white coat was walking from the side cupboards to the beds, back to a microscope, and back to the bed again. He looked up when Greg and Erika entered, and he waved for Greg to come over to him.

"Greg," the man said quietly, "we are going to need more bandages and peroxide. Plus we need some more antibiotics."

"I know, Ryan, but we have already searched all the houses left in Cool and we are running out of options," Greg replied,

"Then we will have to search farther, Greg. More people are going to die without it." The doctor looked deeply worried.

"I will see what I can do, Ryan. We will get it for you. In the meantime, I want you to meet Star's mom, Erika."

Ryan did a double take while he was shaking Erika's hand. "I expected Star's mom to be taller and maybe a blonde like she is. You two don't look very alike. Does she look like her dad?"

"I don't know, Doctor, I found her on the way here. Her real parents are dead and now I'm Mom," Erika replied painfully, remembering the lady she smothered that day.

"That explains it. Sorry to be so blunt but, as you can see, I don't really have time to beat around the bush. I would have brought Star here but we are really full. Oh yeah, and don't call me doctor, Ryan will do. I was only a nurse practitioner, you know," he said quickly.

"Well, I really don't care what you were. I can see from what you're doing now that you're a doctor, and I want you to know, Doctor, that I thank you from the bottom of my heart for everything that you did for Star. Do you think that she will have a full recovery?" Erika could see immediately that this man was a healer. He looked sweaty, like he had been running around for days. His constant care for these patients was evident, as the place was clean and the smell of disease was not too thick in the air.

"Erika, she is going to be fine. The bullet did hit her calf muscle, but it was a clean shot, and as soon as it is healed, she will be back on her feet. As long as she keeps it clean and infection free until then, and staying clean is no easy task around here. That's why I suggested that she stay in bed until it has a chance to heal further; at least then she will stay in a somewhat clean environment," Dr. Ryan replied.

"Doctor... Ryan," a man moaning from a bed called.

"Oh, sorry guys, I have to go. Greg, please remember the supplies," Dr. Ryan said as he ran off toward the bed.

"Bye, Doctor, it was nice to have met you and thanks again," Erika called out softly as she and Greg left the tent.

"Well, he seems nice," Erika said to Greg once they were out in the hot sunshine breathing the fresh air again.

"I don't envy him at all, but he has been our 'savior'." Greg used this term on purpose and shot Erika a wink. "After the quake and the fire, there were a lot more of us that gathered here; we were trying to get things figured out and contact someone who could help, but after a while, it was clear there was no one to contact. Thank God all this happened in the summer when most people are healthy, but some people needed their medications. There is no pharmacy up here, and we couldn't get to a city. The medications they relied on started to run out. For the next couple of months, people were dropping like flies. Ryan tried everything he could think of to make them better, but their bodies had depended on that supply of medicine for so long. There was nothing he could do except make them comfortable and watch them die. It was horrible. Some people have larger stocks of their meds on hand, but eventually, they'll all run out and then what? If their bodies can't learn to survive without it or with a natural substitute, then there is nothing we can do."

"I saw a lot of bodies when I was going through Auburn, but it doesn't look like that here. What are you guys doing with them all?" Erika wondered.

"Over the hill about a half a mile, a huge fissure opened in the earth. We take all the bodies there and throw them down the fissure. That way, disease doesn't spread, and people have a place to go to remember their loved ones. We call it Cool's Trail of Tears. Anyway, there is still stuff left in people's houses, and we need all the supplies we can get. We remove the bodies and any supplies and mark the house so we know we already cleared it. We are working on a pretty good perimeter but it gets old quick, and we never bring back enough supplies to make everyone happy." Greg explained the operation in detail.

"Same old story; you can't please everyone. I am glad you guys are laying the bodies to rest. It really bothered me to see all the decaying bodies just lying there in Auburn. No one cared; I think they even were actually eating meat off of them," Erika said disgustedly.

"Come on, let's not get all bummed out. This is going to be a happy day, darn it! Plus, I still have a surprise for you." Greg knew returning to the mention of the surprise would entice Erika again and get them off of depressing subjects.

Erika had completely forgotten the surprise with all this serious talk, and her curiosity was renewed. "What is it? Come on, you have to tell me."

"No, I don't, and you'll see soon enough," Greg teased back. "Oh man, it is good to have you back, girl. I was so worried." Greg gave her a big hug and added an extra squeeze at the end.

Erika didn't have to say anything. It was good to be with him again too. Friends have always been priceless but nobody had a reason to fully appreciate that fact before. You could come and go and it hardly made a difference, but now everyone knew exactly how important it was to hold on to those little things that really matter in life. Greg started walking toward an area of town that used to be where the feed store was located, but it was no more. It had obviously burned pretty good. Anything that was of use had already been relocated to another survival location. They didn't walk all the way to the feed store though; they made a sharp right and headed for the area that used to be little fenced patios and porches out behind the buildings. This area was darker and had more clutter. Erika followed carefully behind Greg until they came to a board that had a G on it. Greg moved it aside, and the inside of the area looked great. Greg had collected rugs, blankets, candle holders, and so much more. It looked like the inside of some Persian prince's tent. One side of it was more of a sitting area, and the other side was definitely a sleeping area. It was basically stacked with blankets and pillows. While standing there, staring at Greg's setup, Erika didn't even notice Greg's dog, Dakota, sneak up on her. All 180 pounds of his bull mastiff's body bounced at her leg, and his full weight hit her. Dakota knew who it was, and he was excited. His big old butt wagged back and forth and his curly tail wagged furiously.

"Dakota!" Erika screamed with excitement. Erika was an absolute dog lover and she suddenly realized that she had not seen one in over three months. She petted him and hugged him. "Wow, seeing Dakota makes me realize how much I miss Ripper."

"He'll be here soon enough, Erika. Why don't we sit down and chill out for a little bit? Then we'll go over and say hi to Mike and my Dad." Greg found a spot in the sitting room on one of the cushions in the corner. "Hey, Erika, check this out."

Erika was finding her own cushion to sit on over by Greg. It was an old sofa cushion and looked comfortable. She looked over toward him and replied, "What's up?"

Greg pulled back one of the blankets covering the interior of the tent, and he was stocked. He had alcohol, canned goods, and even some more smokes. "Why don't we have a drink and a smoke?"

"Oh yes, no need to twist my arm. I could use a nice break." Erika was looking eagerly at the bottle of Captain Morgan's Spiced Rum that was on one side of the stack. "Greg, grab that Captain Morgan's; everyone needs a little Captain in them, you know."

Greg chuckled and grabbed the bottle. He also grabbed a pack of Camel Lights, Erika's favorite. "Here you go. You can have this pack. Now, where are those freakin' shot glasses?"

"Thanks, Greg. I have a couple left, but I am on extreme rationing now. Aren't those the glasses over there?" Erika had seen some glass sparkling from a corner, but it looked as if another pillow had been accidentally thrown in front of them. "Got a light?"

"Sure do." Greg reached over and lit Erika's smoke and then grabbed two shot glasses from the corner pile. He poured them to the brim and handed one to Erika. "Here's to old times."

Erika raised her glass and added, "It couldn't last forever," and they drank the shots down.

Greg refilled the glasses and they drank the shots slower this time. Erika had never been one for doing shots. She liked the fruity, girly drinks, and the straight rum was a little overwhelming at first. Then as her insides began to warm and her nerves relaxed, she found it easier to drink. It felt wonderful to rest on the soft cushions, having a drink and a smoke. Erika laid back and was just soaking in the restful feeling when all of a sudden a huge tongue licked her right across the face.

"Oh, Dakota!" Erika sat up quickly and was wiping her face. He had slurped a big, gross drool right across her face. Greg was laughing it up.

"I bet you really miss dogs now," he said, laughing.

The two of them laughed and laughed. The stress relief was wonderful. Erika had been so out of her natural element for so long, she had almost lost herself. How easy it would have been to forget her life and give into the disparity of her situation, but she didn't. Now here she was relaxing and drinking with her old friend. A big feast was coming tonight and the most delightful fact of all: her family was coming too. She would see them tonight. She could hardly contain her excitement.

"Greg, I just can't wait to see Vince and Dexter. I never thought I would make it home. I can't believe I am here with you drinking rum." Erika was getting very anxious.

"Honestly, Erika, I can't believe you are here either. I never thought I would see you again. So many people are gone; I figured you were just one more of them. Come here!" Greg leaned over and gave Erika another great big hug. It was one of those hugs that goes straight through to your bones. A hug shared between friends that fills one another with strength and certainty. "All right, we need to keep moving." He was feeling the effects of the alcohol. "We need to go finish visiting and then go help get set up for tonight."

"I will agree with that," Erika was slurring her words a little. "Plus, if I drink anymore of that, I will be way too drunk by the time the boys get back here, and I have a feeling it is going to be a long night. If you know what I mean." Erika had a sly little look in her eyes.

"Oh, I'm hearing ya', sista'. That's what I need, a little somthin' somethin'." Greg had his woman-eater look in his eyes and was staring off into space with visions of grandeur.

"All right, get your mind out of the gutter. Let's go see Mike and your dad." Erika quickly changed the subject.

"Okay, let's go." They got up and headed towards the door of the tent. Greg turned back and gave instructions to Dakota, "Now Dakota, you stay and be a good boy. Protect Daddy's stuff;

I'll be back in a little while to take you out." He closed the tent and they continued walking down a little trail in between tent after tent after tent.

The sun was past the middle of the sky now and it was hot. Inside the tent had been cool, but the sun was blasting outside. Erika was still in awe of how the people were all living together. Normally, everyone would have been in their own individual home with tons of space in between each family, but when the stuff went down, they had all banded together. They did not know one another. Each one had lived their own life before, getting up for work and coming home. They had grocery-shopped together, or bumped into one another in line at the gas station, but never wanted to socialize. They all had their own friends. They all were part of digital social networks. Now here they were all stacked together, all helping one another. It was kind of miraculous and sad that it took total devastation for people to look at one another and ask: How can I help you?

Finally, Greg and Erika came to a deck that used to be the back area of the local bar, The Milestone. The quake and fire had done its damage here as well, but the people had pushed out the debris and put a makeshift roof over the building. This made it possible to pull a bench up to the bar and have a drink. How long would the alcohol hold out? Originally, it had not lasted too long, but they were resourceful. People needed the stress relief and the doctor was in need of the antiseptic virtues of it. The owners had been strictly rationing the original supply, and they were constantly sending out little gathering parties to look for more. But, that did not keep the supply full, so they made a still and were now doing it the old-school way, making their own. It was really strong and tasted like crap but it did the trick for the stress and the medicine.

"Wow, they have really done a lot with the place since I've been gone," Erika said sarcastically.

"Hey, it's a lot better than it was. I thought it was gone but people wanted a bar, so people dug the bar out of the rubble and then they threw this crappy roof on the bar, so here it is." Greg was a construction worker and was having a hard time staring at this world that was so piecemeal. He wanted straight lines and things put together properly, but they didn't have the tools or the materials to make that happen, so he had to deal with it.

"Greg, we're over here," someone called from a table in the corner. Even though it was really bright outside, it was amazing how dark it was inside. Then Erika understood why. There were no windows left. They must have broken out and just been boarded back up. She had to take a moment for her eyes to adjust so she could see who was calling them over to the table. As they neared the corner and her eyes began to adjust, she saw it was Mike Nostrem. Greg's dad, Cliff, was up at the bar ordering another drink for himself and Mike. Erika was kind of curious what form of payment they were using for the drinks. She quickly pushed the thought back and walked up to Mike, who was talking with Cliff's girlfriend, Nancy. Erika did not know Nancy well, so she didn't really react when Erika walked up behind Mike.

When Mike turned around he saw Erika and yelled, "Oh my God, is that you, Erika? Is it really you? Oh my God! Where were you? What happened? Oh my God! Come and give me a big hug."

Mike gave Erika a huge hug and Erika loved it. After being alone for so long, it felt wonderful to be wrapped up in the warmth of old friends who loved you and would take care of you. After a while, Mike released his hug and extended Erika out to the reach of his arms and looked at her. Then he hugged her again. Erika had grown up with Mike's sons, and she knew that one had died. Mike had not seen the other. She did not know how to approach this subject. As if Mike knew exactly what Erika was feeling, he held her closer and whispered in her ear, "Maybe Burt will make it home too."

"I hope so, Mike," Erika choked out. Tears were starting to fill her eyes now. It was as if all the emotions of the day could not be held back any longer.

"Hey, nice to see you made it home, Erika." Cliff had returned with the drinks. Erika and he had not been as close, but they knew one another and exchanged greetings. His distraction from all the emotions was welcome. The alcohol Erika had before did not help to suppress the feelings that the reunion with Mike had created.

Mike had always been friends with Erika's mother as well and quickly asked, "Have you heard from or seen your mom yet?"

"No. Why? Have you?" Erika was excited. She thought Mike may have seen her mom and knew where she was and if she was okay.

"No, I haven't. I was just wondering if you had seen her yet. I have heard that there is a camp down in the Coloma area though, so there's hope. I think Vince was going to check it out," Mike said solemnly.

"Well, isn't this cheery." Greg was up to his classic old tricks again. He never let the tension get too high. He had to stomp it down. That's just who he was and Erika loved him for it. Everyone laughed and it was weird. How could they laugh at a time like this? On the other hand, how could they not? If they gave up and succumbed to the negative energy, they would die right along with everything else.

"Erika, there you are. I have been looking everywhere for you," Joan had come in. "We just about have everything ready to go for tonight. I was wondering if you wanted to come back and get cleaned up at all. Your clothes are dry from this morning if you want to put back on something a little more rugged. Plus, everyone decided you should present the meat tonight for everyone since you are the one who butchered it."

"Oh, okay, Joan." Erika was a little put off by all this attention. She wanted to just blend back in with the group, not 'present' things to them. She knew she would have to tell her story tonight and that was going to be quite enough. The more she thought about what Joan had said about her outfit, the more she thought it might be a good idea to go change out of the delicate clothes that Carol had given her, even though they were very comfortable. But, if she did get a little tipsy tonight, she did not want to make a mess out of them. Plus, she was thinking about Star and wondering how she was getting along. "That sounds good. I would like to change my clothes and check in on Star."

"I'm going to hang out here for now. Margie needs some help getting supplies together for tonight, and I need to go and run Dakota. He has been in the tent for a while," Greg said. "I'll hook up with you in about an hour."

"Sounds good to me, G-man; let's go, Joan." Erika's heart bounced as she left the bar with Joan. She felt so much better, almost fuller. She found a sense of family, and it felt great. Now if her boys would just get here, it would be so much better.

CHAPTER 19

THE SUN WAS just entering an area of the sky that signified late afternoon was approaching. It got hotter and a bead of sweat dripped down Erika's face as they crossed back over the old highway and headed up the hill to where the river group was camped. The wonderful smell of meat roasting was all over the place, and Steve was still over at the fire, drying the meat. Erika noticed a few more men had joined him sitting around the fire and there was a bottle of something that they were drinking. Erika knew what that must be. It was a good deal, alcohol for meat. Everyone would be well fed and having fun tonight. You could feel the energy in the air. The sense of anticipation of something fun. Something people could use to dispel more stress and disparity. It was a chance for people to come together even more, to dance and play.

The first order of business was to check on Star. Erika went over to the tent and peeked in.

"The kids are taking a nap right now," Joan whispered. "I told them that we were going to have a big night tonight, and it might be a good idea to get some rest before the fun begins."

"Good idea. Is my stuff still over in the cart?" Erika asked quietly.

"No, we needed some of that wood to make a bench next to the fire. We put all your stuff in a section of the tent for you. Come on." Joan led Erika into the tent and pointed to a pile on the edge that was her things. There were a lot of little piles and Erika figured out that everyone had their own pile along the edge.

"Thanks, Joan," Erika whispered.

"No problem, I have to go check on the dishes for tonight. You got everything you need?" Joan asked.

"I think so," Erika replied.

"Okay, I'll see you after you change." Joan closed the tent flap and Erika heard her steps move away from the tent.

Erika went over to her pile. Her pile of stuff she had brought all the way from the restaurant. It seemed so long ago now. She looked over at Star, all snuggled up sleeping like a baby. Erika went over and pulled the blanket up around her more, and Star stirred a little.

"Erika, is that you?" she said sleepily.

"Yes, honey, it's me. Are you doing all right?" Erika whispered to her.

"Yeah, my leg hurts, but I'm okay," Star moaned a little.

"Well, I want you to get some good rest because we are going to have some fun tonight," Erika said quietly.

"I'm not supposed to be up out of bed yet," Star said sadly. She looked bummed out that she would be missing the fun.

"You are only young once, Star. I think it would be all right if you came out for just a little while to hear some music and have some fun," Erika said, giving the girl some hope.

"Really?" Star's eyes were wide with anticipation of the fun to come.

"Yeah, really, but I think you better get as much rest as possible so you have all the energy you are going to need," Erika replied quietly, giving her nose a little rub with her finger.

"All right." Star rolled over and snuggled back into her blankets. Erika tucked her in some more and stared for a moment at her beautiful new daughter. Then she headed over to her pile again.

The anxiety of seeing her family was killing her so she decided to stay focused on the task at hand. That way, time would pass faster. Erika decided to change her clothes first. She took off her soft sheet outfit and put back on the blood stained jungle pants. Then she put on her green shirt. She decided to just bring her sweatshirt with her because it was so hot out now, but later it might cool off. The end of September was always unpredictable that way. No more hot August nights. It was usually really warm in the daytime but at night, if there were no clouds to keep the heat in, it was really cold. She looked around and although she liked these people, she did not know where she would actually be sleeping tonight, so she decided to put her things together in a neat bundle. This would be time consuming, and if she decided not to sleep here tonight, it would be easy to move her things.

Erika was at a loss because she did not have a bag or a backpack to put things into. In the end, she decided to spread out one of the blankets that she was carrying and put everything neatly in the center of it then fold in the sides and make it into a sack. She began to pack up her things. The rope that she had went on the very bottom because it was pretty dirty. Then she put one of her blankets on top of it, her bundle of clothes on that, and finally her other blanket. Erika hoped that this way, her good outfit would stay nice. She still had a first aid kit but all it had in it was some gauze, a couple of Band-Aids and some antiseptic. So, she put her two extra lighters, her four kitchen knives, and the five candles she had left in it as well. She put a lighter in her pocket as well as her three-quarter pack of Camels. She put the new pack that Greg had given her, as well as her pack of Marlboros and Marlboro Lights in the first aid kit to save for later. She put the kit, her two remaining boxes of tampons, and the bag of rice she still had on top blanket in the sack. She finished packing her two saucepans on top of that and tied the sack up at the top. Now she was ready to go if she had to.

This was the part of a party that Erika absolutely hated, and this time, it was even worse. It was the time when you are all ready to go but no one is there yet. Usually, she would goof around with Vince before anyone else showed up, but this time he was not even there yet. She thought of his eyes and his warm embrace. He would be coming before too long, and she was absolutely ecstatic. She couldn't take it any longer; she had to get out of the tent and back into the fresh air. When she went out, the sun was going into early evening, and she knew it couldn't be long now. She decided she would go over and give Kit, her horse, some attention. She realized she had hardly seen him today, and he had been so faithful. He was in a little pen that was made from burnt boards crisscrossed in X patterns to form a holding pen. He nickered when he saw her and came over to the edge so she could pet him.

"Hi, Kit, how you doing?" Erika put a hand on his head and closed her eyes.

"I'm doing fine," a very familiar voice said from behind her. Erika spun around so fast she almost fell over.

"*Vince!*" She ran to him and threw her arms around him, and he hugged her. They never wanted to let go. They kissed as tears streamed down their faces. Erika looked into his eyes and soaked in their beauty. She had never thought she would look into those eyes again and then they embraced again. She smelled his smell, his manliness emanating. This was her man, her soul mate; she would have crossed the expanse of the entire world to find him if she had to.

"Oh my God, Erika, I thought you were gone. I thought you were dead! Oh my God, I am never going to let you go again!" He hugged her with an extreme desperation. He squeezed so tight it hurt, but Erika didn't mind. She didn't want him to ever let her go again either. She felt whole again. She had her other half, and now they could both live again as one.

"Mommy, Mommy," Dexter yelled as he ran up. His golden hair shined in the setting sun and his blue eyes shone like the sky.

Their dog, Ripper, was at his heels and ran to Erika with his tail rapidly wagging.

"Dexter!" She picked him up, hugged him, and swung him around in the air. Then Vince grabbed them both and threw his arms around them. He hugged them, and they just stood that way for a long time. They all cried but no one moved. Except for Ripper: he danced and pranced around the family yelping in joy.

Reality was everyone's worst enemy, and it was only a matter of time until it broke the trance of the reunited family. There was so much to discuss. Erika wanted to know it all at once: how did they survive, who else they had been in contact with, the list went on and on. She knew that these conversations would take time, and there were much more pressing issues to discuss right now.

"Baby, there's someone else you have to meet," Erika said excitedly to Vince. "It's a very long story, but I saved a little girl named Star. Her mother and father both died. I had no choice but to take her as my own. I hope you guys will love her like I do. I want you to come and meet her."

Vince held Erika in his arms again and replied, "Erika, I know that whatever happened, I am just so thankful that you are home. If God returned you to me with another child to add to our family, then I say great! Let's go meet her. What do you think, Dex?" His gorgeous gaze moved from Erika to his young son waiting at his heels.

"Yeah, I got a new sister!" Dexter yelled in excitement.

The whole camp was a buzz of excitement when the family returned to the Auburn River Group's camp where Star was. All of the folks from Auburn and most of the people camped in Cool were all standing around the main fire on the hill. A column formed as the family approached the crowd. There, by the fire, was Greg with Star. Greg had known that Star would need an update with all the commotion going on, and he was there for her immediately. He had kept her feeling welcome, and waiting a few more minutes to meet the rest of the family was no big deal. Star hopped as fast as she could over to Erika when she saw the family approach. Erika hugged her and raised her up into the air. Vince, overwhelmed with love for his wife, held the two of them tightly in his arms, and Dexter wrapped onto their legs.

Finally, Vince backed up for a moment and looked at the little girl. He said cheerfully, "This must be Miss Star, the one who I have been hearing so much about. My name is Vince and it is very nice to meet you."

He had always been great with kids. He seemed to know how to communicate with them better than most adults and it was as if Star could sense that immediately.

"This must be the Mr. Vince I have been hearing so much about. Anyone that Erika loves as much as she loves you is A-okay in my book," Star replied smartly.

"Well, aren't you a little gem. You are going to fit right into this family." Vince hugged her again and lifted her out of Erika's hands and raised her high above his head. The whole crowd cheered as he spun her around and delicately returned her to the ground. He had noticed her hobble when she had run up and didn't want her to land too hard on that leg.

The crowd continued to cheer. The people were just happy to have something positive to cheer for, and this reunion story was just what they needed. Greg loved moments like this, and he was just the individual to take advantage of it. He suddenly jumped up on a gnarled stump that was sitting by the fire and addressed the crowd.

"People, people," he cried out, waving his arms in the air. It took a couple of minutes but the crowd began to hush.

"We have all been through absolute hell!" Greg cried out.

The people cheered in agreement and a man yelled out "Yeah we have."

"Now, we have something to celebrate. A *family reunion* for us all!" he shouted out to the crowd.

There was more cheering and shouting.

"Erika was returned to us from the depths of the hell that was once Sacramento, and even I don't know how she did that." Greg paused for a moment and gave the crowd a chance to do more shouting and cheering.

"Well, tonight folks, we are going to hear it." There was a huge cheer that went up from the masses.

"And…"—Greg waited for the crowd to quiet down—"we are going to party!" The crowd erupted into a flood of sound. People were so eager to feel good; they just wanted to feel normal again and a celebration was a perfect way to vent the frustrations of lives that were spiraling out of control.

"So let's party, folks. Everyone, go and get ready. Let's put together a feast to go with all that meat, bring your beverages, and don't forget to do a little clean-up on those grubby faces." Greg was feeling great and the crowd was a vortex of activity: cheering, laughing, and scrambling to get everything ready for tonight.

Erika marveled at how pleasant it was to see everyone smiling and pumped up with positive feelings. She watched the crowd begin to disperse, everyone going off to their respective camps to get ready for the party. She saw some people washing themselves and their kids out of little buckets and others were cooking in salvaged pots and pans. Everyone was busy and the positive energy floated thick in the air.

Erika and Vince were awestruck with the activity. It was a bit overwhelming to be the center of so much attention. After months of being apart, all they wanted to do was find someplace quiet and share each other's company. Dexter and Star had hit it off immediately, and they were already deep in conversation over what they liked and didn't like. Greg knew that whether Vince and Erika liked it or not, they were going to be the stars of the show. Unless someone organized the chaos, Vince and Erika would be bothered by folks all night, wanting to hear their stories and share in their reunion. Now he had cleared the crowd but it had a cost. Erika would have to share her story tonight. Greg jumped down off of the stump and strolled nonchalantly over to the couple.

"Okay, guys. I got you guys a few minutes of time," Greg said. "Where are you guys going to stay?"

Erika and Vince looked at one another and shrugged. Neither of them had thought past finding one another.

"I guess we'll just stay here for now. Until we can figure out what we are going to do," Vince replied.

"Okay, well, I'm going to go back to my tent and get freshened up for the party. That little honey from the watch tower will be around tonight and I plan on getting me some," Greg said slyly.

"Same old Greg," Erika said while rolling her eyes.

"Cool, man," Vince replied after chuckling at Erika for a moment. "We'll see you later and thanks for everything, Greg," Vince said with a hint of a tear in his eye. Greg had returned his wife to him and with her his whole life.

"No problem bro, except she did all the work getting here. All I did was welcome her home," Greg replied modestly.

"Well, thanks anyway," Vince said, choking back tears.

Vince and Erika left to go and spend some well-earned time together in the communal tent that the Auburn group had constructed. Joan had set up another blanket that made an additional private room in the corner area. There was no one else in the tent right now but there would be later, and this addition had made the tent seem much more private and cozy. Star and Dexter decided that they wanted to play outside with Ripper, and since Tyson and Little Jimmy were outside playing as well, Erika did not have a problem with that. Erika had told Star to take it easy, but deep inside, she knew Star would have to stay strong to survive in this world. Joan had also let Erika know that she would be in the vicinity of the kids and would keep an eye on them.

"Things are freaking crazy, aren't they?" Vince stated with awe in his voice.

"You're telling me," Erika countered with a chuckle.

They sat down on the blanket in their little room and laid their heads back to take a much needed rest in the arms of one another.

"Oh, baby, it's so good to see you. I really thought you were gone. That lasted for about one whole minute," Vince said sarcastically with a laugh.

"Why do you laugh? I thought I was going to be a goner once or twice myself," Erika answered back.

"Oh, Erika, I don't mean it like that. I just meant I always knew you weren't gone. I could just... just feel it. I dreamt about you. The dreams were so real and so vivid I knew you were here. So much time went by and everyone said I was crazy to think that somehow you would make it home, but I knew. I knew you were coming home, and I could almost feel you getting closer somehow," Vince retorted with absolute dedication to the one he loved in his eyes.

"I knew you guys were here too. One family I met along the way really wanted me to stay with them. But, I knew you would be waiting for me. I wondered how long you would wait, but I knew you would wait," Erika said, her eyes full of love.

"You wondered how long I would wait. There you go worrying about everything you shouldn't be again. Baby, I would have waited forever. I love you." Vince had tears in his eyes again.

The two embraced and shared a long kiss. Vince put his hands on Erika's head and ran his fingers through her soft brown hair. He put his hands on her neck and felt for her earlobe as he had done so many times before, but he quickly pulled his hand away as if he had touched acid. Erika was horrified. She knew why he had withdrawn; he had felt her new scars and pulled away.

"Oh my gosh, baby, what happened?" Vince was shocked by the amount of scars she had acquired and was more concerned than ever about her. The reality of her journey was smacking him across the face; she really had almost died. The love of his life had been out there all alone and he had been absolutely powerless to help. He would have done anything to have been there helping her and saving her from this pain, and the fact that he had been totally unable to do anything frustrated him greatly.

Erika saw the anger in his eyes and thought it was directed at her. Would he still love her even though her body was so mangled? He had only touched the scars on her neck. He hadn't even seen the worst of it. "I told you that you almost lost me," Erika said rather irritated. "It's just some scars. I'm still me."

Vince saw her defensive side surface and had to reach out to her now. "I know, baby. Don't be embarrassed. I am just so frustrated that I couldn't help you, or stop all the pain you must have gone through. I love you." He turned her head toward him and looked deep into her soul, "And I will always love you." He reached back up to her with his hands and ran his fingers from her ears down her neck, feeling every new crook and cranny of the woman he loved.

"I love you too, Vince. I have just been so worried about what you would think of all these scars," she admitted, trying to pull away from his touch.

"And there you go again, worrying about ridiculous things that you should not be worrying about at all," he said, trying to stifle these feelings she was having.

Erika smiled and Vince began to undress her. He wanted to view his woman and look at the extent of her scarring. He would love her always, no matter what happened to her body, and she needed to know that right now so their love could glow brightly long into the future.

"Well, at least I'm still here, right?" Erika said sarcastically. It was her way of covering the pain of having to bare all of these new scars.

" Darn right! Now get over here, woman, and let me hug you all over." Vince grabbed ahold of her without restraint and wrapped her up in his passionate embrace. He kissed her all over, familiarizing himself with her and relearning all her beautiful curves and embracing the new ones. They made passionate love, quietly, and restrained. They were both modest people. The thought of so many people hovering around in such a close proximity to them made them nervous, but they could not contain their passion for one another. Once their sweet lovemaking was done, they relaxed in the warmth of their love.

Until Joan yelled from the doorway, "The party is beginning and everyone is waiting on you two to start eating."

Then Greg yelled playfully from behind Joan, "So get your butts out here."

CHAPTER 20

WHEN VINCE AND Erika got back outside, it was a wonderful scene. The smells of the food wafted through the air. There were people playing drums and other various instruments in a joyful tune. Since Erika and Vince were the guests of the night, they were given the first place in line to get their food. Dexter and Star joined them, and Vince and Erika helped them with their plates. The food had been set up on a tabletop that no longer had any legs so it was stacked on some extra cinderblocks to make it stand higher.

The food itself was rather interesting. There was the horse-meat roast, plus someone else had provided some venison roast to bolster the meat supply. There were normal side dishes like canned vegetables but there were also things like a dish of prepared cattail shoots, dandelion greens, wild onions, and wild carrots. There were also plates of blackberries, strawberries, and cherries, harvested from wild plants and old groves. Traditional vegetables like zucchini, yellow squash, and tomatoes had been harvested from gardens that had been grown at the homes in the surrounding area. Very few survived the fires but the scavengers knew exactly where to find them. It was a feast for all. It was the first reason they had to celebrate since the big disaster, and this feast was not one that would be available again anytime soon.

To eat the meal, everyone had to bring their own plate to eat off of and their own silverware or knife to eat with. This was a new concept to Erika but not to Vince and Dexter. Vince had brought an extra plate for Erika, but he had no idea that he would be gaining a daughter along with his wife. Erika gave Star the extra plate and Joan provided Erika with the bowl she had eaten her soup out of earlier. It was not as if they could go buy a package of paper plates and given the fragile condition of most plates, not many had survived.

Vince and Erika went through the line, sampling all of the unusual dishes. Then when the family had heaped their plates full, they went to sit by the music players to eat. It was so wonderful to have a nice big meal. Erika had not eaten this well since she left Henry and Carol's and she, like everyone else, would have a full belly tonight. Erika had never heard the great crowd that had gathered here in Cool so quiet. The hush went on and on as the famished people stuffed their faces with the much needed nourishment. When everyone had gone through the line, just about all the food was gone, and what was left was quickly gobbled up by individuals going for seconds. The musicians had plates set aside so they could eat once the music came to a halt. Then the crowd would be entertained by story-telling. It was definitely a new way of life for a people who had become so used to being entertained by televisions, computers, and technology.

A wash station had been set up so that after eating everyone could clean their own dish, plus the dish that they had brought their food for the group in. Any scraps, and the bones were given to any surviving dogs. Ripper grabbed a huge horse bone and ran off to hoard it from the other dogs. It was actually a surprisingly easy process to get all the dishes washed, and Erika wondered why people had not done this before. She figured it was because, before the quake hit, everyone had a machine to clean up the mess in the kitchen. Or, people had opted to use disposable dishes; even though they created a lot of garbage, they sure did make clean-up a breeze. This new method required everyone to be responsible for their own mess.

Now that everyone had eaten and they were feeling fat and happy, it was time for the alcohol to flow and the dancing to begin. The party rolled on. Some people got up and sang to the improvisational tune, while others danced around the fire. Erika and Vince sat in the glow of the fire just enjoying the feeling of togetherness.

"Hey, baby, come here for a minute," Erika whispered to Vince.

"What's up?" Vince questioned.

"Let's go out by the horse real quick."

"Okay, but we're gonna have to be sneaky. These people are watching us like hawks."

Erika got up first and went to check on the kids. She told them to stay put and have fun, and she couldn't help but marvel at how big their smiles were and how wonderful they looked. All the kids were dancing and laughing and it was like watching a dream. In the meantime, Vince had gotten up and made his way over to the back corner of the big tent where Erika soon arrived to meet him. They thought they were home free when all of a sudden a voice called from behind them.

"Hey, where you guys going?" It was Greg. He had watched them execute their clever plan across the crowd.

"Hey G-man, come with us. We'll just be gone a minute," Erika replied quietly. She didn't want to alert anyone else.

"So, what's up, Erika?" Vince was intrigued by all this sneaking away and wondered what Erika had in store.

"Would you like a… smoke?" she said deviously as she pulled a cigarette from her pack.

"Oh you bet. I haven't had one in weeks. Those things are like gold around here now," Vince said amazed that she had hoarded them for so long and hadn't said anything before now.

"Oh, buddies, just you wait. I've got something even better," Greg interjected before they could light their Camels.

"Really?" Erika said questioningly. "What ya got, sucka?"

"How about we…smoke a joint," Greg said all proud of himself.

"Oh, serious?" Vince asked.

"You bet, buddy. I've been saving this for a very special occasion and I think this is the very excuse I have been looking for," Greg said, very pleased with himself.

The three friends smoked the joint and the effects of the alcohol and marijuana blend soon began to take over. They all lit their cigarettes and talked about old times while they smoked them. It felt so normal to Erika, talking about high school mishaps and what if this or that would have happened, but the harsh reality of their current world was never far behind them. Just as they had finished their smokes, Joan came up behind them.

"Hey, there you guys are. Everyone is telling their stories and we are all dying to hear yours, Erika," she said urgently.

"Calm down, we are on our way right now," Erika responded.

"I can't wait to hear this either," Greg interjected.

"Yeah, me neither," Vince said playfully with a wink at Erika.

"All right, all right, if all you all are going to force me to relive that nightmare over and over, then so be it," Erika said in a playfully pathetic voice.

"It's over now, baby. We want to hear what happened," Vince said sympathetically. After seeing all of her scars, he understood why she would not want to drudge through the journey again.

"Oh, poor little baby," Greg teased and Erika gave him a solid whack on the shoulder.

When the four of them got back to the fire, Randy, from the Auburn group, was standing in front of the crowd. He was telling his story of how he survived the quake. He and Taylor had been close friends and used to work on cars in Randy's garage. They were out there when the quake hit. The whole house came down, but the cars and the equipment for repairing cars in the garage had worked as a support and protected them from the crashing building.

Erika was amazed at the great job Randy was doing telling his story. He used sound effects and huge hand gestures. The crowd was entranced, feeling every moment with Randy as he relived it through his storytelling. Erika had been to college and had known fellow students who couldn't even get up in front of twenty people to do one little prepared speech but here was a teen that had no fear. *After the experience that this young man lived through, it was no wonder*, Erika thought. There was nothing left to be afraid of. He had faced death and, so far, he was winning his race for survival. She squeezed Vince's hand and focused on the story again.

After the quake had ended, the two dug themselves out from the rubble that had fallen all over, only to find that the house was completely devastated. Randy told about how distraught he and Taylor were and that their first thought was to save Randy's family. Nothing like this was ever supposed to happen in Auburn, California. All of the quakes happened in San Francisco and LA, but there was no question what had happened. The two frantically searched the home. Just as the two were about to dive into the rubble that had been Randy's kitchen, the gas line that had fed the stove in the kitchen erupted into a ball of flames. The two were blown back from the house and all of Randy's hair on his head and face had been completely burned off.

As the two lay on the ground, flattened by the blast, they scanned the area. They quickly realized that Randy's house had not been the only home damaged, and it wasn't even close to the worst. Everyone's homes were in rubble and some had been completely engulfed by huge crevices that opened up in the earth. They had been so consumed with finding Randy's parents at first that they had not even begun to realize the full scope of the dilemma. Besides the sounds of explosions from gas lines erupting, it was eerily quiet. There should have been tons of people screaming, but they were quiet.

Erika had now become completely entranced by Randy's story. She had a very limited experience with the quake because she had been hidden in a bomb shelter for months while the world fell apart. She was eager to hear more. Vince had found them a place to sit and when he grabbed Erika's hand again, it made Erika jump.

"Come on, babe, let's go sit down," Vince said softly.

"Oh, right," Erika replied distractedly.

When the two reached the log Vince had found to sit on, Erika realized how absolutely spectacular it was to be with Vince again. She felt whole, completed. With him she felt warm and safe, and they sat close to one another caressing each other's hands.

While the two had been finding a seat, Randy's story had continued on. Despite the eerie atmosphere, Taylor had completely freaked when he realized he had no idea where his family was and if they were okay. They ran the five miles back to Taylor's house only to find a very similar scene. The house had killed both his parents and his sister. But while they were frantically searching through the rubble, Taylor heard a soft whimpering noise and knew someone was still alive somewhere. After telling Randy, the two teens searched for the origin of the sound. They realized it was coming from Taylor's neighbor's house. A girl they went to school with, Kim, lived there. Kim's brother, Joe, was older, but he had often helped Randy and Taylor with the cars they had worked on. They found Joe, dead in his room. He had been playing a PlayStation when the home collapsed on top of him, but they still were hearing a whimper.

Randy and Taylor kept searching and, soon, they found the source. It was Kim. She had been putting her clothes away in her closet when the quake hit and this had saved her. She was pinned under what used to be the roof, but besides a few cuts and bruises, she was going to be okay. The three teens were in complete shock from the situation. The landscape had suddenly turned completely foreign, fires burned everywhere, and the explosions were still happening. Since Kim and Taylor's homes had not used gas sources, they were free of flame for now, but they were just piles of rubble on the edge of another crevice that had opened in the earth. Then all of a sudden there was another boom, an explosion ignited in the other neighbor's house. Now, they wasted no time. Quickly, they searched through the piles of rubble and salvaged anything they could. Randy began to list items like sleeping bags, clothes, food, and medicine. He went on and on. They had used an old gardening wagon to help them carry stuff.

The teens had frequently hung out at the lake and figured it would be a good place to go. There was water there, and there would probably be other survivors at the lake as well. The trip to the lake was an intense adventure. Between the aftershocks, the falling debris, and the rapidly changing landscape, it was a miracle they made it anywhere at all. When they reached what used to be the edge of the lake, it wasn't there. That's when they realized the dam had broken so they continued on down the sloppy edge of the land that used to be underwater. By now, they were very thirsty and determined to find water. Their very existence now depended on it. When they finally reached the water, they found other survivors there as well. They stayed there with them and built the river compound for protection from a group of survivors in Auburn that were bound and determined to take all the supplies in the area to ensure their group's survival, even at the expense of others.

When Randy came to this part of the story, the crowd became noisy and restless. Obviously, everyone knew of this group in Auburn and no one was happy about it. Erika herself had begun to resent this group passionately, and she could feel the uneasiness sweeping through the crowd. Before anyone could get too bent out of sorts, Greg jumped up, and he was in front of the crowd in a flash.

"All right, people, let's settle down; we are having a celebration here," Greg yelled out above the noise.

The crowd did not need much convincing and most people were laughing and cheering again.

"And what are we celebrating?" Greg asked the crowd.

The crowd responded, "A family reunion."

"That's right and what story are we all waiting to hear?" Greg questioned the crowd again.

Erika knew the answer but was desperately hoping she was wrong. The crowd quickly confirmed her suspicions.

"Erika's," everyone screamed.

Erika knew she could no longer dodge this bullet and the crowd began to chant, "Erika! Erika!"

Greg looked at her from the front of the crowd and made a motion with his hand for her to join him. The crowd looked toward her as well, and the people parted again as she started to make her way to the front. Erika had never shied from addressing a crowd, but she was not fond of it either. Her body began to shake a little as she reached Greg.

"Thanks a lot, G-man," Erika said as she rolled her eyes.

"Hey, someone has got to keep them focused. We could have had a riot on our hands."

"Oh, that makes me feel much better."

"They won't bite... I hope. Anyway, get on with it; I want to hear what happened too."

Greg quickly jumped down from the log the speakers were standing on, and he went back into the crowd and sat with Vince. Erika looked over the crowd. She was surprised at how many survivors had gathered here, and she couldn't help but wonder what the future would hold for them all. From her high spot, she could see the divisions in the group. The Cool folks had a little separation from the folks that came from the Auburn River camp. The teens separated themselves from the smaller children. She noticed Star and Dexter staring from the crowd, and they waved at her when she made eye contact. She waved back but the silence began to grow very heavy in the air.

The crowd began chanting, "Story, story…"

"Okay… okay, guys," Erika tried to quiet them. "Where should I begin?"

"At the beginning," some smart aleck yelled from the crowd.

Erika had to chuckle at his comment and the tension began to drain from her.

"Well, actually, the story begins right here in Cool." This brought cheering from the crowd. It seemed to Erika that it was a good place to start because people always loved to cheer for themselves. She started telling the tale of being at her in-laws' during the day and then leaving for work. She knew her own family had not heard this story, and she could not help but center in on Vince. Her story began to flow as she looked into his eyes. There she found all the strength she needed to relive the nightmare again. She told all about the annoying guy who was always making a fuss about his wine and how his endless demands had actually saved her that fateful day. She told all about how horrible it had been to be trapped under the wine rack and then realizing that no help was coming. She could see Vince's irritation at the fact that he was not there to help her. She told all about the bomb shelter and the toxic sludge that barred her escape. She told about how she devised her plan to get out of there. Vince, along with the crowd, nodded approval at her ingenious suit and raft. Erika added in some extra gore just to get a rise out of the crowd when she talked about the raft ride and waking up in a pool of dead bodies. The kids were hiding their faces in their hands and Erika wondered if she had added too much. But there was no shelter here, not from this reality; the kids had to face it just like everyone else. Erika told about the volcanic eruption she had seen. The crowd agreed with her that it must have taken place over by the coastal range. Regardless, it had raised the water temperature and her raft had melted. She told all about her desperation of having made it so far and how she was not going to give up then. All of the folks in the crowd were on edge now, wondering how she would survive the heated toxic sludge.

Erika continued on, explaining how she had dragged her raft to the edge but the heat and the pain from the melting plastic caused her to pass out. She looked at Vince again and saw the pain in his eyes. He would have given anything to have been with her then. He would have taken all that pain and shielded her but that had not been an option. All he could do was listen to her story, just like everyone else.

Erika paused here and took a drink. It was strong, and she had never been much of an alcohol drinker. It made her face pucker and she looked at Greg in the crowd, knowing he had been the one making their drinks. He smiled a sly little smile and winked at her. He had made her a very strong beverage, maybe he thought it would loosen her up to have a little extra tonight. The pungent drink made her pause longer than she would have, and she noticed that everyone in the crowd was completely enthralled with the story she was telling. Erika was beginning to like this newfound power.

This enthusiasm caused her story to get more detailed. She went on and on about Henry and Carol. She explained how they had survived the quake and how they had brought her back to life. She even displayed some of her scars to make the reality of her journey hit home. Not only had they saved her, they had given her all the supplies and tools she would need to make it home. They had even provided Erika with the horse that they had dined on tonight. Deep in her heart, Erika felt deeply indebted to Henry and Carol, and this feeling was not lost on the crowd, or Vince. Most people had a tear in their eye and were wondering if they would have been so unselfishly caring if they were given the ways and means to help someone so much.

Erika told about her long horse ride through Auburn and how she had found Star. She left out the part about what the man had been doing to Star's mom and the fact that Erika had been the one who finally ended her life. She simply made it sound like the man had killed Star's mom in an attack and Erika left the scene with Star. Most of the crowd turned to look at the little girl with her golden hair waving in the light of the fire. Erika remembered how the crowd had responded to hearing about the Auburn gang so she talked as little as possible about them when she described the rest of her and Star's journey home. She wrapped it up with "and you all know how I got here."

The crowd cheered and laughed because they knew she had been brought in to the camp, passed out again and soaked with horse blood. She looked back to Vince. He knew there was more to the end of this story than she was saying, but he wasn't going to prod her in front of the crowd. If she was not telling the full story, she must have a good reason for it. Anyway, he just wanted her to finish so he could have her back in his arms again. He had not held her enough and wanted more. Greg too knew that there was more to the story, but he also knew why she wasn't going there. He decided to help her out as long as the crowd was still in a good mood.

"Was that worth waiting for, or what?" Greg had appeared so suddenly that Erika almost jumped out of her skin. The crowd cheered in approval. "Here she is, folks, The Sacramento Survivor." The crowd all cheered again, Erika blushed and shot Greg an evil-eyed look.

"I'd get out of here while you still can," Greg whispered to Erika.

"You don't have to tell me twice," she replied and jumped off the log. The crowd cheered again. Everyone was feeling great.

"And now, folks, for your listening enjoyment, here they are, the only people who have instruments and know how to play them." The crowd laughed in amusement at Greg's jest. Greg was introducing the small group of people who had played the music for dinner. Each one had an instrument and they stood in front of the crowd and began to play an upbeat tune. The crowd began to sway as Erika made her way back to Vince.

"You'll have to tell me the end of that story one day," Vince said with joy in his eyes as Erika approached. It had been so long since he had been able to watch her approach, to watch her move. He loved her more than anything in the world. "But in the meantime, may I have this dance?"

Erika was shocked. It had never been easy to get Vince out on the dance floor and she welcomed the invitation. "Yes, you may," she replied as Vince whirled her out into the dancing throng of people. They were together again, dancing, laughing and holding one another. It was better than any dream and Erika fell into the moment. She could think of nothing but him. She could not smell anything but the scent of his manliness. She drank in his warmth and they swayed to the music, completely immersed in their love. The song played on and on and couples began to disappear back to quiet corners. The kids were laughing and enjoying the night. Erika had glanced over from time to time to look at how beautiful they were with full smiles, all covered in dusty dirt. Joan had noticed Erika's looks and knew that Erika and Vince would be looking for their own private quiet corner before long. She motioned to Erika for Erika and Vince to go. All was well.

"I'm getting tired, Vince," Erika whispered in his ear.

"I'm just waiting on you, baby. What about the kids?" Vince questioned.

"They're with Joan. They'll be fine," Erika assured him.

He had always been such a great daddy and he had stepped it up since he had been Dexter's sole caretaker for so many months. They made their way back to the tent. Erika was still stunned, looking back on all the people. It was like being at some music festival out in some field in the middle of nowhere. Except no one would be going home after the weekend. This was real. A community brought together for the need of survival. People had grown so far apart in our high-tech society. Everyone burrowed into their own homes, communicating by e-mail, text, or some computerized social network. It was amazing how fast it had all been destroyed. *None of those skills would help anyone now, so what was it all for*, Erika wondered. What had been the point? This was the point: people helping people, people sharing stories of pain and love, and people coming together and supporting one another. Erika realized that maybe this little slice of life was more real than any other part of her life that she had already lived.

Vince opened the tent flap for her and they made their way to their little room. Ripper, ever vigilant at Erika's heels, followed them in, and they told him to lie down outside their little room. The noise from outside was intense and it covered the sounds of their passionate lovemaking. It was a hard and dirty event. Drunken sex had always been this way for them. With their senses numbed, there were moments of rough play and furious thrusting. When they had smothered one another completely in blissful fulfillment, they snuggled. They had always fit perfectly together and their love swirled around them like an unharnessed energy source. The alcohol, marijuana, and frantic sex took their toll on the couple, and they fell into a deep sleep. They slept more soundly than either had done since they had been separated so many months ago.

CHAPTER 21

ERIKA AND VINCE woke up to the bouncing of their two children. The children had gotten up early and couldn't help but come in and bombard their mom and dad with hugs and kisses. Star was fitting right in as one of the family. Her leg was still very painful from the bullet that had grazed her delicate skin, but she was tough, and she didn't let it slow her down.

Erika was elated to be woken up by the kids. She snuggled them in tight and hugged them until she thought they would explode. The four of them reveled in the moment of intense love. She ran her hand through Dex's blond hair and savored the scent of his body. None of them wanted to face the harsh reality that awaited them outside of the tent. They could hear the hustle and bustle of people waking up and trying to find something to eat. The feast that they had enjoyed the night before was not a normal occurrence since the great quake. Food was in very high demand, but everyone had felt obliged to contribute to Erika's bounty of horsemeat that she had brought.

"Let's just get out of here today and have one more day of fun before we have to decide what to do with ourselves now," Vince said flatly to Erika.

"I'm down. I haven't had any thought on my mind besides finding you and now that I have, I wouldn't mind some calmness," Erika agreed with Vince. She just wasn't ready to face reality now that she had finally found Vince.

"I know a great place we can walk to from here. It's a rock that was sheered off in the quake and you can look out over the canyon. I spent many a day sitting there hoping I would see you coming up the canyon." Vince said with a sad look in his eyes.

"Well, I'm here now, so let's go enjoy it together." Erika's eyes bounced as she started to get her things together.

"We should let Greg know where we're going in case there's an emergency or something." Vince had more time to adapt to this world and working in a tight-knit community. Erika had been used to just taking care of Star and herself.

"Good idea. We shouldn't be too long though. We need to help out with camp and figure out what we are going to do. I need to go find my mom too." Erika started to stammer with her mind full of plans.

"Slow down, babe. Your mom is alive and well. She is down in the Lotus camp, I have already seen her. Let's just enjoy the day. All our problems will be here when we get back. Trust me," Vince said with a certainty in his voice. He needed a calm day and wanted Erika all to himself.

"You have seen her and she's alive? Well, that makes me feel better. You're probably right. Let's get moving so we don't get stuck doing projects here." Erika was feeling antsy now after her morning of lazy snuggling. She wanted to get moving and do something.

"I know I'm right," Vince said hugging her tightly.

"What do you want me to pack up?" Star asked Erika, trying to be as helpful as possible.

"We are traveling light today, Star, so don't worry about packing; just go rest till we are ready to go," Erika replied. She was concerned about Star's leg and didn't want her to overwork it. "We'll just bring some of that dried horsemeat to munch on."

"G-man found me a good walking stick to lean on yesterday so I'll go get that and Dexter, and I will meet you guys outside." Star had taken over watching out for Dexter. She just wanted to feel useful. She loved Erika so much for rescuing her that she was more than ready to accept her new family as her own. Caring for Dexter was a job that needed to be done constantly, and she knew she could fill that role perfectly.

"Okay, we'll be out in a second," Vince replied. As the kids left, he grabbed Erika and started to fondle her softly.

"Knock it off, you silly man," Erika jested.

"I can't help it. You are so beautiful and I missed you so much; I don't think I'll ever be able to get enough." Vince had a handful of her breast.

"Well, we don't have time for that now," Erika said with her eyes full of love. "The kids will be waiting and the whole camp will hear us."

"Oh, let them hear. I just want my beautiful woman." Vince grabbed Erika and held her close. He gave her a soft kiss and they embraced. The energy between them was palpable and it swirled around them.

"Okay, we need to go," Erika said forcing herself away from him. She was trying to focus on the task at hand and said lightly, changing the subject, "I think I will take Kit with us. We may be able to find some grass for him to munch on along the way."

"Good idea. There's not much grass left around camp but the land is rebounding between here and the Georgetown River camp," Vince replied.

The two exited the tent and greeted the people that were still hanging around the smoldering fire. Most of the camp was off helping accomplish one task or another. Everyone pitched in readily to help ensure the community's survival. Joan was still there cleaning up the morning mess.

"Where are you guys headed?" she asked, noticing that they were carrying packs.

"We are going for a little hike so we can do some much-needed catching up," Erika responded with a wink. "Have you seen Greg around this morning?"

"Yeah, he is over organizing some supplies," replied Joan. "That guy has the hookups. He has stocked up all kinds of goodies."

"Yeah, he has always been a rather resourceful individual, to say the least. Would you let him know where we are when you see him and let him know we should be back within a couple of hours?" Erika didn't want to waste any time traipsing through the whole camp.

"Sure, no problem, do you guys need anything to eat? I think I can still salvage a little food from breakfast." Joan wondered.

"No, we never were very big breakfast eaters and with so little food around, I don't know why we should start now," Erika answered with a sarcastic grin.

The couple walked over and put the leather bridle on Kit. They didn't bother with the saddle because they were having a leisurely day. Ripper ran about their feet happily dancing with the excitement of a new adventure. Since Erika had returned to the family, he had rarely left her side. They used to joke about him being her shadow, and he instantly returned to his old routine upon her arrival. Dexter and Star were not far behind Ripper, and Erika convinced the kids to ride bareback on the horse. Erika thought it would be fun for them, but also Star would not stress her wound. Vince told her it was so that Dexter would not tire too quickly, and Star felt honored to be playing a part in the family game.

As they left camp, Erika was shocked at the landscape. This area was a place she had known so well. It had glistened with green grass during the winter months when the weeds would grow high, and then in the summer, it would turn golden as the sun sucked the life from the growth. The trees had grown tall and proud and cherry trees dotted the landscape. It was her home, and now it felt completely foreign. The earthquake had not been kind to the region. Great scars ripped through the ground, and what had not been destroyed by the shifting ground was burned in the fire that had smothered the area. They walked along quietly. Erika was trying to take it all in. The kids engaged in a quiet chatter about games they had been playing with the other kids in the camp. Vince could see the sense of awe in Erika's quiet gaze. He decided he would have plenty of time to explain it all when they stopped. He just wanted to hold her hand and be near her. Many days he had wondered if he would ever walk along with her again, and now here she was, glowing with curiosity.

It took them a couple of hours to reach the space that Vince had spoken of. It was a rock outcropping that used to sit next to the lake. Since the dam had broken and the river had returned to its natural state, it now overlooked the canyon and river once again. The old Auburn River camp was just barely visible from here if you knew where to look. An individual on watch had seen the explosion the day Erika had fled, but Vince had no idea at that point what had happened down there and that his wife had been involved in the activity. Everyone was scrambling for survival, and approaching the other camps, especially one in obvious turmoil, was not exactly a great idea. So the lookout had watched with curiosity and relayed the story when he returned to the Georgetown River camp.

The lookout space itself sat in the remains of a subdivision that used to dominate the area. Now, it was charred shells of homes that used to house a vibrant community. Survivors in the area had pilfered the remnants months ago and the silence was eerie. Erika recognized where they were. It used to be the backyard of one of their friend's houses. Great big pine trees and pomegranate trees had once stood here. Now it was just charred remains.

"Oh my gosh, baby. This was Jean and Barb's house," Erika exclaimed, shocked at the current state of the property.

"Yeah, it was. Now, it's their grave," Vince said solemnly. "They never made it out. It's a good lookout point though, so it is well used now. You can see a lot of the canyon from here, just like it was before they put the lake in. But you know, Erika, a lot of people didn't survive so let's not think about that now. Actually, it's better to just not think about that at all." Vince was desperately trying to avoid the negatives. He had been immersed in this desperate world and was accustomed to stepping over the world of the past, trying to remake some kind of a future. Today was not about that: it was about spending time together, thinking positively, and enjoying the precious time together as a family.

Nearby, there was a patch of land trying frantically to rebound after the demolition where some grass was growing. They got the kids off the horse and they let Kit graze there. Vince spread their blanket out on the rocks that overlooked the canyon and the river below. The kids were amazingly resilient. They laughed and played with Ripper, leaving Vince and Erika to chat in the sunshine. Vince and Erika sat down on the blanket and embraced. They couldn't get enough of each other. The months away had left them incomplete and now, together again, the two halves were whole.

"So," said Erika gently, "how did you and Dex survive this mess?"

CHAPTER 22

"LET'S SEE... WHERE do I begin?" said Vince. "I had talked with you on the phone when you dropped Dex and Ripper off at your mom's. Not long after that, I got off of work early because we wrapped up that job we had been working on. Remember we had been landscaping that guy's house with the Japanese tea gardens? So, I picked Dexter up from your mom's house. Your mom and I chatted. She was working on fencing that day, and I helped her a little with pulling some barbed wire. Afterwards, we went back home. It was a nice day, not too hot. Remember we had been doing all that watering, trying to keep our grass green? It was so long that I decided to go and mow it while Dex played in the yard. He and Ripper were running amuck, and then all of a sudden, it sounded like a train was coming. The noise was so loud; I heard it over the noise of the mower. I turned it off immediately, wondering what the heck was happening. Then it began shaking like I have never felt before. You could see the ground rippling like a wave and it shook violently. Dexter was over by the shed with Ripper and it was like we froze in time. The earth just kept rippling, wave after wave. Then, in a blink of an eye, the whole town, as well as our house, sank into the ground. It was all the old mining tunnels. They gave way to the movement and everything was devoured. Once all the buildings fell in, fires exploded from everywhere. Most of the propane tanks and gas lines blew, and it felt like a war zone.

"I had fallen into the ground with the house but Dexter was still up on the ground. He was next to that little crappy metal shed. It still stood immune to the shaking. I was knocked out when I fell in and woke up to Dexter's frantic yelling and Ripper's wet tongue. Ripper had run down into the hole to find me. Well, I was pretty shocked and beaten up by the fall, but I slowly climbed my way out of the hole, with Ripper's help."

As if he knew the two were talking about his heroic deed, Ripper ran up and danced around the two of them. He licked Erika as she petted him.

"That's because he is a good dog, aren't you?" Erika praised the animal.

"That day, I thanked the Lord many times that you talked me into getting that dog. It was horrible, Erika. Everywhere, you could hear the screams of dying people and the noise of explosions. I was in complete panic. The first thing I did was grab Dexter. I held him close as I ran around frantically trying to find and help anyone who survived, but I had no idea what to do and the screams began to fade. Honestly, I was scared to move. You had no idea what would fall into the ground or explode next. In the end, I only found four other survivors, and we rescued one man from under his house but he died soon after. It all seems like a blur now. A bad nightmare I can't wake up from. The devastation was so complete.

"The fires burned and spread. Dex and I, along with some other survivors, we didn't know them before the quake, emptied that little shed and stayed there for a few nights until it was obvious that no rescue crew was coming. We salvaged some rope from the wreckage and slowly began sifting through the rubble for anything of use but especially for food. I made Dex stay in the shed because I had never seen so many dead bodies, Erika, and I hope I never do again. That is an image that you can never erase, but there was nothing we could do for them so we just left them there.

"It wasn't too long before the stink of the rotting bodies was unbearable and the lack of water was becoming a real problem. We needed to get out of there, away from the death and near a good source of water. Then, the second quake hit and even more ground was being eaten by the gigantic sink hole. That was the last straw. I had to get Dex to someplace safe. We gathered what goods we could carry and began the long hike toward the lake. Along the way, we ran into a handful of people that had come to the same conclusion. The world was very different then. Smoke was everywhere, and it seemed like everything was in some state of burning. We did the best we could to pick our way along the small trails down to the lake.

I thought about you constantly. Wondering what had happened in Sacramento, but deep down, I knew you were still alive. Anyway, the closer we got to the lake, we realized the dam had broken and it was a river again. All I could think about was you, down there, and all that water coming your way. But I had to stay positive for Dexter. He had no idea about the implications of the dam breaking, and I wasn't about to tell him.

We found some other people from Greenwood that had survived as well, and Big John Green was there. I was feeling much better then. If anyone would know how to survive in this mess, it was him. We decided we would camp with him until I could find you. He looked very unsure that you had survived and urged me to consider the possibility that you had not, but I would have none of it. I knew you were alive. I could just feel it.

So we set up camp there and started putting together supplies for the group. That camp by the river is like one giant mud pit but at least there is water. We made contact with the Cool camp but with resources on such short supply, we decided to keep the groups separated. Big John and I set up snares. Some of them were so cool. I thought of you all the time because I knew you would have loved making them with us. Anyway, we also had some contact with that crazy Auburn group and decided we should set up guards to watch out for looters coming from that direction. I also made a trip over to Lotus to look for your mom. She is doing fine, well as fine as anyone is doing right now. You know her, the little mighty mouse. She decided to stay in Lotus with her neighbors, Bob and Cathy, because there are a bunch of survivors gathering there, and that camp is very well supplied. She begged me to stay with Dexter and Ripper, but I wanted to be close to the river because I knew, eventually, you would be coming that way, and you did! Thank God you finally did. Brett is down there with her. We saw him in Georgetown initially but he wanted to go to find your mom and set off that way immediately. She will be all right with Brett, so don't worry.

"That's about it. I have just been surviving, watching out for Dex, and digging the splinters out of my butt that I accumulated pining away waiting for you." He smiled big as he cracked a joke to lighten things up. "Oh God, I love you." Vince wrapped her up in a big hug as they stared out into the sunset that was fast approaching.

"Holy crap, babe, we have spent all day out here and where are Dex and Star?" Erika said surprised that time had slipped away so quickly.

"They are right over there with Ripper, munching on some of that meat we brought. I can't tell you enough how glad I am you talked me into getting that dog. Since you were gone, he totally attached to Dex and has been like his guardian angel," Vince said, staring off at the kids.

"Dex, Star, come on, let's start packing up," declared Erika.

CHAPTER 23

AS VINCE AND Erika stood up to go, there was that sound again. The sound they all feared, a sound like a train rumbling across the mountains. Their eyes were like saucers as they looked at one another. The sturdy grey rock they had been sitting on was quickly dislodged by the vigorous shaking and in a split second the couple leapt off of it as it tumbled down the canyon side into the ravine. They ran swiftly for the children and the horse that were huddled together in the scraggly grass. Vince grabbed Kit's rope as he began to spook from the fear of the earthquake and the commotion of the people. Erika huddled with the kids and the dog and waited for the shaking to cease.

Finally, the quake came to a halt. The world was transformed again. Houses and shells of homes that had burned in the last fire and had stood there a minute ago were now gone, completely eaten by the earth, or rattled into piles of ash. New fires had sprung up and the smell in the air was nauseating. A dreadful feeling poured over them like hot syrup.

"We have to get back to camp," yelled Vince.

Erika, still shocked, lifted the kids onto Kit, and without a word, they started quickly moving back toward the Cool camp. It took them longer than expected to get back because the trail they had used earlier had a whole new set of obstacles to contend with. Erika and Vince were exhausted when they looked up and saw more smoke on the horizon. As they got closer, they heard screams echoing through the air.

"Oh my God," cried Erika. "We need to help."

They started running toward the camp with Kit and the kids in tow. Ripper was directly beside Kit waiting for orders from his masters. The first thing they saw was that the medical tent was ablaze, and Ryan was running rapidly in and out with his patients over his shoulder. Other people were helping him, and with the whole camp on fire, they were just laying bodies all over the former parking lot.

"I can help them, Vince, make sure the kids and the animals are safe," Erika yelled as she sprinted toward the bodies lying on the pavement.

Besides the people they were hauling out of the medical tent, more people were carrying over bodies both dead and alive from the main camp. Ryan saw Erika and quickly instructed her to start assessing the people in the parking lot. Erika had trained as an emergency medical technician a long time ago but never used the training because having people's lives in her hands was too scary. Now, here she was, staring at rows of screaming, burnt, and bleeding people. Something inside her switched off, and she got straight down to business. She had Taylor from the Auburn River camp and Diana from the Cool camp there to help her.

They started going from body to body to see if it was alive and how they could help. Erika tried to shut off as much of her emotions as she could and barely even noticed if she knew the individual or not. The people that could be saved needed attention and the people that could not had to be left behind, even if she knew them or their families.

Ryan had saved as many supplies as he could from the medical tent before it collapsed into a ball of flames. As soon as the tent fell and there was nothing else he could do, there he was in the parking lot, directing the team to do what they could for the people that could be saved. He instructed Taylor to start hauling away the dead bodies and piling them over by the part of the medical tent that was now done burning. Erika and Diana followed Ryan's instructions, and he listened intently to the analyses of the bodies they had performed. They were all busy wrapping burns and cuts and splinting broken bones long into the night.

Vince had taken the kids up to the tent the Auburn River Group had set up, but that area had not been immune to the blaze and it had burned as well. Richard, Joan's husband, was there watching his son Tyson as well as a group of other kids from both camps.

"Just leave them here, Vince, and go help," said Richard frantically. "They need all the help they can get."

"Are you sure, Rich? Are you all right? Where is Joan?" Normally Joan was the one watching the kids and Vince was full of questions.

"Look, leave the kids. I'm okay, but Joan... she... well, she's down at the medical area," Rich replied with fear in his eyes.

"Oh... sorry... okay, I'll be back." Vince didn't know what to say, so he tied up Kit and got the kids down. He gave them both a kiss and instructed Ripper to stay with Dexter.

He ran down toward the intense fires burning in town. It was chaos down there. The tents had been a great shelter but didn't do well when the quake hit. Candles had been lit inside the tents as the evening closed in. When the tents collapsed, they fell on the candles and lit on fire. The summer had been so long and dry, the fire was just jumping from one tent to the next. Vince was standing in a daze, wondering what to do, when Greg saw him.

"Hey, Vince, come help me get my supplies out of my tent," screamed Greg.

They ran through the burning mess. The buildings that had remained were now all burning down. It was only a matter of time before the fire stretched out to the unburned tents that had been pitched behind them.

"Where is the water, Greg? Why is no one fighting this?" Vince wondered.

"The well caved in, in the quake, Vince. There is no water. Our drinking water won't put this out, and we would have no water then," Greg said flatly.

Greg had gathered a fair amount of canned goods, liquor, blankets, and other supplies. Vince and Greg loaded all they could into blankets and left to go pile it by Erika's stuff in the cart. Greg's old dog came along with them and by the time they returned, the tent was gone.

The full black of night was fast approaching, and the fires were dying down. Everyone who had made it out gathered over in the medical area, trying to do what they could for the injured and see what had happened to their loved ones. Vince immediately noticed Erika when he walked up. Even covered in crusty blood and sweat, she was the most beautiful girl in the world to him. She looked exhausted to the point of passing out.

"Greg, I'll catch up with you later," Vince said as he headed toward Erika.

Vince walked over to her and wrapped her up in a big hug. Erika had been lost in thought and the act of helping. She hadn't even begun to process the reality of the situation when Vince appeared and hugged her; she broke down. She was crying and her legs gave out. Vince cradled her in his arms and carried her over to a quiet corner.

"It's okay, baby, it's going to be okay," Vince repeated to her over and over while he rocked her in his arms.

"No, it's not, Vince," Erika sobbed. "Joan is dead, Mike is dead, Kim is dead, Greg's dad, Cliff, is dead, and so many others. The pile just got bigger and bigger! All those people we were just hanging out with last night! And they were the lucky ones. So many others are burnt to a crisp but still alive. What can you do for them when they are lying in a parking lot? Ryan is doing the best he can but there are just so many, and so little medicine, that some died while they were waiting for help; it was horrible. Maybe if we would have been here…" Erika started to say.

Vince broke in, "Now, don't even start that, Erika. Things happen and God had us right where He wanted us to be. Our babies are safe so just stop. I love you. Just relax now. There is nothing more you could have done and nothing more you can do now."

Erika closed her eyes as the adrenaline left her body. She fell asleep in Vince's arms. Vince picked her up and started the walk back to where he had left the kids. Greg, his eyes full of tears, was already back there with Richard, both sharing in each other's pain. The other survivors had gathered there as well. The group gathered as many blankets as they could and made a huge sleeping area for everyone. They would all be sleeping under the stars tonight. In their exhaustion, there was no need for anything else. Vince laid Erika down with Dexter and Star, who were already asleep. He lay down next to her, covered his family with a blanket, and let the painful evening slip away as he fell asleep.

CHAPTER 24

THE NEXT MORNING was a very different day. There was no noise of hustle and bustle. All of the survivors in camp were solemn from the events of the day before. You could hear screams from the medical area as people who had passed out from the excruciating pain began to wake up to the hell that awaited them. Even the children were quiet and sat talking tentatively amongst themselves.

Vince had awoken before Erika and was sitting with Greg cooking something in a can. Erika got up feeling very stiff, and she was still all crusty with dried blood. Erika really didn't know what to do. Every day seemed so different from the one before. All she could really be sure of was that she was alive and with her family. She sent a silent prayer to God thanking him for returning her to her family and begging him for their safety.

"Good morning, baby," Vince whispered quietly. He had seen her waking up and wanted to go and hug her.

"Good morning," she responded sheepishly.

Vince hugged her tight, and she never wanted to let go. Everything was so messed up and their love felt so right; she wanted to close her eyes and stay there forever.

"There's a little water in that plastic bottle over there but use it sparingly, it's all we have," Vince directed as he pulled away from her to examine her and make sure all the blood on her was someone else's and not hers. "We are going to have to do something about that," he said as he looked at her crusty condition. "I assume once everyone wakes up, we will talk about what to do next. So, get some water and clean your face and come and eat some yummy creamed corn breakfast," Vince said sarcastically.

"Sounds great," Erika countered his sarcastic tone.

She went over and poured a little water in a bowl. As she splashed it on her face and rubbed it on her arms, she stared absently at the bowl as it began to turn red from the blood melting off her skin. She couldn't believe this life. It seemed so unfair that she would have to endure this fate. It seemed like just yesterday they would have been safe at home staring at a TV or a computer. Maybe playing video games with Dex or harvesting vegetables from the garden. They would have been worried about not having enough money to go on vacation, or buy that new car they wanted. It was like a nightmare she could not wake up from. All of a sudden, there was a commotion amongst the quiet of the grieving camp. Erika snapped out of her daydream, finished up her cleaning, dumped the water on the ground, and went to see what was going on.

As she approached Vince, she saw that Big John had arrived. She hadn't seen him since before the disaster, and even though he had lost a lot of weight, he looked really good. His stocky legs had turned to pure muscle and his brownish-gray hair was disheveled.

"Big John!" Erika yelled. "So great to see you." She ran over and gave him a big hug.

He had always been like a big teddy bear, and he lifted her up and swung her around in a circle.

"I had my doubts, Erika. I really did, but here you are. It's a miracle," he said in his gruff voice.

"You can't stop this girl," Erika jested back with him.

"But your will was tested. Wasn't it? Look at you." Big John had stood back to look at her and had her chin in his gigantic hand. He was turning her head back and forth examining the scars that now riddled her neck and stretched up behind her ears. She had done her best to get clean, but with the limited water supply, some blood and dirt had stuck in the ripples of her scars and made them look more pronounced.

"I bet you have some story to tell," he mused as he assessed her.

"Oh no, not again, Big John, it is a long and difficult one to tell," she exclaimed, not wanting to relive the experience every time she ran into someone she knew.

"We don't have time for stories right now anyway. I wish we did, but it looks like you guys got hit hard, and we didn't do much better." He had let her go and was now addressing the group.

"We got freaking screwed, man," Greg said point blank. "Half of the camp is dead, including my father; six people survived with horrible wounds, but we lost our water supply so they have nothing to drink. The fires ripped through our tents, our supplies, and we have about ten more orphaned kids. This is so jacked up!" Greg was usually so calm and jovial, but this last hit and the loss of his father had rocked him hard.

"Calm down, Greg, that's not gonna get us anywhere," Vince snapped.

"Don't tell me to calm down. I'm not calming down. We are screwed, man." Greg was coming unglued now.

The crowd gathering was getting bigger. Erika shot Richard, who was still caring for the children, a sideways look, and he started to shuttle the children off to a quiet corner of the camp. Star would not budge, and she came and sat quietly with Dex, a little ways behind Erika.

"He's right," yelled someone from the crowd. "God's wrath is upon us. This is the end of the world."

"We are all gonna die," yelled someone else. Everyone was quickly unraveling and this situation was getting out of control.

Vince pulled Greg away and started to talk sense to him. Greg had been a charismatic leader, and without him, this group was losing faith, fast.

Erika stepped up on a stump. "Look, everyone, I know this sucks and there is nothing we can do about it. I thought I was dead many times before this but here I am. Humans have been tested by God many times in the past and here we are! If we give up, we are dead, but we are not going to give up. Are we?" she questioned the crowd.

"No," responded some folks.

"*Are we?*" Erika questioned again.

"No!" more people responded this time in a more spirited tone.

"Now we have to decide what to do next. We can't stay here with no water, so let's discuss what to do. Any suggestions?" Erika wanted to include the whole group so no one felt like they didn't have a say.

"Let's go with Big John to the Georgetown River camp. There is water there." It was Ryan the doctor. He was super-concerned about the need for water for his patients.

"Well, hold on now," said John. "I was about to explain before I got interrupted." He shot Greg a sideways look. "Our camp fared better than this one, but we flooded badly. Water came down the river so fast it washed away most of our tents and supplies, but we saved everyone."

"See, we are going to die, everyone one of us," came a voice from the crowd. This time Erika picked out who it was. It was Bob Hawthorne, the moonshine maker. *He was probably drunk already*, she thought.

"Bob, I thought we agreed that kind of talk was getting us nowhere," Erika snapped at him and most of the crowd glared at him. He quietly fell back behind some other folks. He was perfectly happy to speak out when he was anonymous but singling him out made him shrink.

"So, what are you thinking, John?" Erika knew he hadn't finished talking before he was interrupted, again.

"I am thinking we should get out of California. Maybe it isn't as bad on the other side of the mountains. There's no way to know for sure, but let's face it, the coast is gone and who knows when those quakes will stop. We haven't received any help from the East so something must be going on there too, but it can't be as bad as this," John finished.

This is why Big John had come, to get Vince and Erika and leave. He had not planned on taking all these people, or facing all this commotion.

"Where would we go? I've always lived in California," a voice from the crowd questioned.

"I think he's right. Who cares where we go? We need to get the hell out of here," another voice yelled in a panic.

"All right, all right, everyone," Erika broke in. "Let's not get all excited again. Obviously, this gives us some food for thought. It's clear we need to leave here so I think our first stop should be the camp down in Lotus. Hopefully, they fared better than either of our camps. Even if they didn't, they have water and the injured people Ryan is caring for won't survive long without it. Let's go pack whatever stuff we can and make some kind of stretchers for the wounded. Whether you stay here in California or leave with us is an individual's decision, so go pack your stuff and think about it." Erika had no idea how she ended up in this leadership role but she desperately wanted to disperse the crowd so she could talk privately with Vince, Greg, and John.

As the crowd was dispersing, there was another commotion as people started to fend off a raggedy man that had come up out of the canyon. No one had been on lookout and his approach was startling. He was asking for Erika. The crowd began to part as he was ushered over to where she was. Some of the crowd left, but most of them remained. They were curious about who this man was and why he was here asking for Erika.

Vince and Greg didn't like the look of this man and posted up quickly in front of her to protect her from this crazy, looking guy. Vince couldn't help but wonder what this guy had in mind for his wife. Vince and Erika had usually been side by side in the past and each knew each other's friends well.

"Where is Erika? I have to talk to her," the deranged man pleaded insistently.

"Look, buddy, I don't know who you are but—" Vince began to fend him off but was interrupted.

"Harold… Harold Duncan, is that you," Erika questioned in a shocked voice. She began to see through the dirt-layered face, the light brown eyes that looked so much like Henry's, his father. His strawberry-brown hair was smacked down to his head and it looked as though dried blood held it in place.

"Oh my God, Harold, what happened to you? Vince, go get Ryan, he needs a doctor." Erika was scrambling to get past Vince and Greg to Harold and make sure he was okay. Vince was still blocking the two from one another in a defensive pose. "Vince," Erika yelled, breaking his glare at the man. "This man's father saved my life. This is Henry's son. If it weren't for his father, I would not be here at all. Can't you see he needs help? Please, go get Ryan."

"I'm on it," Vince replied. Now that Vince was filled in on the full story, he didn't hesitate to fulfill his wife's wishes and ran off down the hill to find Ryan.

"Here, Harold, sit down over here," Erika said in a concerned voice. There was a stump they had been using as a seat for eating and Erika led Harold over to it. "Now just relax and rest for a minute. Ryan will be here soon and—"

Harold cut her off. "I can't rest, Erika. I have to go," he stammered starting to get up.

"Go? Go where? And where are Henry and Carol and Betsy and the kids?" Erika was very curious now. He was all alone. There was no way Harold would have left them. They had been well supplied with food, weapons, and horses. Now here he was alone and in rags.

"That's what I'm trying to tell you. That Auburn group, they attacked Mom and Dad's house. They took everything from me: my wife, my kids, my parents, all the supplies, all the horses. It was horrible. They caught us off guard. I tried to fight their leader, Doug, I think his name is, and I was winning for a while but then one of his men cracked me over the head and I guess they left me for dead. I woke up and they were all gone, and so were all the supplies." Harold was in tears now looking desperately at Erika.

Just then, Vince came back with Ryan. Ryan had a few of the precious medical supplies with him. As Ryan stepped in front of Harold to treat him, Erika stepped back to fill Vince in on what was going on.

"That sucks, baby, but I don't know what we can do. We just got wiped out and we have to go find your mom." Vince was just trying to face the facts.

"I know, Vince, but we have to do something. These people saved me. They didn't have to but they took pity on me, cared for me, and supplied me for my journey home. Henry even gave me Kit. I would not be standing in front of you now if it weren't for Henry and Carol. Now they need me. I can't just walk away, Vince. I have to do something." Erika's voice was firm.

"Erika…" Vince's voice was more sympathetic now. He had a feeling she was not going to budge on this. "We don't even know if they are still alive."

"They are alive!" Harold had been listening to their conversation as Ryan was shaving his head and stitching up the huge gash on it. "I have been watching my family being held hostage by those animals. I have just been waiting for a chance to rescue them. This last quake really rocked that Auburn compound, but there are still too many men in there for one man to take on. I can't do this alone but I will try if I have to."

"You said they took your supplies too?" It was Rob Burton speaking up. He had stayed behind to see what was going on. Rob used to be in the military and knew it was best to always gather as much information as possible in any given situation.

"Yeah, they did," Harold answered. He was almost appalled that Rob was more interested in the supplies than his family.

"Vince, I don't know if you noticed, but supplies are running really low around here. I've been doing the math and I don't know how we are going to move all these people without more supplies. Those guys at that Auburn compound have really been busy stocking. We could use all that."

Greg stepped in to protect his friend. "Rob you're always looking for a fight. What if we all die? Then all those people we are trying to save would really be in trouble."

Greg's friend Denton spoke up next. "Look, Greg, I know we've been friends for a long time, but I got to agree with Rob on this one. We can't make it very far without more food. Most of what we had left was lost in the fire. We are running out of options."

"We can always rummage the houses that are left along the way," Greg countered.

"Oh, you mean the ones we pilfered last month. There's nothing left, Greg, face it." Denton was right, even though Greg didn't want to admit it.

"Regardless of our supply situation, I am going to save Harold's family or die trying." Erika was just as irritated as Harold that the conversation had gone from rescuing good people to getting more supplies, and her mind was set.

Vince knew there was no changing her mind now, so he simply replied, "Then I'm going with you. Someone has to keep an eye on you." He gave her a wink.

"Then so am I," said Greg.

"I'm in," said Rob.

"I'm in," Denton chimed in.

Big John had been standing off to the side while this drama played out. He finally stepped up, "Okay guys, it looks as if you have some stuff to take care of. My mission is to get us out of California. I am going to go back to the Georgetown River camp and see what they want to do. I will let them know that we are leaving and see how many of them feel the same way. Then I am going to go scout a clear route to get us out of here. I will meet you at the Lotus camp after you have rescued Harold's family and got the supplies. God knows we are going to need them too."

"Sounds like a plan, John," Vince replied. He really wished they could just be going with him now, but he understood why Erika felt the way she did, and there was no way he was leaving her again. "We will meet you at the Lotus camp. That way, we can get Erika's mom and Brett and get out of here."

"Take care of yourself and your woman, Vince," John said with concern in his eyes. "You know what kind of men they are down there. Just be careful."

"We will be. Don't worry. Ain't nothing slowing me down," Vince said with a smile. He was scared and knew exactly what kind of evil men were down there, but he covered it with sarcasm.

Big John left, and after explaining the entire situation to the rest of the camp, they had a group of volunteers willing to risk their life for this mission. There were eleven of them in total. Erika, Vince, Greg, Rob, and Denton had heralded the call for volunteers. Taylor, Randy, and Tom from the Auburn River Group were all young men, but they were strong and ready to take direction. Steve and Jimmy D, also from the Auburn River Group, stepped up as well. They were ready for some payback after the last clash with the Auburn Gang. The last volunteer was Michelle from the Cool camp. Although she was kind of spacey, she was a great shot with a rifle and was a welcomed addition to the group. Even though Richard really wanted to go, in the end, he decided to stay behind with the children and help lead the group to the Lotus camp. There were not too many able bodies left so he would be crucial to that group. After the attack, the two groups would rally in Lotus, where Big John would find them. Then they could all decide their next move after that.

Rob, having military experience, led the attack group. He picked Harold's brain for all the information he could gather about the Auburn Gang's camp. How did they patrol it? Where are their traps set? When did they eat? Where did they get water from? Did they have power? Rob asked a flurry of questions that Erika would have never even considered. This was just as well because while Rob was forming an attack plan, Erika and Vince were busy packing up Kit and his cart. Star would be leading Kit and Dexter was going to ride in the supply cart. Richard would keep an eye on her though, to make certain she was not stressing her injured leg too bad. The pace would be slow because of all the injured people they had to carry, so they all had faith that Star would do fine. Ripper was going with the kids because he could severely hamper the attack if his anxiousness got the better of him. Plus, he would protect those kids with all his being so Erika knew that was the best place for him. They loaded Greg's old dog, Dakota, in the cart with Dex as well. Kota wasn't looking too hot and they wondered how long he would be able to keep surviving in this world.

It felt really wrong to Erika and Vince to be sending the kids off on their own. But they would be well cared for. They had gained a lot of faith in Richard and the group of good folks they had met up with in Cool. Plus, they were headed for Lotus, where Erika's mom was still camped. She would find them and protect them. When Erika had the horse ready to go, she turned and watched Dexter and Star playing in the sunlight. The kids would play. No matter what was going on and how scary the world got, the kids would play. They were so innocent, aware of the world, but not yet fully conscious of its implications. Erika's eyes began to sting with tears. She jumped as Vince wrapped his arm around her. He stood next to her, staring. It was a moment to remember. If she still had a cell phone that worked, she would have grabbed it to capture the moment in a digital image. Those days were gone now.

The two vigilant parents took the time to play a short game of tag with their children. They had no idea when the next time they would get the opportunity to play innocently with their children would be, or if they ever would at all. They ran and laughed. Others joined in the game. Life was going so incredibly wrong, the fun was almost like an addictive drug. You just couldn't help yourself. Other people in the camp stopped whatever they were doing and watched, but the game came to an end all too quickly. Rob appeared ready to head out and the groups were quickly directed off to the areas they were meeting at before departing.

Erika and Vince hugged Dexter and Star as hard as they could and tried to appear positive and optimistic, even though tears were forming in their eyes from the fear of never seeing them again. They tried to savor every sight and smell of the children and hold it tight in their memories. They choked back the tears as they kissed good-bye, but each one knew deep down inside what had to be done. The kids ran off to join Richard and head out for the Lotus camp. Ripper was unsure which way to go, but Erika told him to stay with the children and he hesitantly went off to fulfill his job.

CHAPTER 25

VINCE AND ERIKA dragged their feet as they went to join Rob and the others and gather their weapons. Vince had brought Erika's bow, a quiver full of arrows, her knife, and her rifle with a fanny pack full of bullets. She tucked the knife into the sheath attached to the fanny pack and clipped the pack around her waist. She snapped the quiver to the bow and put the bow over her shoulder. Her hands began to sweat as she held tight to the rifle in disbelief of what they were about to do. Vince carried a crossbow that John had given him with a quiver full of bolts, his knife, and his rifle with a similar fanny pack full of bullets. Michelle and Randy were given the most accurate sniper rifles the group had because they were the least physical individuals and the best shots. They also had knives in case they ended up getting up close and personal with an enemy. In fact, everyone carried a knife, even if it was just an old steak knife. They were not only good protection; they were also convenient eating utensils while they were traveling.

Handguns were not something that the people from the group headed for Lotus were willing to give up but Greg, Harold, Denton, Rob, and Steve all had theirs from before the big quake. Ammo was limited but the amount they had would have to do. Richard had given his pistol to Taylor in exchange for a nice rifle. Besides the rifles that Erika, Vince, and Rob carried, the group had given up three more to the cause, and Greg, Jimmy D, and Steve carried those. Tom only had his crossbow but he was very happy about this because he was very confident in his accuracy and speed. There were some other bows and crossbows that were handed out among the group but, again, ammo was the issue so every shot had to count.

When they were all loaded and ready to go, they turned and watched Cool become a ghost town as the other group moved off slowly toward Lotus. There was a very grave mood as they started the descent down the canyon. Erika was still surprised at the level of destruction these quakes had caused. Great rock ledges and ravines that had seemed so strong and indestructible were leveled.

"You okay, baby," Vince asked. He had been watching her mind wander.

"Oh yeah, just another day in paradise," she replied sarcastically. There had been a song they often sung when they were at home all cozy in their house. It referred to all kinds of domestic problems but how it was all okay and it was "just another day in paradise."

He caught the reference immediately and chuckled. "We can still turn back, you know. We don't have to do this," Vince said. He was still trying to give her an out.

"Yeah, we do," she replied flatly.

"I know we do, but I was just wishing that you might run away with me and we could just stay in each other's arms and be safe forever." He could at least vocalize his dream.

"So do I, but we both know there is nowhere to run to. Carol and Henry need us and our group needs these supplies. We just have to keep going." She was trying to convince herself as much as him.

"Well, at least if we are going to die, we will do it together." He was trying to be sarcastic but deep in the recesses of his mind he believed it might be true.

"You got that right, guys. At least we will die together," Greg teased. He had been listening in and came up behind them. He wrapped his arms around their shoulders.

They had all been friends for so long and the emotions were running hot. They all laughed to relieve the pressure. It was contagious, and the group all laughed at themselves and the task before them. Soon, they were all quietly chatting as they continued their descent. The chatting quickly came to a halt when Rob, who had been scouting out in front with Harold, returned at a quick trot to the group.

"The old river camp is right down there," Rob whispered. "There will surely be scouts out there on the opposite ridge. This is where we split up. I'm going to take Jimmy D, Steve, and Tom, and we are going to go through the river camp to take out any scouts and then go straight at the main gate. We will put on a great show with these pipe bombs I made. In the meantime, Harold says he knows where they are keeping the prisoners. He and Denton will circle around the top of the canyon and sneak in from the back. Erika, Vince, Greg, and Taylor, you guys go with them and protect their rear entry. Randy and Michelle, you will go too. Harold says there is an old juvenile hall with a tower still standing. You will have to take care of the guards posted there. Once you take out the guards, post up there. You can see the whole compound from up there and you will be able to provide cover for us all. We will attack at nightfall. As soon as you hear the first explosion, you guys move in. Any questions?" Rob had laid the plan all out. It sounded easy enough. The adrenaline was pumping now. No one but Rob had combat experience and everyone's eyes had a wild determination in them.

"Let's do this!" yelled Greg.

"Shhh… remember, keep your eyes open for guards and move quietly," Rob warned.

Rob and his group moved off to the left. They were going to cross the river closer to where the dam had once stood. Erika's group moved off to the right. Erika knew as well as Harold where the guards overlooking the canyon were. As they cleared the last of the tree line, they saw the destroyed camp off to the left. They slid down the dried-up hillside toward the river. They crossed it fairly easily. It was the end of September and the end of summer; the mountain water supply was low. Especially now that Mother Nature had destroyed the dams and the natural water flow had returned. The last dam to go went in the last quake. That is what had flooded the Georgetown River camp. Because of that recent flooding, they did stick in the mud around the river but it was managed easily enough. Now they were out in the open, though, and everyone was on high alert.

As they began to climb the other side of the canyon, an intense rumble started again and the ground began to shake. The group clutched to one another and waited as the rumbling shook them to the bone. Vince grabbed Erika and held her close. Erika's thoughts immediately went to the caravan headed to Lotus, and she said a silent prayer for her children en route. Soon enough, the rumbling ended.

"Now what?" said Taylor in a shaky voice.

"We keep going," answered Erika. "We have to. Too many people are counting on us and the wheels are in motion now."

"Let's go then," said Harold. He was a man on a mission, and he turned to continue climbing the hill. He was stopped by an extremely muscular, short, stocky man.

"Stop right there, guys." He sounded really cocky and confident. "Well, well, what's going on here?" he said in a grumble.

The man had a rifle over his shoulder and a handgun pointed at Harold.

"Hey, I know you. You're that guy Doug fought in that barn. Oh, Doug's gonna love to see you. You knocked out one of his teeth," he said with clear recognition in his voice. "He's been taking it out on your lovely daughter ever since," he sneered at Harold. Then he addressed the group, "Now you all are going to put down your weapons if you want your friend to live. Just put them—"

Before he could finish his sentence, a bullet from Greg's gun ripped through the man's head, splattering blood and bits of brain onto Harold's face. The man had been so used to having the upper hand all the time he never saw it coming.

"Whoa, Greg!" screamed Erika.

"What? He would have killed us." Greg was almost as surprised as Erika by his instant action.

"Yeah, but you could have shot him somewhere else. We don't know if he was the only guard. We could have gotten some good info out of him. Plus, who knows who heard that shot." Erika was trying to stay sensible.

"Shot him somewhere else? Where and with what guns once he had all our weapons? Sorry, next time I'll just let him shoot one of us!" Greg was getting irritated with her reaction.

"It's okay; I'm sorry. This is just crazy. Let's just go, quick." Erika was listening to herself and wondering what she was even talking about.

The group moved quickly up to the tree line where they met another man running toward the sound of the gun.

"Oh crap," he yelled as he slid to a stop in front of the war party.

"Hello," Greg said calmly as he grabbed the man by the collar and held his gun to the man's head.

All Erika could picture was a hole in the man's head and brains everywhere. "Wait, wait, Greg!" she yelled.

"I am, just calm down, girl," Greg smoothly replied.

"Who are you people? Please don't kill me," pleaded the man.

"Are you the only one out here?" yelled Greg.

"Yeah, it was just me and Bill. When I heard the shot, I thought Bill killed an animal or intruder or something so I came running. Please don't kill me," he pleaded again as he glanced down the hill and saw Bill's lifeless body.

"There, are you satisfied?" Greg asked Erika.

"Yes," Erika responded.

"Good," replied Greg as he pulled the trigger and put a bullet through the man's head.

" Hold up, Greg! We are not killers!" Erika screamed at Greg.

"Look, Erika, today we are. We are killers. We are going to kill or be killed. What were we going to do with him? Wake up, girl, what do you think we are doing here? You all better wake up." He looked in the eyes of everyone in the group. "If we are going in there, it is to save those people they took as prisoners. It is to take their supplies for our group, and it is to kill anyone who gets in our way. Now if you can't do that, turn back now, because that's reality, folks."

Erika knew he was right and they would all have to flip that switch inside themselves. She had killed before and now she would have to again. Everyone in the group did a mental check and forged on again. They all had faced reality and knew what must be done. There was no more chatting, no more smiling, it was all business as they crept through the tree line that Erika had traversed when she had skirted around the Auburn compound not so long ago. Now they were going to attack it and kill those bastards.

They passed the apartments where Erika had taken refuge and the stench of death rose through the air as they neared the compound. Smoke was in the air and the group realized the compound was in utter disarray from the last earthquake. Finally, a stroke of luck from the quakes.

They had to cross what used to be an interstate highway to get to the hill behind the compound and nature was reclaiming it all. Erika marveled at the marked difference as they went. The group was ready for anything as they mounted the hill in the rear of the compound and kept their eyes fixed on the tower. Night was falling quickly and their vision was becoming very limited, but their sense of smell was heightened and it was being ambushed by a sickening stench of death. Suddenly, they realized it was not deformed ground they were stepping over, it was dead bodies. This area had once been an old Chinese graveyard hundreds of years ago and now it seemed the people from the compound had been using it for this purpose again, except they were just piling the dead bodies here. Most of the bodies were headless. This gang had been putting the heads on spikes to ward off intruders, and the scene was utterly gruesome even in the dim light. Randy held Michelle as she threw up again and again.

"Try hiding in the bodies for days," Harold said with a shudder. "Come on, let's just get through this." In order to find out the whereabouts of his family, that was exactly what Harold had done. He had hid amongst the bodies. He had watched the camp and found out their secrets, and he had been willing to endure all this decay to do it.

"Keep your eyes on that tower. Remember, that's where we are headed," Greg said, trying to keep himself and the group focused. He had never seen anything like this and wasn't doing very well himself.

All of a sudden, they heard an explosion.

"Oh crap, that's Rob. We got to get to that tower, now!" said Vince.

Then *bang!* A shot rang out from the tower, followed by shots at the front gate of the compound. The team broke out into a sprint for the tower, and they were up the stairs in no time. Vince shot a bolt from his crossbow straight through the sniper's heart as he kicked the door open to the lookout tower. The sniper had never seen it coming. They heard, *boom, boom*, as two more explosions rang out from the gate. The team, from their vantage point, could see the group from the Auburn compound manning the front gate. They would never suspect an attack from behind.

"Michelle, Randy, you two stay here and start blasting those guys down there," Greg instructed. "Taylor, you take this rifle and guard that door down there. Don't let anyone up these stairs! Let's go guys!" he yelled to the rest of the group.

The adrenaline was thick in the air now and they had completed step one. Taylor took up his post at the door as the group made their way toward the rear of the compound. It had all looked so clear from the tower but now, as they neared the rear gates, reality began to set in. The camp was in utter chaos. The recent earthquakes had decimated this camp as well. There were fires everywhere and a wild look filled the eyes of the individuals inside. They heard a boom as another explosion rocked the front gate and then *bang, bang!* as Michelle and Randy began firing their rifles from the tower. Creeping closer to the rear gate, they could hear the confused chatter of the guards. They were discussing leaving their post to go help at the front gate. The attack team split up into two groups to flank the guards. With a silent signal from Greg, arrows from their bows sank into the hearts of the guards. Stealth was the key to the rear attack. They must not alarm the compound to their double-sided attack.

Taking lives was not getting any easier for Erika as she stumbled over their dead bodies and stared into their lifeless eyes.

"Come on, baby," Vince commanded as he grabbed her hand and dragged her along.

"Okay, we're in," said Harold in a wild voice. "The prisoners are over here on the left."

"And where are the supplies," demanded Greg.

"They are in a store house on the other side of the camp. Over there." He pointed to a building that used to be a supermarket.

Decisions had to be made fast.

"Okay, Erika, you go with Harold and Denton and get those people the hell out of here. Vince and I will go scope out the supplies and see what we can get."

Vince and Greg started picking their way through the camp as Harold, Denton, and Erika made a break to find Henry, Carol, and the rest of Harold's family. The fires were burning bright in the night, and Erika saw scared eyes peeking out of some of the tents that were not on fire. These folks weren't fighting, and they looked just as imprisoned as the people they were going to save.

Bang! went Harold's gun, as he shot a man coming at him with a spear.

"He was the prison guard. Come on, we are close!" shouted Harold.

Their noses filled with a putrid smell as they entered a building that at one time had housed restaurants and various other stores. It had been turned into a dungeon complete with chains hanging from the walls. *Bang!* went a rifle from the tower as a man that had come up behind Erika fell dead. Erika breathed a sigh of relief, knowing one of those teenagers had just saved her life.

"Whoa, that was close," Denton yelled to Erika, as he gave the snipers a big thumbs-up.

Inside the building, the room was filled with people. The rescuers all gasped as they entered surprised by the sheer amount of people in here. The prisoners were chained to the walls and sitting in piles of their own defecation. They looked thin and hopeless. The prisoners covered their heads and eyes, fearing the return of their captors and shrieking from the light.

"Betsy! Henry!" Harold shouted, searching the miserable victims for his family.

"Over here!" boomed Henry's loud voice.

Harold ran to his family.

"Denton, see if you can find some keys," Erika commanded as she left to follow Harold.

Erika found Harold holding his wife, Betsy, in his arms with his kids smiling as they gazed at their hero, their father.

"Denton is looking for keys," said Erika.

"Oh my God, Erika, is that you?" Henry's voice boomed again. He couldn't believe his eyes. He had wondered if she had made it home alive and now here she was rescuing him.

"In the flesh, Henry, you didn't think I would leave you here after all you did for me? Did you?" Erika teased.

"Praise the Lord," cried Carol. "These monsters have had us locked up in here like animals."

"Well, let's get you all out of here," declared Denton as he arrived with a ring full of keys. He pulled Erika aside as he handed Harold the key ring. "Erika, the guards heard shots over here, and they are headed our way."

"Erika, is that you?" whispered a weak voice down on the floor.

Erika looked down and saw Jaclyn White, from the Auburn River camp, lying in a heap. She had been captured when the camp was attacked. She was barely clothed and very bruised.

"Oh my God, Jaclyn, don't worry, we're going to get you out of here," Erika said frantically. "Denton, go guard the door, I'll be there in a minute."

"Save us too," shouted voices from all over the room.

"We are going to save you all, just sit tight," Erika shouted reassuringly.

By the time Erika got back to Harold, he had his family free and was working frantically with the keys to free the others.

"Good job, Harold, we have to save them all, but I have to go help Denton guard the door. The jig is up and they know what we are doing here." Erika was already headed toward the door.

"I'm coming too," Henry said insistently.

"All right, we can use the help," replied Erika as she handed him a handgun she had retrieved off of a dead guard.

When they got to the door, Denton was already firing at a group of men. They had posted up behind a barricade facing the door. Henry began to fire as well. Michelle and Randy were doing their best to defend the doorway. The gun fight raged on and neither side had a clear shot at one another.

"I don't know how much ammo they have but ours is running low," said Erika when the shooting paused for a moment.

Suddenly, Harold was behind them. "I got them all free, but I don't know how fast they can move. Some of them have been chained there for months."

"Well, get them moving and we'll cover you," Denton urged.

They began to fire a huge barrage at the men behind the barricade as the prisoners slipped out the door and ran toward the rear gate. When the last one was out, Erika, Denton, and Henry ran to follow them. All of a sudden, Henry fell forward as a bullet ripped through his shoulder and out his arm. Harold had been supplying some cover fire and saw his dad fall. Denton turned to cover Harold as he ran up and scooped up his father.

"Run, run!" screamed Denton as he was shot in the heart and fell dead at Erika's feet.

The group finally made it back to the rear gate. They had saved a lot of people, but it had come at a great cost.

"Harold, get these people back to the tower and wait there," Erika demanded.

"What are you going to do?" questioned Henry in a weakened voice. He had been hit but it was not a killer blow.

"I have to go back and find Vince and Greg. I will be okay. Just go!" she yelled at Henry, knowing he would object to her going alone.

To avoid any further protest, Erika turned and left before they could fully register her decision. She was alone in the dark, asking herself what she was doing running off into the heat of a battle alone, but Vince and Greg were in there. She knew where they had gone. She was also an able bodied fighter. She shouldn't just sit and wait for Vince and Greg to return when she could be in there, fighting or helping to relieve the group of some supplies.

Erika had reached the building that at one time had been a huge clothing store. Erika thought back to how new it had smelled inside, the grand spaces and the sight of the new items stacked wall to wall. The Auburn Gang had used this building's shell as a shelter for their power producing equipment. She could tell from the amount of makeshift wiring streaming from the roof. Off to the left of the building in the center, a communal fire was still burning. The tents that were surrounding them were in a state of total disarray. There were scared people still hovering unsure of what they should do. It appeared that all of the Auburn Gang's soldiers had now centered on the front gate and the explosions occurring there were coming at longer and longer intervals. Erika wondered if the men attacking the front were still alive, but if the gang's force was still centered there, they must be. Also, the snipers were no longer firing from the tower. Erika knew they were still alive but they were having the same problem she was having: ammo was running really low.

She crept by in the shadows, in between the tents surrounding the fire and the power building. She was super aware of any movement around her. She slipped past the store and was heading for the building that was at a right angle to the clothing store and stretched out to the left. There was a small parking lot entryway between the two buildings, just big enough for two cars to fit through. She hid next to the building and peeked her head out to check for activity before she crossed. It was dark and difficult to see, but it looked as if two dead bodies now stood guard over an abandoned gate. Fire light reflected off an arrow that was protruding out of one man's head. She chuckled a little and knew that Vince and Greg had definitely been this way. She moved across the pavement and turned to creep along the wall of the next building when all of a sudden a man was right behind her. He came out from the corner of the building. He must have watched Erika cross. Erika had heard his approach and quickly turned to face him. She recognized this man; he was one of the leaders of this group. The one she had seen driving the jeep while she was in hiding in the bushes with Star.

He had a gun in his hand and Erika had one in hers. In an instant, they both raised them up to the head of the other. As they fired, both shots missed as they simultaneously kicked the guns out of each other's hands.

"Oh, you're quick," the man said. Erika knew this was the guy. His name was Steve.

"Hi, Steve," Erika said defiantly as they circled one another.

"Smart too," replied Steve coarsely.

He threw a punch at her but Erika ducked it and countered his attack with a front kick straight to his jaw that sent him flying backwards. Erika grabbed her knife from its holster.

"Oh, you want to play! You're gonna pay for that, little girl!" Steve was pissed off now and bleeding from his mouth.

They circled one another again. Then, in a fit of rage, Steve lunged in to pierce Erika's heart but Erika flowed with his movement and dodged his attack. Steve looked down and saw the hilt of Erika's knife sticking out of his neck. He gasped desperately for air, and she reached up and pulled the knife from his neck. Blood began to bubble from his mouth and ran down his neck out of the gaping hole. His beady eyes stared into hers as he fell to his knees and then he fell flat on his face dead.

Erika stepped back to avoid his fall and sighed with relief, when she was suddenly grabbed from behind. She struggled and kicked but the sudden grab of this new attacker had taken her totally off guard. She slowly stopped struggling as the unknown individual buried the hilt of his gun in the side of her head. Blood ran down her head and her eyes closed.

CHAPTER 26

"**B**OSS, THE FRONT** gate is still holding and we have those two trapped in the supply room," said a strange voice.

"They haven't been captured yet?" Another voice said.

"No, but…" the first voice replied.

"But what?" said the second voice roughly.

Erika's sense of reality was slowly returning. She realized she wasn't dead but what had happened and where the heck was she?

"I want those two scumbags dead!" screamed the second voice.

"Okay, okay, boss, I'll get out there and take care of it myself," replied the first voice hastily.

"You're darn right you will… oh, look, our little pet is starting to wake up," said the second voice. He had noticed Erika starting to move.

"Just let me do her now, boss," said the first voice. Erika heard a click of a gun cocking.

"No, stupid, I've been waiting for this for too long to kill her quick. I'm gonna have some fun with this whore before she dies." Erika heard the man walking across the room. "Hey, little girl, you awake," he said harshly.

Erika slowly and painfully opened her eyes. They felt swollen and when she tried to move, she realized she was tied to a chair. Through the swollen slits she saw a darker-skinned man with a scar on the bottom of his chin staring right into her eyes. She knew him immediately; it was Doug Pennington, the leader of the gang.

"Well hello, sweetie. Comfy?" Doug said softly.

Erika didn't reply. She looked around the room. It was built from old building pieces that had fallen during the quakes. It was lavishly decorated with large area rugs on the walls and floors. The room was partitioned by a rug as well, and she could see that behind it was obviously a sleeping area. The room she was in held a huge desk with papers, and Dave, Doug's right-hand man, stood sheepishly along one wall. His blue eyes made contact with hers.

"Hey, I'm talking to you," Doug shouted in her face and spittle-splattered on her cheek. "Happy to see me, aren't ya?"

"Where am I?" Erika questioned.

"You're in my world now, little girl," Doug snapped back. "You don't know how much I've longed for you to be sitting right there in that chair." He backed off a little and began to pace in front of her. "You put on quite a show down there at the river. It was supposed to be an easy in and out, but no, you orchestrated a resistance. That was a nice touch, the exploding bridge. My brother died on that freaking bridge!" He was back in her face shouting at her. She saw his nasty sweat bead up on his face and then drip onto her body. "The horse was a great touch, very nostalgic, but easily traceable. I followed your tracks back to that junk heap of a barn and I took vengeance on those people. I should have killed them all, but I knew you would come to rescue them. Somehow,

I just knew if I set it up just right, you would come. And here you are. How lucky for me."

Reality hit Erika like a wave. This had all been a setup. They had captured Harold's family and left him alive because they knew he would find her. The truth was almost sickening. Erika turned white with rage.

"Screw you and your dead brother!" Erika snapped as the anger over his attack on Henry and Carol welled up inside her. She spit in his face. Doug punched her across her mouth causing her head to snap sideways and her chair to fall over. Blood poured from her mouth onto the floor. She could do nothing but lay there and wait for his next move.

"Just let me kill her now," Dave shouted as he bounded across the room. He drove his gun's barrel into the side of Erika's head.

"Knock it off, you stupid jerk." Doug smacked Dave across the head. "I told you I was going to savor this kill. Get yourself over to that supply room and kill those bastards. Now!" Doug shouted back at Dave

Dave left in a fury. Erika's eyes followed him as he left. She was terrified for Vince and Greg's safety. Erika heard the door slam as Doug abruptly set her back upright in the chair. She was face to face with him again.

"Now, where were we before that mouth of yours got you into trouble. Oh yeah, I was telling you all about how you lead me straight to that beautiful cache of supplies. So, my fiery little pet, what's your name?" Doug grabbed hold of her chin and looked straight into her eyes.

"Screw you!" Erika ripped her head out of his hand, and spat blood from her swollen mouth onto the floor.

"That can be arranged," Doug hissed at her. He reached down and ripped her shirt down the front. "Well, look at you. Those scars run all over your body. What the hell happened to you?" When Doug had seen her scarring, he was taken back a little. His surprise caused him to step a couple of paces away from Erika, giving her some room to breathe.

She knew her situation was grim and she needed to think fast. It was obvious Doug was not in a hurry to kill her and spike her head somewhere along the wall. She figured if she could keep him talking, it would buy her time to be rescued, or rescue herself. Her face hurt, and she could feel it swelling more and more. At this point, she needed to play damage control. She had to survive; her kids were waiting.

"I made it out of Sacramento," she said flatly.

"You did what?" Doug couldn't believe what he was hearing. "Nobody made it out of there. We looked for survivors, all we found were bodies."

"Lucky for me," Erika commented under her breath.

"You know, you really should control that mouth of yours," he said. He was right in her face again with her chin in his hand. "I don't care if you made it through the gates of hell itself, I'll still kill you right now," he said in a surprisingly calm voice. He looked her up and down as he tilted her head from side to side in his hand. "Oh yeah, there's plenty that can still be done with you." His tongue licked his lips. "Nothing's really damaged here." His tone of voice made Erika's skin crawl.

Erika tried so hard to back away from him she ended up tipping the chair over backwards. This caused Doug to beat on her some more before he once again sat the chair upright.

"You are a spirited one, I have to give you that," said Doug with a chuckle. "You sure are making this fun." He was pacing back and forth in front of her again, obviously taking pleasure in tormenting her.

Both of Erika's eyes continued to swell, and she had sustained a nasty kick to the ribs. She checked the strength of the ropes at her wrists and felt the rope burn on her skin as she twisted her wrists back and forth. They were tight, and pain shot from just about every corner of her body. Her heart beat frantically. From outside, she could still hear an explosion now and again, and she could hear gunfire from every direction.

Doug saw her taking notice of the noise outside. "Don't worry, sweetheart, my boys will kill all those heroes that came with you and no one will come to save you now. You are all mine." Doug rubbed his hands together like he was getting ready to eat a gourmet meal. He watched her puffy eyes start to water. He knew he would break her soon.

Erika prayed he was not correct, but in the back of her mind, she had to wonder if he was. The plan had never been to conquer the whole compound. It was supposed to be so simple, get in and get out, save some people and get some supplies. Now here she was, stuck, and the most sickening part was this had been Doug's plan all along. He had expertly conceived the plan and it had worked. She had no idea that he would be expecting her. She acted on instinct to save her friends and had played right into his diabolical plot. Her mind was racing. *What should I do?* she wondered again and again. Should she appease him and try to survive until she could escape his grasp. She shook the thought from her head. Surrender had never been an option for her in the past, and she certainly wasn't going to give in now.

"So," Doug's harsh voice snapped her back to reality, "you escaped that sludge down there but obviously not unscathed." He was calm and curious now.

"Yes, and those people you took vengeance on, those wonderful people, they saved me. They found me and rescued me. They didn't lock me in a cage or make me a slave. They helped me and sent me on my way back to my fam…" Erika realized she was saying way too much. She had got caught up in her anger over how this monster had devised this plan, and how he had treated Henry and Carol, and all those people, even children.

"Back to your family." Doug had caught the slipup immediately and pounced on her weakness. "And were they alive?" He paced vigorously in his delight while his mind worked on the implications of her statement.

"No, they were dead, even my baby boy," Erika lied, trying to sound convincing.

Doug paced around her chair like a shark smelling blood. Finally, he leaned down so he was in her face again. "You want to know what I think. I think you are lying. You went back home to your little family. You found them and now your man is here, isn't he?" Doug's brain was racing now. Maybe he could have a lot of fun with this. Killing her husband in front of her would be the ultimate humiliation. She would have to submit to him then. He was pacing again. Erika was horrified as she saw a look of realization come over his face. "And I know where he is." Erika's eyes widened. "Oh yes, my little pet, I definitely know where he is." He rubbed his hands together again. "I saw your eyes when I told Dave to go kill those men in the supply room. You looked fiercely concerned. He is one of those guys, isn't he?"

"I don't know what you're talking about." She angrily spat out the words. "I told you my family is dead." Erika was doing her best to sound convincing but she had never been a very good liar. "Of course I would be concerned about my friends." She continued desperately trying to convince him.

"Oh, but I think you know exactly what I'm talking about. Now you just keep your fine self right there and I'll be right back." Doug was excited now.

"You're a monster!" Erika shouted at him.

"You ain't seen nothing yet," Doug seethed as he slammed the door.

Erika found herself alone. What had just happened? That monster was going after Vince. Pain coursed through her body. She took a deep breath and winced from the sting in her ribs. She wanted so badly to just give up. She had endured enough pain for three lifetimes but something inside her said no. This was her chance. What was she going to do? She examined the chair she was tied to. Frantically, she pulled at the ropes on her wrists until she could feel the blood trickling down her hands. There was no working her hands free. She was tied to the back legs of the chair. If only she could break those legs. She rocked the chair so her feet could just barely touch the floor and then she jumped and tried to make the chair land on the back legs. She hit at a horrible angle and fell hard on her side. The pain shot through her. Now, she was down again, and there was no one there to pick her up. The pain surged through her battered body but she had to get up. Working with her tippy toes and fingertips, she finally rocked the chair upright and she was on her feet again. Erika feared the pain from another fall but knew if she could just break those back legs she would be free.

She worked up all her courage, jumped off her feet, and threw all her weight into landing on the back legs. It worked! She heard a loud crack as her hands broke free. She quickly brought one to her mouth to wipe away the blood, sweat, and spit. The rope had been so tight, her hands were still tied to the broken chair legs. She worked at the knots with her teeth and soon her hands were free. She quickly untied her legs. There was no time to lose, any minute now they could be coming back through that door. She stood up. The adrenaline was pumping through her battered body now and she felt no pain. She thought about running out the door, but what about Vince? She couldn't risk the chance that Doug would come back with Vince as his captive, find her missing, and kill him in his rage. She was thinking frantically. She needed a weapon. She scanned the room but saw nothing. She rummaged through the desk but it was just papers and pens. The thought *the pen is mightier than the sword* ran through her head. She didn't think that would be true in this situation.

Erika ran to the back sleeping area. There was a bed with silk sheets. Erika spit a bloody mouthful of saliva on them in disgust and continued surveying the room. There was a table with a sawed-off shotgun lying on it. She ran over and grabbed it. When she broke it open to check for ammo, there was only one shell inside.

"Oh no," Erika said to herself as she looked for more ammo. She found none. "Well, this will have to do."

She quickly hid behind the door to the outside. She waited. She remembered hiding behind her bedroom door waiting to ambush her unsuspecting son. She would jump out and yell "boo." He would be completely surprised and Erika would laugh and laugh at her joke. Hoping this strategy would work, she listened closely for movement outside. She could hear shouting from out in the camp. Every hair on her body was standing on edge. In her moment of calm, she felt the pain in her face, causing the muscles to twitch. Her wrists burned where the ropes had been tied tight. She tried to steady her breathing and prepare for the encounter.

Then from out of nowhere, the door was thrown open. It smashed into Erika but she held perfectly still, holding her breath. Two men with their hands bound were thrown through the door and fell with a crash onto the floor. Erika could see instantly it was Vince and Greg. They both appeared to be badly beaten. Vince looked to be on the edge of consciousness, but Greg fell into an unconscious heap on the floor; his sarcasm must have earned him a much harder beating.

"So, you stupid whore, which one of these bastards is your husband?" Doug fumed as he strut through the door. He had assumed she was still in the chair and his confidence was palpable. "What the heck?" he questioned when he saw the broken chair. He quickly spun from right to left, scanning the room.

Erika's heart was pounding out of her chest as she kicked the door closed to prevent the entry of any backup men. She aimed the shotgun at Doug and without hesitation, *bang!* She pulled the trigger! He blew backwards off his feet as blood flew from his pelleted chest. Behind her, the door flew open again, and there was Dave with his gun pointing right at her. She turned to face him but knew she had no ammo left.

"What did you do," shouted Dave as he looked past her and saw Doug on the floor. In slow motion, Erika could see his finger go to the trigger. He began to pull.

Erika closed her eyes and heard two gunshots but felt no pain. She slowly opened her eyes and saw Dave on the ground. He had turned his back to her. *But why?* she wondered. Why had he turned away? Then she saw another body facing him. She recognized that red hair and that build, but she quickly spun back around to check on Vince and saw Vince with his mouth agape.

"Holy cow, baby, are you all right?" Vince, lying on the floor, was in total shock and awe of his wife.

"I'm all right, but I think that was Henry. He saved me again," Erika said, in shock herself from the chain of events.

"It was, untie me," Vince said quickly. He had watched the whole thing happen. Henry had come up behind Dave while he was focused on Erika. Henry had shot Dave before he could shoot Erika, but Dave turned and shot Henry on his way down. "Go check on him, I'll get Greg."

Erika ran over to Henry. He had already turned himself over. "What were you thinking, old man," Erika jested with tears in her eyes. She could see this was very bad. The bullet had ripped through his chest.

"Now, don't you cry for me," Henry sputtered. He was choking on bubbly blood coming out of his mouth. "I wasn't gonna let you youngsters have all the glory… listen… you just go on surviving… you… youngsters… are the only… hope." He exhaled one last time and his spirit left him.

Erika leaned over and whispered in his ear, "Thank you." She closed his eyes with her hand.

Vince was there with her now. He was supporting Greg's weight on his shoulder. "Erika, look," he gasped.

As Erika looked up, she could see a red sun rising in the east. It cast its light down upon a group of people cheering in the camp. It was over and they had won. The prisoners had mustered their strength, armed themselves, and come in upon the gang full of fury. The people of the camp had decided that this was their chance to escape Doug's monstrous rule, and they helped the prisoners to overrun the remaining gang members and let the other fighters that were out front in. The people had taken their freedom and Doug was dead.

CHAPTER 27

THE BATTLE HAD been much bigger than anyone had anticipated so now there were more decisions to be made. People needed time to heal before they began the long trip over to the Lotus camp. Luckily, Rob's whole team had survived. They had hid and used guerilla warfare to keep the front gate guards occupied. When they finally did rush the gate, Jimmy had gotten his arm broken and Tom had been shot in the leg but they were alive.

Rob took charge and quickly had things in order. He directed the people with medical knowledge to set up a trauma center and was pleased to hear that this camp had lots of medical supplies and a real doctor. There had been a drug store with a pharmacy here, and they had completely raided its contents, even though the building itself was turned into rubble. The doctor was a man named Stan. He had been held hostage here by Doug and his gang because he could patch them up after their raids. He was thrilled by the sudden change of management and stepped forward immediately to volunteer his services for the injured. Erika, Vince, and Greg were all among the injured taken to the trauma center to receive care. Vince was bruised badly but not broken. Erika was in the same bruised state but Doug had broken three of her ribs when he was kicking her on the floor. Greg was messed up pretty bad. He had broken his collarbone and his knee was the size of a grapefruit.

Rob knew that cleaning up this mess of a camp would take time. First, they had to take care of the dead. No one in the camp was happy with the amount of death surrounding it, and they all knew the right thing had to be done for those poor souls. The old rotting bodies scattered out behind the camp and the heads hung as trophies around it were to be piled and burned. The casualties from the battle would receive a proper burial. Next, they needed to take stock of the supplies that were here and this compound was loaded with them. All of these supplies would have to be organized and readied for transport. All this work meant the timeline they were supposed to maintain would be utterly blown.

The group that came in on the attack was very concerned that their friends and families would be worried about them not arriving at the Lotus camp in the timeframe they had planned on. The Auburn group had been capturing and rounding up horses, since they saw how versatile the horses had been in this harsh new landscape. They had a dozen of them so Rob had Randy, Michelle, and Steve eat some food, take a little rest, and then ride immediately to tell the group that had already left for Lotus what had happened and that they would be delayed.

Then Rob met with the new leader of the Auburn refugees, Gloria. She was a nice lady with dark eyes and black hair that was going grey. Her Mexican heritage was obvious, and she took charge with a Latin flare of authority. She had rallied the people of the camp to rise up and take down the monstrous individuals that were holding them under their thumbs. She was fed up with living in fear. Her husband Jose and her son Jose Jr. were fighting with the Auburn gang, but they were just following orders to keep themselves and Gloria safe. In actuality, they were just waiting for the right moment to get away from the compound. When they saw it, they took it, but Jose had died in the struggle. Gloria focused her pain on saving all the people she could and now those people looked to her for leadership.

Gloria knew all the ins and outs of the food preparation and domestic needs of the camp so she immediately directed her people to cooking, cleaning the soiled clothing, and supply organization. All the people who had any carpentry skills were sent to task building carts for horses and carts that people could pull as well. Everyone would have to do their share in order to maximize the amount of the valuable supplies they could carry. Anyone whose clothes had been destroyed in the fight and the people who had been living as slaves were given new clothes. These clothes had been raided from the surrounding clothing stores and there was no way to carry all the supplies they had stocked up. Food and medicine would receive the highest priority.

Erika was extremely happy about this abundance of clothing. The trauma center had been set up outdoors because of the limited indoor space. A cool September wind swept across her bare shoulders as she sat up, holding the blanket to her chest to keep herself covered. She saw a pile of clothes next to her. New, clean jeans and a new T-shirt that was black. There was a new sports bra that was just her size, fresh, clean underwear, and a new camouflage hoodie. Plus, there were even new socks and a pair of boots next to her moccasins. To Erika's surprise, all the items even had the tags on them still.

She began to reach for them when she heard a voice in a German accent. "You may want to clean yourself up before you get dressed."

"Who are you?" Erika had been near exhaustion when she was taken to the trauma center and had not remembered much from then. She was hoping their victory had been real, not some sick dream she had conjured in an unconscious state. "We won, right? Doug is dead, right?" Erika said a little panicky.

"Yes, yes, don't you worry," he reassured her in his thick German accent. "We won and Doug, thankfully, is dead. My name is Stan and I am a doctor," he explained.

"Oh." Erika was still a little light-headed.

"Still feeling dizzy are we? Don't worry, it will subside, but your ribs are going to hurt for a while. Look… there's a shower over there." He pointed to an area that had a water tank perched above a blanket surrounded box.

"A shower? Really?" Erika loved showers and it had been months since the last one she had taken, at home in her cozy house.

"Yes, a real shower. But it's going to get well used today. You better get to it, and then we'll put some fresh bandages on those wrists and wrap those ribs tight to minimize the pain," Stan said in his smooth comforting accent.

Erika looked down and saw the vibrant bruising along her rib cage. She looked at her wrists and saw the burned skin with dried blood on her hands. "Well, that's some more scars to add to the list."

"I would ask about those, but I'll wait till you're ready to share." As a doctor, Stan had seen many things and knew how sensitive talking about her amount of excessive scarring could be.

"Thanks." Erika got up, sleepily wrapping her blanket around herself. Her ribs surged pain through her body as she moved her arms. She winced but remained quiet. This was not the first time she had dealt with the pain of broken ribs. Her martial arts practice had caused a couple in the past.

"Here, take this." Stan had seen her movements and knew the pain would be excruciating. He was taken aback by her lack of reaction to it and knew she must have endured a lot of pain in her life.

"Is there enough? I can handle the pain." Erika was now used to the extreme rationing of pain killers.

"I know you can. You look like a very tough girl. It is just a couple aspirins and we have plenty. Take it," he insisted.

Erika took the pills with a drink of water that Stan had brought her. She continued drinking the water. It was so refreshing. She had no idea how thirsty she was, and then her stomach growled as she smelled the delicious smell of food cooking.

"Mmmm, that smells good," she murmured to herself.

"I want you to take it easy on water and food, sport. Your ribs are broken and with no x-ray, I can't tell if they spurred in toward your stomach or your lungs for that matter. So, we need to keep that stomach small, and I wouldn't recommend any fighting or physical activity for a while," continued Stan. "Anyway, shower first, now go," he ordered.

"Okay," said Erika. She immediately liked this man; no one had called her sport except her grandfather and it conjured fond memories of him in her head. She projected these loving feelings onto Stan and he deserved it. He was very kind and had an excellent bedside manner.

Stan had stooped down and picked up her pile of clothes. He knew if she attempted this motion, it would be very painful for her. "And here's a backpack for your old ones if you want them. But, you will need the pack later anyway, and all your weapons are piled over there." He pointed to an organized assortment of weapons, all waiting for their owners to recover.

"Thank you," said Erika, "for everything."

She took the clothes from him and headed toward the shower. The shower was ingenious. A big plastic tank was stacked on top of a wooden box. The tank was heated from the sun. Besides the arduous task of getting water up there, its design was pretty simple. The wooden box was surrounded by rugs. They were probably raided from the department store. They were the same rugs Doug had lined his den with. Erika shuddered at the thought. Inside the wooden box was a tube that let water out of the tank on top. All you had to do was pull a rope to uncap the hose and unleash the water.

Erika stepped in and removed her towel. She looked down at her body and rolled her eyes. Her body was an absolute wreck. Old scars from the steaming hot plastic were now covered in bruises that came to a vibrant peak of color around her left ribs. She pulled on the handle to start the water flowing and began to rinse away the dried blood that clung to her skin. She thought about just how much blood she had cleaned off her body since the beginning of all this madness as she let the water run through her hair. Reaching for a bar of soap, she noticed there was real shampoo and conditioner too. Erika was thrilled. It had been so long since she had anything other than soap to wash her hair with. The shampoo smelled like coconut and she washed her hair vigorously. Then she conditioned her hair thickly and gave it extra time to work its magic as she lathered the soap all over her body. She remembered that she had absolutely loved the feeling of her soft hair as she rinsed for a final time. It was smooth and silky and she could run her fingers right through it without hitting one snarl. The luscious smells of the soaps filled her nostrils and she was feeling very refreshed.

The pain medicine was kicking in and Erika felt wonderful as she reached for her clean clothes. She smelt the familiar smell of new clothes fresh from the store and it was wonderful. She remembered back to how her husband had always insisted they wash any new clothes before they wore them. He had been right. There was a flame retardant chemical they had used on new clothes that could be dangerous but maybe that additive would be a benefit now. She chuckled to herself. She savored the smell and the crisp feeling as she put on each new article of clothing. There was a bench outside the shower for dressing. She approached it and sat down to put on her boots and pack up her old things. Her shirt had already been trashed. Doug had torn it apart anyway. When she looked up from her bag, Vince was standing there with a pile of clothes.

She jumped up in a joyful bounce and without words they embraced and held one another tightly. The pain of the hug was intense but Erika didn't back away. The pain was entirely worth it. Both of them had tears rolling down their faces, completely enraptured in one another's love.

"I thought I lost you... again!" Vince sighed.

"You should know by now you're not getting rid of me that easily, silly," Erika jested back.

"I love you, Erika," he said very seriously, completely ignoring her sarcasm. Rarely did Vince use her actual name and it amplified the power of his statement.

"I love you too, Vince." Erika looked deep into his eyes. They could feel the love swirling around them like a ball of fire.

"So, you're done? I missed all the good stuff?" Vince broke the seriousness and teased playfully, with a longing look in his eyes.

"Oh yeah, little miss bruise, scar body," Erika teased back but deep down she wondered how anyone could long for this body of hers.

"Now you better knock that off. You are still my beautiful woman." Vince knew her too well and knew what she had been thinking. "Did that shower make you feel better?" He quickly changed the subject.

"I feel freaking awesome. They have coconut shampoo and conditioner in there, babe. Real shampoo and conditioner! Here, smell." Erika put her head toward him and shoved a handful of hair under his nose.

Vince inhaled deeply. She smelled so good to him. He wrapped his arms around her again and squeezed her.

"Ow, ow, ow," Erika yelped. One giant hug had been quite enough for her body to handle.

"Oh, I'm sorry," Vince quickly let go and backed away a little. "You're just so beautiful. I could just eat you up."

"Look at this," Erika said and lifted up her shirt to expose her ribs.

"Ouch... that looks horribly painful, babe." Vince wished he had been able to keep her away from that monster.

"I'll heal. God knows, I'll heal." She rolled her eyes. "Anyway, you better get your stinky butt in that shower. You need it bad," Erika said with a teasing look. She was waving her hand in front of her nose.

"All right, all right, don't get your panties all wrinkled up," Vince said with a wink. "That's my job." He quickly stepped into the shower stall to avoid a smack to his bottom from Erika.

Erika sat back down on the bench to put on her new socks and boots. New boots, she had always hated new boots because they were so stiff and took so long to break in. But, with the feeling of coolness in the air, she assumed the waterproof boots would serve her better than moccasins. She knew the feel of this weather. She was from the Midwest and they have warm summer rains. In California though, it had to get cold to rain. She had always hated that.

When she was done lacing up her boots, Erika went to meet with Stan to get all bandaged up. Even though Erika protested having him wrap her ribs in an Ace bandage, it did feel much better to have them wrapped. Plus, it limited her movement so she didn't accidentally bend at a painful angle. Stan had insisted because he knew that soon they would be on the move and Erika would not shy away from work.

Before too long, the camp came alive. Everyone was awake and well rested. They were all on the move. Most were grabbing some food before they went over to assist their assigned team. There were many more people than Erika had previously assumed. The smell of food was in the air and spirits were high. There was another smell in the air too. Outside of the camp, in the old graveyard, a fire was still burning. It was a big pile of bodies, and it was taking a long time to burn. Erika shook her head in disgust. It was unbelievable to think that people who had acted so civilized could turn to this level of horribleness in less than a few months. No one had any idea how fragile the world was. It was just taken for granted.

By the time Stan was done working on Erika, Vince had rejoined her fresh from his shower. They went to visit with Greg before they left for the food area. Greg was in a particularly bad mood. The combination of the condition of his knee and the broken collarbone prevented him from moving very much. He couldn't even use crutches to get up and move around because the crutch had to sit in his armpit and it messed with his broken collarbone. He would have to make the journey to Lotus in a pull cart with the supplies, and he did not like that prospect one bit. Vince and Erika left him pouting like a baby. They assured him he was going to be fine, but he just sat there and watched them go.

They walked to the food area, feeling jovial. When they got there, Rob found them and proceeded to fill them in on all the plans while Erika and Vince ate. They were thrilled that a message had been sent back to the Lotus camp so that the children would not worry about them being dead. Rob told them that they were currently packing up all the supplies, and they were properly taking care of all of the dead. Erika noted the smoldering smell coming from that direction. He explained that it was taking a long time to dig all the graves so some of the graves had to hold multiple bodies, and they were burning a lot more bodies than they thought they were going to have to. But, at least they would be laid to rest in a respectible manner.

Rob had decided that as soon as all the carts were finished being built, they were going to leave. He was trying to get as many carts built as possible from the available building supplies. They needed to bring as much as they could. It felt completely wrong to leave behind anything that could be of some use in the future because who knows when you would find it again. Rob explained that there were lots of people that wanted to come with them to the Lotus camp. There was nothing left for them here. He had considered the implications and saw it in two ways. It was good because there would be plenty of hands and horses to move the goods. But it was also bad, because the group in Lotus might not want to take the people in. At least the amount of supplies they were bringing might make the Lotus Group much more welcoming.

He had also surveyed all of the power making equipment that the Auburn group had scavenged. They had gathered a lot. Generators were stacked on one side of the room. Some were being used for parts and others were in great shape. They had gasoline stocked in just about every kind of container imaginable. Solar panels were in use on the roofs of any of the building that were still standing. The gang had been raiding them from just about everywhere they found them so there was a stack of panels inside that weren't even in use yet. They had rolls of wire to run the electricity stocked up as well. It was a gold mine of power goodies, and he wanted to take as much of that as he could as well. It made sense but it would be heavy. That was why he wanted to leave as soon as they could. The going would be very slow.

CHAPTER 28

IT WAS A crisp morning when the caravan set out. Rob had as much inventory as possible organized and strategically packed into all the carts they had built. The group lined up like a human and horse train. They left that sad place behind and no one looked back. Jaclyn, the lady from the Auburn River camp who had been held captive, was only going to travel with them down to the river and then she was headed back up towards Foresthill, a town on the same side of the river as Auburn but further upstream. She was going to finish the mission she had started before those monsters had altered her plans. She wanted to find out what had happened to her kids. The carts slipped and slid but everyone made it down to the river in good shape. Jaclyn hugged Erika tightly and said good-bye to everyone. Her blue eyes had tears in them as she took her heavy pack and began to carefully make her way along the river bed.

The main group had to stop there at the bottom of the canyon and rebuild a makeshift bridge. The carts were too big and heavy to make it across the river without one. They were already having a hard enough time making it though the muddy mess by the river. While they were stopped, fires were built and everyone ate another meal. Building the bridge ended up taking longer than they thought because supplies were scarce. People had to be sent back up the hill to gather materials and then come all the way back down to build. In the meantime, camp was pitched for the evening. Going uphill with the carts would be much harder than it was going down and that had been difficult enough. No one wanted to attempt the climb in the middle of the night.

This whole attack had been a way bigger production than anyone would have thought it would be. Erika was in awe as she looked out over the group. There had to be at least forty people in all. Each pair of two had a cart to pull, except for those who were injured. They were being towed behind the horses. It was a sight to see. Makeshift gear had been constructed so that the horses could be put into teams of two and pull a much larger cart. This in itself was a feat.

Having horses pull a cart is much more difficult than one would assume or the old movies portrayed. These horses had been pets. Used for pleasure rides now and again. Now they were being asked to do so much more than they had ever been trained for, and with the choppy terrain and jimmy-rigged equipment, the task's difficulty was amplified to near impossibility. But the group was determined and needed the horses' power so the horses gave it their best shot.

Erika sat down at the warm fire by Vince. It burned brightly in the evening dusk. Surprisingly, they didn't talk about their experiences at the compound. Each was too much in conflict in their hearts. They were thinking about different decisions they could have made so they made small talk about nothing important and enjoyed one another's company. When their meal of tuna and rice was done and the dishes were washed, Vince decided he wanted to go visit Greg and talk with Rob about tomorrow's plans. Erika had other things on her mind.

She slowly picked her way through the camp. It was a solemn night full of self-reflection. Most folks had built small private fires to cook their food and were keeping to themselves. Still, there was a communal fire where mostly young people had gathered and were chatting quietly. She headed toward the glow. When she got there, she saw a familiar face. Michelle was there chatting with Randy. Erika knew they were talking about their sniping fury because of their gun-like hand movements. Love was in the air and it looked as if these two were really starting to hit it off. Why not, they were about the same age and let's face it, the pickings were pretty slim nowadays.

Erika chuckled to herself as she interrupted, "You guys did a great job out there that day. I don't think I've had the chance to properly thank either one of you yet."

They both blushed with pride and Randy said, "Thank you, Erika, we just did what we had to do."

Such a mature response. Here was this kid, seventeen, who should have been finishing his junior year of high school, and here was this ditsy eighteen-year-old girl who should have been finishing her senior year. Now, they were being turned into snipers and facing a hopeless world. They were looking fear straight in the eyes, and they were even falling in love in the process.

Erika decided to leave them be. Who knew what tomorrow would bring. To change the subject and get out of their hair, Erika queried, "Do either of you know where Harold and his family are camped?"

"Yeah," answered Michelle. "If you follow this line of carts"—she pointed over to the right—"they're down there, kinda by the horses."

"Cool, thanks," Erika said.

"Are you going to see them?" There was something wrong in Michelle's tone of voice.

"No, I was just asking for the sake of it," Erika jested back.

"Well, I was just asking because…"—she lowered her voice and leaned closer—"well, don't say I told you but…" She was stammering a little.

"Just spit it out, for God's sake!" Erika was getting a little impatient with her slow reply.

"Well, I went over there to visit with them. After all, they were pretty much the reason why we went to that compound in the first place. Anyway, Harold's oldest girl, Jen… well, she's fifteen, and I thought maybe we could be friends. Well, Harold said I could visit with her but it probably wouldn't do any good. It didn't." Michelle was just as ditsy as ever, and Erika wasn't following her explanation at all.

"Why? What's wrong?" Erika shot right to the point.

"Those guys, Erika… those guys screwed that girl up, literally. They beat her and did… stuff to her; she just sits there, staring," Michelle said in one breath.

Erika should have figured. She had heard what that guard had said before Greg shot him that day on the side of the canyon. Doug had been taking his hatred for Harold and Erika out on Harold's daughter. Erika knew the whole story. She had heard it from the mouth of the beast himself. Erika had killed his brother and set Doug's horrible plot into motion. Then Harold had put up more of a fight than Doug had intended, knocking out one of his teeth in the process. The two of them had been on the top of Doug's list and he had directed this anger at Jen. What a horrible thought. The poor girl. Erika had only tasted a little of Doug's rage, but Jen had endured it for days. The fear that Erika had experienced for only a matter of minutes must have been minuscule compared to the fear and desperation that Jen must have felt. Erika thought about those silk sheets and his beady, hungry eyes. An innocent fifteen-year-old girl had those eyes fixated on her and had felt the sickening touch of those sheets. Erika wanted to puke. There had to be something that Erika could do.

"Thanks for the heads up but let's not give up on her." Erika felt horrible for the girl and wanted to make sure Jen would have a friend if she wanted one.

"I won't," Michelle whispered. "But I really hope she can snap out of it. Honestly, I don't know if I could, though."

"I hope she can too," said Erika, ignoring the second part of Michelle's statement. Deep in her heart, she wondered if she would be able to overcome that experience as well. She turned to head toward Harold's camp. She walked down the row of carts and saw at the very end Carol and Betsy whispering quietly as they finished the family's dishes.

"There she is!" Harold boomed as Erika walked up. For a moment, he sounded exactly like his father. He walked up and gave her a big hug. Carol and Betsy had left their work to join in one big hug.

"What are you guys doing camped way out here?" Erika felt their joy and wondered why they hadn't camped closer in to the other folks.

"Well, Kim here"—Harold hugged Kim closer—"has been reunited with Lightning, her horse, so we wanted to be close to him. He has a big job to do, but Kim has been quite a help with the horses."

Erika could tell he was holding back the whole story, and she had to wonder if it was for Jen's benefit as well. Erika was surprised that, for the most part, the family was very cheerful. The family was reunited and free and that was the focus. Horrible things had happened, and Harold was having a hard time coping with the fact that he was not there to protect his baby from those men. There was a spot in him that was very hardened because of it, but he would work with it and appreciate the fact that his family was alive and together.

They talked about Henry, and Erika could see that Carol was very lonely without her love, but he would not have wanted her to give up. She was here with her family and she was going to thank God for every moment she had with them. Carol did mention, however, that the traveling had been very hard on her. The arthritis in her joints was flaring and she didn't know what pace she would be able to keep. Erika advised her to go talk to the doctor and see if she could get some medicine. Plus, he would have more ingredients to make salves.

Jen was quite a contrast to the high spirits of the rest of the family. She just sat there staring off into nothing. The bruises on her face and body were healing, but the bruises on her soul would take a lot longer to heal. Erika did not know how to approach her or what to say, but she knew she had to say something. She had to think of something to reassure her that the bastards who had done this were dead and her family would give their lives to protect her. Her grandfather had proudly given his for that very reason.

Erika went and sat next to Jen. The family had seen Erika make the move to contact Jen through her veil of depression so they moved to the other side of the camp to talk quietly. Jen's light brown hair blew in the breeze. Erika remembered her vigor when she had first met her and that she had loved basketball. They sat there quietly. Erika still did not have the words.

"You gonna tell me how everything is okay now and nothing will ever happen again." Erika was startled by the tiny voice, so full of hatred.

"Nope." Erika was still unsure and paused for a moment. "All I would say is those guys are scum, sent from the devil himself. I am sorry for what happened but you're going to have to live on. Your grandfather died to make sure you would never have to face those men again. If I know your grandfather, he died a little more inside each time they hurt you and he was unable to stop it. He killed that man, Jen. To protect me and to protect you, and if you give up now, his sacrifice will mean nothing and that's not acceptable to me. Nothing will erase what those men did but you can be strong and learn to protect yourself so that you can ensure that nothing like that ever happens to your little sister."

Jen just sat there. She didn't say anything more, and Erika had nothing more to say. It would be up to her now. Erika got up and said her good-byes to the rest of the group. It was late and tomorrow would be painfully exhausting. She headed back towards her cart. Her ribs screamed with pain as she looked at it. Pulling that thing was hell but it had to be done. She looked around for Vince. He wasn't back yet so she stoked the little fire, put on another log, and climbed under her blanket. At least sleep would dull the pain.

Vince returned to the camp just as Erika was falling asleep. Vince tended to the fire again and climbed in next to Erika's warm body. They talked about Harold's family and about the plans Rob had for tomorrow. Then they discussed how Greg was acting like a big baby, sulking around because of his injuries and inability to be the center of attention, even though all the single females had stopped by to check on him. Then they chuckled, remembering the past and how it was almost impossible to get a night alone without the kids.

Vince snuggled up closer and fondled Erika's nipple in his fingertips. Erika tried to play coy and back him off because of the pain in her ribs, but soon, Vince took her erect nipple in his mouth and began to suckle on it, pressing the issue. Erika gave in to the erotic moment and kissed his neck. He proceeded to reach down and rub her soft fuzz. Erika could feel his erect penis rubbing up against her and reached down to take it in her hand. They moaned softly in the loving embrace. Vince spun his body around so that their heads were at each other's pelvises. Erika kissed the soft tip of his penis and gently licked the head with her tongue. Vince thrust it into her mouth and Erika's lips moved up and down it as he thrust it in and out of her mouth. He slid his finger into her soft folds and felt her moist readiness. He gently caressed her mound with his tongue and slid his finger in and out of her. Erika's body began to tingle as she moaned and felt the intense orgasmic feelings. Once he knew she was ready for him, Vince turned back around. They kissed and embraced one another as he slid his hot member into her moist folds. Vince thrust in and out of her. He held his body in an arch so that she would not feel his weight on her ribs and she willingly accepted his body. They moaned as the raw energy grew into a final climax of thrusting, joyful orgasm. With his essence spent, Vince slowly slid his penis out of her. He looked deep into her eyes and they kissed. He snuggled up to her again. They cuddled into one another and fell asleep enraptured in the pureness of their love.

CHAPTER 29

VINCE AND ERIKA awoke the next morning with loving, sleepy eyes. When they emerged from the blankets, it was to a cloudy sky. Nobody liked the looks of it but Erika had known it for days; rain was on the way. The riverbed was not where you wanted to be camping when it started pouring so they packed up as quickly as possible. The bridge was completed and there was nothing keeping them there now. Breakfast would have to consist of dried fruits and nuts that you could eat on the move.

Coming down the canyon had been much easier when they were on foot with no carts to pull or horses to worry about. Obstacles could be easily jumped or climbed around but now they would have to be methodically calculated. They had planned to take essentially the same route to Cool that the main river group had taken on their trip up the canyon, but the current group had much larger carts than that group had. Also, the quakes kept the landscape in a constant state of change, so areas you had just traveled through days or even hours before could be completely altered.

The group slipped and slid their way up the slope where the lake had been. Tediously avoiding stumps from old trees and new crevices that had been opened up. When they finally made it to the tree line, the rain came in. Any tarps they had were used to cover wagons that had water-unfriendly products in them. The situation became dreadful. They contended with the weight of the carts, the moist slippery ground, and drenched clothing. No one smiled anymore; they simply put their heads down and pulled up and up.

The group was halted for a tree that had come down in the pathway and would need to be cleared. Everyone sat around huffing and puffing while people took turns hacking through the huge pine. No one felt like conversing and everyone just wanted to reach the top before night fell and all light was lost. They huddled under the carts and corners of tarps, trying to find somewhere dry to rest. Finally, the tree was cleared and cut up into rounds that were small enough to be carried. With the limited supply of firewood in the burn zone between Cool and Lotus, it was decided that the extra weight of the wood would be worth carrying. It was loaded onto multiple carts wherever it would fit. The only positive thing about carrying more weight was it helped to hold down the tarps in the rain and wind.

The caravan was on the move again. The horses leading the way heaved their heavy loads up the mountain. Then, one by one, the groups of people with their own hefty loads passed through where the tree had fallen. Erika and Vince had lagged at the spot where the tree had been to make sure everyone made it through. Before long, the heads of the horses popped up over the side of the canyon. As night began to fall, the last of the handcarts arrived in Cool with Erika and Vince helping to push it up.

The day had been completely exhausting. It seemed Greg, having been hauled up the mountain in a cart, was the only one with any energy to spare. Erika and Vince found him at a communal fire, the only fire that was built tonight, cooking and telling funny stories to try to lift everyone's spirits. They sat down on a blanket in the throng of people by the fire. Each person was given a little portion of rice and beans with canned roast beef. It appeared that Rob and Gloria had taken careful stock of their food supplies and were rationing them out accordingly. The servings seemed awfully small given that they had worked hard and eaten very little that day, but no one complained. They were all so tired. They were just happy to have something warm in their bellies.

The rain had slowed while they were eating but soon it came back with a vengeance. The people were wet and needed someplace dry to sleep. Tarps were very limited so they decided to move the carts as close as possible to one another so one tarp could cover multiple carts. In the end, two tarps were spared. One of them was used for everyone to sleep on and one was hung from the surrounding carts as rain cover. Everyone packed in like sardines in a tarp sandwich. It was a huddled mass of humanity that smelt of musty wetness, but it was warm. The warmth was welcomed as the night turned cold and the storm raged on.

In the morning, the sun turned the clouds a strange shade of green, and theories went round the camp about the volcano fallout or a toxic meltdown, but the mission before them was still at hand. Rain or shine, the group had to keep moving. There was no water, except what they had carried from the river and could harvest from the rainfall. If they stayed put, it was only a matter of time until they would run desperately low. Even though the tarp covering their sleeping area had been hung low and you could only crawl and sit under it, most of the camp stayed there to eat breakfast. It kept the area warm and people talked with one another about how miserable the day would be if this storm kept up. Then they were forced out. Rob had called everyone into action. The horses stomped in the rain as they began the long march into territory Erika had not entered since the mega-quake had happened. This had once been a very familiar drive for her not so long ago. Her son was going to preschool down this road and she had driven it at least twice a week to go visit her mother's ranch in Lotus.

Erika's thoughts wondered off to her mother as the line began to move; Vince and Erika dug in their heels and began to pull the cart. This was the longest time she had ever not talked with her mother. Normally, she would have called her on her cell phone every morning just to say good morning and see how she was doing. They had always been such good friends, sharing all their thoughts and stories together. Erika could not wait to see her and it made all this pulling worth it.

"This is earth calling planet Erika." Vince had been trying to get her attention.

"Oh, I'm sorry, what?" Erika said startled.

"I was just saying I wish this rain would stop and do you really think all this stuff is worth all this work?" Vince questioned.

"I agree about the rain, but I think Rob is right about the supplies. No group would take in all these people without a huge incentive. The group from the river was way smaller and the Cool group still didn't want to take them in. It's all about food and numbers now, Vince. More mouths means less food, so I have to agree with Rob. The more these people can bring to the table, the better, literally," Erika said thoughtfully.

"I guess you are right, but it still doesn't make this cart any lighter," he said sarcastically.

"I hear that," she returned his sarcasm.

Much to their relief, the caravan came to an abrupt halt. Most people had left their carts and were moving to the front of the line to see what the problem was. Erika and Vince had taken the moment to rest before they too went to see what was wrong. As they were walking to the front, Vince saw someone unusual at the rear of the line. There were two men that had come out from behind some rocks. Both were very ratty and dirty, and they were peeping under the tarps of the last three carts.

"Erika, get your rifle!" Vince commanded quietly.

"Why? What's up?" Erika had not yet seen the men.

"Just do it and cover the left side of the carts." Vince was already pointing his rifle down the right side.

Erika grabbed her rifle and looked down the sight through the pouring rain.

"Maybe they are from our group," Erika cautioned Vince, but he had seen them come from behind the rocks, and they both knew they weren't. Their actions were those of thieves who had been watching the caravan proceed, just waiting for an opportunity to pounce.

"On the count of three," directed Vince. Vince was so calculated in his actions, Erika had no choice but to follow his direction. "One… two… three."

Their guns fired, *bang!* in the same instance, and the two men fell dead at the same time.

"There's a third," Vince yelled but the man ran left behind the cart. Then, *bang!* Erika had fired a second shot and the third man was down. Rob with a group of fighters, including Michelle and Randy, came running back to them. The rain was pouring down.

"What are you guys shooting at?" questioned Rob.

"Three guys trying to rob us," Vince answered in a cold tone of voice.

"Well, let's go check it out," Rob said amused. He always did love a good fight. Rifles were at the ready as the team walked to inspect the thieves but there was no need. Two men lay dead, taken out with extreme precision, and the third was clinging to life. Rob stood over him.

"We… just… wanted… to eat," the man said in a weakened voice.

"Should have looked somewhere else," Rob said as he fired his gun and killed the man.

Everyone in that team felt mixed feelings. They were happy to have protected their goods but it was horrible to have killed these men. Maybe their only crime was hunger.

"Vince, Erika, good job. Don't look all sad. You made the right choice. We can't save them all," Rob said trying to quiet their minds.

"Did we?" said Vince. "Not too long ago we were the thieves."

"No, we weren't," countered Rob. "We went to save people and maybe get some stuff in the process, but our intentions were completely different. We would never have even been there if it was solely to steal. We were in the right then and we are now, and as long as we continue to do what is right, we are still good people." Rob was trying to convince himself as much as Vince. Decisions had to be made and lived with, and none of them were going to be easy. "Now, Michelle, Randy, and Tom, you three stay back here to watch the rear. The rest of you come with me."

"It's okay, baby," Erika grabbed Vince's hand. In reality, she was just as distraught as he was, but this was no time to show it. They had made the choice. "Anyway, that was an awesome shot we made!" She had been impressed by their combined accuracy and teamwork.

"How can you say that? Those men are dead by our hands." Vince was appalled.

"Yeah, they're dead, but they are dead by their own hands. They didn't come and ask. They were going to rob us, or kill us, or rape men's daughters. They can all die for all I care. I am done feeling sorry. I am done wondering what if. Screw them, baby, screw them!" Erika had snapped. All this death and maliciousness was too overwhelming.

Vince saw the hate in her eyes, but he still wondered if they had made the right decision. Deep down, he knew Erika was right, though. It was time to quit wondering and just keep on doing. "Well, I guess it really was a good shot, wasn't it?" He smiled at her and saw the love come back into her face.

They had finally reached the front of the line of carts and saw the dilemma. The quakes had completely ravaged the landscape ahead. Normally, this area was filled with rolling hills that could be easily skirted if you followed the highway. Now, it was full of cracks and crevices with rocks teetering in unstable positions. In the pouring rain, it was difficult to see to the bottom of this particular crevice. The people were discussing a rather obvious trail of tracks that skirted the crack in a direction that headed left. But the former people that traveled through here, which included Erika's children, hadn't faced this decision in the rain. It appeared that the rain runoff was channeling through the crevice so who knew what the top looked like. Plus, the wildfires that had cleared the landscape had created a perfect environment for mudslides.

All kinds of scenarios were discussed. If they turned right and tried to blaze a new trail they had no idea how far they would have to go to find the river and then backtrack all the way up through land that didn't have any kind of road before the quakes. Even with the road before them in shambles, at least they were more familiar with it.

It was also suggested that they just wait out the rain. It was a valid suggestion because usually, in California, the rain wouldn't last more than a couple of days. But what if it didn't let up? What if it got worse? People were living in terror and waiting for anything normal to happen didn't really make sense right now.

So, in the end, they turned left, following the tracks in the mud, hoping against all odds for survival. The giant ravine loomed in darkness on their right and the flow of the mud pushed them toward the edge. The horses snorted deeply as the mist from the rain blasted through the air. Everyone was back in position now, and it wasn't long before Vince and Erika turned left and began their fight with gravity and the pull toward death.

Finally, the caravan halted again. Most people were afraid to leave their carts on the edge of the cliff to go forward and see what the holdup was now. Erika left the cart in Vince's care and went to find Rob. As she passed the horses, she saw that the ravine did indeed have an end. It ended right into the side of one of those huge rolling hills. To get around the top of the ravine, the carts would have to be put almost completely on their sides. Her eyes followed the line that a cart would fall down and to her shock there was a cart down there. Then her worst fears were realized, she knew that cart! It was the same one Kit had pulled with her kids in it!

"Oh my God!" she screamed. She immediately started down the crack but she was stopped short.

"Whoa, whoa, whoa," Rob said as he grabbed her by the arm. "I already sent Taylor down there. There are no bodies there, not even a horse, so calm down."

"My God, Rob, I was so freaked." Erika sighed as she realized the implications of his statement.

"I knew you would be; so was I, honestly. Now the biggest problem is how do we get past this? Our carts are way bigger than that." He pointed to the cart in the ravine.

Now that the shock was over, Erika focused on what could be done. The rain was still pouring down and she was so tired of being wet and cold. The water was driving down into the ravine, which made the crossing even more perilous. Everyone knew the supplies were too precious to leave behind, but they were running out of options. To make matters worse, it would be dark soon.

They decided there were basically two options. They leave the supplies behind and continue on, or they hunker down on the edge of the cliff for the night and dig. The rain was already cutting the hill and, if they could make the crossover flatter, they could get the carts by safely. They would take shifts digging and sleeping all night until it was passable and with any hope that would be sometime tomorrow. This would have to be a group decision, though, so Erika went back down the line of carts and informed them one by one of the options. Then when she had reached the end, she turned back and asked what decision they had made. No one wanted to leave the supplies. They all knew that this was their ticket into a community, or their start to a new one. They had come so far already and there was no way they were going to leave it all.

It was a horrible night. The carts had to be constantly readjusted because of the sliding mud trying to suck them into the ravine. Anyone not tending to carts was digging at the hill. Mud caked everyone and the rain continued at a steady downpour.

When the morning light shown, it was through fierce clouds that had a green hue. The rain had halted but the clouds were threatening. Food was distributed and everyone had a small rest before they were ready to start the crossing. Suddenly, a buzz ran down the chain of people on the cliff. Steve and Randy had ridden back from the Lotus camp. They had informed the people there of the delay but knew that this crossing would be difficult so they had ridden back. He ensured the group that, after this crossing, the road ahead was manageable. He also informed them that a large group of people were coming from the Lotus camp to help but they were on foot so it would take them longer to get here. Relief ran through all of them. They would be accepted and they would have help.

It took about another hour before the people from the Lotus camp showed up and, even though people wanted to mingle, it was all business. The rain had started again and it was time to move. All the carts made it past the ravine safely, and feelings were very good as they trudged the carts through the mud toward a new home. As they neared the river and their destination, Erika saw snipers on the hills. These folks were organized. Soon they reached high wooden walls with guards posted on top. The walls had been recently constructed from old buildings and fallen trees. Erika was impressed as the gate opened.

CHAPTER 30

ERIKA'S HEART RACED as she went through the gates. She had no idea what this camp would be like, but she knew her mom and kids were in there so she went on in with the group. She could tell everyone was nervous. A lot of these people had been living under the rule of a monster for months, and they were hopeful that this place would be different. They were corralled into a large area on the other side of the gates where men with guns stood watch from the fences over the top of them. Erika was beginning to feel like a cow in a cattle roundup when a militant man with sandy gray hair took center stage in front of them.

"My name is Andrew Bingham. I have been chosen by the people of this community as their leader and, as such, let me explain some things to all of you. Now, you are a very large group and we just took in the group from Cool, so obviously things are getting a little tight around here. But Steve and Randy have informed me that you have brought an extraordinary amount of supplies with you, so for that effort, we thank you. Plus, I hear you have a doctor and medical supplies, and we have many here in need. To get to the point, we can make this work if we all work together. The supplies, minus your personal belongings, will be stored in our central supply area across the bridge. When we are done here, you can take the carts there to be sorted and stored. The families here have already divided tasks among themselves. Some provide wood, some provide food, some security, and so forth, so we will make a line over by the supply area, and each newcomer will provide their skill set so they can be placed into the appropriate family group. They will show you your new home and explain things to you. Anyone not okay with this can leave now. If you cannot be of use to the community, we have no use for you. We all work together and survive together." A murmur went through the group, but no one headed for the gate. "Okay, now that we have that straightened out. Welcome, everyone!" Andrew said joyfully, "and congratulations on surviving!"

The crowd cheered and started to mobilize the carts toward the bridge as Andrew had instructed. Men that had been standing idly around now smiled brightly and jumped in to help with the gear. Vince and Erika hung back as the caravan continued on toward the storage area. Erika approached Andrew and saw the two men near him with guns perk to attention.

"Andrew, right?" Erika questioned tentatively. "My name is Erika."

"Oh, Erika Moore, I have heard a lot about you." Andrew smiled wide and the men with the guns relaxed. "I bet you are looking for your mom."

Erika was relieved. "Yes sir, I am!"

"She's waiting for you at the supply area. She's helping organize the food stores. You can head over there—oh, and it's very nice to finally meet you." Andrew was very welcoming and Erika could understand why he had been chosen as a leader.

Erika felt her heart pounding out of her chest with excitement as she and Vince pulled the last cart with Greg in it across a suspension bridge that had been resurrected where the old bridge that had crossed the river had once been. As soon as they reached the other side, Ripper came running up to meet them. The mud could not cover their scent from the dog. He barked and danced at their feet as Vince and Erika showered him in pets and praises. On the right, where an old hotel had stood, were tons of tents and shanties made from the wrecked wood of the hotel. People they didn't recognize stood on the hill by the tents; some were waving with smiles and some were attending to tasks with grim faces dripping in the rain. They continued to follow the caravan.

Lotus and Coloma were side-by-side towns with very little distinction between the two. Coloma was where gold was originally discovered in California and a historical area had been kept to remember the past. Ironically, it was mostly these buildings that had survived so far. The area they were taking the supplies to had once been a museum filled with tools from the past. The people were putting them back into use and horses pulled the historical carts around the camp, busily rebuilding a town for survivors. There was a *clang, clang, clang* coming from the old blacksmith shop, which was now back in full operation. Erika could not help but feel that she had stepped back in time.

"Mom!" Erika said excitedly to Vince as she nudged him. She had seen her mom up by the supply house, but she was met by another family member first. "Dexter!" He ran to meet them, and Erika was almost breathless as she reached out and hugged him, spinning him around in the air. Vince jumped in and wrapped them both up in his arms. They all fell on the ground, laughing.

Greg poked his head over the side of the cart and watched with a loving smile at the three of them all wrapped up in love, rolling and laughing on the ground. "What about uncle G," he said. "Where's my hug?" Dexter got up in the cart and tackled Greg, giving him a huge hug.

"Where's Star, Dex?" Erika questioned with urgency.

"She's in helping Grandma. They said I was too little and should just go play with the other kids, but I'm not too little, Mom. I'm strong and I can help," he said in a pouty voice.

"I know, Dex, you're my big boy right?" Erika said lovingly.

"That's right!" Dexter said confidently.

"Well, let's go see where they are then." Erika smiled so wide she thought her cheeks would bust.

"Come on, Mom, I'll show you." Dexter grabbed Erika's hand and began to pull her along.

Erika looked at Vince, asking him with her eyes if it was all right to go.

"You guys go ahead. Greg and I can get in line with this stuff. I'm sure we can find someone to help get the cart over there," Vince said, knowing what her look meant.

"Are you sure, Vince, I can stay here and help." Erika wanted to double check.

"Just go and I'll catch up," Vince replied.

"Come on, Mom," Dexter yelled pulling Erika along as hard as he could.

Erika felt like a little kid at Christmas as she followed him through a mass of people. With all the supplies coming in, it was all hands on deck. Some people were sorting and storing, food was cooking, some were leading the new folks off to camp areas, and everyone was busy doing something. Dexter led Erika past the line of people and through the main sorting area. Erika could smell the food cooking strongly now as they entered the food storage area. She waved at Clay and Laurie Roberts as they went by. They were right at home preparing food for the camp. Erika and Dex walked past a big pile of boxes and there was her mom. Erika had stopped so she could just take in the image. She was alive and well and just as busy as ever. She was in her element, surveying each item and directing people to where that item would be stored.

"Come on, Mom," Dexter said as he pulled at her again. "Grandma, look!" he yelled.

Erika's mom looked up from her task, almost disgusted with Dexter's latest distraction. She saw Erika and dropped the box in her hands. She ran over to her daughter with tears streaming down her face.

"Oh my God! Thank you, God! My baby!" The words were hard to find so she just gave Erika the hugest hug she could muster. "I thought... I thought you were..."

"I know, Mom," Erika said, not wanting her mom to say what Erika knew she was going to. "Everything is going to be okay."

"My baby... I love you so much!" she said as she held tight to her daughter.

"Erika!" Star yelled. She had heard the commotion and came running out from a stack of boxes.

"Hey, girl," Erika replied lovingly. They all hugged and no one wanted to let go.

"I got to get in on this," Dexter said and it was a big ball of loving hugs all over again.

They were interrupted by a man saying, "Hey, Nancy, where should I put this?" He had a big box in his hands.

"Just put it there and I'll take care of it," Erika's mom, Nancy, replied.

They all wanted to hug forever but necessity was knocking at the door and there was work to be done.

"Erika, don't you go anywhere, but I have to sort and store this stuff," Nancy commanded her daughter.

Erika could see that her mom was torn between visiting with her daughter and the task at hand. "Just tell me what to do, Mom, and I'll help." Erika didn't want to leave her mom right now either.

"Oh, but look at you, you're all a mess. You should go get cleaned up," Nancy admonished as she stepped back to get a look at her daughter.

"Nonsense, I'm always a mess nowadays. That can wait." Erika didn't care what she looked like; she wasn't going anywhere.

Erika did take a little scrub in a nearby bucket of water that was going to be used to wash dishes after the camp was fed. Then she jumped right in stacking boxes and unpacking cans with her mom, Star, and a lady named Cathy. Cathy was her mother's neighbor before the quake. There were other men and ladies about but they were busy cooking a feast for the new arrivals. From her vantage point amongst the incoming boxes, she could see the folks from Auburn all lined up outside like cattle. First, they would pull their cart into the unloading zone and have a brief conversation about its contents with a receiver. Then, they would take their personal belongings, which usually consisted of a backpack or two, and get into another line. Here, they would discuss what they did before the quake and what use they could be now. Then they would be led off to an area where they would live now. Most of the folks looked completely exhausted. Their trek had been long and their lives were obliterated.

Erika talked with her mom while they were working. Her mom had always been in touch with all the local drama and was a wealth of knowledge about the goings on in the community. Erika found out that one man she had met at the Auburn River camp, Jim Harlow, was heading up an electricity team, and they were able to get power to the kitchen and a couple of other buildings. Erika informed her that they had brought a bunch of equipment for power production and Nancy agreed that it would be put to good use. Richard, who had been watching over the children in his wife's stead, was now putting together a school so the kids would have some structure. Dexter and Star would be attending as soon as Richard had it all set up.

Nancy was ecstatic that Greg had made it back with them but saddened by the loss of his father. Greg had helped her in the past with landscaping and carpentry needs around her property, and Nancy told Erika, time and time again, how highly she respected his skills. Erika explained his current situation and Nancy assured her that she would help him get back on his feet.

Nancy went on telling Erika about folks Erika would know. Ryan Crest, the nurse who had been thrust into life as a doctor, found a few volunteer firemen who were also EMTs and greatly improved their medical area. No one had really given it structure before him, and the community was very happy to have someone to treat everyday issues, not just trauma. Erika told Nancy that another doctor and tons of medical supplies had come with them. Nancy assured Erika that Ryan would welcome him with open arms.

"Margie Cassavoy and her partner, Bob Hawthorne," Nancy continued, "were very welcomed for their moonshining skills. Some local men helped them set up a series of stills and they have not only been making alcohol out of everything possible, but they were purifying water as well."

"Sounds like you are well informed," Erika said sarcastically. In reality, she was thrilled about the normality of the conversation. It was just like when she used to sit on the counter as a kid and listen to her mother talk about this and that. "Where's Brett?" Brett had been her mother's best friend before the quake, and she knew from Vince that he had survived the quake and headed this way.

"Oh, he's around here somewhere," Nancy replied whimsically. "You know him. He's probably out getting firewood or building housing or fences or something."

Finally, she saw Vince with Greg hobbling along beside him in the line. They were the very last ones. They didn't need to get in the second line because they would be staying with Nancy, so once they had their supplies checked in they came over to join Erika.

"Vince! Get over here and give me a hug. You too, Greg," Nancy demanded. "You son of a gun, you told me she was alive... that she would come home. I didn't believe it. I wanted to... but I just couldn't. But thank the good Lord above, here she is. You son of a gun; you were right. Then you idiots go tramping off toward death and send your kids here alone. I should kill you both right here where you stand for even thinking it, but here you are all safe and almost sound. Now, no more forays seeking victory over one group or another."

"Mom, knock it off. We had to go." Erika had to stop the scolding. They had already been through so much.

"I know the story and I understand why you all had to go. That's why I am not going to say anything else except this, you all better stay safe, or I'll kill you myself." Nancy winked and everyone laughed. "Now let's finish getting this stuff put away so we can get you all settled."

"Nancy"—Greg was looking puzzled—"I thought that Dakota would be here. I sent him with the caravan."

"Didn't Steve tell you, Greg? Dakota didn't make it. The trip over here was just too much for his old body and he died along the way. I'm sorry," Nancy said solemnly.

"I knew he was on his way out, bummer," Greg said sadly.

"They took the time to bury him under a tree. Steve felt really bad so it's no wonder he didn't say anything." Nancy tried to console him.

"It's okay, I just wish I could have been there to see him off." Greg had known for a while that Dakota was living on borrowed time so the pain didn't bite too hard.

Nancy gave Greg a big hug. "Come on and help me with these boxes; it will take your mind off it."

Everyone pitched in and, soon, the boxes were put away. By the time they were finished and walking outside, the lines of people were all gone. All that was left was a buzz of voices coming from all around the camp.

CHAPTER 31

NANCY'S TENT WAS located clear on the other side of the gated area known as the Lotus camp. They had to go back past the old hotel, which was now a clutter of people moving from one sleeping area to another. The current residents were consolidating so that there was room for the new residents. At the old hotel, they turned left along what used to be a road but was now a broken landscape next to the river. It appeared that every flat spot had a tent or lean-to erected on it, except along the trail they were following. They walked past an area that used to be a pristine park on the river but was now filled with tents, temporary structures, and people. Finally, they neared another gate where the road to get to her mom's old house had been. There was a rafting company located on that corner just inside where the new gate was, and the remnants of the building had been rebuilt into tented sleeping areas.

"Well, this is it, guys," Nancy said as she pulled back the curtain on a wooden makeshift structure. The structure had a fireplace built in the main room and three little curtained coverings in the back that were tents with their openings connected to the main area.

"Nice, Mom." Erika was impressed. She had been sleeping in balls of humanity and it would be nice to have some privacy.

"Brett added on the extra sleeping areas after we saw Big John and heard you were alive and headed this way. He figured we could use the tent on the left, you and Vince can have the middle, and we'll put Greg on the end. The kids can crash here by the fire or wherever they fall down. There are even mattresses in the sleeping areas," Nancy boasted.

"Are you serious? A real mattress?" Erika was thrilled. She had hated camping in the past just because she could never get comfortable on the ground. She hadn't slept on a mattress since the quake; it would be like heaven.

"Oh yeah, where is Big John now?" Vince questioned. He was impressed with the sleeping arrangement as well, but he was more concerned with the safety of his friend.

"Big John went back up through Georgetown to scout a way out of California. It's kind of a touchy subject; he and Brett got in a big argument. Big John doesn't think this is over and he says the worst is still to come," Nancy said in a hushed voice.

"Well, neither do I," Erika said loudly.

"Shhh…" Nancy commanded quickly. "Let's not worry about that now. Let's get you settled in and cleaned up. There's going to be lots to eat tonight, and everyone will be there. There will be music and dancing." Nancy was strategically changing the subject.

Erika noticed the quick change of subject and decided to leave it alone for now. Besides, they had cheated death again and reunited as a family: it was time to celebrate. The horrible world they faced would be there tomorrow, so why not enjoy the evening.

"Mom, why camp all the way out here if you are helping with the kitchen all the way over there?" Erika wondered.

"I just help stock the kitchen and I used to cook sometimes. Now that Clay and Laurie have arrived, they have things in perfect order. I mostly hike out toward the old property where the farms are," she replied.

"Wow, farms. You guys really are rebuilding here," said Erika, truly impressed with their level of organization.

"Well, people have to eat and Andrew runs this place like clockwork. He has set up military training, food production, the blacksmith shop, carpentry shops, and now the school, so folks can survive and be useful. The soldiers repair the roads, get wood, make weapons, hunt, and, most of all, protect our supplies. It's really coming along," Nancy said with pride.

"Sounds like it." Erika gave Vince a sideways look. She wasn't sure how she should feel about this. On one hand, she wanted to believe the disaster was over and they could just rebuild and live, but on the other hand, she had this sickening feeling that Mother Nature wasn't finished. There was more to this changing Earth than anyone could guess.

Vince could feel her dilemma and tried to get her mind off it. "Look, babe, here's all your stuff that we sent back with the kids."

"Well… almost all your stuff. I found a pack of Marlboro Light 100s in your first aid kit and I have to admit that I took it," Nancy said honestly.

"That's fine, Mom, I had been saving it for you." The pack had instantly reminded Erika of her mom, and she knew it would be cherished.

"Thank you, Erika. I can't tell you how bad I've wanted one of these." Nancy gave her a hug. "Oh Vince, Big John even brought your stuff from your camp. I washed all the clothes you both had so you guys will be all fresh. Now each little camp has their own bathrooms so you have to take your stuff and head over there. Once you go out the tent, it's over on the left. It's not very nice but at least there are showers, kind of, and a place to potty. I'll get the kids cleaned up and make sure Greg is okay, so just get going." Nancy was always the organizer and she was in full swing again.

Erika and Vince got their tent organized and made sure that the kids were in order. Then they grabbed their piles of clean clothes and headed out into the camp. This group looked to be about ten of the same setups that Nancy had and, at the end, was a wooden structure with a small crowd gathered around it. They headed toward the group. There was a line for the shower so they waited in it. The line moved slowly. People were saying small pleasantries, but most were focused on the night and not much for chatter right now. They recognized the couple in front of them. Dan was a gentleman with an average build, jet-black hair, and matching eyes. He had been a firefighter in Georgetown before the quake. His wife, Val, was a taller woman with a very strong build. She had blue-grey eyes and sandy blond hair. Vince knew them best so they quietly chatted. They had owned a horse farm in Georgetown that Val ran. Although they had lost most of their horses when the barn collapsed, they had saved five and were currently in charge of horse care along with another man named Drew Goddard. They were training some horses for military use, plowing, and cart pulling. Val had told Erika that Kit was out there, and she was more than welcome to stop by and see him anytime. Finally, the two couples got to the front of the line. Because of the amount of people needing to use the facilities, it was normal for couples to shower together to save time and water, so Dan and Val got in next.

Erika noticed a man, Glen Wales, was his name. He was in charge of keeping the shower reservoir full and informed Erika that the best time to get a hot shower was at the very end of the day but before everyone else got there. That way, the sun had time to heat the water and it had not been drained and refilled. He was a talkative man, and Erika was sick of hearing about showers by the time it was their turn to step in.

Vince and Erika gave each other the thank God he shut up look and giggled at one another. With so many people around, you didn't want to be overheard saying something derogative, but a look could be worth a million words. As they undressed and began to wash the mud away, they looked longingly at one another, but their modesty overpowered their urges. There was soap but no shampoo and conditioner. Erika figured maybe the new supplies had not been allotted to the individual camps yet. They finished up, re-dressed, and headed out.

There, in line, were Harold and Betsy, still all covered in mud.

"Hey, you two," Erika said cheerfully.

"Hey, Erika, Vince," Harold replied.

"How about this place?" Betsy said enthusiastically.

"It's really something," Erika agreed. "You guys staying over here too?"

"Yes, we were assigned here because of Betsy and Carol's farming knowledge and Kim's horse skills. I'm going to attempt to set up a communications center with Jimmy D using some of the gear we brought back from Auburn," Harold replied.

"Cool, do you think it will work?" Erika questioned. She hadn't even thought of trying to communicate with other survivors.

"I think so, but we'll see if the gear is still useable and who is actually out there." Harold was trying to stay optimistic.

"Well, good luck," said Erika. "We'll see you guys tonight."

"See you then," Betsy replied.

When they got back to the house, Brett was back from his day's tasks. He was going to help Greg get to the showers. They said their hellos and hugged one another and then Brett and Greg left. Dexter and Star were playing with a couple of trucks that Dexter had and Vince joined in the play as Erika and her mother chatted quietly at a little table. Erika told her mother all about her ordeal of escaping Sacramento and showed her some of her scarring.

"Good God, girl, look at you," Nancy said as she looked over Erika's extensive scarring. "I am damn lucky to have you back."

"You don't even know," Erika replied. She was getting used to her scarring. It was almost like they had always been there now. The old scars had healed a long time ago and new ones had formed over the top of those.

Erika went on to tell her mom about Henry and Carol and how Star came to be in the family.

"She watched the whole thing?" Nancy was outraged as she listened to what had happened to Star's mother.

"Yeah, Mom, she was right there in the bushes." Erika was still horrified by the story as well. She couldn't believe what an animal that man was, or what she herself had done. It was like she was someone else that day, but she was really thankful to have Star in her life so you have to take the good with the bad.

As if reading her mind, Nancy said, "I really like that girl. She is such an in-charge little lady. I never would have thought… that she… she went through…"

"I know, Mom. That's just life now. That was the first time I killed. I was sick, but now I have killed so many more." Erika paused for a moment to reflect. "I have killed, Mom." Erika was trying to rationalize these feelings. Her mother knew every fiber of who Erika was. Her mother knew she was totally capable of killing if she needed to, but she saw the moral struggle clearly in her eyes.

"Erika, you had to survive and you had to protect what's good in this world. I am so proud of you." Nancy squeezed Erika's hand in her own. "It's going to get better," Nancy finished.

Erika wanted to believe that so deeply. She wished it with all her heart, but she knew it was not over. It was merely the beginning of the end. Vince had been listening to their conversation while he was playing with the kids and stepped over to them. He had never heard Star's whole story and it all made sense now.

He knew that the kids had also been listening in and wanted to shield them.

"So my lovely ladies, you all ready for a night on the town?" Vince jested.

"Are we ever!" Nancy said lightheartedly. They were soon laughing and teasing one another.

"So, who's going to be the sober driver?" Erika chimed in.

"We definitely don't have to worry about that now." Nancy was saying as Greg and Brett walked back in.

"Worry about what?" Brett questioned curiously.

"A sober driver," Vince said winking at Greg.

"No more DUIs!" Greg continued the game. "Hell yeah, maybe this place isn't so bad."

"If you weren't such a ding dong, you wouldn't have had to worry about that before the quake," Erika poked at Greg.

"Oh yeah, Erika, I'll still kick your butt with a bum leg and shoulder." Greg was trying to put up his dukes like he was going to do something. "I didn't have anyone to take turns driving with when I was at the bar like you two."

"Like you would have had a sober driver, even if you did have someone to trade off with," Vince jested again.

"You're probably right," Greg said and put down his fists, defeated.

"I'm gonna get ya, Uncle G!" Dexter yelled as he ran over to hug Greg. He nearly knocked him down.

"Well, come on then." Greg was always romping with Dex. "Oh, darn kid. I think you grew while I was in the shower."

Dexter tried to wrestle with him for a little while but was quickly scolded for the behavior given Greg's current condition. Star was also excited about the evening and the air was thick with joy.

"We better get going," Brett said matter-of-factly.

They all gathered up anything they would need for the evening into a couple of backpacks and headed out together, with Ripper close on their heels. Outside, they met up with the folks from their little camp that were headed for the communal space. They all walked down the trail together, and as they walked, they were joined by more and more people from all the other little camps along the way. Erika had no idea how large the Lotus camp group actually was but it was huge. Everyone from the surrounding area that had survived was here. As more and more people joined the procession, the chatter from the crowd increased. Despite the recent rain and their current situation, spirits were high.

Tonight, there were lots of reasons to celebrate. The current group just got a ton of food and miscellaneous supplies, plus a doctor and loads of medical supplies. The Cool group found a more stable home with plenty of water. The Auburn group had found a new home free from the tyranny of a psychotic leader. Plus, many families had been reunited today. Everyone was happy and smiling.

The procession had to file through many areas of the trail, where the quakes had completely disrupted the landscape and turned it into a walkway, only big enough for a couple people to fit through but everyone was polite and courteous. Little children were helped over the rough spots and elderly people received any assistance they needed as well. Seeing the elderly people made Erika realized there weren't many of them around. With their limited mobility, many had died in the first quake. Many of those that survived the quake were on medication that they could no longer get and perished because of it. People were calling it the great die-off after the quake. Even though Erika had been in her own hellish situation, she was glad she had not been around to bear witness to that.

"Pretty warm tonight because of those clouds; I hope the rain holds off," said Nancy, snapping Erika out of her thoughts.

"Seriously, I don't think I could handle any more rain after the trip here." Erika was thinking of the arduous cliff crossing.

"Well, at least, we won't be dragging Greg's gimpy butt through two feet of mud," Vince said sarcastically.

"Hey, I told you guys to just leave me. You guys are the ones who brought me so it's all on you now," Greg said in a pouty voice.

"Come on now, that's enough picking on each other. We are going to have fun tonight," Nancy said with a wink. She didn't want the teasing to go too far and someone's feelings getting hurt. "You'll be right as rain in no time. Now get your butt over here so we can go get some hot food."

Greg smiled and Nancy wrapped her arm around him. They were headed toward the food building and the crowd was thick. Their procession had blended with the rest of the camp and the mass of people was awe inspiring. It was like being at the fair, a concert, or a festival back in the old days.

"Usually, the camp comes in shifts to get food so we can stagger the groups. There is going to be a long line," Nancy muttered.

"Oh well, there's going to be food. Remember, we are going to have fun tonight," Vince said poking Nancy's words back at her in jest.

"Food!" Dexter yelled joylessly.

"You hungry, little man?" Erika questioned.

"Oh yeah, Mom, I'm so hungry I could eat a whole cow!" Dexter said ambitiously.

"A whole cow? Wow! Let's just start with a heaping plateful and we'll go from there. Okay, buddy?" Erika quieted him.

"K', Mommy but the line is so loooooong," he said as if he would die of starvation. He began to run a circle around them in the line.

"I'm gonna get you!" Star yelled as she ran off after him. Her limp was becoming less noticeable as her leg began to heal.

"You guys can play around over there if you want while we wait in line. I'll call you when it's our turn." Erika knew the pain of waiting as a child.

The kids ran off screaming. Soon they joined up with other kids from the rest of the camp and the games began. Ripper had found the other dogs that were there and they were all fighting over scraps from the kitchen. Erika had to admit it was a painful wait because the line was long and the food smelled delicious.

"This is worse than watching cooking shows when you're hungry," Erika told Vince.

"No kidding. I'm beginning to notice a pattern at this camp, long lines!" Vince replied.

"Greg, why don't you go and see if you can weasel your way in at the front. That way you won't have to stand here on that leg," Nancy told Greg.

"Good idea, Nancy," Greg replied. "At least I can get something good out of this bum knee."

Greg hobbled off towards the front while they all waited. A huge fire could be seen in the middle of the field with lots of people around it and a group of people that had saved or made instruments were beginning to strike up a tune. Erika just couldn't shake the feeling that this was like being at a festival. It was the only time in her life she had camped in such a mass of people. The noise of voices, the clatter of things being done, and the sound of music was everywhere.

Before long they were at the front of the line. The kids had not rejoined them yet so Vince and Erika each made extra plates for them. The food was an assortment of canned foods that had been salvaged. In addition to wild game, fish, vegetables, and herbs that had been gathered from the land. One particularly interesting dish was a plate of a weird nutlike root. Laurie explained to Erika that a woman from the Lotus camp had found a good cache of them nearby. It was called Yampa and it had a flavor similar to that of water chestnuts. Tonight, they had found enough to make a whole dish of them, but they could also be used as a seasoning like caraway seeds. This dish they had baked, and Laurie said it definitely was worth trying. Erika took a little bit just to try. She had never been a big fan of water chestnuts so it didn't sound too interesting to her. Overall, the food was delicious and piping hot. No one talked while they devoured the nourishing food. They just sat huddled over their plates. The kids had finally rejoined the family and dug into the food with a fury. Once everyone at the camp had made it through the line, the people were allowed back in for seconds so nothing would go to waste.

When the food was gone, the music really started rocking. It seemed the camp was alive with song and dance. Erika and Vince held each other close and danced. Rarely had Vince danced in the past, and Erika was surprised that he would want to do it so often but there was no holding back now. Life was too precious. He had watched couples dancing during the months Erika was gone and wished so badly he could have been dancing with her. He was not going to pass up any opportunity to do so and Erika was in heaven dancing with her man. Young children and old folks joined in the fun and smiles were everywhere. Drinks flowed from Margie's makeshift bar and Bob was hard at work refilling bottles from the stills. Erika saw everyone she knew merrily enjoying the evening. When she and Vince began getting tired of dancing, they sat at the large fire enjoying the company of their friends. Ripper finally showed back up and lay down behind them.

Randy and Michelle had officially become an item. They were holding hands and relishing in the fact that they were allowed to drink. They were old enough to fight and the rules of the old world didn't exactly apply now. They told Erika that Andrew had taken them into the militia and they were housed over by the training area. They were assigned training times and guard duties. They also told Erika that Rob had been an especially welcome addition to the militia and was quickly becoming Andrew's right-hand man. He was an experienced military man and knew training techniques. He was also an accomplished hunter and was now assigned to leading hunting expeditions and salvage parties. They also said that Taylor and Tom had joined the militia and were camped in the same area as Randy and Michelle. Soon they left to go and dance again and Erika was pleased to hear that they were fitting in so well.

Jimmy D arrived full of jokes and smiles. During their conversation, he informed Erika that, with all his knowledge of electrical issues, he had teamed up with the other Jim, Jim Harlow from the Auburn River camp, as well as Harold and a guy from the Lotus camp. They were camped close to the kitchen and they were working on getting power to the medical building as well as getting a communications station up and running. Before long, Diana Walker from the Cool camp arrived and sat next to him. Diana's husband had been killed and she had two sons—John and Rain—who used to go to school with Dexter. She was a pretty woman and judging from the smiles and flirting that she and Jimmy were passing back and forth, it was clear they had something going as well. Diana used to work in a doctor's office so she was handling incoming patients and supply maintenance and inventory over at the camp's doctor's office. She was camped over in the doctor's area, which was not far from Jimmy D.

Steve Dunch came and sat down with Brett. Erika learned from him that he did not want to participate in the militia anymore even though he was a valued fighter. It was just too much for him. He had done construction in the past and was involved in building homes and salvaging wood. He was working daily with Brett and their friendship was growing.

To Erika's surprise, Richard also showed up. He was finally childless for the evening. All the kids were keeping themselves busy and he joined the adult conversation. He said he really missed having adults to talk with, but the whole time all he did was talk about the school and how well the children were doing. It was his way of focusing on the now and not reliving the pain of losing Joan.

Clay and Laurie Roberts also sat down to talk with Erika and Vince, once the kitchen duties were done for the night. Having owned a restaurant in Cool before the quake, they knew most of the former Cool community very well. They knew that Vince's parents had been in Washington and told him that they were saying prayers that they too were alive. A little tear came to Vince's eye and you could see he was touched. It was a very hard subject for him to face. He was the kind of guy that usually kept all his feeling bottled up with a thick cork. When they mentioned his parents, it was obvious that they had popped the cork, but Vince was doing his best to keep the emotions contained. When Clay and Laurie left to go mingle with other folks, Erika held him tight. Eventually, he pushed away, assuring her he was "just fine."

Despite some hard topics, it was so awesome to sit and visit with everyone. It was almost normal except that they were out in the open by a big fire, instead of huddled in some building somewhere. As the night wore on, the people began to feel the effects of the liquor. The dancing began to mellow and the storytelling began up on stage. It was a much more elaborate show at this camp. Actors backed up by the musicians played out the parts of stories both old and new. There was a rendition of "The Hobbit" playing out and the kids loved it. Survival stories were also acted out. Erika learned the story of the coming together of the people of the Lotus camp. They also told the story of someone's family member who had come and found his family all the way from the Yosemite area. He had been out camping when the quakes hit, so he had all his supplies and just started hiking back to find his family.

Soon, Erika found out she was also the key character of one of the plays: a camp favorite. It was a play based on her experiences that she had told when she reached the Cool camp. It was obvious to Erika that certain areas had been embellished, but everyone was surprised by a survivor coming from the west. From what Erika understood, the entire western side of California was in dire straits. The ocean had not been immune from the quakes and great waves had ravished the coastline and the cities all the way up to the coastal mountain range. Thankfully, the mountains had seemed to create a barrier for the rest of the state, for now.

Erika's mom broke up Erika's daydreaming. "I didn't want to tell you. I had already heard your story before you told me; I wanted to hear it from you."

"Wow, that's crazy. How long have they been doing a play from my story?" Erika was shocked that her story would now be played out but she should have realized after she saw them playing out the other stories.

"Since they heard the story a few weeks ago. A man from our camp had been up gathering information when you arrived and told your story. I was so thankful to know you were alive. That's why I was so upset it took you so long to get here," Nancy replied.

"Mommy, Mommy, it's about you and Star," Dexter yelled excitedly.

"I know, honey; it's crazy, isn't it?" Erika said.

When the story had finished, the crowd roared. Thankfully, they had left out the part about Star's mom being raped and just played that part out with Erika finding a girl in the bushes. The next play was about how a small group had invaded and conquered the monsters in Auburn. When that one was over, they announced that the stars of the shows had arrived and asked the whole attack party, including Erika and Star, to stand up and be recognized for their heroic achievements. Everyone cheered for them and Erika blushed. She did not enjoy being the center of all this attention. After that, her night became more miserable than joyful. People kept asking her about the story and if they could see her scars. These were two things she just wanted to forget and they were shoved at her all night. She was surrounded by a crowd when suddenly Vince broke through and grabbed her hand.

"You want to get out of here?" Vince saw she was tired of the attention, but he was also a little jealous and was sick of sharing her.

"Hell yes," Erika replied.

They quietly snuck away and found Nancy and Brett. They let them know that they were going back to their little camp. Nancy said she would make sure the kids got back safely. Ripper knew something was up and was at Erika's side in a second. They crept over to where the trail home was. Greg was there with a woman. They had been quietly chatting in the dark.

"Sneaking out on me again?" he asked. He had his eye on them and had seen the tide turn during the night. Even though he had met a wonderful woman who had let him into the food line in front of her, he wanted to be with his friends and brought her along. "This is Penni, and look what we snuck away." He held up a bottle of vodka—real vodka, not the homemade stuff.

"Sweet," said Erika, "let's go then."

"Getting a little too crazy for you?" Greg questioned sarcastically.

"Just a little," said Erika with a sigh.

The four of them made their way back to the home camp and lit the central fire there.

"I am so sick of smelling like a bonfire," Penni said. She seemed like a nice woman. She had sandy blond hair and green eyes. She seemed older than they were; maybe in her late thirties.

"I know," replied Erika politely, "seems like there is no escaping it."

The ice was broken and the two women hit it off grandly. Penni was so feminine and Erika had never been very girly. It was an uncanny matchup but it worked perfectly. The four of them drank and talked the rest of the night away. Erika dug out the few cigarettes she had left and they had a couple of them along with a joint that Greg had been saving. It was perfect. Erika had never enjoyed large groups of people and she was much more comfortable in this setting.

As the night wore on, other folks from the family camp returned. Some joined in the conversation around the fire and others went right to bed. Nancy and Brett returned with Dexter asleep in Brett's arms and Star sleepily dragging her feet along.

Once the kids were put to bed, Erika and Vince stayed for a little longer at the fire then they went to bed as well. They made love. A fast, hot, drug-induced extravaganza that drove them both into a deep sleep.

CHAPTER 32

LIFE WORE ON fairly peacefully at the Lotus camp over the next few days. Erika and Vince decided to train with the fighters. They practiced their martial arts and shooting skills, but they also learned many new wilderness survival skills. Greg was getting much better. He trained a little when he was feeling up to it, but he mostly spent his time with Penni. They were really getting close. Greg was ignoring all the other girls and only wanted to be with Penni; Erika was impressed. Erika and Penni were getting really close as well. Erika learned that it was probably best that Dakota died on the trek over here because Penni really wasn't too much of a dog lover, especially not one that stunk and drooled a lot. It was an excellent friendship for Erika to have because most of the time she was off training with the guys and it gave her a chance to be feminine and discuss girl things. They complained about kids and guys and discussed how to handle that time of the month now that supplies of sanitary napkins were running low. Most of the women needed them once a month, and there was no way that there would be enough for everyone so the women had to get creative and go old school with piles of rags sown into washable pads.

The kids went to school with the other kids. There they learned everything from history and math to fighting and survival skills. They had a great opportunity to learn, be active in the community, and play with other kids. Everyone welcomed the idea of the children attending school because no one wanted bored children running underfoot all the time.

Even though things seemed to be going well and no one wanted to admit it, no one felt the trauma was over. It was a hushed subject. The people here just wanted to focus on the now; taking care of their families, and carving out some kind of normal life for themselves.

The rain came and went in scattered showers. This was a weird, early October for California. Even without the quakes, it was not normal to have this much rain. It was still pretty warm though, so Erika was confident it was raining and not snowing up higher in the mountains. Snow now would totally crush their hopes of crossing the mountains this year. They would have to wait for the snow to melt and that would keep them here far too long.

Even though life seemed to be going fine, Erika was still itching to go. She thought about it all the time and discussed it with Vince, but Nancy and Brett didn't want to hear it. They were warm and safe and didn't see any reason to go off into the unknown. Erika kept quiet and just went on training, all the while planning what they would need to pack.

Nancy could feel Erika's restlessness and thought if she could just get Erika to take an interest in things at the camp instead of just training and hunting all the time, then she would have something to look forward to here in the future. Maybe this would settle her down a little. It was a sunny day when Nancy woke up Erika and asked her if she would like to forgo training today and go out to the gardens instead. Vince, overhearing the request, was very interested in going out to see what they had set up. He had always loved growing gardens and landscaping. Erika was hesitant. She was keeping her focus on training her body to match any threat that she encountered. She was honing her hunting skills to ensure she could always provide food for her family. Vince had enough of the military training, though, and he was very persuasive.

"Come on, baby, let's just blow the day off and go check it out," he pleaded. "We are going to have to know how to grow food too; we can't just hunt for everything we need." He was trying to find a way of enticing her that would make sense to her.

"You know how to grow food, Vince, and we were supposed to be working on defense techniques in the yard today. We may miss something good," Erika retorted.

"Look, it's like our master instructor used to tell us, there is only a handful of basic techniques. Then it's all about application from there. We have been training nonstop since we got here. Don't get me wrong, I have loved hunting and learning, but come on, we need a rest. What would be so wrong with a walk through the woods with your sweetheart," he said with a wink. "Plus you could stop by and visit with Kit on the way home. You haven't seen him in a while." She had shrugged off his wink so he continued to dig for enticing reasons for her to come.

"You are right. I haven't seen Kit in a while. Plus I would like to see the horse set up and training area." She was being swayed.

"Well, you two need to make up your mind because I am headed out," Nancy yelled from the other room.

"All right, all right," Erika yelled back, "just give us a minute." She put down her martial arts training gear and loaded her holster with her pistol.

"I'm going to check on the kids and make sure they are getting ready for school," Vince said with a wide smile. He was excited for the change of pace.

Erika headed out to go see her mom. Nancy was just finishing loading bags of compost she had been harvesting from the kitchen into a cart so they could take them out to the garden sites.

"Oh, now I see why you wanted us to go. You want us to drag all that stuff out there," Erika said teasingly.

"No, I was looking forward to spending the day with you but since you're coming... I might as well put all those muscles you two have been building to use," she said, engaging in the game.

Erika helped her finish loading the bags and before long, Vince appeared with Dexter and Star. Erika gave them each a kiss and they trotted down the trail toward the school which had been built in the central area of the main camp. Erika noticed that some clouds were rolling in and she was glad she had chosen to go to the gardens. The training field would probably be a muddy mess by the afternoon. Ripper tagged along at her side watching the kids go. Sometimes he would follow them, but today, he knew they were doing something different so he decided to go along with Vince and Erika. They had asked Greg if he wanted to come but he was going over to help Penni at the kitchen. He said Penni would not want to go hiking if the sun was not shining. She would rather stay indoors and wait for a warmer day. The kitchen would be plenty warm and she was busy putting together table cloths and decorations for the eating area. She said that they should still have some class even in this screwed-up situation. Erika thought it was kind of silly but she had to admit that the little changes Penni was making did make the area seem fancy and more normal.

Erika, Vince, and Nancy headed through a side gate to the camp and down a trail that used to be a road that Erika had known well. She had traveled this road to get to her mom's ranch at least twice a week. It was a long, winding road right next to the river but it was a mess now. The quakes had shifted it this way and that. Trees and rocks had shifted and fallen, making an even more treacherous path. There was a little bridge on the road not far in from where one can turn onto it and it had been completely destroyed. The little creek that moved under it was now swollen from the recent rains and it made the crossing interesting. Fallen trees had been moved and carved into a bridge. They carefully pulled the cart across the shifty structure. Nancy was so glad that they decided to come. She would have had to have some of the other garden hands pull the cart otherwise, and she had specific plans for this load of compost.

After the bridge crossing, the walk became easier. It was nice enjoying the peace and quiet with her family and not worrying about life threatening issues like attacks and defenses. They stayed to the right side of the trail along the river. Soon they came to where the summer crops had been planted and were being harvested. Erika and Vince were impressed. There were rows and rows of squashes, tomatoes, and pumpkins. They had been planted in close proximity to the river so that the water could be diverted to irrigation ditches with the push and pull of a board through a box system. The plants looked healthy and their bounteous vegetables were providing well for the Lotus camp. Erika and Vince saw Betsy out picking weeds and harvesting ripe vegetables. Nancy went off to talk with the head gardener. Vince and Erika did not know the gentleman well so they went over to talk with Betsy.

"Hello, you two, nice to see you out here today," Betsy said in her sweet voice.

"Hey, how are you?" Erika asked.

"Doing fine; isn't this something?" Betsy said as she looked over the garden site.

"It really is," said Vince. "How did they pull this off?" He was dumbfounded by the amount of plants and the system they had.

"Ricardo Manuella, that man your mom is talking to, he came up with the idea. I guess a lot of people out this way had little family gardens so the garden team from camp went around and found all the plants that they could salvage. Glen Wales, the man who fills the shower too; he has lived in this area for generations and he knew how to maximize the river so that they could save all the plants they could find. Instead of hauling water all the way out to the plants, they moved them all here and developed this irrigation system. Pretty cool, isn't it?" she said rhetorically.

"Wow, this is awesome!" Vince was enthralled. He immediately wanted to know all about how the whole system functioned, where they had got plants from, and what they were using for fertilizer. He started wandering about talking with the various workers and eventually ended up over with Ricardo and Nancy.

Erika stayed behind with Betsy. Erika had liked planting and harvesting a garden in the past and she had to admit that this garden was certainly was doing its job to feed the camp. Deep down, though, she knew they would be leaving so it seemed kind of silly to focus on something that needed time in one place to be productive. She started to help Betsy with her harvesting and engage in some small talk.

"Where is Carol?" Erika wondered.

"Her arthritis was flaring up and she did not want to walk all the way out here today. She decided to stay home and take care of laundry." It was a direct answer for a direct question.

"So, I know this is a touchy subject but how is Jen doing?" Erika never was one to beat around the bush with a topic. She just blurted it out.

"She is doing better," Betsy said with a far-off look in her eyes. "She is still not the same girl I knew not so long ago but it's getting better. She is talking more and she has taken an interest in going out to the horses with her sister, Kim. The animals bring her peace, she says."

"I can see that," Erika agreed. "I always loved just spending time with my horse when I was little. I even had a hammock hung in the stall next to his. I used to read and even sleep out there. I am glad to hear she is doing better. I couldn't help but feel somewhat responsible."

"I have to admit to you, Erika, that I was a little angry when everything first happened and I blamed you a little as well. But you know what, life just happened. You had no control over what those animals were doing and you came back. You would have given your life to save me and my children and that is a debt that can never be repaid. All I can say is thank you." Betsy had tears in her eyes.

The two women hugged one another deeply. They had become sisters in life and felt an intense love for one another. They continued tending to the vegetables and discussed the daily goings on of life at the Lotus camp.

Finally, Vince and Nancy returned to collect Erika. It had not been very long and Vince still had the compost wagon in tow. Obviously, this was not the last stop of the day. They continued on past the garden site. Erika began to recognize the road they were on despite the devastation that had ravaged the area. Ripper knew where they were headed as well. He had always perked up in the car and gotten excited whenever they had headed down this way. He was dancing about, happy to be in an area he knew. They were headed out to her mom's ranch.

When they neared the ranch, Erika couldn't believe what had happened. Her mom had occupied a corner lot and a huge hole had opened up across the street to the left. Besides the home being in shambles, Nancy's property still looked good. The pastures remained and even the fencing still stood intact fairly well. Her old neighbors, Bob and Cathy Meyer, had removed all their supplies and solar power equipment because there was no place to live here anymore, but their property was in decent shape as well. Erika immediately noticed they had built windmills to pump water from the wells. There were three of them scattered throughout the properties. It was sad to see the condition of the homes but there was hope of utilizing what was left.

"Still working on the property, Mom?" Erika questioned sarcastically. Nancy had always been busy working this land. She loved it. It filled her days with a peaceful energy.

"You know me, gotta stay busy," Nancy answered as if it was any old day.

"I can't believe all this," Erika said with a sigh. "All the memories in that house, Dad and Bob; do you think we'll ever see them again?" Erika had not wanted to talk about her father, Roger, or her brother, Bob, before. It was too painful. They had been across the country in Michigan and in Canada when things went down. Both of them lived where they did because of their jobs. They loved to work and make money and it had taken them away from their families often.

"All we can do is pray, Erika," Nancy replied, obviously shaken. She hadn't said it out loud either. "Now look here"—she quickly changed the subject. She had one of her children here and life had to go on—"we are hauling all this compost out here so we can plant these fields next season. Remember, Bob and Cathy had those lamas, and I was always saying how we should sell the poop for money. Well, good thing we didn't, because we are spreading it all out so that we can plant in good fertile soil."

"What happened to the lamas?" Vince wondered.

"They are still over there at Bob and Cathy's. We figured why move them. They are fed and supplying fertilizer. We are going to shave them for their wool next summer and, eventually, Cathy is going to try to turn them into pack lamas, but for now, they are fine," Nancy replied. "Let's dump all that compost we brought out over there. Ricardo said he would send out a crew tomorrow to spread it and check the windmills."

Erika remained in deep thought while they emptied the wagon. She just couldn't get her father and brother off her mind. She wondered what had become of them and if they still lived. She maintained small talk for her mom's sake but she couldn't let it go. Vince knew that Erika was not impressed by all this.

If anything, it had just brought up more issues that she would be preoccupied with. Being that they had no control over any of these issues, Vince found it all rather pointless to worry. He had his own family worries buried deep in his mind and didn't want to think about any of it. Staring at Erika and reading her mind, Vince knew she wanted to leave this place and had no interest in what would be happening here next summer. Nancy still hoped that Erika would take an interest and want to stay, but she understood Erika's feelings as well. Nothing felt safe anymore and seeing the old ranch again and again did just bring up memories of much better past times.

It did not take long to unload the compost and soon they were walking back. They had shaken the bad feelings and were enjoying the afternoon sun that had decided to cut through the clouds. Ripper plodded along, worn out from all the excitement of returning to a familiar stomping ground. When they were returning, the wind had shifted and Erika could smell the horses, strongly. The horse training grounds were actually close to the bridge they had crossed at the start of their day. This proximity kept the horses close but far enough away that their mess did not muck up the camp. The creek that ran under the shifty bridge supplied water to the horses. This ensured that water did not have to be bucketed in from far away. They had been so preoccupied with the crossing of the bridge Erika had hardly noticed the facility they had set up when they had headed out to the gardens.

Vince saw her interest and had promised her earlier that they would go see Kit. "Want to head over and see Kit now, baby."

"Sure," Erika replied. "I wonder if Kim and Jen are out there too."

"Let's go check it out," Vince said positively. "Do you want to come with us, Nancy?"

"No, I am whooped. I am going to go back to camp to shower before everyone comes in for the day. I'll meet the kids when they get home. You guys have fun, maybe go for a ride." Nancy was tired from the long hike and exhausted from trying to convince her daughter of something that she knew wasn't what Erika wanted.

"All right, Mom, I love you," Erika replied, giving her a big hug and kiss. "Oh hey, will you take Ripper with you?" Ripper had always had a knack at spooking horses and Erika really didn't want to worry about him getting kicked or causing trouble.

"Sure, no problem," Nancy said reassuringly. "Now go have some fun!"

They headed down a wagon rutted trail. It looked like something straight out of the Old West. The property had been someone's home at one time but the home was demolished and the property was all that remained. It had been cleared of most of the trees and, even though the ground had shifted dramatically, the horse activity was stomping it back down to some kind of flat area. There was an area where the horses slept at night by the creek so they had access to water, and adjacent to it was a circular ring used for training. When Vince and Erika arrived, no one was around except for some horses tethered to the area where they slept. It smelled richly of horse, not manure, but the smell of animal. The whole area was meticulously cared for. They had salvaged manure rakes and had put them to good use. The manure was hauled out biweekly to help boost the quality of the soil in the gardens and make teas to feed the existing plants.

Erika and Vince surveyed the setup, impressed with the cleanliness and innovative thinking. Before long, a tall, skinny man approached with about eight horses in tow. He introduced himself as Drew Goddard and explained that he had been a horse trainer and ranch hand before the quake so he was right at home here. He had a tent out here with the horses, explaining that he felt more at home with them than being in the midst of all those people. He came in once in a while to use the shower over at the garden camps where Erika and Vince lived. Erika thought she had seen him before, but there were so many strangers around, she couldn't be sure. He was a very nice man but spoke as little as possible. He told Erika that Val would be back soon. She was out collecting horses as well. Erika asked him where Kim and Jen were and he said they were going to go out that afternoon and were getting ready to leave when he went to get the horses that had been in use in the main camp. The military horses would be brought back by the soldiers that utilized them for the day. Each soldier was training in basic care as well.

Erika explained to him that Kit was her horse, and he told her what a wonderful animal he was and that he was not being used for cart pulling. He was such an easy ride that he had been used mostly for scouting missions. He had rested today and Erika was more than welcome to take him out for a ride if she wanted. Erika was thrilled that he was receiving such wonderful care, and she also felt a little ashamed that she had not been out sooner to see him. She had just been so preoccupied with hunting and training. Drew told her that he knew lots of good fighting techniques he could teach her to do from horseback, and it probably wouldn't hurt to get him more used to being around gunfire even though he was a very calm animal and handled it well already. Erika assured Drew she would be out much more often to work with Kit and help with the horses.

Erika got her bridle from the station where they were all hung and Drew gave Vince one for another horse that was tied up by Kit. She was a bay like Kit and had very much the same demeanor as him. Drew was happy they were going out. He informed Erika that Kim had taken out a young horse that they were trying to get more trail-friendly and he hadn't liked the idea. Vince put a saddle on his horse, but Erika had always loved riding bareback so she chose not to saddle Kit.

They headed out down a trail that headed away from the main camp and the gardens. It wound through a mountain pass and the silence was eerie. Vince rode next to Erika and they chatted and enjoyed the peace of riding and taking in the quiet. The birds chirped tentatively and the squirrels ran and hid. It was so relaxing and quiet but there was some haunting feeling on the breeze. The horses began to get nervous which was very unusual for this set of horses. All of a sudden their ears perked as two horses came flying down the trail toward Erika and Vince. It spooked their horses, but given their calm demeanor, Vince and Erika were able to keep them under control.

"Is that the girls' horses?" Erika questioned Vince in a frenzied voice.

"I think so," said Vince. He caught hold of the bridle of one of the animals as they were running by and the other slowed to a stop by its partner.

Then they heard a scream from around the bend of the trail. Erika kicked her heels into Kit and they galloped off around the corner. Vince was dumbfounded by the sudden sequence of events. He jumped off his horse and tied the other two to a tree nearby. He quickly remounted the nervous horse and galloped off after Erika.

Erika rounded the bend and saw Jen standing over her sister with a large stick in her hand. She quickly assessed the situation. A mountain lion paced around the girls. Erika flew off her galloping horse and pulled out her handgun in one motion. She was running at the girls and the lion but could not shoot for fear of hitting the girls. The mountain lion became spooked by this sudden divergence to his easy meal and began to charge at Erika. It covered the ground so quickly it was like lightning. Erika shot once, twice, three times, but the lion kept coming. It launched in the air with its paw extended straight at Erika's head, when *bang!* A blast came from Vince's rifle. His horse reared and yelled. The shot blew the lion back through the air away from Erika. It lay on the ground with its head blown open. Blood began to run and stain the ground as the four of them stood in awe at what had happened.

Vince jumped down off his horse and hugged Erika. "Oh my God, baby, are you okay?" He backed off and was frantically looking her up and down.

"Yeah, I'm fine, but what about the girls?" Erika was still in shock and was only thinking about how bravely Jen had been standing guard over her obviously injured sister.

"You girls okay?" Vince questioned as he carefully stepped around the lion and ran toward the two girls.

"I am fine but it got my sister!" Jen was still standing over her sister, breathing heavily.

Erika followed Vince over toward the two girls. "Holy crap! That was crazy!" Erika said, heavily feeling the effects of the intense adrenaline boost.

Kim lay motionless on the ground. Erika grabbed Jen off of Kim while Vince checked her for injuries. Her leg had been swiped by the lion and would need immediate medical attention. It appeared that the horse had reared when the lion attacked and Kim had fallen off. She had hit her head when she fell but her skull was whole, and she was probably just knocked out.

"Jen, you did it! You saved your sister, with just a stick!" Erika was praising her bravery heavily.

"You sure did, Jen," said Vince, "but she is going to need to see Stan right away."

"I did?" questioned Jen. "Yeah, I did! Thank God you guys came when you did. How did you know we were even up here?"

"Drew told us, it was just lucky we arrived when we did," said Erika.

"What about our horses?" asked Jen.

"I have them tethered just around the bend," Vince reassured her. "Look, guys, I am going to take my horse and Kim and ride her down into camp. Can you guys manage the other horses?"

"You bet, babe." Erika was still pumped from the adrenaline. "I am going to gut that thing and bring it back with us. That hide is too valuable to leave for the scavengers. Plus it is a nice trophy for a wild experience." She was almost joyful about the ordeal.

"You guys just be careful, the scavengers are exactly what I am worried about. Get it done quickly and meet me at the medical building. I will stop and tell Drew to alert Harold and Betsy on my way." Vince was concerned about the girls, but he knew Erika would not let this animal go to waste. It was best to just let her gut it and bring it. She was fast at gutting anyway.

Erika and Jen got Kim up on the horse in front of Vince and the two of them rode off down the trail. Erika had her knife out and was quickly splitting the belly of the lion. Jen had never seen an animal gutted before and she watched attentively. Before long, its innards were lying on the ground in front of it and Erika wondered exactly how they were going to get it and the three horses back to the camp. Erika tried to put the lion up on Kit, but even with his good temper, he was not going to have a predator of that status on his back. They ended up strapping the animal to a couple of logs with some extra leather from one of the saddles and pulling it behind the horse that Jen had been riding. Erika rode Kit and guided the horse that was pulling the travois. Jen ended up riding the jittery young horse that Kim had been riding.

It was not an easy ride home. Jen's nervous horse smelled the animal that had attacked them not far behind and was dancing all the way. Jen pulled at its bridle and talked softly to it but the thing was spooked badly. Its eyes rolled in its head and it almost went sideways down the trail instead of straight. Kit, upset by the other horse's nerves and the smell of the lion, danced a little as well. Usually, if Erika was riding bareback and the horse was spooky, she would just hold a handful of mane but she had Kit's reins in one hand and the lead rope for the other horse she was towing in the other. She gripped hard with her legs and held on for dear life.

Finally, they reached the horse paddocks. Each girl was sweating heavily and the horses were completely exhausted. Drew had already returned from alerting Harold and Betsy and was there waiting for them when they came down the trail. He quickly grabbed Jen's horse and tethered it to a post. It stamped nervously in the setting sun. Jen jumped down and breathed a sigh of relief.

"I hear you are the hero of the day," Drew said to Jen as he reached for Kit and winked at Erika.

"I wouldn't say that. I just protected Kim, but it was a good thing Erika and Vince showed up when they did or I think we would have both been in big trouble," Jen said in an exhausted voice.

"I don't think you're giving yourself enough credit. You stood with a stick, fending off one hell of a mountain lion to protect your sister. That takes guts, girl," Erika said proudly. She knew this was the perfect opportunity to get Jen out of her shell and proud of herself again. "Check it out," Erika said to Drew as she unhooked the travois from the other horse.

"Wow, that thing is huge! I would call you a hero for sure," Drew said to Jen.

"It is pretty big. I never even thought about it. I just knew I had to protect Kim." Jen was staring at the lion again, impressed that she had even thought she could beat that animal with nothing but a stick.

"You're darn right it is," agreed Drew as he led the other two horses off to the tether. He had some buckets of water ready for them. Not only did they need some feed and water to settle down but they were getting baths as well. He cared deeply for the horses and knew they had a traumatic day and would need some loving. "Now get that thing the hell out of here, you two, before it spooks all the horses and I have a stampede on my hands," he said with a wink.

It wasn't far back to the garden camp so they each grabbed one of the travois poles and pulled the beast all the way home. Darkness was closing in as they entered the light of the fire. The whole garden camp minus Vince, Harold, and Betsy were there, clapping for the two heroes. Dexter and Star ran to Erika and just about knocked her down with a hug. Erika's mom just stood there with a look like *I told you not to get yourself back into something dangerous.* It was a great feeling and Jen's smile stretched from ear to ear. Everyone gathered around the lion and gawked at the size of it. They looked at the claws and wished they could have seen its teeth but they had been blown out of its head. Erika and Jen left the animal in Brett's capable hands. He didn't care for hunting anymore, but he certainly knew how to survive off the land and he was quite skilled at skinning. Erika and Jen were bloody and messy with horse sweat and dirt so they headed off to the showers.

After the shower, they left for the main camp. The night had fallen and most people had already come and gone from the food line but Nancy assured them there would be something they could eat, and they needed to go and check on Kim. They headed off down the trail, pretty tired but still in high spirits. The camp was buzzing with the news of what had happened. The main fire was burning bright and people were gathered around it. They knew eventually the participants from the big drama of the day would show up. Penni and Greg were at the kitchen when Erika and Jen arrived. Clay and Laurie were exhausted from a long day of preparing food for the camp and when they heard everyone was okay, they had gone to bed. Penni, being the excellent caretaker that she was, knew Erika and Jen would still need to eat something, especially now. She had some hot leftovers ready for them. Erika thanked her deeply and immediately knew why Greg was so smitten with her. She was always so considerate and kind.

They ate their food at the communal fire, while they enchanted people with the tale of what had happened. Vince had heard the commotion from the medical tent and came over to meet with them. He assured them that Kim was going to be fine. She had bonked her head solidly when she fell from the horse but she had come to and was answering basic questions with accuracy. Stan was more concerned with the slashes the lion had put on her leg.

They would fester with infection for sure. At least they had a supply of antibiotics and antiseptics, but it was still questionable if he would be able to save her leg or not. The animal had just about ripped her calf muscle off. He would have to stitch the muscle and the skin, and he was still not sure if it would ever function like it did before. He congratulated Jen again for her extreme bravery and Jen smiled wide with pride.

Before long, Betsy joined them at the fire. She hugged her daughter fiercely and told her how proud she was of her. Erika didn't think it was possible for anyone to smile any bigger than Jen already was but receiving this praise from her mother did the trick. Betsy thanked Erika and Vince again and again for helping her daughters and bringing them home safely. She thought it would be very hard to let any of her children out of her sight again and commented on how many more gray hairs she would have now. They all said a prayer for Kim before Betsy left to go and attend to her.

It was deep into the night before they all headed back to the garden camp. They thanked Penni for keeping the food warm and wished her and Greg a great evening. Greg was now staying with Penni at her tent, which left a room for the kids at Erika and Vince's tent. The fire there was burning low but Nancy was waiting up with Brett when they arrived. He had taken care of the animal and the pelt was salted and awaiting tanning. He had saved all the claws and gave Jen and Erika each half of them. They could be tradable in the future, especially with the story that came with them. They talked quietly for a little while before everyone headed off to bed. They all slept soundly that night. Thankful that they all had their skin attached.

CHAPTER 33

TIME PLODDED ON at the Lotus camp. Erika and Vince trained vigorously, but Erika made more time to spend with the horses. Kim kept her leg but was recovering slowly, as she was racked with infection and fever. Jen had a whole new attitude and worked with the horses daily. Greg and Penni's relationship grew strong. The injuries Greg had received at the Auburn compound had healed, and he was soon at full strength, training, and building around the camp. Nancy was busy with garden plans and kitchen duties. Life was good and the quakes were few.

Erika still could not shake the feeling of impermanence, though. The more she enjoyed each day at the camp, the more she feared the feeling. She knew they would have to go. She should have been happy. Her family was together, their days were full, but she couldn't get complacent. She blamed the past overwhelming circumstances for her feelings. She tried to drive them away, but it still seemed to her like she was standing on the train tracks just waiting for the train to come around the corner.

Finally, the issue came to a head. John Green returned from his scouting mission. He was tired and raggedy from his trip. Big John pitched his tent near Erika and Vince's, scarfed down some food, had a shower, and went to sleep. He hadn't said much, and rumors of his arrival spread through the camp like a wildfire. Folks were already forecasting the outcome of his mission. The horrors he must have seen. Erika's skin crawled with the fear of the unknown that was palpable in the air.

Erika had heard the news when she was over at the horse paddocks working with Kit and returned immediately. She found Vince busy cutting firewood for the camp. When their eyes met, they knew this was it. They would be on the move before the week was done. They chatted quietly about nothing while they waited. Vince just kept on splitting while Erika paced around the ground, her mind alight with curiosity. Before too long, Erika could see her mom coming up the trail from the kitchen. She had been organizing food inventories and collecting compost that was ready. It was much earlier than she was supposed to come back. Erika figured the ladies at the kitchens had probably sent her for information, which Nancy was probably desperate for anyway. Who could blame her, they all were. Nancy was lost in her own thoughts and didn't see Erika watching her approach until she started to climb the hill to the campsite.

"Oh, you're home early. I didn't expect to see you here," Nancy said startled by Erika watching her.

"I could say the same," Erika said with a gleam in her eye. It was pointless to put on charades with one another. Each knew the other too well.

"So, where is he?" Nancy went right to the point. It wasn't her normal beat around the bush style and Erika stammered for a minute.

"Vince said he went to sleep," Erika replied flatly. "Poor guy must have been beat."

"Well, thank goodness he made it back safely," Nancy said, full of concern. "I didn't see him at the kitchen. Did he get some food?"

"Vince gave him a can of soup we had in the tent," Erika answered. Big John was going to force an issue they had been avoiding talking about for weeks and Erika knew it.

"Well, what did he say?" Nancy was bursting with curiosity.

"I don't know, Mom. He just went to bed. Probably wants to recharge before getting inundated with questions." Erika was just as curious but trying to hold it altogether.

"We'll know soon enough, I guess." Nancy's disappointment with this lack of information was obvious. "Andrew will probably want to talk with him first anyway," she continued almost to herself.

"I'm surprised he isn't here yet," Erika said with a chuckle.

"No, I heard"—Nancy lowered her voice—"from some of the guards that there are problems with another group that is camped over closer to Placerville. We have had to go further and further to hunt and so do they. I guess there have been a couple of confrontations now. Andrew doesn't want to alarm the whole camp, but they are putting more and more guards at the gates."

"I know, I have gate duty in the morning." Erika was hunting often and training with all the soldiers so she already knew about the looming threat.

"You do? Why didn't you say anything?" Nancy was offended at being left out of the loop.

"Because Andrew didn't want to alarm the camp, Mom," Erika said, knowing her mom would have told someone at the kitchen and then she would have been to blame for letting the cat out of the bag.

"But I'm your mother and I wouldn't have told a soul." Nancy's eyes glinted in a mischievous way.

"Oh yeah, sure," Erika teased and hugged her. Nancy couldn't help it; she loved gossip, and if it was happening, she would know. The kitchen was gossip central. Everyone relaxing and enjoying meals discussed the day's events. Nancy was frequently there. She relayed information and supplies from the garden to the kitchen. She was always talking with the kitchen ladies and knew all the stories.

"Where's Star and Dex?" Nancy questioned, looking around. It was their day off from school and they were usually hanging around.

"They went out with the garden crew this morning. Ricardo said he would keep a sharp eye on them. They'll be back before dinner." The children had been restless in the morning and they had begged and begged to go out to the gardens where they could play in the waterfalls by the river.

"They'll sleep good tonight then," Nancy replied. "The garden crews are trying to plant some chard seeds and broccoli seeds that we found. I think the seeds are still good and it's worth a shot anyway. It's a little late for a summer crop but we are going to need the food. Stocks are going quick and finding food is getting harder and harder," Nancy rambled on with a look of concern in her eyes. "There's just too many of us," she finished, staring at Erika absently.

"Let's not get into it now, Mom. There's no sense in starting this conversation when we don't know what Big John has to say." Erika was used to being on the defense on this issue.

"No, Erika, I'm saying it may not be an argument anymore." The tone of Nancy's voice made Erika take notice. "I work in the supply house and I work out in those gardens we have going. I can see the reality of our situation. Every day, more and more gets used up and less and less comes in." Nancy was concerned.

Erika was shocked. For weeks they had argued this question of staying or going. "Still, Mom, let's see what Big John has to say before we make any decisions. Plus, have you talked with Brett about this? You know how he feels about it."

"He's the one who threw the obvious in my face," Nancy replied with a little disdain.

"Really?" That was even more shocking. Brett had argued fervently about staying put. He knew this area. He had stomped these grounds since he was a child, and he made it very clear he was not going to leave now. They had come to find out he had doubts all along and now was changing his tune altogether.

It was just before dinner when Big John woke up. Andrew had arrived to talk with Big John but was waiting patiently, sipping tea with Erika, Vince, and Nancy. Groups had returned home from their day's forays. They commenced to the evening events of getting cleaned up and getting ready to head over for dinner. They chatted about the day's events and discussed the garden details with Nancy. Harold had been over at the communications building where they were finally making some headway on communications rather than energy supply. They had not had contact with anyone yet and were very curious about what Big John had found as well. Dexter and Star returned home with the gardeners. They were full of pride over how much they had accomplished out in the fields and what they did while playing in the river. The evening noise grew louder and louder. No one wanted to leave for dinner because they were all eager to hear what Big John had to say. Even some folks from the other camps close by were showing up, which was very unusual given that the garden camp was the furthest camp from the central area.

"Good evening, John," Nancy said when she saw him stagger out sleepily from his tent. A hush fell over the crowd.

"Hey, Nancy, so good to see you," Big John said in a deep voice. They hugged one another.

"Are you all right? Do you need anything?" Nancy wondered.

"Nope, all in one piece," Big John beamed as he shook off the sleepiness.

"How about some tea then?" Nancy scurried to grab him a cup. "Here, sit here," she said as she pointed to a seat on the way by to get him a cup.

Everyone greeted Big John as he sat down. He had met Andrew before he left and he greeted him warmly as well. Dexter was playing with Star and John commented how big he had gotten and how nice it was to see everyone again. In this uncertain environment, you never knew how things would go. Each meeting could be your last. The curiosity over his journey could not be contained for long, Erika had to ask.

"So, did you make it to Tahoe? What's out there?" she blurted out.

All eyes went to Big John but time before dinner was limited so John laid it out simply. He explained how the hole that had engulfed Georgetown was massive. Once you passed that and headed east into the mountains, a lake called Stumpy Meadows that they all knew well had broken out of its manmade boundaries and had flowed down the mountain side. There was little left but a puddle with dead fish surrounding it. The bears had found this especially enticing. John explained that, as he continued on up into the mountains, it looked as if the earthquakes had rippled the landscape like waves in the ocean, but he could swear that the mountains were pushing upwards toward the east. He also joked about how he wished he was a cliff climber because of the fragmenting but that he had found a passable route. There was a little cabin on the way through the backwoods called Uncle Tom's Cabin. It was gone, but the mountain people that lived there, forever without power, were still there living much the same minus their cabin. The high mountain lakes were still intact for the most part. Some were smaller due to the draining of water through the newly opened crevices, but there was water available to drink. He had made it to Tahoe. The pass was still walkable and horses would only speed the trip along.

Some people had survived in Tahoe and had small camps, but there was a fear of trying to stay there through the winter. The snowfall could be sudden and deadly, and they all knew it. Big John had stayed briefly with them but had quickly turned back because of his duty to return to those he had promised. Erika and Vince thanked him for his efforts. Their minds were already made up. They would be leaving with Big John. The conversation was brought up short because it was time to leave for dinner before the kitchen was closed for the night. Andrew cautioned John about talking too much about this. He didn't want to rile up the camp before he had a chance to do crowd control. But it was too late. Andrew's fears were quickly realized. There was no keeping this quiet. The whole camp was in an uproar faster than if someone would have tweeted the message to everyone in a not so distant past. They were quickly inundated with people who were waiting for the garden camp group to walk by so they could get the news. The crowd continued to grow bigger and bigger around them as they headed for dinner.

Andrew knew he had to act fast. He set up a tall stump near the food line and yelled, "All right, all right, everyone!"—all eyes turned to him—"we all want to know how Big John's trip went and there will be plenty of time for that. Let's all get some food, so the kitchen workers can finish their night's work and then we will all hear his story together. Big John"—all eyes looked from Andrew to Big John—"would you please start the line as our guest of honor?"

Andrew had focused the group masterfully. Sending John through the line first would focus the group on the line and then their food so they could orderly hear the news rather than mobbing poor Big John. Erika scanned the full length of the line. The camp typically came for food in shifts, depending on what group they were part of. It was rare that the whole camp came at once and she had not seen this since they had arrived. Big John's return was reason enough for everyone to eat together and tell stories long into the night. Seeing the people all in one area was overwhelming. Erika had seen the supplies the camp had and their raid on the Auburn camp had added greatly to the supply. They had been hunting, fishing, and gathering as much as they could, but still she had to wonder how long they could sustain this vast group. There were no grocery stores. No trucks bringing food from the four corners of the world. Next summer, the gardens would be productive and they had planted some winter crops, but this bountiful harvest was still a long way off. Erika had to wonder how long the fragile balance of the camp would last once the food ran low. They were already on pretty tight rations, and everyone was working much harder than they were used to just to survive in this altered reality.

"Hey, guys, what's up?" Greg's cheerful voice snapped Erika back to reality.

"What's up G-man?" Erika replied.

"Hey, buddy, what's going on?" Vince said in unison with Erika.

"Big John's back, he came to your camp first, right? So, hook a brother up with the 411," Greg insisted.

Erika noticed ears perking up in the crowd around them. "Big John's going to tell the camp what he saw after dinner," Erika said loudly for all to hear. Then she lowered her voice to a whisper, "we are outta here, Greg. Start packing."

"Really?" Greg's mind was wandering. He was obviously considering the implications.

"Is it Penni?" Vince questioned. He knew his best friend inside and out.

"Yeah, she just got our tent all situated to make room for me with her kids and all. She's not really into trekking into the unknown. She loves Cali, you know? She loves the sun and she has always lived here." Greg was obviously torn.

The crowd was perking up again, listening in on their conversation.

"Guys, let's talk about it later, okay?" Erika warned as she motioned toward the crowd tuned into them.

Before long, they reached the front of the line and got their carefully allotted dinner. Penni and her kids had not been far behind them in line, and they all went to a grassy area to eat. Nancy and Brett were already there with Big John. Even though everyone was going insane with curiosity, they gave Big John space so he could eat in peace. There was a hardwired social law in effect and no one was about to step out of line.

After the meal, Big John took center stage. He never liked crowds but he laid it all out for the whole camp. He told them how widespread the quakes were. He explained how lucky they had been to not have been continuously rocked at this camp because the quakes were still shaking everywhere else. He explained how he was not staying and the best route seemed to be to go east, possibly all the way to the Rockies. The crowd was enraptured. A murmur would run through every once in a while, but for the most part, they were quietly reflecting on personal choices that would have to be made. Even Andrew sat with his hand on his chin, wondering how the group would respond and what he personally would do. Erika and Vince weren't considering the options. They were out of here. They were only thinking about packing.

When Big John finished, he told the crowd that he was leaving as soon as possible to beat the winter that would inevitably come to the mountains. He was through. He had laid it out for the whole group, and now it was up to every individual to choose their path. Neither choice would be easy, but then, life never was easy, not now and not before. The crowd was abuzz with talking and arguing. Everyone had broken into their own private groups and each had to take a hard look at reality.

Andrew took the stage next. He laid out a whole new set of issues for everyone to consider. He explained that their supplies were rapidly dwindling and hunting was very scarce. They had retrieved some cattle that had become scattered after the quake, but in order to have more in the future, they could not slaughter that many. The water was becoming more and more polluted, not only from their large camp, but from other camps utilizing it upstream, and this would affect the health of the gardens and their water for bathing. If they kept supplying this many people, they would have to start raiding other camps in the area so they could take their supplies and resources, and he was very opposed to that idea. It was clear something had to be done. He acknowledged everyone's hard work in building this camp into a place that could self-sustain and was not happy about the prospect of losing guards and hands, but the truth was they were coming to the end of a rope that may hang them all if something wasn't done and quick. They had simply taken in too many people and everyone had to eat.

The crowd was now alight with talking. Vince and Erika left with their family group. They had already made their decision and there was nothing left to do but pack.

"Mommy, are we leaving?" Dexter questioned.

"Yes, baby, we are. Big John says it doesn't look good for this area and we should go someplace safer." Erika never liked shielding her kids from reality.

"Where are we going? What about my friends?" Dexter was so innocent and his questions reflected it.

"Each family will have to decide what is right for them, Dex. But I am sure some of your friends will be coming too," Erika replied sweetly to him. "Hey, Star, you ready for some more hiking?" Erika wanted to include her in the discussion.

"I guess," she answered quietly.

"What's up?" Erika questioned.

"I was just getting used to this place and I loved going to school again and going out to the gardens and visiting with the horses. Now, we are just leaving?" Star said in a sorrowful voice.

"Well, I'm sure we'll find some place where we can do all those things again, and I know we will be taking some of the horses." Vince stepped in to cheer the conversation up. "And we'll all be together. It won't be so bad."

"Okay," Star answered more cheerfully. She was a resilient girl and would flexibly glide through any problem.

They returned to their camp and started repacking. Each individual would carry their own pack. Plus the horse carts had to be redesigned to handle the treacherous road ahead. The carts would be more lightweight with better suspension systems to be more agile but still support the weight of the supplies, while putting less tension on the horses.

Within two days, everything was packed and ready. About fifty people ended up coming along. Greg had convinced Penni and her family to come along. Harold was also coming with his family. Kim was still recovering from her run-in with the mountain lion so she would have to ride in a horse cart. Stan the doctor decided he would be coming as well. He was convinced Ryan could handle the camp, and he would be needed more in the traveling group. Andrew saw the logic of leaving but his position as the leader of the camp held him here. He did all he could to supply them with traveling resources and he gave them ten of the horses. One horse for every five people, that way they could all carry an ample supply of materials. Rob decided to stay as well. He was now in charge of multiple military activities at the camp and was not about to walk away from it.

A lot of other people that Erika had met through her travels were staying as well. Jim Harlow, who had been diligently putting his electrical knowledge to use around the camp, was too involved in projects here to leave it. Jimmy D decided to stay. He didn't want to leave California and had become very involved with Diana, who was determined to stay and help Ryan with the medical facility. Clay and Laurie Roberts decided to stay as well. They were in the groove of running the kitchen operations here in

Lotus. Margie Cassavoy also decided to stay. She loved her new liquor setup and, with her knowledge of distilling water, she was too valuable to the camp to leave. Andrew made that very clear. Her partner Bob was not as convinced, and he decided to leave with the traveling party. Gloria, from the Auburn compound, was at odds with her son. He wanted to go but she had started a relationship with Ricardo the gardener, who was definitely not going anywhere. In the end, Jose decided to leave his mother and go. Glen was just as attached to the gardens as Ricardo and was staying put. Finally, Drew, the horseman, was not about to leave his post. He had all the horses to take care of and a lot of his hands that had helped him were leaving, including Dan and Val. He felt responsible to care for the horses that would remain and now he had the cattle to care for as well. Dan and Val, who had a horse farm in Georgetown, had already lost so much they decided they were ready to try something new and felt very confident that Drew could handle the horses here without them.

Many other people decided the best choice for them was leaving. Taylor and Tom had been with Erika since the Auburn River camp and decided if she was going, they were too. Randy and Michelle also felt the same way. Michelle was now pregnant with Randy's child and although, traveling would be risky, they still wanted to go. Steve Dunch also decided to go; he had nothing to lose. Even though Richard had his school for the kids, there was no shortage of capable people to take his place, and since he had been through so much with Erika, he decided to take his kids and come as well. Bob and Cathy Meyer, who had been Nancy's old neighbors, saw the writing on the wall as far as supplies and decided if Nancy and Brett were up to the adventure, they were too. There were about eighteen other folks that were strangers to Erika but decided that leaving was the best decision for them as well. Big John was a little taken back by the size of the group he would be escorting but he was a good man and was dedicated to making sure everyone made it across the mountains safely.

CHAPTER 34

I T WAS A chilly October morning when the party set out. There were many tears shed. People staying behind had to watch their friends leave, and the people going had to say farewell to their friends. Spirits in the traveling party were high, though. They were stepping out into the unknown, but then again, staying at the camp would have been a big unknown as well. Erika was ecstatic. She had been waiting for this day since she arrived at the Lotus camp and the day had finally come.

They covered ground quickly that first day. Most of the group that had known Erika was at the front of the pack with her. The other folks that had come along made up a second pack following behind. Erika saw the division, but she knew it would dwindle as everyone got to know one another and time ticked by. Anyone who could not walk speedily rode in the carts as they made their way through the broken terrain. They were headed back toward the little town Erika and Vince had called home. Erika was shocked at how unrecognizable Georgetown was. This town had been torn to pieces. At one time, she had known this place like the back of her hand. She had walked her dog and her baby through the town and down all the back roads almost daily. She had taken her son to the library for story time and played at the park. Now, it was as if it had been run through a shredder. As they passed the town, her heart sank and her jaw dropped. She held Vince's hand and squeezed it tight, marveling at the fact that her family had been here when the town was destroyed and they had survived. She silently thanked God for his leniency. No one talked much as they passed by. They all just stared in wonder at the level of destruction that had occurred here. From the edge of the hole, dirty people clinging desperately to life watched them pass. The skinny stragglers didn't wave or ask questions; they simply watched the people go by. They looked tentative and it seemed that they were just thankful they were not being attacked for the meager supplies they were sustaining life on.

The group continued on into the broken landscape that was now strewn with fallen trees from the surrounding woodlands. Progress slowed to a crawl. They reached an area where a restaurant had once stood and decided to stop for the night. It was a tough decision. This place would have been looted and re-looted by any survivors for the precious food that might still be inside. The hope was that any survivors in the area would have already picked it clean and now avoided the sight. Everyone was on super high alert as the group made dinner preparations. There had to be other survivors around, and the smell of food cooking was an invitation to attack for the reward of a meal. Without the safety of their high walls at the Lotus camp, they were vulnerable.

Once the camp was set up for a long night, people's moods began to improve. Every scrap of food that was prepared was eaten and, afterward, musical instruments were brought out. In the group of newcomers, there were a couple of people that played the guitar. Penni's son, Mitchell, was learning to play as well. Jen was learning to play an old clothes washboard and it was a nice accompaniment to the guitars. Steve Dunch broke out a couple of spoons and the beat began to flow. It was a delightful evening, full of dancing and singing. Greg was in his element and entertained the crowd with his great voice and dancing skills. Dexter watched him closely and was really picking up on some of his moves. A little girl from the group that Erika was not familiar with from Lotus came and danced with him. Her name was Willow. She had blond hair and a very slender build. She matched his skills perfectly and it was so cute to see the children dancing together.

It was nice to have the two distinct groups merge finally. The children had been the little ambassadors. Erika and Vince introduced themselves to her parents. Their names were Susan and Edward Cooper. Edward had worked with computers before the quakes started and Susan had cleaned homes. Besides Willow, they had three other children—two girls and one boy. They said they kept trying until they got the boy. Zoey was the oldest at ten, Willow was five, Summer was three, and then there was Jensen. He was only two but cute as a button. He had blond hair and blue eyes and the cutest little round head. He usually clung tightly to his mother who was still breastfeeding him but took an interest in Ripper, and before long, he was climbing on his back and tugging at his ears. Ripper, with his vast patience, just sat there and let the baby play.

Everyone talked and enjoyed the fun atmosphere long into the night, but it was the last time they would smile for a while. That night, toward dawn, they were attacked by a group of stragglers. Michelle and Randy had been on watch duty and their rifles had met their mark. When the attackers had seen the first two of their party fall and realized how well armed this party was, they backed off immediately. The noise had everyone up and since they were already up, they decided to start off the day early. They left the bodies of the people that had come in to attack. They figured the scavengers would be back to claim them. Some people did feel bad for the folks that were barely surviving around here but everyone decided that if they left anything for the people, they might just be inviting future problems.

They made really good time that day. They stopped by the former mountain lake in the mid-morning to have a rest and some food. Big John had been right. There were a lot of bears in the area. They had been scavenging the fish that had once lived in the lake. Big John took one down with his rifle and the team of hunters had it gutted, skinned, and butchered in no time. This meat was rich with fat and would be a welcome addition to their food supplies. By noon, they were on the move again. They made it all the way to the little cabin known as Uncle Tom's Cabin before the evening set in once again.

Big John went to liaison with the people there. Big groups could be rather intimidating and Big John had already met up with the people here just a few days before. It was not long before Big John returned to the group.

"So what's up?" Vince asked John.

"We are not going over there, Vince," John answered with a weird look in his eyes.

"Why not?" Vince wondered. "We have plenty of meat to share."

"They are dead, Vince," John choked the words out. "Someone killed them all. They must have been really desperate too because it was all done with clubs and axes. They must have come in the night, just like those guys who attacked us. The people here must have got drunk and lazy and let their guard down. It's a horrific scene, though. We don't want the women and children to see that. Let's just keep going and put some distance in between us and that."

Without any argument, the group pushed on. It was a very long evening trek and they made it all the way to where the only two roads in this area merged. While the camp was pitched, the older folks who had rode in the carts for most of the trip prepared dinner. Big John had sent Taylor and Tom back to make sure that no one was following them. He was scared that the group of stragglers would tail them all the way over the mountains. There was really nothing they could do about it, except keep their eyes open and stay ready. The exhausted travelers ate and relaxed, watching the fire, and listening to Mitchell fiddle with his new-found skills on the guitar. Taylor and Tom returned to camp and told Big John that they hadn't seen anyone, but more people were put on watch that night anyway.

The threat of the stragglers was the least of their worries because during the night, the quakes returned. In the darkness, the earth awoke and shook the very gates of hell. Whole chunks of the mountain slid down the hillsides and huge gaping cracks opened. The camp awoke in a frenzied panic. The horses were frantic and people scurried about trying to ready themselves as fast as possible. The camp was packed in the blink of an eye. Big John was a true leader, driving his herd of people on towards the mountain peaks. The line weaved through the black morning like a snake.

The horses snuffed, shuttered, and blew their smoke-filled breath into the air. Every horse trainer was worth their weight in gold that day, and they stepped up into their roles with ease. Erika had Kit in the lead. He was always calm and helped to calm the rest. The other trainers, Jen, Dan, and Val, were dancing from horse to horse instructing its leader on how to proceed and keep the animal calm. Taylor and Tom had been training to use the horses in a military fashion and weren't much help with handling the carts, but they knew the horses and provided a calm shoulder for the horses to nuzzle up to. It was quite a sight to see; the trainers calming the spirits of the animals while their own danced wildly in their hearts. They hid it well from the animals.

Quake after quake struck and shook, trees fell, and the very rocks under their feet melted away to quicksand. There was nothing to do but continue on as best they could. The sun slowly rose over the mountains they were trying so desperately to conquer. Amazingly, they had made fairly good time in the early morning. It would have eased all their worries to stop for breakfast but the quakes were relentless and no one knew what to do. Ripper was freaked and stuck to Erika's side like a tick. Big John, driven by an unending sense of responsibility, drove them fearlessly forward. Until his worst fear was realized. They had just passed a little lake called Loon Lake. It was a beautiful mountain lake, clear blue straight to the bottom. Erika had loved swimming in it when it was hot even though the water was freezing. The party had to halt during a fierce shaking, simply to stay on their feet, when *swoosh!* A huge crevasse opened like a can of tuna and half of their party was swallowed like plankton into a whale's mouth. The screams of people and horses were deafening. Children and babies were instantly lost into the deep abyss. The people on the edge clung to the dirt and roots. Erika and Vince had been at the front of the line, chatting with Big John, Greg, Nancy, and Brett about the route they were going to take when the chaos struck.

"Keep going, Vince, do not stop, do not look back, *just keep going!*" Big John screamed as he saw the disaster behind them unfolding.

"But we can help!" Vince was not a man to turn tail and not assist where he could.

"Look, Vince, you need to think about your family, get them to safety. *Just go!*" John was direct and there would be no argument. He was afraid it would be like breaking ice. Once someone fell in, any attempt to save them would just break the ice more, and more people would end up in the water.

"Vince, what are we going to do?" Erika was wild-eyed.

Looking into his wife's eyes, full of fear for her children in the cart, he knew he had but one choice. "We are going on, Erika. We have to get over the mountain. Let's go!" he yelled back to the people behind him.

They were totally distressed and took his direction eagerly. They were happy to follow any order in this chaos. There would always be time later to count the remaining folks and mourn the losses, but if they never made it over the mountain, that time might never come. The horses screamed and scrambled up the edge of the mountain. The carts were pulling them back into the ground that had now turned to a substance more like quicksand than rock.

"We have to leave the carts!" The voice came from down the line. It was Jen. She had been caring for these animals long enough to know their needs inside and out.

"We cannot leave the supplies!" It was her father, Harold, speaking out against her. His concern for his family's future outweighed his concern for the safety of the horses.

Father and daughter were now in a heated argument that no one had time for.

"Quickly, unpack the carts and load as much as you can onto the horses and our backs," Vince had gone back and stepped in. "Jen is right; the horses will die if we ask them to continue on under this strain. Plus, we will move more efficiently without the carts. Just let them go."

The order was followed immediately and everyone was rushing to get the supplies packed onto their backs.

"Did you see Big John?" Erika questioned when Vince returned to her side.

"No, but we must unpack the cart and carry as much as we can on the horse. Give the kids their packs." Vince was straight to the point. There was no time to worry who had made it and who hadn't.

"I wondered how long it would take to come to that realization," Erika replied under her breath. She had watched Kit struggle under the heavy load for far too long. She quickly packed up the kids while Vince loaded the essentials onto the horse.

"I will walk the horse, you walk with the kids, *let's go!*" Vince was completely driven. He would not stop until they were safely over the mountains.

Erika fell in behind Vince and Kit with the kids in tow and Ripper still stuck to her side. She looked back for a moment to see who she could. Nancy and Brett were right behind them. Penni and her two girls were behind them. Greg and Penni's son, Mitchell, had gone back to the end of the line to make sure everyone was keeping up and check for any stragglers that may have survived the chasm. This worried Penni greatly, given the tragic past they were outrunning. Harold's family was behind Penni and they had put Carol on one of the horses. Jen danced between the remaining horses making sure they were still all right and staying as calm as possible. But the trees were so thick and strewn about that Erika could not see farther beyond that. She thought of her friends and wondered who was still with them.

They were now passing the high mountain lake. It was empty. The cracking was relentless. They trudged on and on. They took very short breaks now and again to rest the children, elderly, and horses, but the constant shaking was like a whip at their backs driving them on and on. There was no time to count the remaining folks. When they stopped, everyone just stood in line, panting, and gathering their strength. Each time they did stop, Vince was hopeful that Big John would catch up with some survivors, but it never happened. Then Vince's fear for his family and the remaining people would get the better of him, so he got the train moving again. Erika was quiet. The strength in her husband's eyes was reassuring and she watched the children and carried Dexter when his feet could no longer carry him along.

Night fell and they still kept moving. A compass ensured they were still moving east and the slope of the mountain intensified. The people and animals were so tired and the endless shaking had rattled them to the bone.

Erika was startled by a hand touching her back. "Are you doing all right?" It was her mom. "Brett said he could carry Dex for a while if you want."

"That would be great, Mom. I see Star is starting to falter a little and I can't carry them both," Erika admitted.

"Let's get Vince's attention and stop for a second so we can regroup." Nancy knew they had to keep going, but the whole group needed a chance to reposition their kids and supplies if they were going to keep up this pace.

Erika passed Dexter to her mom and rushed up next to Vince to relay the message. He was not pleased with the request but he didn't protest either. They were getting close to Tahoe now and he needed to make sure everyone was prepared to make the final push. Plus, he was holding tight to the thought that Big John was going to catch up.

The kids were asleep on their feet, so most of the supplies were unloaded off the horses and onto people. The kids were loaded onto the horses. The shaking wasn't stopping and it worried everyone fiercely. They took a much-needed breath and pushed on for the final climb up the side of the mountain. People stumbled and slipped over a massacred landscape. In the dark, they just kept walking. The sound of trees cracking and falling was deafening, but they continued on. They climbed over the debris and prayed that no trees would fall on them and no falling rocks would crush them. Many prayers were said that night and by some miracle they stayed safe, for now. As they cleared the last ridge of the mountain, the shaking became so vigorous no one could stay on their feet. Even the horses laid down and hugged the earth, hoping it would not give out underneath them.

"Is that water?" Erika yelled to Vince.

The sound of gigantic waves crashing was overwhelming and drowning out all other sounds.

"No, *it's Big John!*" Vince yelled back.

There was a faint cry of a man screaming over the sounds of the gigantic wave that was chasing him. The shaking continued and the edge of the mountain was about to go. The remaining group scrambled with their horses to the eastern side of a huge crack that was forming along the ridge. Vince and Greg took a look at one another and ran for the edge of the crack as one side began to break away from the other. Big John leapt into the air as the mountain began to sheer in half. He flew in slow motion through the air with his arms extended and *bam!* Vince and Greg each caught one of his hands and hoisted him to safety.

The shaking suddenly stopped. Everyone made one final effort to get away from the newly formed edge and then they collapsed. No one bothered to pitch camp, no one spoke; they just collapsed into little family heaps of people. Even the horses laid back down and silently fell asleep. Slight aftershocks shook them during the night on a few occasions, but no one noticed. Compared to the shaking they had endured, it was insignificant. Their escape had been so extreme that adrenaline had been the only factor pushing them forward. But now their bodies were toast and they had nothing left to give.

CHAPTER 35

THE MORNING SUN rose crisp and clean. The remaining horses had found an area of grass and were munching away, enjoying the calm that had finally come over them. The elderly were up, keeping the children—who had slept through the final panic—busy and quiet. That way, the adults and teenagers, who had carried the bulk of the load, could rejuvenate their bodies. Slowly but surely each individual started to awake, Erika and Vince had fallen asleep in each other's arms and there was not a more welcome sight than opening their eyes and staring into the others.

"We made it," Erika said in a sigh of relief.

"Oh my God!" Vince gasped as he stared out over the cliff.

"Holy crap!" Erika agreed.

The whole side of the mountain had sheared off and the Pacific Ocean had filled the void. The surf crashed into the mountain about fifty feet below the top of the cliff and ocean mist flew in the air.

"I wouldn't stand so close if I was you," Big John said as he, Greg, and Penni walked up to them.

"All those people," Penni said with tears in her eyes.

"We made it, girl. The kids are safe. That's all we can think about now," Greg said trying to reassure her. In reality, they all felt the pain.

"I'm serious, though, guys. We made it safely and let's keep it that way. I don't know how the mountain will hold up to the ocean," Big John said as he turned his back to the new coastline and walked away.

"He's right, come on, guys, let's go," Vince agreed as he held Erika's hand and went to follow John.

The group was alive and kicking when they returned. Everyone was talking about how lucky they had been and thanking Big John and Vince for being the slave drivers that had kept them moving and alive. Jen and Mitchell had gone out to check on the horses. Besides some scrapes and bruises, they too had made it safely.

Erika began to take stock of who had not survived the trip. Three of the ten horses had not survived. The group now numbered thirty-two individuals. That meant eighteen had died. Susan, who she had just met, had lost her husband and first born daughter, Zoey. Edward had tried to save her and fell in the abyss along with her. Dan and Val Winslow had been helping with the horses in the back and had died as well. The loss that saddened her the most was the loss of Randy and Michelle. They had fallen back because Michelle was pregnant and the fast pace was hard on her. Erika began to cry when she thought of them and their unborn child that would never know life on this earth. Maybe it was for the better. What were they supposed to do now?

Once the group was counted and back on their feet, they decided it would be best to leave the new coastline as far behind as possible and set up a more permanent camp where they could recoup and stay for a couple of nights before heading out again. They needed to figure out what direction they were headed.

They hiked through the day to the east side of Lake Tahoe. The ocean had flowed into the lake but the lake had stayed for the most part within its boundaries. There were dead fish everywhere around the edges. Some were dead from the surge of the lake boundaries when the ocean and lake had combined, and some were dead from the new salinity level of the lake. The group collected and gutted all they could carry. They would make an awesome feast and the extras could be dried for the future.

They found a gorgeous area, free from any other survivors. The people here in Tahoe had all fled down the mountain toward Nevada in the shaking, leaving behind plenty of goods for this group to pillage. The camp was set and food was prepared. Everyone stuffed themselves so full they could hardly keep their eyes open after a meal like that.

Vince, Erika, Nancy, Brett, Big John, Greg, and Penni went to sit high on a hill where they could watch the children playing in the meadow below. They sat and talked. The smell of fish drying wafted through the air. From their vantage point, the conversation from the camp could just barely be heard. The horses played and ate in the grass. Off to the side of the hill, Mitchell and Jen were quietly snuggling and talking. It was so peaceful and beautiful. Erika thought back to a life she had once known. Everyone so busy they had no time for one another. Technology so intrusive, it occupied the few extra seconds of life they did have. Having been through so much and looking out over this beautiful scene, Erika realized maybe this was not the beginning of the end, but a return to innocence, a finding of oneself.

The End